PRINCE OF THIEVES

CHUCK HOGAN

BLOOMSBURY

First published in Great Britain 2005

First published in USA by Scribner, an imprint of Simon & Schuster Inc.

Copyright © 2004 by Multimedia Threat, Inc.

The moral right of the author has been asserted

Bloomsbury Publishing Plc, 36 Soho Square, London W1D 3QY

A CIP catalogue record for this book is available from the British Library

All papers used by Bloomsbury Publishing are natural, recyclable products made
from wood grown in well-managed forests. The manufacturing processes conform
to the environmental regulations of the country of origin.

ISBN 0 7475 7875 3
ISBN 13 9780747578758

10 9 8 7 6 5 4 3 2 1

Printed in Great Britain by William Clowes Ltd, Beccles, Suffolk

PRINCE OF THIEVES

To my mother:
How great the darkness.

For where your treasure is, there will your heart be also.

—Matthew 6:21

Charlestown, Massachusetts's reputation as a breeding ground for bank and armored-car robbers is authentic. Although faithful to the Town's geography and its landmarks, this novel all but ignores the great majority of its residents, past and present, who are the same good and true people found most anywhere.

While Charlestown is home to some of the most decent people in the city, it has, like no other neighborhood, a hoodlum subculture that is preoccupied with sticking up banks and armored cars.

—*The Boston Globe,* March 3, 1995

. . . a community to which more armored-car robbers are traced than any other in the country, according to FBI statistics.

—*The Boston Globe,* March 19, 1995

This self-described Townie spoke . . . on condition of anonymity, describing what it was like to grow up in Charlestown. "I'm mighty proud of where I come from. It's ruined my life, literally, but I'm proud."

—*The Boston Globe,* March 19, 1995

First, a toast. Raise a glass. Solemn now:

To the Town.

To Charlestown, our one square mile of brick and cobblestone. Neighborhood of Boston, yet lopped off every map of the city like a bastard cropped out of a happy family portrait.

This is the heart of the "Old Eleventh," the district that first sent the Kennedy kid to Congress. The one square mile of America that shipped more boys off to World War II than any other. Site of the Battle of Bunker Hill, the blood of revolution sprinkled like holy water over our soil and our souls. Turf and Tribe and Townie Pride—our sacred trinity.

But now look at these outsiders snapping up our brownstones and triple-deckers. Pricing us out of our own mothers' houses. Yuppies with their Volvos and their Asian cuisine, their disposable incomes and contempt for the church—succeeding where the British army failed, driving us off our land.

But sure, we don't go away so easy. "Don't fire until you see the whites of their eyes!"—that was us, remember. This carnation here may be a bit brown at the edges—but see it still pinned to the tweed lapel over my beating Townie heart.

Be a hero now, reach me that jar. We'll have a hard-boiled egg with this last one, see how she goes down. It's caps off, gents. Here's to that towering spike on a hill, the granite battle monument that'll outlast us all: the biggest feckin' middle finger in the world, aimed right at good brother Boston and the twenty-first century beyond.

To the Town. Here's how.

PART I
PRIDE

1
THE BANK JOB

DOUG MACRAY STOOD INSIDE the rear door of the bank, breathing deeply through his mask. Yawning, that was a good sign. Getting oxygen. He was trying to get amped up. Breaking in overnight had left them with plenty of downtime to sit and eat their sandwiches and goof on each other and get comfortable, and that wasn't good for the job. Doug had lost his buzz—the action, fear, and momentum that was the cocktail of banditry. *Get in, get the money, get out.* His father talking, but fuck it, on this subject the old crook was right. Doug was ready for this thing to fall.

He swung his head side to side but could not crack his neck. He looked at the black .38 in his hand, but gripping a loaded pistol had long since lost its porn. He wasn't there for thrills. He wasn't even there for money, though he wouldn't leave without it. He was there for the job. The *job* of the job, like the *thing* of the thing. Him and Jem and Dez and Gloansy pulling pranks together, same as when they were kids—only now it was their livelihood. Heisting was what they did and who they were.

His blood warmed to that, the broad muscles of his back tingling. He rapped the hard plastic forehead of his goalie mask with his pistol barrel and shook out the cobwebs as he turned toward the door. A pro, an athlete at the top of his game. He was at the height of his powers.

Jem stood across from him like a mirror image: the dusty navy blue jumpsuit zipped over the armored vest, the gun in his gloved hand, and the white goalie mask marked up with black stitch scars, his eyes two dark sockets.

Happy voices approaching, muffled. Keys turning in reinforced locks, strongbars releasing.

A spear of daylight. A woman's hand on the knob and the kick of a chunky black shoe—and the swish of a black floral skirt walking into Doug's life.

HE SEIZED THE BRANCH manager's arm and spun her around in front of him, showing her the pistol without jamming it in her face. Her eyes were green and bright and full, but it was his mask that scared short her scream, not the Colt.

Jem kicked the door shut behind the assistant manager, smacking the cardboard caddy out of the guy's hand. Two steaming cups of coffee splattered against the wall, leaving a runny brown stain.

Doug took the bank keys from the manager's hand and felt her going weak. He walked her down the short hallway to the tellers' row behind the front counter, where Gloansy—identically dressed, masked, and Kevlar-bulked—waited. The bank manager startled at the sight of him, but she had no breath left for screaming. Doug passed her off to Gloansy, who laid her and the gray-suited assistant manager face-first on the carpeting behind the cages. Gloansy started yanking off their shoes, his voice deepened and filtered by the mask.

Lie still. Shut your eyes. Nobody gets hurt.

Doug moved with Jem through the open security door into the lobby. Dez stood beside the front door, hidden from Kenmore Square by the drawn blinds. He checked the window before flashing a blue-gloved thumb, and Doug and Jem crossed the only portion of the lobby visible from the ATM vestibule.

Jem unfolded a deep canvas hockey bag on the floor. Doug turned the stubbiest key on the manager's ring in the night-deposit cabinet lock, and silver plastic deposit bags spilled to the floor like salmon from a cut net. A holiday weekend's worth. Doug gathered them up five and six at a time, soft bags of cash and checks bundled in deposit slips, dumping the catch into Jem's open duffel.

After raiding the night drop, Doug went on alone to the access door behind the ATM. He matched key to lock, then looked over to the tellers' cages where Jem had the branch manager on her feet. She looked small without shoes, head down, hair slipping over her face.

"Again," Jem commanded her. "Louder."

She said, staring at the floor, "Four. Five. Seven. Eight."

Doug ignored the choke in her voice and punched the code into the mechanical dial over the key. The door swung open on the ATM closet, and Doug unlatched the feeder and pulled the cash cassette. After the long weekend it was less than half full. He scooped out the sheets of postage stamps as an afterthought and dumped them with the tens and twenties into the bag. Then he flipped the service switch, reloaded the empty cassette, and hustled back past the check-writing counter, running the bag through the open security door to the tellers' cages.

There, he retrieved a small strongbox from a drawer at the head teller's station. Beneath some dummy forms and a leftover stack of flimsy giveaway 1996 desk calendars was a brown coin envelope containing the cylindrical vault key.

THEY COULD HAVE BEEN a couple waiting for an elevator, except for the gun: Jem and the manager standing together before the wide vault door. Jem was holding her close, exploring the curve of her ass through her skirt with the muzzle of his .45 as he whispered something in her ear. Doug made noise coming up behind them and Jem's gun moved to her hip.

Jem said, "She says the time lock's set for eight eighteen."

The digital clock built into the vault door said 8:17. They stood for that one minute in silence, Doug behind the manager, listening to her breathing, watching the hands of her self-hugging arms grip her sides.

The clock changed to 8:18. Doug inserted the key over the thick black dial.

"We know all about panic codes," Jem told the manager. "Now open it clean."

Her hand came out stiffly, steadying itself against the cool steel door and leaving a brief, steamy palm print there before starting in on the dial. When she hesitated after the second turn, Doug knew she had made a mistake.

"No fucking stalling," said Jem.

She dried her quivering hand on her skirt. The second time, she made it past the third number of the combination before her nerves betrayed her, her fingers twisting the dial too far.

"For *Christ*!" said Jem.

"I'm sorry!" she wailed, half in anger, half in terror.

Jem put the gun to her ear. "You have kids?"

She veered away from him, her voice strangled. "No."

"A husband? Boyfriend?"

"*No.*"

"Christ! Parents, then. Do you have parents? Who the fuck can I threaten?"

Doug stepped in, easing Jem's gun away from her face. "How many attempts before the lock triggers a duress delay?"

She swallowed. "Three."

Doug said, "And how long until it can be opened again after that?"

"I think—fifteen minutes."

"Write it *down*," said Jem. "Write out the combination, I will fucking do it myself."

Doug looked at her grimacing face in profile, feeling her fear. "You don't want us here another fifteen minutes."

She considered that a second, then reached fast for the dial, her hand darting like a bird from a cage. Doug caught her wrist, held it firm.

"Slow," he said. "Take your time. Once you start, do not stop."

She wrapped a fist around her thumb. When he released her, her hand went cautiously to the dial. Her fingers obeyed her this time, shaking again only as she approached the final number. The interior *clack* was audible.

Jem spun the locking wheel and the door released, opening on massive hinges, the vault emitting a cool, cottony yawn after a long weekend's sleep.

Doug grabbed the manager's arm and walked her away. She paused in sight of her office, their entry point, where they had brought the ceiling down on top of her desk.

"It's my birthday," she whispered.

Doug walked her fast out to Gloansy, who put her back with the assistant manager, facedown on the floor. Dez stood near with his scarred mask cocked at a quizzical angle. A radio check, him listening to the unseen wire rising up from inside his jumpsuit collar.

"Nothing," Dez said. The police frequencies were all clear.

As A CONQUEST, VAULT interiors always disappointed Doug. The public access areas such as the safe-deposit rooms were kept polished and showroom clean, but the actual money rooms were no more impressive than utility closets.

This vault was no exception. The main cabinet door containing the cash reserves was made of thin metal and fastened with a flimsy desk lock, which Doug busted open in one stroke. Despite the vault's hard-target exterior, once you were in, you were in. He ignored the heavy racks of rolled coins and instead pulled down stacked bundles of circulated paper currency. The color-coded paper straps that banded the bills told him the denominations at a glance: red for $5s, yellow for $10s, violet for $20s, brown for $50s, and beautiful mustard for $100s. He snapped them off as he went, fanning the wads of cash, spot-checking for dye packs and tracers.

Four cash-on-wheels teller trucks lined the back of the vault. The top drawers held about $2,500 each, and Doug cleared out all of it except the bait bills, the thin, paper-clipped bundles of twenties laid out at the bottom of each slot. The first drawer was the one tellers drew from during routine transactions, the one they emptied in the event of a stickup.

The second drawers were deeper than the first, containing higher denominations for commercial transactions and account closings, more than four times as much money as the first drawers. Doug again emptied each one down to the bait bills.

They ignored the safe-deposit room altogether. Opening boxes would have meant drilling each door individually, ten minutes per lock, two locks per box. And even if they did have all day, the Kenmore Square BayBanks branch served a transient community of Boston University students and apartment renters, so there was no point. In an upscale-neighborhood bank, the safe boxes would have been the primary target, since branches in wealthier zip codes usually carry less operating cash, their customers relying on direct deposit rather than paycheck cashing, purchasing things with plastic rather than paper.

Dez's blue palm halted them on the way back. "Asshole at the ATM."

Through the blinds, Doug made out a college kid in sweats playing the machine for allowance money. His card was rejected twice before he bothered to read the service message on the screen. He looked to the door, checking the bank hours printed there, then lifted the customer service phone off the receiver.

"Nope," said Dez.

In the middle of this, Doug looked at the manager lying behind the second teller's cage. He knew things about her. Her name was Claire Keesey. She drove a plum-colored Saturn coupe with a useless rear spoiler and a happy-face bumper sticker that said *Breathe!* She lived alone, and when it was warm enough, she spent her lunch hours in the community gardens along the nearby Back Bay Fens. He knew these things because he had been following her, off and on, for weeks.

Now, up close, Doug could see the faintly darker roots of her hair, the pale brown she treated honey blond. Her long, black linen skirt outlined her legs to the lacy white feet of her stockings, where jagged stitching across the left heel betrayed a thrifty mending never meant to be seen.

She rolled her head along her bent arm, just enough for a peek up at Gloansy, who was hunched over and watching the kid on the ATM phone. Her left leg began to creep toward the teller's chair. Her foot slipped underneath the counter and out of Doug's sight, poking around under there, then gliding swiftly back into position, her eyes returning to the crook of her elbow.

Doug exhaled slowly. Now he had a problem.

The kid in the ATM gave up on the dead telephone and kicked the wall before shoving bitchily through the doors out into the early morning.

Jem dropped the loot bag next to the tool bag and the work bag. "Let's blow," he said, exactly what Doug wanted to hear. As Gloansy pulled plastic ties from his pockets, and Jem and Dez lifted jugs of Ultra Clorox from the work bag, Doug turned and walked fast down the rear hall into the employee break room. The security equipment sat on wooden shelves there, and the system had tripped, the cameras switched on and recording, a small red light pulsing over the door. Doug stopped all three VCRs and ejected the tapes, then unplugged the system for good measure.

He brought the tapes back out to the front and dumped them into the work bag without anyone else seeing. Gloansy had the assistant manager in one of the teller's chairs, binding the guy's wrists behind the chair back. Bloody snot painted the assistant manager's lips and chin. Jem must have flat-nosed him on their way in.

Doug lifted the heavy tool bag to his shoulder just as he saw Dez quit splashing bleach, setting his jugs down on the floor.

"Hold it!" Dez called out.

Dez's finger went to his ear as Jem emerged from the vault, jugs in hand. Gloansy stopped with the manager seated behind the assistant manager now, back-to-back, a tie for her wrists ready in his free hand. Everyone looked at Dez—except Doug, who was looking at the manager staring at the floor.

Dez said, "Silent alarm call, this address."

Jem looked for Doug. "What the fuck?" he said, setting down his bleach.

"We're done here anyway," said Doug. "We're gone. Let's go."

Jem drew his pistol, keeping it low at his hip as he approached the seated bankers. "Who did it?"

The manager kept staring at the floor. The assistant manager stared at Jem, a black forelock of hair hanging ragged and sullen over his eyes.

"We were gone," said Jem, pointing at the back hallway with his gun. "We were out that fucking door."

The assistant manager winced at Jem through his hair, eyes watering from the bleach fumes, still sore from his cuffing at the door.

Jem locked on him. Wounded defiance was the worst possible play the assistant manager could make.

Dez picked up his bleach, hurriedly finishing splashing it around. "Let's go," he said.

"We've gotta move," Doug told Jem.

Another few seconds of staring, and the spell was broken. Jem stepped off, relaxing his gun hand, slipping the piece back inside his belt. He was already turning away when the assistant manager said, "Look, no one did any—"

Jem flew at the man in a blur. The sound of knuckles against temple was like a tray of ice being cracked, Jem holding back nothing.

The assistant manager whipped left and slumped over the armrest, the chair tipping and falling onto its side.

The assistant manager sagged, still bound to the chair by his wrists. Jem dropped to one knee and hammered away again and again at the defenseless guy's cheek and jaw. Then Jem stopped and went back for his bleach. Only Doug's hooking his arm stopped Jem from emptying the jug over the man's shattered face.

That close, Doug could see the pale, nearly white-blue of Jem's irises within the recesses of the goalie mask, glowing like snow at night. Doug twisted the bleach out of Jem's hand and told him to load the bags. To Doug's surprise, Jem did just that.

Doug soaked the night drop in the lobby. He soaked the carpet where they had filled the loot bag, jumpy near the windows, expecting sirens. He shook out the jug over the ATM cassette, then returned to the counter.

The assistant manager remained hanging off the overturned chair. Only his wheezing told Doug the guy was still alive.

The bags were gone. So was the manager.

Doug walked to the back, bleach fumes swamping his vision. The bags were stacked and waiting, and Dez and Jem both had their masks off, standing at the rear door, Jem's hand clamped on the back of the manager's neck, keeping her from seeing their faces. Dez picked up her brown leather handbag where it had fallen upon entry, shooting Doug a hard look of warning.

Doug whipped off his goalie mask, his ski mask still on underneath. "Fuck is this?"

"What if they already got us walled in?" said Jem, wild. "We need her."

Wheels skidding on alley grit, the work van pulling up outside, and Gloansy, unmasked now, jumping from the wheel to throw the side doors open.

Dez started out, two-handing the first duffel bag, swinging it aboard.

"Leave her," Doug commanded. But Jem was already rushing her out to the van.

Doug's ski mask came off, crackling with electricity. Seconds mattered. He carried the work bag into the glaring sunlight and dumped it into the van with a crash. Jem was next to him, trying to load the manager into the van without her glimpsing his face. Doug took her by the waist, boosted her up, then cut in front of Jem, leaving Jem the third bag.

Doug pushed her down the length of the soft bench seat to the windowless wall. "Eyes shut," he told her, stuffing her head down to her knees. "No noise."

The last bag thudded and the doors slammed and the van lurched up the sharp, ramplike incline, bouncing off the curb and onto the street. Doug pulled his Leatherman from its belt pouch. He opened up the largest blade and tugged the hem of her black jacket taut, cutting into the fabric, then collapsing the blade and tearing off a long strip. She flinched at the noise, shaking but not struggling beneath him.

He looked up and they were headed around into Kenmore Square, the red light at the end of Brookline Avenue. The bank was on their right. Doug kept his weight on the manager's upper back, watching. No cruisers yet in the square, nothing.

Gloansy said, "What about the switch?"

"Later," Doug said, through his teeth, sliding the Leatherman back onto his belt.

The light turned green and the traffic started forward. Gloansy went easy, bearing east on Commonwealth Avenue.

A cruiser was coming, no lights, rolling west toward them, around the bus station in the center island of the square. The cruiser lit up its rack to slow traffic, making a wide U-turn and cutting across behind them, pulling up curbside at the bank.

They rolled past the bus station toward the Storrow Drive overpasses. Doug wrapped the fabric twice around the manager's head, tying it tight in a blind-fold. He pulled her halfway up, waving his hand in front of her face, then made a fist and drove it at her, stopping just short of her nose. When she didn't flinch, he let her sit up the rest of the way, then slid to the far end of the bench, as far away from her as he could get, tearing off his jumpsuit as if he were trying to shed his own criminal skin.

2
CRIME SCENE

ADAM FRAWLEY PARKED HIS Bureau car in the slanting shadow of Fenway Park's Green Monster, jogging across the short bridge over the Massachusetts Turnpike with his folder and notebook trapped under his elbow, pulling on a pair of latex gloves. The fence along the side of the bridge was high and curved at the top to keep Red Sox fans from hurling themselves off it every September. At the tail end of Newbury Street, two windbreakers from the Boston Police crime lab were crouching inside yellow tape, dusting a graffiti-tagged metal door and bagging loose alley trash near a plum Saturn coupe.

Newbury Street was the tony promenade listed in every Boston guidebook, beginning downtown at the Public Garden and riding out in orderly alphabetical blocks, Arlington to Berkeley to Clarendon, all the way to Hereford before skipping impatiently to *M,* the broad Massachusetts Avenue that formed the unofficial western border of the Back Bay. Newbury Street continued beyond that dividing line, but with its spirit broken, forced to run alongside the ugly turnpike more or less as a back alley for Commonwealth Avenue, its humiliation ending at the suicide bridge.

Frawley rounded the corner to the front of the bank, at the tail end of a block of brick-front apartment buildings topping street-level retail stores and bars. Kenmore Square was a bottleneck fed by three major inbound roads, Brookline, Beacon, and Commonwealth, converging at a bus station where Comm boulevarded into two lanes split by a proper grass mall. Curbside clots of police cruisers, fire engines, and news vans were squeezing traffic down to one lane.

An industrial-sized fan blocked the bank's open front door, broadcasting pungent bleach out onto the sidewalk. A handwritten sign on the window said the branch was closed for the day and directed customers to area ATMs or the next nearest branch at the corner of Boylston and Mass.

Frawley opened his credentials holder, pressing his FBI ID card and his small gold badge against the window near the FDIC sticker that was his ticket inside. The Federal Deposit Insurance Corporation guaranteed all deposit accounts up to $100,000, making any bank crime committed on U.S. soil a federal offense. A Boston cop holding a handkerchief to his mouth stepped into the ATM vestibule and switched off the big fan in order to let Frawley inside.

"Here he is," said Dino, greeting him beside the check-writing counter, clipboard in hand. The smell of violation was not so strong there as at the door.

Frawley said, "I was fine until I hit the expressway coming back."

The Boston Bank Robbery Task Force operated not out of the field office downtown but out of a resident agency in Lakeville, a small bedroom community thirty miles south of the city. Frawley had been pulling into the industrial park there when he got this call.

Dino had a pair of paper bootees for him. Dean Drysler was Boston Police, twenty-seven years, a lieutenant detective on permanent assignment to the task force. He was local product, tall, long-boned, sure. Boston saw more per capita bank jobs and armored-car heists than anywhere else in the country, and Dino was indispensable to Frawley as someone who knew the terrain.

Frawley was thirty-three, compact, laser-sighted, a runner. He had less than two years with the Boston office, eight overall with the FBI following rapid-fire assignments in Miami, Seattle, and New York. He was the youngest bank robbery agent in the country, one of a platoon of five Boston agents assigned to the BRTF, investigating bank crimes throughout Massachusetts, Rhode Island, New Hampshire, and Maine. The working partnership he and Dino had formed was of the teacher-student variety, though the roles of teacher and student flip-flopped day to day, sometimes hour to hour.

Frawley pulled the bootees on over his size-eight-and-a-halfs and organized his rape kit: paperwork folder, notebook, tape recorder. He scanned the various uniforms and acronym-proud windbreakers. "Where is she now?"

"Break room in back. They let her go at Orient Heights, north of the airport. She walked to a corner market, they called it in. We already had a cruiser here on the silent bell."

"From?"

"Teller cage number two." They walked through the security door behind the counter, where the vapors were stronger, the industrial carpeting already blanching in spots. Dino pointed his clipboard at a floor button. "Panic bell. The assistant manager is down the street at Beth Israel, he caught a pretty good beating."

"Beat him, then took her for a ride, let her go?"

Dino's eyebrows arched satanically. "Unharmed."

Frawley set his suspicion aside, trying to go in order. "Anything on the vehicle?"

"Van, seems like. I put a BOLO out for car fires."

"You talk to her?"

"I set her up with a female officer first."

Frawley looked at the open vault door behind Dino, its round piston locks disengaged. Two techs in jumpsuits and bootees were going over the inside walls with blue lasers. Print dust on the outer door showed a beautiful handprint over the dial, but small, likely the manager's. "Morning Glory?"

"Morning Glory and a Jack-in-the-Box. Worked a bypass and busted in overnight. Phones here are all dead. BayBanks central security tried a callback on the silent and got no answer, dispatched the patrolman. Security chief's on his way over with the codes and specs, but I'm figuring two hard lines and a cellular backup. They tricked out the cell and one of the Nynex lines."

"Only one?"

"Waiting on a Nynex truck to confirm. I'm guessing the vault is hardwired, bank-to-station, same as the teller panics. Our guys let the time lock expire and had the manager open sesame."

"Under duress."

"That is my understanding."

Frawley jotted this down. "Easier than humping in SLICE packs and oxy tanks and burning through the vault walls."

Dino shrugged his pointy shoulders. "Whether they could have jumped the vault bell or not."

Frawley considered that. "Neutralizing the vault might have tipped their hand too much."

"Though with some of these guys—you know it—burglary is pussy."

Frawley nodded. "It's not a payday unless they're robbing someone face-to-face."

"Bottom line is, they know phone lines and Baby Bell tech."

Frawley nodded, surveying the fouled bank from the perspective of teller station number two, his cop eyes starting to sting. "These are the same guys, Dino."

"Throwing us curveballs now. Look at this."

THE TREND IN "COMMUNITY BANKING" was to feature the branch manager's office up front, prominent behind glass walls, playing up accessibility and putting a friendly, local face on a corporation that charges you fees for the privilege of handing you back your own money. Kenmore Square was a prime location—high foot traffic with the student population, the nightclubs, the nearby ballpark—but the space itself was an odd fit for a bank, deeper than it was wide, owing to the ending curve of the road. The manager's office was tucked away behind the tellers, along the back hallway near the break room and bathrooms.

A police photographer was inside, his flash throwing shadows off the chunk of ceiling concrete atop the desk. It had crushed a telephone and a computer monitor, cords and keyboard dangling to the floor like entrails. Neatly sheared rebar and steel mesh lay among rubble of plaster, ceiling corkboard, concrete dust, and mottled gray chips.

Frawley looked up at the layers of flooring visible in the square ceiling hole, seeing an eye chart above an examining-room sink. The robbers had broken into the second-floor optometry shop and cut through overnight. This was the hidden cost of doing business in an older city like Boston, and why banks preferred to open branches in freestanding buildings.

A red helmet appeared in the hole, a fireman doing a pretend startle. "Thought you guys were bank robbers!"

Dino nodded upward with a smile. "Off your break already, Spack?"

He said it old-city style, *Spack* instead of *Spark*. Dino could turn the hometown accent on and off like charm.

"Just getting my eyes checked. This your whiz kid?"

"Special Agent Frawley, meet Captain Jimmy here."

Frawley waved at the ceiling with his free hand.

"A perfect square, two by two," said Captain Jimmy. "Nice work."

Dino nodded. "If you can get it."

"Hope you two catch these geniuses before the cancer does." He pointed down through the hole. "Those gray chips there, that's asbestos."

Frawley said, "Any tools up top?"

"Nope. Nothing."

Frawley eyed the smooth cut, turned to Dino. "Industrial concrete saw."

"Yeah, and a torch for the rebar. Nothing very fancy. Our boys are blue-collar bandits. Real salt-of-the-earth numskulls."

Frawley said, "Numskulls who can bypass alarms."

"Spack's gonna cut out this hole for us," said Dino, turning to leave. "Hey, careful up there, Spacky, you don't pull any muscles, have to take a year's disability vacation on my account."

Chuckles from firemen above, and Captain Jimmy saying, "Dean, you know there's only one muscle I'd pull for you."

OUTSIDE THE BACK DOOR Frawley heard the cars on the nearby turnpike, speeding into and out of the city. The small parking spaces and chained Dumpsters sat lower than the street, a culvert gathering sand, grit, and trash.

A Morning Glory score was typically the most successful and lucrative type of bank robbery. Ambushing employees before the bank opened meant fewer people to control. The branch's cash stores were still centralized in the vault, not yet disbursed to tellers or spread around in secondary safes or backup drawers, and therefore easy to find and carry with speed. The typical Morning Glory involved a distracted branch opener getting waylaid in the parking lot at gunpoint. Breaking in overnight and lying in wait for the manager to arrive—the Jack-in-the-Box—showed a deeper level of preparation and, among notoriously lazy bank robbers, an aberrant affinity for hard work.

Frawley saw a photographer laying a ruler next to the tire treads in the road sand. He almost told her not to bother. The stolen getaway van would turn up in a few hours, in a vacant lot somewhere, torched.

He envisioned them loading the van, hustling but not panicked, the silent alarm ringing only in their heads. Why take the time to beat the assistant manager? The vault was empty, and they were already on their way out. Taking the manager was schizo. It was a piece that didn't fit, and as such, something for Frawley to key on.

THE SHAPE OF THE bloodstain soaked into the carpet behind the tellers' cages resembled the continent of Africa. A lab technician was sampling it and depositing fibers into a brown, coin-sized envelope.

"He was cuffed to the chair." Dino held up an evidence bag containing a snipped plastic bundling tie, the kind with locking teeth. "Cracked his jaw, maybe his cheekbone, the bones around the eye."

Frawley nodded, the odor at its most pungent there. Bleach effectively fragged DNA. Criminalists at the FBI lab used it to blitz their work surfaces clean, to avoid any evidentiary cross-contamination. Pouring bleach was something he had heard of rapists doing, fouling genetic matter left on the victim, but never bank robbers. "Bleach, huh?"

"A little extreme. But camping out here overnight, you can never be too careful."

"They sure don't want to get caught. These guys must be facing a long fall." Frawley slid his beeper to his hip and crouched behind the third teller's cage, noticing blond crumbs on the paling carpet, partially melted by the bleach. "They sat here and had a picnic."

Dino crouched with him, his mechanical pencil tucked behind a hairy ear. "Gets hungry on a job, Frawl. I told you, these are blue-collar bandits. Boiled eggs and thermos coffee. The Brown Bag Bandits."

Dino stood again while Frawley remained on his haunches, imagining the bandits hanging out there as the sun came up, the bank theirs. He rose and looked through the teller's cage to the windows along the front of the building, the square outside. He had a vague memory of passing through it the day before—a sense of entering the home stretch, his legs burning, the crowd cheering him on. "Marathon runs right by here?"

"Holy shit, Frawl, I forgot. Look at you. Twenty-six point two miles and you're up and around like nothing happened."

Frawley returned his beeper to the front of his belt. "Broke three and a half hours," he said. "I'm happy with that."

"Well, congratulations, you loose screw. That is one lonely sport you got there. What is it you think about the whole time?"

"Finishing," Frawley said, now looking at the lockbox open on the back counter. "So the eye doctor was closed all day."

"Top-floor gym was too, but some employees got together to watch the race—picture windows, good view up there. They were out by six. Traffic control ends around eight at night outside, even with runners still stumbling in. Our guys didn't need more than a few hours to load in, punch their hole, and drop down."

"Young guys. Lowering themselves through a two-by-two hole in the ceiling."

"Not the old masters, no. The older generation—lockpicks, plumbers—they'd need a bed to land on."

"How'd they access the building?"

"Another rear door. Separate entrance for the shops upstairs."

"Exterior security cameras?"

"Not for the bank. But we'll check. Though if it's our guys—"

"Yeah, they'll already have been busted." Frawley put his hands on his hips, his thighs and calves still stinging. "So what's your call?"

"Early call?" Dino sucked in a breath and joined Frawley in looking around. "It's a good pick here. The holiday, the hundredth running of the marathon. Nice weather, a square full of hungry race fans. The bookstore, clothing stores across the street—though they're mostly credit-card transactions. But the convenience store, the McDonald's, that Espresso Royale coffee thing. Plus the Sox are in town, that ups the neighborhood restaurant and bar cash big time, over three days. Plus—Jesus—the nightclubs on Landsdowne Street. Their combined Saturday-Sunday takes?" Dino worked his tongue around the inside of his cheek. "I'm gonna go large here. With the vault, the night deposits, the ATM? Put me down for three and a quarter. Plus or minus ten percent, yeah, I'd say a good three and a quarter."

"I'm going three-five," said Frawley, turning toward the open vault. "*Fuck,* I want these guys."

FRAWLEY NEEDED THE VAULT. The vault was his vic. Not the corporation that owned the bank, not the federal government that insured it and employed him. The vault: emptied and plaintive and violated. He needed the vault in the same way that homicide detectives generate sympathy for the corpse to fuel their hunt.

The safe-deposit room had not been touched. Drilling each individual box demanded a blind man's patience and a lottery player's devotion, a hundred-to-one gamble on finding anything of value that wasn't insured and traceable.

He moved through the open interior door into a well-maintained cash hold. Frawley sometimes found tellers' jackets and umbrellas hanging inside vaults. He had seen vaults used as break rooms.

Fingerprint dust coated the cabinets and doors. Only traveler's checks, scores of torn, color-coded paper straps, and the manager's tally sheets remained inside the forced cabinet. Frawley tried to shut the bent door with his elbow, the hinges whining as it crept open again.

Six rigid bundles of cash had been set aside, left behind in a small, neat pile over the cash drawers. Frawley cracked open one of the short stacks of retired bills, finding a dye pack nestled in the hollow. He recognized the SecurityPac brand. Dye packs worked when removed from the bank's premises, triggered by electronic transmitters hidden near the doors. The device was timed to delay detonation for twenty or more seconds, the pack burning at 400° Fahrenheit, too hot for the thief to grab and throw. It released an aerosol cloud of indelible red dye powder that turned note-passers into human smoke bombs, voiding currency and staining human skin for days. Less well-known was that many dye packs also emitted a small burst of incapacitating tear gas.

He examined the drawers without touching them, empty but for the bait bills clipped together in the bottom of each slot. Bait bills were $10 or $20 notes whose denominations, series years, and serial numbers were recorded and kept on file by the bank, per federal deposit insurance regulations. This established a paper trail linking a suspect and the cash in his pocket to the crime scene.

Many bait bills also contained a tracer in the form of a thin magnetic strip that, once removed from the drawer, triggered a silent alarm signal to police dispatch. Known as B-packs, these particular bait bills acted like tracking bugs, the same way a LoJack device works in a stolen automobile. Many counter-jumpers, arrested at their home hours after what seemed to be a successful $1,200 job, never learned until their court date how it was that the FBI fingered them.

With no carpet to absorb it, the bleach odor was dizzyingly potent, but Frawley remained inside as long as he could. He wished that the vault could beg him for justice. That it was someone whose hand he could take in a gesture of reassurance, offering a covenant, cop to vic. Then he wouldn't have to bring so much to these empty repositories himself.

* * *

THE TECHNICIAN SWABBED THE insides of the branch manager's cheeks, collecting elimination DNA along with her fingerprints while Frawley made a copy of the manager's contact sheet on the bank's Xerox machine.

Claire G. Keesey. DOB 4/16/66. Frawley looked again and realized that today was her thirtieth birthday.

Dino wanted a look upstairs, leaving Frawley to do the interview solo. She was wiping ink from her fingers as Frawley introduced himself, making their perfunctory handshake awkward. He had snagged her a Poland Spring, which she thanked him for, uncapping it and sipping a little before setting the bottle down on the table beside them, next to an empty Diet Coke.

Frawley sat in the corner with her facing him, so that the police passing outside the door would not distract her. The bleach odor was only mild here. She shifted in her seat, making herself ready for the interview, smiling a little, uncertain. She rubbed her stained hands together in her lap as though chilled. Her arms were long and bare.

"No jacket today?" said Frawley.

"Someone took it," she said, looking back at the door. "For evidence. They . . . they cut my blindfold out of it."

"Would you like . . . ?" He opened his own jacket, and she nodded. He stood and draped it over her shoulders, though as he sat back down, she slipped her arms into the sleeves. The cuffs hung just an inch too long. If he had known a woman would be wearing his jacket that day, he would have chosen a newer one. "And you're sure you're okay, you don't want to go get checked out?"

"Just stiff," she said.

"No bumps, bruises?"

"No," she said, realizing only then how odd that was.

Frawley showed her his microcassette recorder, then turned it on and set it on the table. "Ms. Keesey, I want to start with your abduction, then take you back through the robbery itself."

The word *abduction* brought a blink and a deep swallow. This trauma had many layers and she was in only two or three deep.

"It's unusual to see a bank employee kidnapped during an otherwise successful robbery. But it means you spent a fair amount of time in the company of the bandits and perhaps possess some information that can benefit our investigation. I am the local bank robbery coordinator for the FBI, and this is all I do, work bank crimes, so nothing you can tell me is too trivial. Let me also say that if I don't ask a question you want asked, go right ahead and answer it anyway."

"Then, if I could . . . no one's been able to tell me about Davis."

"The assistant manager?" said Frawley. "He's being checked out at the hospital, but he's going to be okay. He's hurt, but he's going to make it. That's what you wanted to know?"

She nodded and rubbed her cheek with her hand, the dried stain leaving no exchange.

"You saw them beat him?" said Frawley.

She looked down and nodded.

"It was brutal," he said.

"I didn't . . . I looked away."

"Now I'm assuming these bandits threatened you upon your release. Told you not to cooperate in any way with the police, the FBI, correct?"

"Yes."

"Okay. And could you detail the exact nature of that threat for me?"

"It was after they stopped. One of the ones in front—he was the same one with me at the vault—he had my handbag."

"Okay, hold on. Now, you were blindfolded for the entire ride, no?"

"Oh—yes, he shook it. My big Coach bag—I know the sound of my things. He unsnapped my purse, told me he was pulling out my driver's license. He read it to me. Said he was keeping it."

"In his words, if you can remember them?"

She crooked her head, looking down, repeating them quietly. "'If you tell the FBI anything about us, we will come back for you and fuck you and kill you.'"

"Okay," said Frawley, pretending to write that down, coming back up with a neutral smile. "Of course, intimidation is a bank bandit's stock-in-trade. What I can tell you is, they have their money, they think they have gotten away, and I can assure you they want no more involvement in this investigation. No way they would risk exposing themselves now."

"I . . . all right."

He had her take him slowly from the bank into the getaway vehicle. "You're sure it was a van?"

"Yes. That van-sound of the doors. The bouncing as it drove."

"Do you remember seeing a van outside when you arrived at work this morning?"

She winced, shaking her head. "I don't know. A white one, maybe?"

She took him through the drive. "You couldn't see anything out of the blindfold? Not even at the very bottom?"

"Sometimes a narrow strip of light. My lap against the seat. The seat was white, or cream."

"Any sensation of light passing? Windows in the back where you were?"

"I . . . no. I can't say. I don't remember."

"It was a passenger van."

"I guess. Yes."

"You're not certain."

"I don't know what a 'passenger van' is. If that's a minivan, then, yes, I'm certain. We went skiing up in Maine last winter—myself, some friends—and I rented the van. It was a Villager, I remember, because that's a strange name for a car, and we called ourselves the Villager People. I don't know if this was that, but it was like that."

"Okay, good. Like that how?"

"Two separate seats up front. The middle bench I was in. Another bench behind." She winced again. "I'm bringing too much to it, maybe. At least, this is how I see it in my mind."

"That's fine." He wanted to encourage her without flattering her, keeping her account honest. "Where were you sitting?"

"The middle bench. Yes, the middle."

"How many sat there with you?"

"Just one."

"To your . . . ?"

"My right."

"On the door side. You were against the wall. And you don't think there were any windows there. How many in front?"

"Two men in front."

"Anyone behind?"

"Yes."

"Two men in front, one next to you, and one behind."

"I think . . . yes."

"And they didn't have their masks on in the van."

"But I don't know how I know that for sure. Maybe I don't know that."

Frawley chided himself for focusing on the van. The van was going to turn up torched. "How did they communicate? Did they speak much?"

"Very little. 'Right.' 'Left.' 'No.' 'Yes.' Like that." She looked up at him. "That's how I know they didn't have their masks on."

"By their voices."

"They were so *beastly* in the bank, with them on. So distorted and . . . not even human. Like monsters. Can I . . . should I talk about the masks?"

"Go ahead."

"They were all the same. Like Jason, like *Friday the 13th*."

"You mean hockey masks."

"Yes, but—with these scars drawn all over them. Black stitches."

"Stitches?" said Frawley.

"Like hash marks. Sutures." There was fear in her distant gaze. "Why do that? Why *scars*?"

Frawley shook his head. It was a strange detail and his investigation welcomed strange details. "So they didn't speak much in the van."

She was reluctant to return there. "No."

"Did they seem to know where they were going?"

"Maybe, yes."

"Did they tell you where you were going?"

"No."

"Did they tell you you were going to be released?"

"No."

"Did you think you were going to be released?"

"I . . ." She stared into the middle distance, almost in a trance. "No."

"Did the van make stops?"

"It did."

"What for?"

"Traffic, I guess."

"Okay. No doors opened, no one in or out?"

"No."

"And you never tried to escape?"

A blink. "No."

"Were you ever on a highway?"

"Yes. For a while."

"Were you wearing a seat belt?"

She touched her lap, aiding her memory. "Yes." Then, green eyes focusing on him: "I didn't try to escape because they had guns."

"Okay." Wanting not to break the spell. "You asked them no questions?"

She shook her head.

"And they never addressed you?"

"No."

"Nothing was said. Basically they left you alone in the backseat."

"The middle seat."

"Right."

"Yes. Except . . ."

"Go ahead."

She was far away again. "The one who was sitting next to me. Not *next* to me . . . but in the same seat, the same bench, the two of us. The one who blindfolded me. I could tell somehow . . . he was looking at me."

"Looking at you."

"Not like that. I mean . . . I don't know. Maybe it was just a feeling."

"Not like what?"

"Not like, you know, *looking*. Just, I don't know. Just *there*."

"You had his full attention. And then what?"

Her eyes swelled in the recalling. "They just drove and drove. Seemed like hours. I guess I have a sort of . . . it seemed like it went on forever, but now it's like there were whole blocks of time . . . I'm just blank. I know that at some point I realized we were off the highway, making lots of turns. I was praying they would stop, praying it would be over—and then all of a sudden they did stop, and all I wanted to do was keep on driving. The engine was still running but I could tell the ride was over. That's when they shook my Coach bag." She found Frawley's face. "My credit cards, my car keys . . . ?"

"If they turn up, you'll get them back. The one in the seat next to you, he made the threat?"

"No. No, the voice came from in front of me, the angry one. The one who took me to the vault." She pulled at her stained fingers. "I had trouble with the combination."

"Was he the driver?"

"I don't . . . no, I don't think he was. He wasn't—because I was on the left, and his voice came from the right front."

"Would you say he was in charge?"

"I don't know. I know he did the talking then."

"What about the one next to you?"

She lifted the lap of her skirt to cross her legs, and Frawley noticed that her shoes were gone, just dirty stockinged feet. "I think there might have been tension."

"Between them? How so?"

"The angry one, he was the one who wanted to take me."

"From the bank. And the others?"

"One of them questioned him—I'm not sure, it happened so fast. I think it was the one who sat next to me."

"So the angry one, as you call him, he takes your license."

"And then the side door opened. The one next to me helped me out."

"Door slid open or opened out?"

"I . . . I don't remember."

"And the one next to you—you say he 'helped you out'?"

"Just that—I was afraid of falling. I was afraid of *everything*. But he didn't let me fall."

"So he didn't pull you from the van?"

"No. He grabbed my arm and I went. It didn't feel like I had a choice."

"Did he lift you down, walk you down?"

"I wasn't—I mean, of *course* I was scared, I was very scared, *terrified*." She uncrossed her legs, sitting still. "But it wasn't, like . . . I didn't think he was . . . maybe I was naive. If it was the angry one taking me, I would never have left the van on my own. I wouldn't have been able to *walk*."

"Okay, slow down. Did you get a sense of his size?"

"Yes. He was big."

"Big as in strong?"

"As in strong, tall."

"Would you say he was friendly?"

She picked up on Frawley's implication. "No. Impersonal. Just, not angry."

"Okay. So you're out of the van."

"I'm out of the van, and we're walking fast. He's got me by the arm. The ocean stunk, really foul, and the wind was hard. I thought I was at the airport— I heard planes—but it wasn't a runway because the ground was sand around my feet. It was a beach. And basically he told me to walk to the water until I felt it on my toes, and not to take off the blindfold until then. It was so windy, and the sand was blowing up, airplanes screaming overhead—I could barely hear him. But then suddenly my arm was free and I was on my own. I know I stood there for like a minute, idiotically, until I realized I had to be walking. I took very short steps—not even steps really, dragging my feet through the cold sand, arms out in front of me, because I had this image of myself stepping off a cliff. It took, literally, forever. The longest walk of my life. Another plane roared over-head, a rising roaring, a terrible noise, like pulling all the air up with it—and then the sand was different and I felt water washing around my heels. I pushed off the blindfold and I was alone. And I had only walked maybe, thirty feet." The toes of one foot rubbed the heel of the other as she looked at her ruined stockings. "Why did they take away my shoes in the first place?"

"To keep you from kicking or running, don't you think?"

She reached for the water and swallowed some down, her hand shaking more now. "My first day of kindergarten, I pitched a fit when my mother tried to leave, and Mrs. Webly took away my new patent leather shoes as punish-ment. And just like that, I stopped crying." She rubbed at her stained fingers.

Frawley let her burn off more residual adrenaline, then focused her on the robbery itself. She took him through it with mixed results, returning again and again to the garish black stitches on their masks. Tears pushed to her eyes but did not spill as she recounted Davis Bearns's beating at the hands of the "angry" bandit. "He had fallen . . . he was just sagging off the chair . . . and that one just kept hitting him . . ."

"Did you see Mr. Bearns activate the alarm?"

She reached for her Poland Spring again but held the bottle without opening it, watching water slosh around inside. Car-wreck eyes. Something was up, but he couldn't tell if it was her account or just trauma bleeding through.

"No," she answered softly.

The foot traffic outside the break-room door had quieted. "Ms. Keesey, are you sure you don't want to go somewhere and get checked out?"

"I'm sure. I'm fine."

"It was a long ride. And you said yourself, you can't really account for the entire trip."

"I just . . . spaced. I shut down, that's all."

"It's available to you now. It couldn't hurt."

Her eyes came up on him, cooler, assertive. "Nothing happened."

Frawley nodded. "Okay."

"But that's what everyone's going to think, isn't it?"

He tried to distract her. "Is someone coming here to—"

"He rubbed his gun against my butt." She blinked a few times, fighting back tears and exhaustion. "The angry one. While we were standing at the vault. He said some things, told me what he wanted to do to me. That is *all*."

Frawley started off shaking his head, shrugging, searching for something to say, then ended up just nodding. "Do you want to tell me what he said?"

Her smile was fierce and cutting. "Not particularly."

"Okay," said Frawley. "Okay."

"Now you're looking at me like I'm some stupid . . ."

"No, no, no."

"Like I'd jump in a van with *anybody*."

"No. Look—"

He reached over for his tape recorder. In fact he had nothing to say to her. He only hoped the act of pressing STOP would provide a distraction.

She sat there breathing deeply, thinking deeply. "When I was walking to the ocean . . . I thought of nothing. Nothing, no one. But in the van, driving, blindfolded like that—I saw my life. I saw myself as I was, as I am, my life up until this day. Today—it's my birthday."

"I see," said Frawley.

"Sounds crazy. Just another day, I know. I don't know why it matters." She crossed her arms, her stockinged foot bobbing. "It doesn't matter."

A quick thank-you and a handshake could have ended it there if she weren't still wearing his coat.

"Look," Frawley said. "I've seen people—bank customers standing in line to cash their check when a two-time loser comes through the door and announces a robbery—who come away never looking at life the same. People think of bank robbing as a victimless crime, an insured crime, but when a teller gets a gun pointed in her face—that can change a person's life forever. I'm only telling you this so you can prepare yourself."

"I haven't even cried yet—"

"The adrenaline's fading, you're probably going to feel a little depressed for a while. Sort of like mourning—just let it happen. It's normal. Some people bottom out all at once, others just gradually get better until one day they don't wake up thinking about it. For a little while, you'll see these guys behind every closed door. But you will get better."

She was staring at him, rapt, as though he were turning over tarot cards. He knew he had to watch himself here. A pretty girl, hurt, vulnerable. Taking advantage of that would have been like pocketing the bait bills from the vault. She was his vault now, his vic.

"And stay off the Diet Coke," he added. "No caffeine or alcohol, that's key. Stick with water. In the breast pocket of my jacket, you'll find my card."

She fished one out as he stood. "What about my car?"

"You should be able to pick it up whenever. It'll take a hand-washing to get all the fingerprint dust off. If you don't have spare keys, you should be able to get them from your dealer."

She curled her toes. "And my shoes?"

"Those, we'll have to hold on to for a while. Crime lab people, that's how they are. If they could wrap you up in a paper bag and put you on a shelf for a few weeks, they would."

"Might not be such a bad idea." She slipped out of his jacket as she stood, smoothing the sleeves before returning it to him. "Thank you." She read his card. "Agent Frawley."

"No problem." He dropped it over his arm, its tempting warmth. "And don't worry about those threats. Just focus on yourself."

She nodded, looking at the door, not yet moving. "Actually, my license—it had my old address anyway."

No point in telling her that the bandits had likely been following her for weeks before that morning. Frawley felt up his jacket for a pen. "Let me get your current."

FRAWLEY WATCHED HER HUG a pink-faced, white-haired man in a pin-striped suit inside the door fan.

"Seemed like a good wit," said Dino. "You want to handle the summary narrative?"

Frawley shook his head, still watching her. "Gotta do my 430 case-initiation form for D.C."

"Uh-oh," said Dino, coming up closer to Frawley. "That look in his eyes."

Frawley shook his head, watching daughter and father walk past the front windows and away. "I was ready to write her off completely, except . . ."

"C'mon. I can take it."

"Except that she moved about a year ago. The address we had is out-of-date."

"So she has a new address. And?"

Frawley turned back, watching the wise smile dawn on Dino's seen-it-all face.

"Nah," Dino said, playing at disbelief. "Can't be."

Frawley nodded. "Charlestown."

3
THE SPLIT

DOUG CARRIED A HAM and cheese sub from the Foodmaster out across Austin Street and up Old Rutherford Avenue to the O'Neil Memorial Ice Skating Rink.

"Hey, hon," said the oaken woman smoking behind the rentals counter, and Doug waved hello with a genial smile that belied his down mood. Nailed to the wall behind her was a yellowed newspaper photo of Doug in his Charlestown High hockey uniform, which he took care to ignore.

The rink inside was only half-lit, Boston Bruins and Charlestown Youth Hockey rafter flags hanging high over the day-care kids leaning on milk crates and chop-stepping their way around the overweight instructor in a slow parade. Two teachers stood outside the boards, sloppy, elephant-legged neighborhood girls in long shirts and stretch pants who checked out Doug as he passed them for the skate-scored bleachers.

Jem and Gloansy were halfway up the risers where the bleachers ended at center ice, splitting a sausage-and-burger pizza and drinking out of paper-bagged bottles of beer the shape of artillery shells.

"What are you two pedophiles up to?" said Doug, rapping their fists and sitting one row above them.

Freddy "Gloansy" Magloan of the Mead Street Magloans wore the same splotchy freckles that were the birthright of his seven brothers and sisters. His face was jaw-heavy, jocular and dumb, his ears so mottled they were tan. His pale hands were tarnished with the same sun rust.

Jimmy "Jem" Coughlin of the Pearl Street Coughlins was all shoulders and arms, his head a small squash under swept-back hair that was thick and old-penny brown. The pronounced ridge beneath his nose didn't help, and then there were those blue-white snowflake eyes. The Jem machine operated at two speeds: Mirth or Menace. The gang of knuckles around his emerald-studded gold Claddagh ring were still purple and swollen from his tune-up of the assistant manager.

"Here's the criminal mastermind now," said Jem. "Where's the Monsignor?"

"Coming," said Doug, setting his bag down over some ancient racist knife-scratchings.

"Cheryl, man," said Gloansy, crooking his head at the teacher with the dark, frizzy hair squeezed off in a leopard-print scrunchy. "Ever I see her, I think of third-grade class picture—Duggy, right? Front row and center. *Little House on the Prairie* dress with ruffles, pink plastic shoes. Hands folded, legs crossed tight at the ankles."

"Last time that happened," chewed Jem.

Doug remembered one day in fourth grade, coming out of school to find Cheryl waiting. To kiss him, she said, which she did—before shoving him backward off a curb and running home laughing, leaving him scratching his head about girls for the next few years. Home for her, then as now, was the town-within-a-town of the Bunker Hill Projects, a brick maze of boxy welfare apartments whose architects had taken the word *bunker* to heart. A couple of years ago her younger brother, known around Town as Dingo, got dusted and leaped off the Mystic River Bridge, catching a good shore breeze and only missing his mother's gravel roof by two buildings. One of the black kids tripping over the ice out there now was Cheryl's.

"Think about her mouth and where it's been," said Jem.

"Don't," said Gloansy, his own mouth full.

"That girl could give a plastic soup spoon gonorrhea."

Gloansy said, garbled, "Let me swallow first, for fuck's sake."

"You know she had to take a Breathalyzer once, came back blue-line pregnant?" Jem took a mouthful of beer and gargled it. "Think of Gloansy's shower drain trap, all gooey and hairy—that's Cheryl's tonsils."

"For Christ!" protested Gloansy, choking down his food.

Desmond Elden entered the rink, muscled though not to the extent of Jem or Doug, but with an added bookishness, thanks to his thick-rimmed Buddy Holly eyeglasses. He wore lineman's boots, fading jeans, and a denim work shirt with the Nynex logo over the pocket, his fair hair matted down from wearing a phone company helmet all morning.

Dez gave Cheryl and her posse the courtesy of a *Howzitgoin'* before mounting the bleachers, his insulated lunch sack in hand.

Jem said, "I should dock you just for being polite."

Dez sat down one riser below them. "What, you didn't even say hello?"

"Fuckin' softie," said Jem. "Anything with chicks."

Doug said, "Where'd you put the truck?"

"Foodmaster parking lot. Cruiser there, so I walked the long way around, just in case." Dez unzipped the nylon bag between his knees and pulled out a thick sandwich wrapped in wax paper, smiling. "Ma made meat loaf last night," he said, then bit in big. "Gotta snap to. I'm due in Belmont in like forty minutes, install a ISDN line."

Jem took a long pull on his beer and pointed at Dez. "That's why I hadda swear off work. Too many commitments."

Gloansy toasted that. "Amen, brother."

Doug cracked open his Mountain Dew. "So let's do this."

Jem ripped a burp and none of the kids on the ice even turned their heads. Doug liked the rink for its awful acoustics. He was worried more and more about surveillance around Town, but no bug could outwit those rumbling refrigerators.

"Not much to say," said Jem. "Looks like we're out clean. Newspapers got everything wrong, as usual. Nothing went sour until the end, when everything did."

Gloansy said, "Duggy, man, you said banks train their people not to hit any alarms until after."

"They do. It's a safety issue. Plus banks carry kidnap and extortion insurance, and shit like that voids it."

Jem shrugged. "So the homo pissed himself. Thing is, it shouldn't of happened. Could of been real fucking bad. Time to settle up now, and these things get counted. Gloansy, my friend, it's time to pay the piper. You're docked."

Gloansy's face fell, his open mouth full, looking at Jem. "What the fuck?"

"It was your watch. You knew Monsignor Dez had to leave the vault and teller bells hardwired."

"*I'm* getting fucking docked? *Me?*"

"All you had to do. Keep the citizens down on the floor and away from the bells."

"Fuck you." Gloansy was teary, he was so shocked. "Fuck you, all I had to do? Who boosted the work van? You think you fuckin' . . . think you *walked* to and from this job? And who torched the rides after the delayed switch?"

"Who was watching that kid at the ATM instead of the bankers at his feet?"

"Fuckin' . . . so who delayed the switch? You're the one that brought the manager along. Why'n't you dock yourself?"

"Plan to. Same as you. A hundred-dollar whack to the each of us."

"A hundred—" Gloansy's face relaxed, pulling back into a fuck-you frown. He punched Jem's left triceps hard, saying, "Fuckin' ass munch."

Jem smiled tongue-out and slapped Gloansy's cheek. "Fuckin' *this* close to bawling, Shirley Temple."

"Fuck you," said Gloansy, shaking it off, all better now, taco-ing another sloppy slice into his freckled mouth.

Doug took a bite out of his sandwich, so fucking tired of the whole fucking thing.

"So, the magic number," said Jem, tearing open packets of salt over the closed pizza box. "This is per, now, and net expenses." With his finger he traced out a five-digit sum: 76750.

Gloansy worked on the upside-down figure until his eyes grew big.

Dez nodded, a smile flickering before he checked on Doug.

Doug finished chewing, then leaned down and blew the salt figure away.

Jem went on, "That's minus a chunk I dropped into the kitty for the next one, replace the tools I dumped. And some short bundles of new consecutives, I incinerated, not worth worrying over. And then ten percent off the top for the Florist. Overall, a fucking dynamite haul. Oh—yeah." He reached into his back pocket. "From the ATM. Stamps for all."

Doug said, "What's this with the Florist?"

Jem passed out the stamp sheets. "His tribute."

"And why you involving him?"

"It's not like he doesn't already know about it. It's the right thing to do."

"How'd he know?" Doug let his sandwich drop back onto the wrapper on the bench. "I didn't tell him. I didn't tell anybody. Unless someone here told someone, he didn't know."

"Duggy. People know. People in the Town."

"Tell me how they know."

"They just know."

"What do they know? What? Yeah, maybe they *think* they know something. But *thinking* you know something, and actually *knowing* something—that's two different things. The cops and the G, maybe they *think* they know something. But not *knowing* it is exactly what keeps us on the street, keeps us in the game."

"Fergie knows a lot of secrets, Duggy."

"And now he's got one more on us. I don't see the point of putting it out there."

"We don't duke him, there could be trouble down the road."

"How?" Doug felt himself getting carried away and not caring. "Trouble how? What trouble, explain that to me. This 'Code of Silence' trial now, everybody in town is an opera star. Clutching their hankies and belting it out for the cops and the papers. The fat lady, she's singing. Just tell me you didn't visit him in his shop."

"I saw him out on the pier. He's my mother's cousin, Duggy."

"We're not Italian, Jem. Third or fourth cousin means maybe a nice Christmas card, not 'Here's my kidney, you should need one.' The G is all over his shop, that is guaran-fucking-teed."

"It's so. But you think *he* don't know that?"

Dez piped up, "That thirty-five grand or so you gave him—he gonna wash that clean before sending it out to the IRA?"

Jem scoffed and said, "All that's rumor. That's just for street cred."

Doug said, "Dez *thinks* he knows that Fergie fronts for the IRA. He doesn't *know* it—not like he *knows* that Fergie puts dust out on the street, not to mention has a taste for it himself. This is a sixty-year-old man on angel dust you're meeting out there on the pier, Jem kid. Chatting with, handing bank money to."

"Look, Fergie's always putting things into motion. You're working on our next, sure, but he said, and in not so many words, that he's got some big things that would suit us nice. That we could buy from him."

Doug thought he was going to levitate out of his seat. "Why the fuck would we want to work for someone else? *One* good reason."

"These are marquee scores."

"Marquee scores!" Doug waved at the vanished salt. "You got kids in braces or something, that's not enough? We got more than we can conveniently wash as it is. Marquee scores mean marquee busts, Jem boy. Fergie's got room on his roster exactly because Boozo's crew got lazy up in New Hampshire and Boozo's tweak-freak son, Jackie the Jackal, shot up that armored guard. And the heat from that is *still* out all over the Town. Jackie's what, he's our age? Younger? And he's gonna die in prison. He'd fucking die there anyway, for being stupid and running his mouth, but eighty years is not something he's gonna survive. And that's without a murder charge ever being brought—that's the racketeering thing, interstate, plus the firearms mandatories. This isn't kid stuff anymore. We all of us, except the Monsignor, got strikes against us. We take a fall now, with twenty-year gun mandies, we're never gonna land. Got it? I gotta spell this out in salt for you?"

Gloansy said, "I ain't taking no more falls."

Doug said, "And I ain't taking any falls before you. The only thing the law likes less than pro outlaws are reckless outlaws. The G—they don't like it when you rob banks, that's fine, fair. Honest heat is honest heat. Toss in kidnapping and assault, their fucking palms start getting sweaty. They take that personal. Suddenly they got jobs on the line—reassignment, whatever. They need results. And we can't win going up against them nose-to-nose. This crazy Cagney shit you pull, it draws them out. Things go wrong on every job. Trick is, keep moving, don't fix one fucking mistake with another."

In the silence that followed, Doug realized he had gone on what was for him a tirade. He was the only one who could talk to Jem like this, and even he was pushing it. Gloansy, or especially Dez, they would have been on the floor with Jem's knee in their throat.

Jem was making a show of fishing food out of his teeth with his tongue. Doug had been sitting on this stuff too long. He didn't even know specifically why he was so pissy himself. It was the jokes, it was the beer on their breath and the hour of the day. It was all of their youth going round and round in circles on the ice down there.

"Fuck it," Doug said with a wave. "You want to duke the Florist, fine, duke the Florist. Keep him happy? Fine. But I won't work for him. We are pros here, not cowboys in a Wild West show. We're different. That's what keeps us ahead in this cat-and-rat game. Free agents, we gotta stay smart, full-time, else we'll get beat. I will walk away before I became some gangster's personal fucking ATM machine. If I even *thought* that was coming, I'd walk away right now."

Jem put on a grin. "Bullshit. You could never walk away."

Doug said, "Have to, someday."

"You'd make a real good old woman, you didn't have such a fucking nose for crime. Only you could be raggy about this score."

Doug chewed and watched the kids make their way off the ice, skate-walking to the doors.

"Duggy's share is back at my place," said Jem, proceeding as if nothing had happened. To Gloansy and Dez, he handed over orange-headed locker keys. "Your pieces are out front. Remember, it's all dirty linen and's got to be washed. Now, last thing—bank manager."

Looking at Doug. Doug shrugged and said, "Yeah?"

"You grabbed her license from me. What's the scoop?"

"Nothing."

"Thought you said she lives in the Town."

"Hasn't been back home yet. I think we can forget about her. So long as you ditched the masks, she's got nothing."

"Course I ditched the masks."

"Well, you seemed pretty fond of your artwork, I want to be sure."

"Masks, tools, everything ditched."

Doug shrugged. "Then whatever."

Gloansy said, "I saw her on the news, being walked away, her father. She's too shaken up to tell them shit anyway."

"Yeah," said Doug, swiping his nose like the manufactured cold was getting to him.

"Done, then," said Jem. "We're clear. With that, this investment club meeting is officially adjourned."

Dez packed up his trash. "Gotta rock."

"I'm behind you," said Doug, bagging his.

"Whoa, where you running off to?" said Jem. "What clock you on?"

"I got some stuff," said Doug.

"Blow it off. Free ice now. Me and Gloansy gonna skate."

"Can't," said Doug, rising, Dez already smacking fists and starting out.

Jem frowned and said to Gloansy, "Guy lives in my house, I never see him."

Doug said, "I gotta breeze. You know how I get, between things."

"So stay. Have a few tall boys with us, relax. Gloansy brought his goalie pads, he's gonna let us take shots at him."

"Fuck you," sang Gloansy, lifting out the last skinny slice.

"I'm walking," said Doug, starting down the scarred planks. "Besides, you're wrong. I do got a job. Keeping you homos in line."

"Ho, shit," said Jem, their little tiff passing like a storm cloud. "That's some full-time work right there."

DOUG CAME OUT THROUGH the doors as Dez was pulling his cut from the rink lobby lockers, the size of two thick phone books wrapped in butcher paper. Jem had left a Filene's shopping bag folded in there and Dez dumped the package inside, rolling the bag into a bundle and tucking it up under his arm, football-style. They walked together through the doors out into the hard, white daylight.

Dez said, "Ma's been after me to get you over for dinner again."

"Yeah, we'll do that soon." The high sun summoned up in him a tremendous, satisfying sneeze.

"God bless," said Monsignor Dez.

Doug squinted. "You going up to drop half that in the collection box right now?"

"No time. Later."

"St. Frank's gonna put a hot tub in the confessional before you're done."

Dez looked at Doug without a smile. "The split's light," he said. "Isn't it."

Doug rubbed his eyes. "Ah, fuck it."

"Why? Why let him be in charge? You know you run things. And that whole dock thing, that was a charade."

Doug shrugged, truly uninterested. "Hey, what's a IDSN line?"

"ISDN," Dez corrected. "Data streaming, high-speed Internet. Like if I was a plumber bringing you your water, this'd be a much wider pipe. Fiber optics. Makes World Wide Web surfing like changing channels."

"Yeah? That the future?"

"Today it is. Tomorrow, who knows? Someday there'll be no wires, I know that. Someday there'll be no linemen."

"Maybe you oughta think about getting something going on the side."

Dez smiled in the direction of the highway. "I gotta roll." They rapped fists, Dez taking off down the incline with the bundle of cash under his arm.

Doug turned and went the other way, up Old Rutherford, habitually scanning the parked cars for snoops as he went. He turned right on Devens and followed it around to Packard, a one-way street, one of the few in the tightly packed Town with a back alley. The narrow alley showed bow windows and Juliet balconies over brick walls separating tiny parking spaces. Empty trash cans stood at every cobblestoned parking court except Claire Keesey's, the plum Saturn still gone. A poker hand of takeout menus was fanned inside her back screen door.

Keep moving, he told himself, jamming his fists inside the pockets of his warm-up jacket, pretending he was satisfied. All he had done was save her from a beating. He lowered his head like a regular citizen and walked on.

4
PLAYSTATION

T HE BACK OF THE hill was Charlestown without the gas streetlamps. It was wooden row houses with stepped roofs and front doors that opened onto sidewalks sloping at forty-five-degree angles to the sea. During the Blizzard of 1978, on plastic Super Saucers and collapsed cardboard box "project sleds," neighborhood kids got up over twenty miles an hour bombing down the sheer faces of Mystic, Belmont, and North Mead before bottoming out hard onto Medford Street below.

The gentrification that had made new virgins out of other Town fiefdoms such as Monument Square, City Square, and the Heights, had embraced but not yet transformed the uncapitalized old lady known simply as "the back of the hill." Its curbs saw a few Audis and Acuras, designer water bottles lay in some recycling bins, and most exteriors had been power-washed and painted smooth. But Irish lace still fluttered in a few windows, a handful of Boston firefighters and city employees still calling it home.

Doug ate two buttered corn muffins out of a wax paper bag at the crest of Sackville Street. His large tea, thick with milk and sugar, steamed out of the tall Lori-Ann's cardboard cup set on the roof of his rust-pocked 1986 Caprice Classic.

Breakfast there was for him a regular thing. The house he was looking at across the street, with its rich red siding and nurse-white trim—formerly dove gray over flaking charcoal—was the home of his youth. He still considered it his mother's house even though she had abandoned it, and him, when he was six years old. His father managed to hold on to it for ten more years, meaning, and this seemed impossible, that Doug had lived half his life away from it now. It still ruled his dreams: the monster oil tank in the stone basement; the dark wood parlor with cabinet radiators and custard wallpaper; his corner bedroom on the first floor, swept by passing headlights.

This was the place he went to get his head together. A bungled job—this one had netted them plenty, but he would forever think of the caper as failed—always left him in a sour mood, but never with the mental mono like this one had. He returned to the heist over and over in his head, trying to untangle its faults, only to get caught up again in the image of the branch manager blind-folded next to him in the van. This image possessed him, how fragile she had appeared, yet also how composed. How she had wept tearlessly beside him—he had felt her shaking, her hands limp and empty in her lap—like a statue of a blindfolded woman crying. Having followed this stranger around, he now felt himself getting sucked into the mystery of her existence.

He was breaking out of that rut today. It was April and the sidewalks of the Town were teeming with Claire Keeseys, drawn to the neighborhood by its cheap rents and safe streets, baring their shoulders and legs after a long winter's hibernation. The Town was a stocked lake and fishing was back in season. This fog, whatever it was that had descended on him at the beginning of the bank job and lingered in the days that followed—it was finally lifting.

He shook his head and crumpled up the muffin bag. His not telling the others about her triggering the alarm: that was not going to haunt him anymore. It was over with. In the past. Time to move on.

"CHECK THIS OUT," said Jem.

Doug set down his liter slam of Mountain Dew and accepted the wrinkled Victoria's Secret spring catalog. On page after page, Jem had applied a drop of water to each of the lingerie models' breasts, puckering the thin paper and raising persuasive nipples.

Doug nodded, turning the pages. "And you say this project only took you half the morning?"

"Some days, you know? You just wake up horny. I have all this fucking energy, I already worked out twice today, shoulders and calves. What do you do, days when you can't focus on anything because your mind keeps running back to your dick?"

"Some call it 'applying the pine tar.'"

"No, no," said Jem, shaking his head. "No, I don't do that anymore."

"Excuse me, what?" Doug smiled. "You don't do that anymore?"

"They say weed saps your ambition? I say, yanking it does. Saps your drive. Makes you soft, more ways than one. Always leaves me tired, dopey. I'm serious."

"You'll be down in the basement *three* times a day, working out, and all that's gonna happen is, spume's gonna back up into your system, turn you gay. I seen it happen, man. It's tragic."

"Voice of experience here."

"Radical idea just came to me out of the blue. How about going easy on yourself, getting a regular girlfriend?"

"I think I do awright. And I'm gonna start doing even better. Abstinence makes the dick grow fonder. Hey, you're the last person should be giving shit. Mister fucking life change already."

Doug dragged the remote off the glass-topped coffee table and opened up the cable menu over the soft-core pool-table scene playing on Jem's black box Spice Channel. He found a kung fu movie on pirated pay-per-view, put it on the huge TV. "Your eyesight improves, maybe you can get a smaller screen."

"Hey, how about this. Tonight, right? They say yanking it also gives you hairy palms, right? Okay, we get that spirit gum like we used for the Watertown job, the stuff that gave us fake chins and cheeks? Slop it on our hands instead, then shred up a wig, stick fur on there. Walk in the door at the Tap with all the yuppies, give the place a big wave. High-five the bartender with our furry mitts."

Doug grinned. "You walk in reading your catalog?"

"I will spill water on my *crotch* before I walk in, a nice round little cum stain." He mimed walking into the bar for Doug, open hand raised, hips thrust forward, big Irish smile. "Evening, friends!"

Doug said, "This, right here, is why we don't have regular girlfriends."

"*For Christ,* then it's working." Jem hopped down Fonzie-style onto his green leather couch and grabbed a PlayStation controller. "Bruins," he called.

They played NHL '96 on Jem's Trinitron, first a couple of straight games with the crowd noise roaring in stereo, then they ignored the puck and skated their players around the ice looking for trouble, doling out hard checks until helmets popped off and the view zoomed in and the computer men threw down their gloves, the announcer bellowing in sim surround, *FIGHT!*

At one point, Jem turned to Doug, eyes bleary with game glee. "Like old times, kid! Can you tell me why we don't do this every fucking day?"

Eventually Doug had to step out past the tower speakers to take a piss. The worn checkerboard bathroom tile, the rotten shower curtain, the foam-coated pipes running up through the ceiling into his own third-floor bathroom: it all seemed virtual to him, flickering, pixilated. At that moment the computerized rink with its frictionless ice was more real to him than Jem's mother's house.

He stepped back into the narrow hallway with its undulating walls and twitching corners, a world with seams, the framed photograph of Cardinal Cushing hanging over the long-dry holy-water bowl looking poor-graphics fuzzy.

The sound of the glass rattling on the downstairs door sent a dead feeling through Doug, the caffeine and carbonation draining from his alter world, his game buzz gone flat.

"Krista's home," he said, returning to Jem.

"It's cool, man, she won't bug us."

"Let me get my take, get it squared away."

Jem smiled icily. "You're gonna breeze."

"No. Just get my shit squared away, then come right back down."

Jem stood, unconvinced, going to the frame of the doorway between the parlor and the neglected second-floor kitchen. He yanked on the molding and brought it loose in one long piece, revealing plywood shelves nailed in between the old walls like a row of mail slots. Jem withdrew Doug's bundle, leaving many smaller newspaper-wrapped parcels behind, many ripped open and spilling cash.

"You stash here?" said Doug.

"Why not?"

Doug nodded at Jem's room full of toys. "You take a search warrant and they see all this hardware against your tax return, then the electricity you steal, the cable you pirate—you don't think they're gonna tap on the walls?"

Jem shrugged and fit the molding back over the wall edge, hammering it in tight with the heel of his hand. "Always so fucking panicked. What, where you keep yours? You don't spend it, I know that."

"Not upstairs." Doug weighed the bundle in his hand. "Speaking of, how you fixed for clean linen?"

"Could always wash some."

Doug nodded, feeling residual good humor from the game. "We could go native tonight."

"Native it is. But only if we eat down there. Make a night of it this time, Duggy, do it right, not just up and back like going to the cash machine."

Doug nodded, cool with that. "I'll run this upstairs. You call the two homos."

DOUG RETURNED DOWNSTAIRS CARRYING a suede Timberland jacket with eight thousand dollars in twenties and fifties tucked inside the quilted lining.

Jem's mother's house was a classic Charlestown triple-decker of stacked, identical apartments. Diabetes had claimed Jem's mother's body in pieces, toes and feet first, then fingers, knees, kidney, and finally her heart. The disease had since spread to her house, rotting it room by room.

Doug's rent for the entire third floor was a couple of grand a year in real estate taxes. Jem, on the second floor, took care of all stolen utilities. The first floor was Krista's.

Kristina Coughlin was Jem's Irish twin, exactly eleven months and eleven days his junior. They bickered like husband and wife, she doing his laundry and occasionally cooking a meal—her mother's gooey chicken à la king her specialty— while he handed her money and generally laid around watching TV.

Krista shared her brother's wild streak. She had smoked her twenties down to the filter, the wear and tear just now starting to show, though she had snapped back from her pregnancy like a fresh rubber band. Merit Longs kept her in fighting trim. She had the Coughlin white-blue eyes, not so bad as her brother's, but when she drank, which was often, they glowed like demon jewels. Something she did to her hair with a razor kept the layers jagged and sharp. Like her partying soul, her dirty-blond hair lay flat and useless during the day, only to be teased into action every night. Her chest was criminally small, her long legs usually done out in stonewashed denim and heels in order to show off her proud, heart-shaped ass.

The three of them had grown up together, Doug spending so much time at the Coughlins' house as a kid that, when Doug's father went away, Jem's mother's taking him in presented little change. Krista and Doug had been a longtime, on-and-off couple, bad for each other in every way except carousing and sex. But now she couldn't let go. She had even tried to get clean with Doug after his release from prison, just weeks after her mother's death, but after a few months of sobriety fell out rather dramatically. For Doug, this had been a source of secret relief. She had been the heaviest of many stones roped around his neck. A couple of months later she was a couple of months pregnant and going around Town telling everybody that Doug was the father.

Now Krista sat at the table, watching Jem down half a High Life at a gulp. "And you wonder why he don't come down no more?" she said with smoke in her voice.

"Fuckin' Duggy doesn't mind—do you, kid? His will is *strong*." Douche-bag grin as he killed the bottle. "Maybe too strong." The dinged-up cordless phone trilled and he snapped it off the table, answering, "Gloansy, you fatherless prick," rising and wandering away down the narrow hall.

Almost nothing had changed on the first two floors in the three years since Jem's mother's passing. They were sitting now in the first-floor back parlor, directly below Jem's game room. A maple chair-rail border ran between velvety milk-white parchment wallpaper stained nicotine yellow and scuffed white wood. The only new addition was an empty walker sticky with old juice, and the padded plastic high chair with the nineteen-month-old girl strapped into it.

Shyne gripped a gnawed graham cracker in one hand, the pink ribbon of a sagging Mylar heart balloon in the other. Despite the name and its inventive spelling, Shyne was a white child, an alabaster doll with fine, threadlike copper hair and sad, small, Coughlin-white eyes. She looked nothing at all like Doug, eliminating any sliver of doubt remaining in anyone's mind—even his own—as to Krista's paternity claim.

Shyne chewed on her cookie and stared across the table at him. The little

girl was like a clock running slow. At a glance, you might not notice that anything was off, but spend any amount of time with her and you'd see she wasn't
ticking with the rest of the world. The few times Doug had brought this up
with Jem, Jem always countered with some pap he had heard on television,
about children developing at different paces. And he could never bring it up
with Krista, who was always reading him for signs that he was ready again to
care.

Alone with him now, Krista shook out her ash-blond hair and sat back from
the table, looking small and tired in the old armless chair. "I don't ask him to do
that."

Doug watched the perfectly still, half-inflated red balloon, wanting the year-
and-a-half-old to bounce it, something. "Do what?"

"Leave us alone together like this. It's fucked-up, his pushing. Sometimes I
swear he wants it more than I do. Like it's you and his friendship he wants to
save."

"Where are you getting all this?"

She shrugged as though it were obvious. "You don't come around. I mean,
he's an asshole, but you guys are like brothers." She combed up her hair with
her fingers, lifting it high off her ears, then letting it fall. "Or maybe it's me.
Like I'm so radioactive now you can't come around."

Doug sat back and sighed.

"It's you who's radioactive," she said. "Your X-rays got inside me young,
altered me permanently." She picked at a waffled, clover-shaped place mat, the
old food dried into it. "You came home late from your meeting last night."

"Jesus," he said. "That fucking glass rattling in the door."

Jem blew back into the room. "Gloaner's in," he said, dropping down in
front of Shyne and plucking at her balloon string, trying to grab her attention.
She gazed up at the sagging, slow-drifting heart. "Talking about your meetings
again?" Jem said. "Like fucking church with you."

Doug said, "It's in a church."

Jem gave up on his niece and turned to the gored table, rolling an Irish-flag
Zippo lighter over and over in his hand. "Hey, I go dry. Days at a time. Good
to step back now and then, reset the clock. Healthy. But this is, what, you're on
like a year or more? That's fucking hitting pause, kid."

"Two years next month."

"Key-reist almighty. Real comfortable up there in the front seat of that
wagon. I'm remembering one time you fell off—Dearden's wedding."

Krista smiled at the memory. Doug wondered why this always came up.
"That was a mistake."

"A mistake where you rocked the house, buddy. That was a night."

"I had almost a year in, until that slip."

"Slip? Yo, a *slip*? That was a high-dive, Rodney Dangerfield. A *Back to School* Triple Lindy belly flop. My point is, Duggy—you went right back. Look at you. Unshakable. Better, stronger, faster. So what's the fucking harm now and then, breaking down and getting a little wet with your poor, misguided, dry-throated friends?"

The phone rang and Jem snapped it up, answering, "Monsignor Kid-Toucher, what's the word?" again jumping to his feet and wandering away.

Krista sat there with her arms crossed, watching her daughter, lost in thought. "You're no priest," she said.

Doug turned to stare at her. "The hell are you talking about?"

"Even the Monsignor, Desmond the Nearsighted—the Pope of the Forgotten Village—even he lowers himself to drink with the boys."

"Because he can handle it. I can't."

"'Cause you're an *alcoholic*."

"Right. 'Cause I'm an *alcoholic*."

"So proud, though. Proud of your disease."

"Jesus, Kris," said Doug. "You were asking why I don't come down anymore?"

"So what's your high now? Just banks? Being the prince of these thieves?"

Doug frowned, done. He never talked about this with her, and she knew he didn't like her talking about it at all. "Any more shots you want to take before I go?"

Krista wiped some cracker mush from her daughter's mouth before turning on him. "Yeah. What's it gonna take to wake you up from whatever dream it is you're dreaming?"

When he didn't answer, she stood and carried her crossed arms into the kitchen, leaving him alone with Shyne's staring eyes.

THEY DROVE SOUTH THROUGH Rhode Island into Connecticut in Gloansy's tricked-out '84 Monte SS, black with orange trim. With three convicted felons on board and riding with a lot of cash, Gloansy couldn't be trusted to keep his Halloween-mobile under the speed limit, so Dez had the wheel. Doug sat up front with him, working the radio and using his side mirror now and then, idly checking for tails, while Jem and Gloansy split a six in back.

Two hours to Foxwoods, door to door. Careful as they were on the job, even a circulated bill could be marked, and washing the money was one of Doug's rituals. Insisting on it had the added benefit of slowing Jem's and Gloansy's spending.

Jem liked the roulette wheel and usually ended up dropping half of what he came to wash, drinking Seven and Sevens on the house and overtipping like a fifteen-year-old out on a date.

Gloansy bought a $12 cigar and set out to lose at high-min poker.

Dez floated back and forth between rooms, paranoid about pit bosses and floor managers with their cop eyes.

Doug worked steadily at the blackjack tables. He started by laying out sixty twenties on the felt of a $50 table and watched the dirty bills get dunked, forty-eight $25 chips pushed over to him. He drank Cokes without ice and played not to win but *to not lose,* which is different. Not losing means staying in every hand as long as possible, sitting on fifteens and sixteens and letting the dealer do all the busting. When he cashed in thirty minutes later, he was down only six chips. He folded the clean $1,050 into his zippered pocket and moved on to a $100 table, washing another quick $1,300 there before cashing out and rotating again.

It took him less than three hours to roll over the entire eight grand, ending hot, dropping a total of $320 in play and tips, a minuscule 4 percent commission to what the papers said was the most profitable casino in the country.

He met up with Dez again by a revolving red Infiniti. They made two complete circuits of the floor before an Indian war cry brought them to Jem, finding him doing a rain dance around the $50 roulette table, having finally scored on double zero. They cashed him in and steered him away.

Jem wanted to stop for a quarter-hour massage at one of the jack shacks near the casino, but Gloansy refused. "The red man just jerked me off for nineteen hundred dollars, I'm not going to pay some greasy geisha half a yard to do the same."

Instead, Doug drove them a few exits north to a steak house, where they filled a booth by the window in sight of the back-finned Monte. Soon the table was cluttered with steaks, High Lifes, and Doug's large no-ice Mountain Dew.

"So what's next, Duggy?" asked Gloansy.

"Strip club," chewed Jem.

"I mean, for us. For the team."

"I don't know," said Doug. "Think we need to mix it up a bit. I'm looking at a few things."

Jem said, "You talked about hitting a can."

"Maybe. Might be looking at something softer first."

Jem waved that off. "Fuck softer."

"Hitting a can means daylight. Armed guards, crowds, traffic. Going in strong like that, I don't know. We need a win."

Jem pointed his steak knife. "You're losing your edge, DigDug. Startin' to worry about you. Used to be you were the first one to throw down gloves and go."

"Used to be I got a hard-on every morning, homeroom. But now it's 1996 and I'm thirty-two, and I got that shit together."

Gloansy said, "Whatever it is, I'm ready. Anytime you say, Duggy."

Jem speared one of Gloansy's pinkest morsels and pushed it into his own mouth. "Anytime *I* say, corn hole."

Gloansy watched his steak get swallowed, poured ketchup on more. "I'm sure that's what I meant."

They ate and drank and got loud and stupid as usual. Doug tried to hustle them along like children, like he was running a fucking field trip outside the Town.

Gloansy said, "If I had to go one hundred percent legit? One of those batting cages things. Indoor/outdoor. Snacks and shit. Town needs something like that. What about you, Jem?"

"Liquor store, man. Also sell smokes, lottery, and porn. That's one-stop vice shopping."

Gloansy said, "That was Duggy's brainchild once upon a time."

"Duggy don't drink anymore. So that million-dollar idea goes to me."

Dez said to Jem, "Maybe put in a photo-developing booth too?"

Jem stared at him, Dez holding the look for another few seconds before cracking, Doug too, both of them falling into snorts of laughter.

"What is that?" said Jem. "The fuck is that, 'photo-developing booth'? It's not funny. He's not funny. It makes no fuckin' sense."

Jem's fury only made them laugh harder, the nearby tables starting to get annoyed. Doug went to use the head, and on his way back he saw what the other diners saw sitting there at the side booth: Gloansy and Dez playing goalposts with a packet of butter, Jem draining another longneck and staring out the window, bobbing his head to some interior tune. The glamorous life of the outlaw; the majesty of being the prince of these thieves.

The waitress delivered the check as he returned. "Let's split," Doug said.

"Got a stop to make on the way back," said Gloansy, grinning. "In Providence."

Doug was tired, he wanted to get back to Dodge. "Losers."

"No," Gloansy corrected him. "*Horny* losers."

The munching sound next to Doug was Jem eating the food bill.

DOUG RECEIVED A BEAUTIFUL lap dance from a long-haired Portuguese girl with teardrop-shaped breasts. He succumbed to the hypnotizing power of cleavage, the pendulousness of femininity, as she ran her small hands over the muscles of his shoulders and leaned boldly into his face. When she turned and ground herself into his lap, waist and hips undulating, the swelling in Doug's jeans reminded him that he was already four months in to going 0-for-1996.

Afterward, as she dressed in the seat next to him, Doug felt shitty and alone. Even a guy without a girlfriend had to admit that patronizing a strip club was like cheating on womankind in general, and with this vague sense of guilt came a philandering husband's determination to repair and repent. She relieved him of his $20 wad with a wink and a smile, then paused, giving his face a pursed-lipped look of concern. She reached out and explored, gently, the sliver of skin where Doug's left eyebrow was split, planting a soft kiss on the old scar there before walking off in search of her next dance.

The free kiss threw him. Twenty doughnuts for tits and friction, and then a gratis moment of actual intimacy? She could have saved the dance and charged him twenty just for the compassion.

Hitting the sidewalk outside the Foxy Lady was like quitting PlayStation, gravity reclaiming Doug, the night air a chilly hand cupping the back of his neck. Laughter gave way to honking snores at the Massachusetts border, the Monte reeking of spicy Drakkar Noir and stripper sweat as Doug sped back toward Dodge, his orphan mind once again returning to the image of Claire Keesey sitting blindfolded in the van. He crossed the bridge back into Town, turning toward Packard Street for a quick detour—just one look, her door, her dark windows—before shuttling his slumbering Townies back home.

5
INTERVIEW

"IN A WAY," said Claire Keesey, shrugging, "nothing since that morning's really seemed real to me."

She was curled up on the maroon cushions of a college rocking chair, the Boston College seal emblazoned over her head like a small sun. Her father's home office took up half of the living room, a desk-and-shelf unit of austere mahogany behind brass-handled French doors. Claire's mother—tight smile, anxious hands—had tucked a quilted paper towel beneath the tin BC coaster supporting Frawley's glass of water, as an extra layer of protection. Her father— gull-white hair over a rare-meat complexion—had taken the early Friday train to be there to answer the door and eyeball this agent of the FBI.

Frawley glanced at his Olympus Pearlcorder on the bookshelf near the head of the rocker. The handheld tape recorder had been a gift from his mother on the day of his graduation from Quantico, and every Christmas since, along with the sweater or turtleneck or pants from L.L. Bean—one year she mailed him bongo drums—she included a four-pack of Panasonic MC-60 blank microcassettes, *For your stocking!*

It clicked over, the tiny spools reversing, thirty minutes gone by. Claire sat with her legs tucked beneath her, arms folded, hands lost inside the cuffs. Her eggshell sweatpants announced *BOSTON COLLEGE* in a maroon and gold banner down one leg, her loose, green sweatshirt whispering *BayBanks* over her breast. It looked like a sick-day outfit, though her hair was brushed and smelled faintly of vanilla, and her face was scrubbed.

"My mother doesn't want me to work at the bank anymore. She doesn't want me to leave the *house* anymore. Last night, after three or so vodka tonics, she informed me that she had always known something bad was going to happen to me. Oh, and my father? He wants me to get a gun permit. Says a cop friend told him pepper spray is useless, only good on scrambled eggs. It's like, I'm *watching* them take care of me. Like the thirty-year-old me has gone back in time but is still a child in their eyes. And the scary thing? Sometimes I like it. Sometimes, God help me, I *want* it." She shuddered. "By the way, they don't believe me either."

"Don't believe what? *Who* either?"

"About nothing happening to me out there. My mother treats me like the ghost of her daughter, back from the dead. And my father's all '*Brrrhrrrhrrr,* business as usual, let's rent a movie . . .' "

Frawley's first impulse always was to counsel. He reminded himself that he wasn't there to help or to heal, he was there to learn. "Why do you think I don't believe you?"

"Everyone handling me like I'm porcelain. If people want me to be fragile, watch out, because I can be *very* fragile, no problemo." She threw up her handless cuffs in surrender. "So stupid, getting into that van. Right? Like a six-year-old on a pink bike, pulled into a van, and not even screaming or kicking. Such a *victim*."

"I thought you had no choice."

"I could have struggled," she argued. "I could have let them, I don't know, *shoot* me instead."

"Or ended up like your assistant manager."

She shook her head, wanting to relax but emotionally unable.

Frawley said, "I went out to visit Mr. Bearns. He said you haven't been by yet."

She nodded at the floor. "I know. I need to go."

"What's holding you up?"

She shrugged hard inside the baglike sweatshirt, avoiding the answer. "We're trained to help robbers," she said. "You know that, right? To actually *help* the criminals, and not to resist. Even to repeat their commands back to them, so they know that we're following their orders *to the letter*."

"To put the bandit at ease. To get him out of the bank more quickly, away from customers, away from yourself."

"Fine, okay, but—*helping* the thief? Like, rolling over for him? You don't think that's a little whacked?"

"The vast majority of bank theft is drug addicts looking to score. Their desperation, their fear of being sick, makes them unpredictable."

"But everything is like, *Do what the robber says*. Like—*Don't give him dye packs if he tells you not to*. Hello? So why do we have them? And—*Be courteous*. What other business do they say that in? 'Thank you, bank robber, have a nice day.' "

Through the side window, Frawley watched two boys tossing around a tennis ball a few backyards away, making showtime catches on a late Friday afternoon. "Speaking of training," he said. "It's written policy at BayBanks for the openers to enter one at a time, the first one confirming that the bank is secure, then safe-signaling to the second."

She nodded contritely. "Right. I know."

"And yet this was not your usual practice."

"Nope."

"Why not?"

Shrug. "Laziness? Complacency? We had an all-clear for the tellers."

"Right, the window shades. But the tellers don't arrive until a half hour after you two. And setting off the silent alarm—you're trained to wait until it is safe to do so."

"Again—what is the point of sounding an alarm *after* a robbery? Can you tell me that? What is the *point*?"

"Mr. Bearns put you both at risk."

"But you couldn't *know* that while it was going on," she said, angry suddenly, tearing into him with her eyes. "They were inside the bank, *waiting* for us when we walked in—outnumbering us, scaring the *shit* out of us. I didn't think I was ever walking out of that bank again."

"I'm not placing blame, I'm only trying to get at—"

"So why haven't I gone to visit Davis? Because I couldn't stand to let myself fall to pieces on him. *Me,* little suburban *me,* not a scratch on her, safe and fine and hiding out—at her *parents*?" She pushed hair off her forehead where there was no hair and looked away. "Why, he asked about me?"

"He did."

Her shoulders drooped. "The hospital won't tell me anything over the phone."

"He's going to lose most of the sight out of one eye."

Her handless sleeve went to her face. She turned to the window, toward the boys playing catch. He pushed it here, needing to be sure.

"Broken jaw. Busted teeth. And, unfortunately for me, no memory of that day. Not even of getting out of bed that morning."

She kept her face hidden. "I'm the only one?"

"The only witness, yes. That's why I'm sort of counting on you here."

She watched outside for a while, without actually watching anything.

"The rest of your staff," Frawley went on. "Anyone there you might consider disgruntled, or whom you could imagine providing someone else with inside information about bank practices, vault procedures—"

Already shaking her head.

"Even unwittingly? Someone who likes to talk. Someone with low self-esteem, who has a need to be liked, or to please others."

Still shaking *no.*

"What about someone who could have been blackmailed or otherwise coerced into providing information?"

Her face came away from her sleeve—sad but tearless, squinting at him. "Are you asking me about Davis?"

"I'm asking about everyone."

"Davis thinks that being gay—he's crazy, but he thinks it will hold him back. I told him, look around, half the men in banking live in the South End. This Valentine's Day, he asked what I was doing, and I said, you know, renting *Dying Young* and watching it alone, what else? And he had no one, so we went out together instead, for Cosmos at The Good Life, had a great time. We've only been real friends that long."

"Was there anyone new in Mr. Bearns's life? Maybe a relationship gone bad?"

"I wouldn't know. I never met his friends. He didn't talk about that with me. He was just fun. It was nice having a guy around who noticed when I got my hair cut."

"So you don't know if he was promiscuous?"

"Look . . . they *beat* him, remember? He's *innocent*."

He absorbed her disappointment in him, wondering if there wasn't something behind her flash of anger. The way Bearns was *innocent*. "So he was ambitious, he was looking to move up?"

"He was going to business school nights." Defensive now, firmly in Bearns's corner.

"Not you, though."

"Me? Nooo."

"Why not?"

"Business school?" she said, like he was crazy.

"Why not? Promotions. Advancement. Four other assistant managers you trained have leapfrogged over you to corporate. Why stay on the customer end?"

"It's been offered." A little pinch of pride here. "The Leadership and Management Development program."

"And?"

Claire shrugged.

Frawley said, "You can't tell me you love being a branch manager."

"Most weeks I hate it."

"Well?"

She was bewildered. "It's a *job*. It pays well, really well, more than any of my friends make. No nights, no Sundays. Nothing to take home. My father—*he's* a banker. I'm not a banker. I never saw banking as my career. I just—my career was being young. Young and uncomplicated."

"And that's over now?"

She sank a little in the chair. "Like my friends, right? They were supposed to be taking me out that night. My birthday, the big three-oh, whoo-hoo. They rented a limo—cheesy, right? So I wind up bailing because I'm still in shock from this, and I tell them, you already got the limo, go ahead without me. So they call the next day, going on and on about dinner and the cute waiter with tattooed knuckles and the guys who bought them drinks, and driving up Tremont Street singing Alanis Morissette out of the roof, and Gretchen making out with an off-duty cop outside the Mercury Bar—and I'm like, my God. Is this who I am? Is that who I *was*?"

Frawley smiled to himself. He found her vulnerability attractive, this confused girl with her soul laid bare, struggling with newfound introspection. But he resolved to keep his pursuit pure. He was after these Brown Bag Bandits, not a date with Claire Keesey.

"I should feel worse, shouldn't I," she said. "People I tell, they give me these looks like, *Oh my God*. Like I should be in intensive therapy or something."

He stood and snapped off his tape recorder. It felt like they were done. "It was a robbery. You were an unwilling participant. Don't search for any meaning beyond that."

She sat up, anxious now that he was preparing to leave. "So weird, my life suddenly. FBI agents showing up at my door. Do you know, I barely recognized you when you walked in today? I only mean that—I was so out of it when I talked to you last time. It's all a blur."

"I told you, it's normal. Robbery hangover. Sleep okay?"

"Except for these dreams, my God. My grandmother, she died three years ago? Sitting on the edge of my bed with a gun in her lap, crying."

Frawley said, "That's the caffeine. I told you, leave it alone."

"So you haven't made any arrests yet?"

He stopped by the doors. Was she stalling him because she wanted information? Or was she interested in him? Or was it simply that she didn't want to be left alone with her folks? "No arrests yet."

"Any leads?"

"Nothing I can really talk about at this time."

"I read about the burning van."

Frawley nodded. "We did impound a torched van, yes."

"No money inside?"

"Sorry—I really can't say."

She smiled and nodded, giving up. "I just—I want answers, you know? I want to know why. But there is no why, is there?"

"Money. That's the why. Pure and simple. Nothing to do with you." He tucked his kit under his arm. "You staying here a few more days?"

"Are you kidding me? It's like, if I don't get out of here now, I never will."

"You're going back to Charlestown?"

"Tonight. I'm counting the minutes."

Frawley wanted to remark on the irony of her moving back to bank bandit central, but decided that would only spook her.

FRAWLEY STEERED HIS BUREAU car, a dull red Chevy Cavalier, past mini-mansions with landscaped lawns swollen like proud chests, looking for a road out of Round Table Estates.

"Everything about her says squeaky-clean," Frawley said into his car phone. "Except for the fact that she's lying about something."

"Uh-huh," said Dino. "That the only reason you're buzzing around her?"

"I'm not buzzing," said Frawley, thinking back to her stalling him.

"Then what are you doing out there, Friday after six?"

"Canton is on my way home."

"Every single town on the South Shore of Massachusetts is on your way home, Frawl. You waste three hours a day driving back and forth between Charlestown and Lakeville. I like your devotion to living among the bandits, but this is getting to be an addiction. Frawl."

"Yeah, Dean?"

"Spring is in bloom. Know what that means?"

"A young man's fancy turns to . . . ?"

"Bank robbing. And buzzing around pretty flowers. You've got approximately sixty hours off ahead of you. That's your weekend, federally mandated and enforced. Take off the tie and get yourself laid. No more running ten miles, stopping to yawn, running ten more. For my sake."

Frawley hung a left at the end of Excalibur Street. "Copy that. Over and out."

6
THE SPONSOR

THEY HUDDLED AT THE back of Sacred Heart like father and confessor: the middle-aged man sitting relaxed, his left hand gripping the pew in front of him, gold band glowing brassy in the candlelight; and the younger man, half-turned in the row before him, watching bodies rise from the basement like ghosts wearing the raincoats they died in. The coffeepot downstairs had been emptied and rinsed, all the munchkins eaten, the stirrers and sugars boxed away, the trash bagged and pulled.

"Good meeting," said Frank G., the middle-aged man, fingers drumming the dark wood. "Crowded tonight."

"Weekends," agreed Doug M., as he was known here.

Frank G. was a Malden firefighter, father of two young boys, on his second marriage. In three years, that was the sum total of personal information Doug's sponsor had let slip. Nine years dry, Frank G. was devoted to the program, especially the *Anonymous* part, even though—or maybe because—Sacred Heart was apparently his neighborhood parish. Doug drove fifteen minutes north from Charlestown for every meeting, specifically to avoid having to pour out his soul to familiar faces, which seemed to him very much like taking a nightly dump out on his own front porch.

"So what's the word here, studly, how's things going?"

Doug nodded. "Going good."

"You spoke well down there. Always do."

Doug shrugged it off. "Got a lot to talk about, I guess."

"You have a tale to tell," agreed Frank G. "Don't we all."

"Every time, I say to myself—just stand up, speak your piece, two or three sentences, sit right down again. And I always end up doing five minutes. I think the problem is, meeting's one of the few places where I make sense to myself."

Frank G. nodded in his way, meaning *I agree,* and *I've been there,* as well as *It's all been said before,* and at times, *Go on.* He had the sort of dour, everyman face you find on the can't-sleep guy in a cold-remedy commercial, or the beleaguered car-pool dad suffering from occasional acid indigestion. "It's a gift, having a place like this to go. To sort it all out, keep focused. Some people, it's addictive. Too generous a gift."

"You noticed," said Doug.

"Sad-eyed Billy T. Getting off on the shame like that. It's opening night every night with him, rising to sing his song and spill his tears until they drop that curtain. That's his drunk now."

"Gotta feel that shame, though. Someone like me—I got nobody to let down, except myself. Nobody at home keeping me honest. Back in the Town"—in meeting, Frank G. had once mentioned growing up in Charlestown, though with Doug he never acknowledged their common background—"I don't feel it."

"The stigma."

"I talk about going to prison for beating someone up in a bar, there it's like, 'Hey, it happens. Some guy needed fine-tuning, but you did your time, you got out'—like something I hadda endure. Like I been in the army two years. People downstairs here? I mention prison and their eyes bug out, they pull their purses closer. And this is Malden, not some soft suburb—but it reminds me I'm not always living in the real world, where I am."

"Nobody's here looking for friends," said Frank G. "This here, you and I, this isn't friends. This is a partnership. What we have is a pact. That said, I don't know what all this is exactly about your being out there on your own."

"Okay. You're right."

"I'm your wife in this. Me, I'm your kids. I'm your parents and I'm your priest. You let yourself down, you let us all down, the whole system crumbles. And as to the others listening to you—hey, so they're not asking you for a ride back to the T. They respect the work. You're doing it. Coming up on two years? That's getting it *done*. I'd take respect over back pats, any day."

An old man came shuffling up the center aisle, shrugging on his raincoat, saluting them before hitting the door. "Billy T.," said Frank G., waving good-bye, watching the church door close. "Wonder what he goes home to, huh? If he's got anybody but himself to answer to." He shook his head at the character of the guy, then shook him all the way off. "But one thing I don't get about you, and it's a big one. Why you're still doing your two the hard way. After all you learned here—why you don't know you can't be around people who drink."

Doug made an impatient noise, knowing Frank G. was right and also knowing Doug wasn't about to change. "You choose your friends, right? But not your family? Well, my friends—they are my family. I'm stuck with them, they're stuck with me."

"People grow up and leave their families, guy. They move on."

"Yeah, but the thing with that is—they actually keep me sober. That's how this works. By their example. Seeing them fuck up over and over—that works for me."

"Okay. So hanging around with knuckleheads makes you feel smarter."

"It's like lifting weights. Resistance training. The temptation is to give in, to skip that last rep, short the weight, arms burning. I ignore all that, finish out my set. Being with them reminds me that I'm strong. Reminds me I'm doing this. Without that, I could get lazy."

"Okay, Doug. And I hear you, right? And I still think you're packed full of crap. This uncle of mine, right? His wife died, he's getting ready to go to a nursing home, and I'm helping get him set up there. Decent attitude, all things considered. Month or so ago, we're sitting in Friendly's over grilled cheeses. All-around good guy, telling me how now he looks back over his life and thinks, *Hey, if only I knew then what I know now*. Not regrets necessarily, just his perspective now, you know? That whole, *Youth is wasted on the young* thing. And I was polite and all, sucking my Fribble through a straw. But I'm looking at him, this uncle of mine, struggling to get that flat yellow sandwich into his mouth, and I'm thinking—no way. He'd do things *exactly* the same way he did them before, even knowing what he knows now. Drop him back into his life at twenty-one, twenty-five? He'd slip right back into the moment, make all those same mistakes. Because that's *who he is*." Frank G. leaned closer to the back of Doug's pew, resting his forearms on the top and lacing his fingers. "So who are you?"

"Me?"

"What makes Doug M. think he's different from everyone else."

"I guess—only because I *am* different from everyone else."

"Fine, good. We got a problem here, let's address it." Frank G.'s hands grappled with the air. "You don't seem to realize that you *are* your friends. That's who you are—the people you attract, who you keep around you. Now, I'm a part of you, right? Just a little taste, maybe—lucky dog, you. A bigger part is this goddamn cancer tumor part, I'm talking about your knucklehead friends. Seeing them tonight?"

"Yeah."

"Okay. Do this for me. Take a good long look around. Because those faces you see staring back—that's you."

Doug wanted to answer that, wanted to lodge his protest. He wanted Frank G. to know he was more than the sum of his friends.

The priest was out in his black suit and Roman collar, cupping his hand around the candles on the altar, blowing flames into smoke. "Looks like last call," said Frank G.

Doug said, "I think I might've met someone."

Frank G. was quiet awhile, a silence more meaningful than a simple pause. Doug suffered through it, alternately sickened by his desire to please Frank G. and hoping he had succeeded.

"She in the program?"

"No," said Doug, surprised.

Frank G. nodded like that was a good thing. "What does it mean when you *think* you meet someone?"

"I don't even know. I don't know what that means."

Frank G. rapped a knuckle on the back of Doug's pew, like a blackjack dealer knocking a push. "Take things slow, that's all. Take care picking who you hook up with. Attraction does not equal destiny, the thirst teaches you that too. Not to break your tender heart here, kid, but nine times out of ten, romance is a problem, not a solution." Frank G.'s brows remained high over long-sober eyes. "Aside from not walking into a bar alone, my friend, this is the most important choice you're ever gonna make."

7
SATURDAY NIGHT FEVER

DOUG CONTINUED ON TO the Tap that night because he had told them all
he would. Upstairs was filled with warm bodies arranged around a glass
bar underneath some nouveau lighting, lots of laughter and clinking and
the general hubbub of people working on their weekend buzz. Whiny guitar
chords warned drinkers away from the doorway leading to the smaller rear
room and its one-light, one-stool stage. All the young professionals who
couldn't get into the Warren Tavern on a Saturday night, this place was their
Plan B.

Doug turned down into the narrow stairway just inside the front door,
descending into the haze of smoke. Downstairs was old-Town style, brick-
walled and low-ceilinged, a dungeon of piss and beer. A glass bar here wouldn't
last one night without shattering. Cases of empties formed benches along the
walls, and a CD jukebox pumped in the corner like a beating heart. The bathrooms were grim but never crowded, drawing buzz-emboldened ladies from
Upstairs, picking their way through the hometown crowd like debutantes at a
sewerage convention with minced *Excuse me* faces, French-tipped nails pointed
toward the His and Hers.

"MacRaaay!" hailed Gloansy from the bar, jumping up on the iron-pipe foot
rail. He had that crazed, this-night-will-last-forever burn in his army-green eyes.

Doug made his way there, letting maniacal Gloansy hug him and slap his
back. "'S'up?"

"I'm getting there, man. You good?"

Splash, the wet-handed barman, saw Doug and shouted something along
the lines of *Long time, no see,* then slapped down an automatic soda-water lime.
Splash spilled every drink he served. Doug answered Gloansy by taking a slurp
of soda water, then looked around the room.

Gloansy had already signaled Jem, who detached himself from two sour-
looking kids Doug didn't know and made his way toward the bar, a lane opening up for him. Jem, in turn, thinking Doug couldn't see him, gestured to the
corner to hail Krista, and like half-drunk chessmen on a crowded, sticky board,

the pieces made their moves. Krista stopped stirring her bourbon and Coke and placed a hand on Joanie Lawler's forearm, starting away from their conversation, and Joanie—a sturdy, frog-faced girl from the projects, the mother of Gloansy's boy, Nicky, and Gloansy's longtime bride-to-be—shooed her on, mouthing something encouraging.

Dez fed the corner juke a dollar bill and The Cranberries' "Linger" came on, a recent favorite on the all-Irish Downstairs playing list. Another hour or so and Dez would be firmly installed there for the night, the self-declared DJ, enforcing the mood, clearing out any malingering yuppies with a barrage of Clancy Brothers and accordion jigs before getting serious with a late-night set of U2.

Jem came up and telegraphed a roundhouse right, following through at half-speed, Doug playing along, snapping his head back in mock contact. Doug returned a sharp, *Star Trek* jab to the face that back-stepped Jem, who in his zeal for Hollywood splashed a pair of idle, hoop-earringed girls with foam out of his High Life longneck.

"The mastermind," greeted Jem.

"The masturbator," said Doug, smacking Jem's fists.

"Not anymore," Jem reminded him, killing his beer with a muscular flourish and pointing hard at Splash. "Four Highs."

Gloansy smiled, never tiring of the horseplay. "Jem kid, I think you shot a little beer cum on those ladies there."

Jem turned, the neighborhood girls glaring at their blouses like they'd been bled on. They were sore but receptive, and any politeness at all—an apology, a napkin, the offer of a free drink—might have opened the door to opening their legs. But Jem dismissed them with a nasty grin. He'd only be kissing beer bottles tonight.

"Fuckin' packed Upstairs, huh?" he said, under a belch. "We should open a bar. *I* should. Front somebody the liquor license. Drinking and money, combine my two loves."

Doug said, "Not so sure how well a gay bar would do here."

Gloansy howled, stamping the floor, Jem smiling like he had the secret murder of a thousand men on his mind. Doug turned, seeing himself in the bar mirror, Krista having arrived at his side without a word.

"Bully's was fucking hoppin'," said Jem. "We started there. Pitchers, he serves. And no cock-ass tourists."

"Bully's clears maybe twenty cents a beer," said Doug. "And no ladies show up there without they wheel in their own oxygen."

Splash was yelling at them from the end of the bar, pointing upstairs, disappearing.

"Old McDonough chased us outta there," said Jem. "Weaving around the place, waving his fucking walking stick, offering up laments for the Town. Weepy, bandy-legged old fraud."

"Lived all his life three streets down from me," said Gloansy, swiping at his nose with glee. "So how's it his brogue gets thicker every year?"

"It's the fucking brain damage," said Jem. "This guy needs to be put down humanely. Bumming pitcher hits off everybody, singing his songs. Making his toasts. How the old Town is gone, gone, gone . . ."

Doug felt Krista lean into him, making *Hi, I'm here* hip contact. Of all the associations the Tap Downstairs held for him, hers was the strongest. Once upon a time they had ruled this cellar together, back when Doug's nights never ended. Downstairs was old territory and so was she. Old habits he had kicked but kept close. The only difference being, beer bottles couldn't jump down off the shelf and rub against him.

Doug started a little trouble to distract himself. "Isn't it, though? Isn't it all gone now?"

Jem smacked the air with a grandiose backhand. "Fuck that."

"So it's not gone? It's just hibernating? Taking a little break?"

"These things're cyclical," said Jem, the last word rising up on him like a curb.

"Sickle-lickle," said Doug. "You think those bananas upstairs're going to drop all this money on real estate here, and someday just walk away from it?"

"Run, not walk," said Jem. "I got a plan."

"You got a plan," said Doug. He looked to Gloansy. "He's got a plan."

"I do have a plan," said Jem. "You know sometimes I feel like the last fuckin' sentry on the watch here. The only one who fuckin' cares about the auld Town at all."

Dez came up on them then, rapping knuckles with Doug and singing, "Here he is among us!"

Doug slowed him down with mock-seriousness. "Jem has a plan."

"Ah," said Dez, draining his High Life, eyes shining behind his eyeglasses. "About blowing up synagogues again?"

Jem horselaughed, then punched Dez in the left tit.

"Taking back the town," said Doug. "Turning back time. Being Marty McFly and all."

"Ho, yeah, great idea," said Dez, rubbing his chest, but not backing down. "I'm all nostalgic for those busing riots and street-corner stabbings."

Jem feigned at Dez again, then let it go, confident enough in his drunken scheme to proceed, showing them a scarred-knuckle peace sign. "Two options."

Doug repeated this for the benefit of the others. "Two options."

"F'r'instance, lookit these twats right here." They came off the rubber-carpeted stairs together—safety in numbers—like candle-holding virgins entering a horror-movie cave. One wore a shapeless black blouse, the other a mint green cashmere sweater hanging over her shoulders, sleeves knotted into a tit-covering bow. "The papers're right—it's single women overrunning the Town. Neighborhoods're safe, there's street spaces for their fuckin' Hondas and Volkswagens, and so on. Now I ask you, are we seeing any of this action?" He pointed up. "I think not. We gonna go sit Upstairs with the turtlenecks, sipping Chablis, fuckin' sweaters tied around our waists?"

"Sipping Chablis." Gloansy appreciated that one.

"Gotta scare them all out of Town. How? Okay. First thing would be, a chemical spill. The environment, bad air. Fumes. They start worrying about their ovaries, all that. So fucking health-conscious it makes *me* sick. Then? Like, a serial rapist."

Doug nodded at his reasoning. "You planning on handling that work yourself?"

"Just rumors, that's all you need. Put it out there. This 'safe neighborhood' rap—that's what's bringing them in by the carload. Make it unsafe. Put a little fear in them, and—*ffft!* The sound of housing prices falling all over Town."

"So basically," said Dez, upon a moment's reflection, "you'd shit in your own backyard just to keep people away."

Doug said, "I think it's foolproof."

"Fucking *genius* is what it is," said Gloansy.

Splash reappeared with four uncapped High Lifes tangled in his fingers. "You guys're onna tear tonight. Hadda hit Upstairs for more cold ones."

"And four more again," said Jem, dealing out the brews, setting one down on the bar in front of Doug.

Miller High Life had always been their weapon of choice. A tawny brew, cold gold in a crystal-clear, long-neck bottle. The Champagne of Beers. Something about the label always reminded Doug of a bill of currency, the easy-twist cap a serrated silver coin.

Jem had laid a loaded gun down in front of him—the bottle waiting, misting. Krista leaned around Doug. "Jesus, Jimmy."

Jem guzzled his, coming back angry. "Fuck's your problem?"

"You."

"*I'm* your problem? Think I'm more like your freeloadin' fuckin' solution."

"Don't be a drunk prick. Pick one, be a drunk or a prick, but don't be both."

"So long as you're drinking on my dollar, why don't you just *shut the fuck*."

She squinted at him like he was so far away. "What's wrong with you?

This is like the same thing with you bringing Ma all those fucking pastries."

Jem's eyes went dead white. If he reached around to smack Krista, Doug would get dragged into it, and the last thing he wanted to do was rescue her from anything. The truth was that Krista preferred Doug drunk and pliable too, but right now her brother was a convenient, common enemy.

And then, just as suddenly, some blue leaked back into Jem's eyes and he smiled, if only to himself. He leaned in close to Doug's elbow. "You understand me, right?"

"Well as anyone," said Doug.

"We always said, did we not—one of us takes a fall, the others keep the split going four ways, hold his cut. That's what this is. I buy a round? I buy four, always four. You die tomorrow, and I buy a round tomorrow night? I buy four. You're always in for a quarter. Even in this jail of yours, serving your own self-sworn sentence. In my head I been count-culating your share these past two years—"

"*Count-culating?*"

"I—fuck you—been *calculating* your share, and you're in for a motherfuck-ing bitchload. When the floodgates open, brother, you drink free and long—on me. This is my *brother* right here!" he announced to the bar, standing up on the foot pipe as four more beers arrived. "This is my *sister* here, and this is my fuckin' *brother*!"

Heads turned, but there were no cheers, nothing like that, the Downstairs accustomed to his outbursts. Jem killed his beer, then traded his empty for a new one, his sudden affection carrying him away into the room. Dez extracted from Doug the promise of an ass-kicking later at the bubble hockey table, and then Gloansy disappeared, Doug finding himself alone with Krista at the bar.

She pushed aside her half-empty bourbon and Coke and took up Doug's untouched beer. He tried not to watch as she drank half of it. "Proud of you," she said.

"Yeah." Flat smile.

"I mean it. Strongest guy I've ever known. Stronger than any of these—"

"Yeah, okay." Doug got Splash's attention, pointed for another soda.

Krista took another pull, running her knee along the outside of Doug's thigh. "What was it that happened to us? Haven't we come through all that bullshit now? I mean—here we are, the two of us. Still."

"Still."

"If you think about it honestly," she said, choppy, dirty-blond hair falling off her ears in daggers, "is there anyone else for either of us? All this history that we have."

The tilted bar mirror gave Doug a good scope on the room. Dez had retreated to his jukebox confessional. Joanie sat on a stack of Beck's cases, one hand gripping a Bud bottle, the other hooked in Gloansy's back pocket while her drunken fiancé tossed off a nasty compliment at a woman walking past. Jem was back with the two unknowns—Townie kids, young and eager—regaling them with his stories, hands out like he was revving a Harley, getting laughs. The kids listened like bright-eyed disciples, and Doug felt an immediate distaste.

Frank G. saying, *Those faces you see staring back*. The haze of the room and Krista's closeness was working on him like déjà vu.

"I don't want to spend the rest of my life down here," said Krista. "I really don't."

Doug didn't quite believe that. He didn't quite believe anything Krista said, even the stuff he knew to be true.

"Can I tell you a secret no woman should ever tell a man?" She leaned in close, her warm breath tickling his ear. "I'm starting to feel old here."

She hung on Doug's reaction. "I'm feeling like I'm a hundred fucking years old," he admitted.

"I think we're being replaced."

Doug nodded and shrugged, dunking the lime wedge in his soda water. "Maybe that's not such a bad thing."

Her beer was gone. "Not if you got someplace else to move on to. Someone else to be."

So routine was the sensation of Krista's hand inside his thigh that Doug only registered the touch when her fingers started to creep along his inseam.

"How long has it been for you?" she said.

They say drowning men feel the water get warm before they slip under. The pull of familiarity here was like the tepid bath of sleep. *That's who you are—the people you attract, who you keep around you.*

"It's been too long for me." She had a magician's ability to keep talking into his ear while her trained hand worked. She was all over him now like the humidity of the room. "You know what I miss? Your high-mileage sofa. The grip I used to get on that armrest. I like thinking that every day you walk by it and see my nail marks there."

Doug stayed focused on her forgotten bourbon and Coke, the stirrer standing in melting ice, its tip nibbled. He felt a stirring himself.

He smelled her foxy grin along with the High Life on her breath and lips. "The strongest man I know. . . ."

As the first chords of "Mother Macree" reached him, Doug stood, her hand sliding off his leg. "Be right back," he told her. He set out in the direction of the john, but once in the crowd of merrymakers he cut back, slipping through the doorway and moving up the rubberized steps two at a time.

SURFACING UPSTAIRS WAS LIKE climbing out of a subway station into a cocktail party. A room full of pleated pants and necklace-twiddlers and roving, impatient eyes. Kids with drinks in their hands, aping their parents, trying to outshine one another. Guys pretending they cared, girls pretending they didn't. The big charade.

The hand-stamper at the door asked if everything was all right, making Doug wonder what the look on his face said. An alcoholic's rage, his apartness. The line waiting to get inside stretched almost to the corner, and Doug walked fast, stuffing his hands deep inside his pockets so he wouldn't hit anybody, heading south on Main.

Closer to Thompson Square, the sidewalk beneath his feet changed from cement to Colonial brick. He noticed a pale light inside the hazed glass of Fergie's flower shop across the street, glowing faintly like the withered power of the old mobs that, until just a few years ago, ruled the Town like royalty. Fergie, Doug figured, knew about as much about flowers as Doug did, which was zilch. The light winked out as he passed, the front door opened by a big white-haired mick in a tracksuit: Rusty, a supposed ex-IRA gunner who was Fergie's guy. Rusty scanned both sides of the street, warily tracking Doug's shadowed form—then Fergie appeared behind him, a head shorter, his boxer's hands tucked into his sweatshirt pouch, the tight hood stretched like a cowl over his head. The old mobster filled out the zip-up pretty well, though Doug could recall his father telling him long ago that Fergie wore women's sweatshirts because the female cut accentuated his size.

Doug took only that one brief glance before switching his focus to the lit point of the monument. Best not to gaze curiously at a gangster, especially not on a dark street at night, and especially not at one so paranoid and tweaked as Fergie. Triple especially if you're already feeling pissed off: true killers can read that shit and turn it back on you, and next thing you know there's rounds whistling into your chest. He heard the car doors close and the engine rumble as the living ghost of the old Town sank into his black, hearselike Continental and cruised away.

If the Bunker Hill Monument was the needle of the Charlestown sundial—the Town an irregular circle bleeding yolklike to the northwest—Doug had left the Tap at about nine o'clock, now headed for eight. His mother's house on Sackville stood at just after eleven, Jem's mother's house on Pearl ticking closer to midnight.

Packard Street, Claire Keesey's address, stood at about six thirty.

That previous night, he had found her plum Saturn returned to its brick-walled space. The no-haggle, sporty-cute coupe had been parked nose-in, the wasted spoiler and happy-face *Breathe!* sticker turned to the alley. It was while sitting there in his car looking at her dimly lit, second-floor windows that the question *Now what?* had occurred to him. He was wasting his time cruising a stranger's house, looking for . . . yeah, for what?

Pride had finally made him peel out of there, racing the Caprice up narrow Monument Avenue—a tunnel of brick row houses rising to the stage-lit granite dick. He returned home and slid her driver's license out of its hiding place behind the sill of his kitchen window. The ID had seen a lot of action, its plastic laminate curled at the edges, creased from long nights in tight pockets. In the unflattering photograph she looked startled, like someone bumped from behind in mid-smile.

The plastic blackened and sagged before it burned, her image melting, crying, the license suffering in his ashtray before curling up and surrendering oily black smoke. A simple ceremony to put an end to his wrongheaded infatuation.

Then this very evening, on his way out to Malden for his meeting, as he pulled into the Bunker Hill Mall to grab a Mountain Dew—there it was, pulled up to the curb outside the Foodmaster like a bomb waiting to go off, the bumper sticker screaming at him, *Breathe!*

He parked one row away, sitting there, his hands relaxed on the steering wheel, watching the ticking Saturn in his rearview mirror. Then, cursing himself, he was out of the Caprice and cutting across the parking lot, guessing CVS and moving inside, checking the store aisle by aisle.

He spotted her halfway down in Hair Care. She wore a red sweatshirt, gray sweatpants, Avia ballcap, running shoes, and amber sunglasses. It was a familiar look around Town, the frumpy weekend girl, yuppies doing their errands behind hats and glasses and baggy clothes, no one in the Town much worth impressing.

He fooled with packs of playing cards at the end of the aisle while she weighed conditioners. Some ballcaps on women looked wrong, joyless, severe—but Doug could see her running out a slow grounder up the first-base line, her sunny blond ponytail flying. She chose a tube the color of butterscotch, and Doug tailed her across two aisles to the magazine racks, where she pulled down *People*. She sidetracked into the wide central aisle, looking watchful all of a sudden, grabbing a quart-sized carton of Whoppers malted-milk balls and folding the magazine around it before walking to the front.

Doug pulled a Cadbury crème egg out of the clearance bin and fell into line behind her. He smelled the vanilla that was maybe the last of her old conditioner and eyed the faintly freckled slope of her neck. He worried that she would pick up on his presence with some self-protective sixth sense of fear, but she looked only at her small, red key-chain purse, its plastic driver's license window empty.

Doug stepped back for her as she left, then spilled some coins for his candy while she helped an old woman tug a handcart full of no-name toilet paper through the folding doors to the sidewalk outside. Doug exited after her, feeling like a ghost, watching her climb into her car and check her mirror before backing up and pulling away.

See? Nothing special, said the class-conscious part of himself—the thirty-two-year-old bachelor in him answering back, *Yeah, right.*

Why he went on to tell Frank G. he might have met someone, he still didn't know.

And now here he was, back again, on foot this time, gazing up at her window. Mornings outside his mother's house, nights outside hers: Since when had he become such a sad sack? Was this what he had kicked the juice for? To spend his Saturday nights standing in alleyways like a bashful thief?

This was all he had ahead of him. You couldn't even call it a dream. It was the opposite of a dream, and the opposite of a dream is not a nightmare but nothingness. Dead sleep. The Town was one big walk-in cooler, and her window up there, its yellow light, was the last cold one sitting on the shelf. The bottle he could not open; the one he was never to touch.

HE WAS FLIPPING DROWSILY through *Vette* magazine and watching the cable rebroadcast of that afternoon's Sox game when his door tapped sometime after 1 A.M. He walked barefoot in boxers and a T-shirt through the parlor that, one floor below, was Jem's playroom, and below that, Jem's mother's old dining room, now the ground floor domain of Krista and Shyne.

Prison time had left Doug with a meticulous, almost military appreciation for order—Jem called it fussiness—and his place reflected this. Clean house, clean life, clean mind. By choice, he never had visitors anymore.

He stopped before the locked hall door and the shadow in the stripe of light beneath it.

"Duggy."

Krista, her voice bar-hoarse and bourbon-hushed. The tapping became a fine scratching, and he could almost see her body leaning against the door, her ear pressed to it the same way she used to listen to his heart through his chest. Her hand would be close to her mouth, telling the door a secret.

"I know you're in there."

All the drinks he didn't drink that night, all the mistakes he could have made but didn't—coming back for him now. Picking at his door, one last chance.

"Tell me what you want me to do," she said. "Tell me why wanting you isn't enough."

He lay his palm flat against the door, in the hope that some sort of current of understanding might pass between them. Then he turned off all the lights, passing by his sofa with her nail marks in the armrest, going to bed.

8
FRAWLEY AT THE TAP

"WHERE'D YOU GO?" asked Frawley.

"Bathroom downstairs," said June, hanging her bag on the stool back and easing his knee aside with her hand as she returned to her seat. "No line."

They sat together at a black Formica tabletop the size of a small steering wheel. The same people kept walking past.

"There's a downstairs?"

"Sure. All the girls know it."

She had a lot invested in that word, *girls,* did June, a thirty-six-year-old Realtor whom Frawley had met one night at Store 24, she buying cream cheese, him size AA tape recorder batteries. They both lived in the navy yard, she in a water-view condo with glass furniture and indirect lighting, he in a highway-view, two-window sublet with milk-crate bookshelves and most of his clothes still in cardboard boxes. For some reason, being and remaining a *girl* was inordinately important to her, with streaked blond hair crowding both sides of her face, hiding—like a terrible family secret—the margins where lines and creases were starting to form.

"You've never been here before," she said twinklingly, ever amused.

Frawley shook his head, still looking for the stairs.

"But you've been to the Warren," she said.

"Nope."

"Olives? Come on, you've at least been to Figs."

"I've walked past both."

"My God, Adam." She put her hand on his wrist, like offering a prayer for his speedy recovery. "Do you know that I had reservations at Olives last weekend, nine o'clock—and it was *still* a forty-minute wait? When I moved here, in '92—way ahead of the curve, by the way—there were only two restaurants I would even think of setting foot in, the Warren and the Tavern on the Water. Now look." She gestured proprietarily at the room. "All this you see here—this is happening *right now*. This is *the* hot neighborhood, the South End of a few

years ago. Only instead of gay men, now it's single girls leading the charge."
Girls again, thought Frawley. "The only drawback is the negative stigma, with
the gangsters and dockworkers and all that—which by the way is fading every
week. This is boomtown right now, I'm fielding a dozen calls a day from girls
looking for apartments." She sipped a fresh margarita, cleaning the salt off her
lip with a small tongue, Frawley hearing Motley Crüe's "Girls, Girls, Girls" in
his head. "Even Thai food now. That says all you need to know right there. Thai
food in Charlestown? Run up the white flag."

Frawley nodding, still wondering where those stairs were.

"There's a new bistro and wine bar opening up next month—where the old
Comella's was? The space was vacant for almost a year. We'll have to try it."

"Great," he said, thinking, *Uh, no.*

"And you have to take me running with you sometime. They say it's great
training for cardio-boxing."

Training for a workout class, that was something new. Frawley touched the
"fun" margarita she had talked him into ordering. A bad experience in his fresh-
man year at Syracuse—he had never before or again since vomited purple—had
taught him never, ever to trust tequila. "So," he said, "what was it that made
you move here in '92?"

"Honestly? The parking. And now this whole neighborhood has exploded
around me. My first place, before I bought in the yard, was over on Adams, this
rickety condo with a girl who answered phones for Harvard Health. She lived
in her pajamas all weekend and cried every Monday morning before work.
Utterly manic, and I mean up until three in the morning painting walls. She
had this absolutely dreadful, hopeless affair with one of the jerks who lived over
us—got herself *pregnant* and was lucky that was all she got from him—then
wanted me to go with her, you know, to get it taken care of, and I had to cross
the protest lines with her, outside the clinic through all these crazy—what are
you looking for?"

"Oh. Nothing. Our server."

"He'll be back," she said, grabbing a strand of her streaked hair and twirling
it. "But why do *you* live here, *Special Agent Frawley*?" She loved that. "Your
commute sounds insane. It's not really about the bank robbers, is it?"

"I guess it is."

"You're like some Sigourney Weaver observing the apes by living among
them?"

He deserved this for trying way too hard to impress her on their first date.
"Just like that," he said.

"Because that's all fading away. That meteor that killed off all the old
dinosaurs? Coming down on this town like thigh-high boots with a thirty-foot

heel. That's girl power." A shrill tone rang between them, barely audible. "Ah," she said, a smiling frown, tugging her bag off the stool back and sliding out a flip phone, pulling up the antenna. "I was afraid this might happen." She answered it, covering her opposite ear. "Hi, Marie." Eye roll. "I can barely— hold on—" She covered the mouthpiece. "A client, signed a purchase-and-sale today, a two-bed with roof deck on Harvard, court parking, my exclusive. Needs some hand-holding." She unfolded a pair of flat-framed specs and slid them on. "Two minutes, cross my heart." She resumed the phone call. "Okay, Marie, June's here . . ."

Frawley excused himself and wandered through the crowd until he found the stairs near the entrance, a downward flight of beer-slicked, rubber steps without a sign. It looked like he was headed into the Tap's storage basement until a twist cut off the clatter Upstairs, blending in laughter, yells, and music below.

He came off the steps into a catacomb of brick walls and sticky stone floor. There was a short, dirty-mirrored bar, a jukebox pumping in the far corner, stacks of empty cases, a plastic-domed foosball table, and plenty of hothouse sweat. The music beat a blood pulse through the crowd, Frawley recognizing "Bullet the Blue Sky," placing it somewhere around law school: faculty-student cocktail hours, driving his guacamole green diesel Rabbit to his FBI interview. The *Joshua Tree* album? Or *Rattle and Hum*?

A fair-haired type in comically thick-rimmed eyeglasses was grooving at the jukebox, mimicking Bono's midsong rap, "Peelin' off those dollar bills / Slappin' 'em down . . ." Then every voice in the room cheered as one:

One hundred!
Two hundred!

Frawley noticed the tequila in his system now, tasting it in the sweat along his upper lip. This was where Frawley needed to be, not Upstairs with the smart set but underground, in the furnace room where the beast was nightly fed—the real Charlestown, the authentic Charlestown—Bono growling, "Outside it's America . . ."

The bump shocked him back into himself. It was a professional bump, almost a cop's bump, making out Frawley's service piece on the shoulder rig beneath his jacket.

Frawley looked up, met the bumper's eyes. They were bloodshot, the pupils a misty, near-white blue, close set. Those and the pronounced ridges beneath the bumper's nose stuck out in Frawley's mind: the memory of a face with a number board beneath it. A mug shot from the thick Charlestown files back at Lakeville.

The stare went on, Frawley still digesting the pro bump as well as the mug, too stunned by it all even to begin competing with the bigger guy's prison-yard stare. Downstairs not a full two minutes, and already he was made.

"Jem, you're up!" yelled someone—the bartender, turning the bumper's head.

The bumper grinned hard and angry. "Bathroom's that way," he said, shouldering hard past Frawley toward a quartet of beers opened and waiting on the bar.

9
THE GARDEN IN THE FENS

AFTER BREAKFAST OUTSIDE HIS mother's house on Sackville Street, Doug crossed the bridge into the city, bought a *Herald* and a *Globe* from a shaking, grizzled hawker outside the veteran's shelter on Causeway, then piloted the Caprice up onto the expressway, riding south against the morning traffic.

He spent much of the morning cruising suburban banks, trying to work up some enthusiasm for a low-margin score. He was looking for something he could control, something he could get them into and out of quickly and that would show a decent payday for their efforts—which was to say, the same thing any thief went looking for. Taking down scores was a game of momentum, and the Kenmore Square job had thrown them off their winning ways. They needed a nice medium-weight take to get back their confidence, and city banks were getting too complicated.

He eyeballed a co-op in East Milton Square, a Bank of Boston on the Braintree–Quincy line, a credit union in Randolph—but nothing that lit up his switchboard. He tried to figure out if it was the size of the scores or his mood that was putting him off. Cash was out there, everywhere he looked: the trick was finding enough of it concentrated in one place, however briefly, to make a job worth the risk.

ATM machines were cropping up all over, in bars, gas stations, even all-night convenience stores. These droids were fed by armored-car couriers making as many as fifty stops per day, sowing cash around metro Boston like uniformed Johnny Appleseeds. Unlike bank runs, ATM couriers never picked up cash, they only distributed, starting at the beginning of the day with a full whack and dropping between fifty and eighty grand at each jump, returning at end of day with only printouts and receipts. These couriers therefore had to be hit early, within their first few stops, and this had worked for Doug before, but now contractors were getting hip to the routine. They were showing more care early in their daily runs—using two-man deliveries, maintaining constant radio contact, even hiring out the occasional police escort—then easing off coverage after lunch.

Convenience stores and the like took only twenties, usually from commercial armored trucks like Loomis, Fargo, & Co. or Dunbar—but their delivery times and routes varied due to demand, and there was no outside way for Doug to track that. Banks required tens as well as twenties—some of the downtown machines even took neat stacks of hundreds—distributed separately from branch deliveries, generally by unmarked armored vans with specially plated exteriors and bulletproof windows. But the bank bills were usually new and serialized—and therefore highly traceable.

It had gotten to the point where Doug was willing to look beyond banks, but businesses doing even half their sales in hard cash were getting harder and harder to find. There were nightclubs, but that was often goombah money, and stealing from the government was a lot safer than getting tangled up in a lot of spaghetti. Fenway Park had caught his eye during prep for the Kenmore job, but though he had enjoyed working out a scheme in his head, it was too much of a name job, "a marquee score" as Jem termed it, and good only for unending scrutiny and heat. Never mind being sacrilegious. Sometimes just knowing you can pull off a job is enough.

What he had been looking at more and more were movie theaters. The big ones, the multiscreens. Only a portion of the ticket sales were done by credit card, and all the concessions remained strictly cash. As with ballparks, theater profits weren't in their ticket prices. Food and drink were their main action. Theaters made most of their coin on the appetites of captive audiences, and big summer movies meant row after row of shiftless kids with nothing better to do than spend. The multiscreens lived off these opening weekends, and Monday mornings found them sitting as fat as a bank on Friday. Jump a can making a pickup, and maybe they'd have themselves something.

But possibilities and probabilities, that was all he had. He scoped out a few movie houses on his way back into the city, just drive-bys, him trying to get his head together. Whether by accident or intent, his return route took him in past Fenway and over the turnpike bridge toward Kenmore Square.

The Saturn was there in its regular space behind the bank, jumping out at him like something thrown at his windshield. The spike he felt in his chest was the same charge he got as a kid whenever he thought he spotted his mother in a crowd. For a year or more after she had disappeared, he'd faithfully cataloged his daily activities in a Scribble Pad, so that when she returned, he would be able to catch her up on everything about him she had missed.

He banged a one-eighty around the bus station and cruised into the parking lot beneath the landmark Citgo sign, the same spot he had used to case the bank from, all the time wondering if there was a name for this virus he had. He thought he might just sit there awhile, watch the bank across the square.

A minute later he was slamming the door of the Caprice and crossing the street. From Uno's, he told himself, he could get a better look. Then the Walk sign stayed white, and his feet carried him all the way across Brookline Avenue to the sidewalk outside the bank.

One quick pass by the windows was all he could afford. The bank door opened as he approached it, him reaching out to hold the door for a black lady in a wheelchair—and the next thing he knew, he was inside, telling himself to scrawl something on a deposit slip and get the fuck out.

Then he was in line for a teller, smacking himself on the thigh with his rolled-up *Herald*. This was something a sweaty-eyed arsonist did, returning to the scene of the crime. A whiff of bleach hit him, even if it was present only in his mind.

"Oh, hi." She made him right away, Jesus Christ, this skinny-necked black teller with her hair flour-sacked on top of her head, smiling. "Haven't seen you for a while. Meter change, right?"

"Yeah, thanks." He pried a dollar bill off his damp fingers and pushed it through. He had the slimmest of angles on the hallway to the door of the manager's office from there. Someone was moving around.

The teller leaned toward the perforated bulletproof partition. "Did you hear we got robbed?"

"Yeah, was that this branch?" Cameras perched on the wall behind her like little one-eyed birds, him keeping his head down, making himself watch her hands. "Everybody okay?"

"I'm fine, I wasn't here." She made a four-quarter stack with dry, delicate brown fingers and pushed them forward like casino chips, speaking low. "But our assistant manager was beaten. Badly—he's still in the hospital. The manager was supposed to be back today—you know the blond girl, carries her keys on a strap?"

"Okay, maybe."

"Not to open, just to be here—her first day back. She never showed."

The words actually rose in his throat, Doug almost informing her that the plum Saturn was parked out in back. A brain virus, it had to be. He choked on his swallowed words, scooping up his quarters and walking away, half-blind, not even trusting his mouth with a cordial *Thank you.*

DOUG WAS SAFELY BACK inside the Caprice when it hit him, his theory, and he would not sleep again unless he proved it right or wrong. That was what he told himself as he drove back over the short bridge toward Fenway, parking there and jogging a block under the warming sun to Boylston, across Park Drive into the Back Bay Fens.

The Fens was a park laid out around a dead-river pond, a city oasis glowing hormonally emerald in the full-on puberty of spring. Inside the bike paths along Park Drive were the Fenway Gardens, five hundred fenced lots staked along meandering dirt-and-pebble lanes. A couple of times in early April he had followed Claire Keesey here on her lunch hour, watching from a distance as she sat on a crumbling stone bench, picking through a Tupperware salad under the pale green fingers of a willow tree. She had sat with perfect posture, as though posed for one of the pictures in the thick fashion magazine open at her side. She usually embezzled a few extra minutes of lunch hour beyond her allotted sixty.

His landmark for locating her plot was a rain-hatted scarecrow dwarf at the end of the row, fashioned out of basket wicker and tilted on a crucifix of broken ladder. Nothing else anywhere looked familiar to him. Spring had sprung and the gardens were completely transformed.

He saw her kneeling on the ground, going at it hard with a hand fork, clawing the soil as though it were a memory that would not die. When she stopped and got to her feet for a water break, Doug saw that she was dressed not for gardening but for work—a soft pink sweater-blouse over a long, muddied skirt, both ruined. She reached for a spading fork and pushed up her dirtied sleeves, resuming her all-out assault on the earth.

People on bicycles or walking their dogs slowed as they passed her, one feisty little gay pug yapping at her with concern. Claire Keesey never looked up. A shirtless man eyed Doug from three plots down, and Doug bashed him with a look, starting back quickly to his car, the mystery of Claire Keesey clouding his mind.

10
STAINED

D UE TO A QUIRK OF either geography or city planning, the C branch of
the MBTA Green Line subway made twelve stops along a three-mile
straightaway between Boston's Kenmore Square and Boston's Cleveland
Circle—all of them in the town of Brookline. The old-fashioned trolleys ran
aboveground there, on tracks that cleaved the length of Beacon Street. At the
St. Paul stop stood a half-block-long, three-story Holiday Inn hotel with a
glassy corporate atrium, where on four Tuesday mornings each year the Boston
Bank Robbery Task Force and associated agencies assembled for a breakfast
meeting.

The BRTF was formed in late 1985, at a time when alliances of federal,
state, and local law enforcement agencies routinely failed due to conflicting
mandates and general bad blood. It was a shotgun marriage: the Massachusetts
region had seen fifteen of the nation's sixty-five total armored-car robberies in
that year. By the early 1990s, the task force had halved that number—signifi-
cant progress, but not enough to shake Boston's title as the Armored Car Robbery Capital of America. Gains had also been made in reducing the number of
bank robberies, pushing the regional total below two hundred per year, and
showing a whopping 73 percent clearance rate, as compared to 49 percent
nationwide.

The full-time investigative arm of the BRTF, headquartered at Lakeville, was
composed of five FBI agents, two Boston police detectives, and three Massachusetts state troopers. Today's informational meeting included associated
members of the Massachusetts Department of Corrections, the Cambridge
Police Department, a guest speaker from the Drug Enforcement Administration, liaisons from every major area bank chain and armored-transport company, and a representative from the Federal Reserve Bank of Boston—all
sharing information and identifying trends over croissants and cranberry juice.

That morning found Frawley unusually impatient. He had spent the entire
day before in his Cavalier with Dino, shadowing a Northeast Armored Transport truck on a tip from the Organized Crime section. Fifty-four stops at super-

markets, convenience stores, and nightclubs throughout Saugus and Revere, and they'd be back at it again tomorrow—leaving him little time to pursue the Brown Bag Bandits from the Kenmore Square heist.

Frawley was a doodler and a good one. As the suit from the Federal Reserve Bank outlined concerns regarding the Big Dig—the Central Artery reconstruction project that included, as part of its ten-year overhaul of the city's crumbling highways and fallen arches, a major tunnel within a few dozen yards of his institution's gold bullion vaults—Frawley added hash-mark scarring to the egg-eyed hockey masks lining the margins of his schedule memo. He did them mug-shot style, full-face and profile: two small bean holes for the nostrils, a flat, expressionless slot for the mouth, and the twin tribal triangles at the pits of the cheeks. Tracing the masks was a dead end: a visit to a Chinatown costume store showed him dozens of easily adaptable *Friday the 13th* party masks staring down from the walls.

Hunting a disciplined crew was most difficult because it eliminated Frawley's two greatest advantages over bank robbers: their stupidity, and their greed. He could not rely on their compulsion to pull reckless jobs, leaving him fewer opportunites to capture them.

He wandered back to the raided vault in his mind. The yawning cabinet, the plundered cash drawers: he tried to let that feeling of violation wash over him again. He remembered the bait bills and dye packs left behind, untouched. Pro bank bandits, like practitioners of any arcane craft, were a superstitious bunch. Frawley hadn't touched them either, being superstitious in his own way, himself the student of a dying art. He was the last in the long line of bank detectives. The bloodline traced directly from the first stagecoach Pinkertons to himself. If he couldn't be there at the beginning, he figured the second-best place to be was right where he was, at the tail end. Credit cards, debit cards, smart cards, the Internet: the dawn of the cashless society meant the twilight of the modern bank bandit, and the coming of a new breed. Identity theft and electronic embezzlement were the future of financial crime. The next Adam Frawley would be a pale, deskbound Net-head hunting cyber-thieves with a mouse and a keyboard instead of an Olympus Pearlcorder and a blue Form FD-430. Adam Frawley would soon become obsolete. The techniques, the tradecraft, everything he knew about banks and vaults and the men who robbed them, and all he had yet to learn—it would die with him, the last bank robbery agent.

Below the cartoon masks, he sketched the handset of a telephone and connected the two by a coiled wire. This wire was his only tangible lead now. It was the phone company tech the Brown Bag Bandits exhibited, in the Kenmore Square job as well as the others the task force now suspected them of: credit unions in Winchester and Dedham; the Milk Street Pawn cut-in; ATM jobs in

Cambridge and Burlington; a co-op in Watertown; two banks just over the
New Hampshire border; last September's weekend spree of three Providence
storage facilities, for which they had disabled the ADT Security System network across most of eastern Rhode Island; and the nontech armored-car heists
Frawley hunched them for, in Melrose, Weymouth, and Braintree. All three-
and four-man crew jobs, all of them spread out over the past thirty months.

Frawley had found fresh wounds running up a telephone pole around the
corner from the BayBanks, left there by a lineman's spikes. A Nynex crew in a
cherry picker worked for three hours to diagnose and repair the junction-box
reroute.

No one Frawley had talked to inside the Monopoly game that was the
booming telecom industry could satisfactorily explain how a thief could locate
the particular cellular antenna—disabled one and a half miles away, on the roof
of a Veterans Administration Hospital on Roxbury's Mission Hill—responsible
for bouncing the bank's backup alarm signal to the Area D-4 police station.

He sketched a cell tower with suturelike antennas, then fleshed out the
tower, letting it grow into the Bunker Hill Monument.

The bleached crime scene, stolen surveillance tapes, and torched work van
left them with no physical evidence at all. Frawley's only hope now was that the
subpoena would prove out, this one seeking not just Nynex service logs but
employee records and home addresses. He would run down any leads involving
phone company employees residing in the Town—possibly opening up the case
to a "Charlestown witch hunt" defense at trial, but right now it was all he had.

On top of all this was the phone call he had received just prior to the start of
this meeting, informing him that Claire Keesey had yet again failed to return to
work.

His felt pen moved incessantly, all these things playing inside his head, finding expression here and there in automatic writing: gloved hands aiming
BANG! cartoon guns; fat moonshine jugs labeled BLEACH; dollar signs hash-
marked with stitching scars.

He willed himself not to check his wristwatch again as an enormously pregnant DEA agent outlined the positive impact that falling heroin prices might
have on note-passers. Apparently a price-and-purity war was raging between
the Colombian cartels and the traditional Asian heroin producers, the Colom-
bians gaining East Coast market share by wooing needle-wary smokers and
snorters. At $5 per thumbnail-sized bag, street H was now stronger than coke
and cheaper than beer.

Heroin use was also rising in Charlestown, but along with the institutional
anachronism of the neighborhood, Townie drug addicts retained their affinity
for the bad-boy drug of the late 1970s, angel dust. Dust came sold in small

packets, or "tea bags," the powder acting as an anesthetic, a stimulant, a depressant, and a hallucinogen—all at the same time. Its status as the outlaw drug of all drugs surely accounted for its special appeal within the Town.

But his mind was wandering again. He focused on the tablecloths, their bright coral pinkness reflected in the water glasses like floating lilies. Outside the right-hand wall of windows, the dreary street was drawn in charcoal pencil, smudged by the all-morning drizzle.

Frawley's and Dino's pagers went off at the same time. Frawley sat back to read the display on his hip, showing the Lakeville office phone number, followed by the code 91A. The FBI offense code for bank robbery was 091. *A* was shorthand for "armed."

Dino had his phone, Frawley rising with him, both of them in suits for the meeting, moving away from the tables. Dino held his phone elbow high, as though cell-phone use required a more formal technique than regular telephones.

"Ginny," he said. "Dean Drysler. . . . Uh-huh. . . . Okay. When was that?" He stepped to the wall, looking out the weeping windows to the western end of Beacon. "Got it." He hung up, turned to Frawley. "Note-passer. Just happened. Claimed gun but didn't show."

"Okay." Hardly anything to shake them out of a meeting for. "So?"

"Coolidge Corner BayBanks, intersection of Beacon and Harvard." He pointed out the window. "Two blocks that way, across the street."

Frawley tensed, then looked for the door to the lobby. "I'm gonna run."

Frawley was out of the room fast, new-shoe-running over a slippery carpet into the lobby, blowing past the doorman in his silly vest and out into the gray mist. Down a steep, turnaround driveway, across busy Beacon against the light, then following a low fence along the trolley tracks until he could cross the slick inbound lane of Beacon ahead of onrushing traffic, up the rising sidewalk past a Kinko's and a post office and a whole-foods market.

He covered the quarter-mile in no time, arriving outside the corner bank with his hand on his shoulder piece. The sight of a dapper man dancing back and forth there with keys in his hand, searching hooded faces, told Frawley the thief was already gone. Frawley drew his creds out of his jacket, flapped it open.

"My *God,* you got here fast," said the branch manager, silver eyeglasses perched ornamentally on his face.

"How long?" said Frawley.

"One, two minutes. I came almost right out after him."

Frawley scanned in all four directions, the intersection calm in the rain, no one reacting to a man running, no cars tearing out of handicapped parking spaces. "You don't see him?"

The manager craned his neck until the rain specks on his glasses made him draw back under the overhang. "Nowhere."

"What'd he have, a hat? Sunglasses?"

"Yes. Scarf around his neck, tucked into his jacket, to his chin. A caramel brown chenille."

"Gloves?"

"I don't know. Can we go back inside?"

Frawley saw blue cruiser lights about a half mile up the inbound lane, cars pulling over for them. "After you," said Frawley.

It was a handsome old bank, well-appointed, underlit. Customer service was corralled in the center by a low, wood-railed office gate with a thigh-high swinging door. Green-shade banker lamps illuminated boxy computer monitors. The teller booths and a currency-exchange window lined the rear.

The customers and service reps stopped their buzzing, all eyes turning to the manager and the overdressed FBI agent. In back, the tellers had left their windows to huddle with their co-worker in the rightmost window.

"Make the announcement," said Frawley.

"Yes," said the manager. "Umm—everyone? I'm sorry to say that there's been a robbery here just now, and—"

A collective gasp.

"Yes, I'm afraid so, and we're going to have to suspend our transactions for at least an hour"—a confirming glance at Frawley—"or two, perhaps even just a bit more, so please, if you would, bear with us for a few minutes, and we'll have you on your way."

Frawley's call for a show of hands of anyone who'd seen the bandit leave the bank got him nowhere. Customers are usually never aware that a note job is going down until afterward when the manager locks the front door.

Dino arrived at the same time the police did, shaking their hands and generally keeping them out of the way while the manager let Frawley in back with the tellers.

"CCTV or stills?"

"What?" said the manager.

"Close circuit cameras or—" Frawley looked up and answered his own question. The video cameras were placed too high on the wall. "Those aren't even going to get under his hat brim," Frawley said, pointing. "Seven and a half feet high, max—make sure those get lowered. Do they slow to sixty frames after the alarm is punched?"

"I—I don't know."

The others remained huddled around the rightmost teller, hands of support on her shoulders and back. She was an Asian woman in her midthirties, Vietnamese perhaps, tears dripping off her round chin and spotting her salmon silk shirt, her nude nylon knees chunky and trembling.

Her top drawer was open, its slots still full of cash. "How much did he get?" asked Frawley.

A woman wearing a long hair braid of gray and silver answered, "Nothing."

"Nothing?" said Frawley.

"She froze. She's a trainee, this is her second day. I saw she was in trouble, and I saw the note. I hit my hand alarm."

The note lay just inside the window slot, scribbled on a white paper napkin, wrinkled like a love letter held too long in a sweaty hand. "Did you touch this?"

"No," said the Vietnamese teller. "Yes—when he first pass it to me."

"Was he wearing gloves?"

The head teller answered for her. "No."

"Anybody see the gun?"

The Vietnamese teller shook her head. "He said bomb."

"Bomb?" said Frawley.

"Bomb," said the head teller. "He was carrying a satchel on his shoulder."

The note read, in a shaky, frightened slant, "I have a <u>BOMB</u>! Put ALL MONEY in bag." Then, larger, bolder: "PLEASE NO ALARMS OR ELSE!!!"

The word *please* jumped out at Frawley. "A satchel?"

The head teller said, "Like half a backpack. Not businessy. Gray."

Frawley lifted out his capped felt pen and used it to flip the note. On the back was the familiar pink and orange Dunkin' Donuts logo. Dino appeared on the other side of the teller window like a customer. "Still smell the coffee," said Dino. "There's one across the street here—right, ladies? And you can see the bank from the window, correct?"

Yes, mm-hmm, they all nodded.

Frawley said, "He sat there and wrote out the note, crossed the street with it in his hand inside his pocket. . . ."

"Impulse, maybe," said Dino. "Not a hypo."

"Not a bomber either." Frawley turned back to the Vietnamese teller. "The note mentions a bag. The same bag the bomb was in?"

She was sniffling now. "No, a white bag, trash bag. He took with him."

"And just left? Walked right out?"

She turned to the head teller then. "I need the lady room now."

The head teller said to Frawley, "He got nervous. I think it was me noticing him. He turned right on his heels."

Frawley looked back at Dino. "Guy needs money, like now."

Dino nodded. "Trolley's free outbound from here."

Frawley said to the head teller, "What's the next bank down the line?"

"A . . . another BayBanks branch. Washington Square."

Dino said, "Ladies, I need their telephone number, pronto."

Frawley was moving past the head teller toward the opened security door. "Hat? Jacket?" he said over his shoulder.

"Bucket hat," she answered. "Some kind of golf thing on the crest. Jacket was short, tight. Heavy for spring, but not cheap. Hunter green—he dressed nice."

"Dino?" said Frawley, moving fast.

Dino waved him on, picking up a phone, "Go, go."

Frawley stopped on the wet curb outside. Dino's Taurus was pulled up there, his grille blues and headlamps flashing. Double-parked cruisers had jammed up traffic in all four directions.

A trolley came clanging up the rise, the only thing moving. Frawley crossed the street and ran to intercept it, darting inside the opened doors. "I need you to go straight through to Washington Square," he told the toothpick-chewing conductor.

The guy squinted doubtfully at Frawley's creds. "Small badge."

"It's real enough." This was Frawley's first commandeered vehicle. "Let's go."

The driver thought a moment, then shrugged and closed the doors. "Fine by me."

The trolley nosed through the honking cars, gaining speed past the intersection, passing boutiques, a high-end pastry shop, a RadioShack, apartment houses.

"So what kinda money you people make?" the driver asked.

"Huh?" said Frawley, standing next to him, heart pounding, creds still in hand. "Less than you probably."

"Any overtime?"

"Mandatory ten-hour day."

"Thought you guys supposed to be smart."

The driver sounded his horn as they failed to slow for waiting raincoats and umbrellas at the next stop. "Hello, excuse me!" said a woman behind Frawley, grocery bags sagging at her feet like sleepy dogs.

"FBI's driving the car now, ma'am," said the driver.

They blew another stop to a chorus of middle fingers. Then, suddenly, the roadside on Frawley's right separated from the track, rising on a hill above them. "Hey! Where's that going?"

"It'll be back, don't worry," said the driver. "Listen. You people gotta unionize. It's every American's right."

"Yeah, noted," said Frawley, looking for the road. "Where the hell is Washington Square?"

"Washington Square, next stop!" sang out the driver.

The roadside plummeted back down to realign with them, the joined road opening into another intersection. Frawley saw the green and white BayBanks sign on the near right corner. The trolley braked, wheels squealing, turning every head in the square—but none so dramatically as that of the man in the green jacket, tan scarf, and bucket hat exiting the bank door with a travel satchel on his shoulder, a white plastic trash bag in his hand.

The nature of his work dictated that Frawley dealt almost exclusively with crime scenes. In his eight years of chasing bank bandits, he had never once witnessed one in action.

"Open!" said Frawley, banging on the door. The driver opened it before he stopped, and Frawley jumped out and hit the ground running, sprinting into the intersection, suit jacket flapping, darting around cars.

The suspect strode across the side street as though unaware of this man yelling, *"Hey!"* and running after him. A car in Frawley's way forced him to go wide and intercept the suspect at the far curb.

Up close, the guy looked like a blank, not at all menacing, a nose and a mouth under a gray rain hat, big sunglasses, and the coiled caramel scarf. The L.L. Bean walking shoes, mossy corduroys, and gray travel bag—those did not compute. Not your standard note-passing outfit. Frawley was close enough to him now to see loose fifties static-pressed against the white, one-ply trash bag hanging limp in his left hand.

"Hold it!" said Frawley, one hand opened toward the man, his other up on the butt of his holstered gun. The suspect's jacket was zipped to the collar; any move he made would have to be a clumsy one. "FBI," announced Frawley, feeling good as he said it, the suspect stopped before him in the light, misting rain.

There was a crackling sound that was almost fuselike, coming from somewhere on the suspect. Frawley remembered the guy's bomb threat—then the sidewalk went blind red.

Frawley reeled backward, certain the guy had exploded into pieces in front of him. Something struck him hard—the pavement—and his throat began to burn, eyes stinging and tearing. He brought one hand in front of his face and saw it painted red.

Frawley tried to right himself on the sidewalk, his respiratory system closing up on him. Through slitted eyes he saw the suspect on the move, stumbling backward, tripping off the curb. Something fluttered up into Frawley's face like a bloody bird and he fought it off—then another, and another, one sticking to his hand. Gray-green and red. He held it before his swelling eyes, trying to focus.

It was a fifty-dollar bill, stained and burned.

A dye pack. Not a bomb but half an ounce of red dye and tear gas bursting from a tiny, pressurized CO_2 canister sandwiched inside a hollowed-out stack of retired bills.

Frawley turned on his knee, forcing open his bleary eyes and seeing the dappled bills fluttering across the square like fall leaves off a money tree. The red-splashed trash bag tumbled empty and dreamlike toward the stalled Green Line trolley.

Frawley got to his feet. He found his way off the curb. His pace grew more certain with every step, and he yelled both to stop the suspect and to keep his airway open.

The form before him trailed a long scarf. Something small lay in the road—the dropped satchel—and Frawley followed the vague shape between two parked cars. It turned right at the end of a fence, the fringed scarf slithering away.

A chorus of high-pitched screams as Frawley reached the corner. An elementary-school playground, Frawley's appearance sending them squealing toward the school.

The sight of the children slowed the suspect just enough for Frawley to dive for the end of the scarf, clotheslining the guy, bringing him down. Frawley got on him fast, wrestling the guy's flailing arms behind him and kneeing his face into the turf.

Frawley carried no handcuffs. He hadn't collared anyone without an arrest warrant since his first office assignment. He whipped off the perp's gloves and squeezed the guy's thumbs together, pulling up hard on his arms, immobilizing him with pain.

The guy spat something into the dirt. "What?" said Frawley, adrenalized to the max, ears ringing, nose running.

"Shoot me," the guy said. Frawley realized then that the guy wasn't fighting him, only sobbing.

Sirens coming now. Kids still dropping off the monkey bars, Frawley yelling at teachers to get them indoors. He eased up on the guy, unwinding the muddy scarf from his neck. The guy looked maybe forty, despairing, already ashamed.

"Mortgage or sick kid?" said Frawley.

"Huh?" the guy sniffed.

"Mortgage or sick kid?"

A defeated, wincing sigh between sobs: "Mortgage."

Frawley fished out his creds yet again, holding the gold badge high for the screaming cruisers. "Should have refinanced."

The cops came up all loaded for bear, weapons drawn, and Frawley shielded the bandit with his body, bellowing at them, *"It's okay, back off!"*

They finally holstered, Frawley so furious by then that he snatched a pair of handcuffs out of one of the patrolmen's hands and hooked up the bandit himself. Then he stalked off toward the now vacant playground, stopping at the short fence, wiping his draining eyes and nose on his suit sleeve and checking himself out. The suit was ruined, his shoes, belt, and tie, all stained. He rubbed at his left hand, his palm a bright red, the clinging aerosol powder already adhered to his skin. He looked up to clear his vision and found rows of little faces at the classroom windows, teachers trying to pull them away. He touched his own face, cringing, fearing the worst.

Dino was climbing out of his Taurus, hustling across the sidewalk toward Frawley, then seeing Frawley was okay, slowing down. "Now this," he said, baring dentures perfect and white, "is a definite first."

Frawley held his arms out from his sides as though he were soaking wet. "You okay there, Dean?" Frawley said, congested. "All that getting in and out of the car, I was worried."

Dino took in the full view. "Everything but the paint can over the head. Do me a favor? Hold out your gold badge like this, say, 'Jerry Lewis, FBI.'"

Frawley showed him a brilliant red middle finger instead. He looked back to the bandit, now bent over a cruiser for a pat-down, his ear to the hood like it was whispering his children's future. Then they straightened him up, folding him sobbing into a cruiser.

Dino said, coming up next to Frawley, "Fun job, innit?"

11
JAY'S ON THE CORNER

NEW DRY CLEANERS WERE popping up all over the Town. The modern
career woman required first and foremost a dependable local launderer.
So much so, even old-style wash-'n'-drys such as Jay's on the Corner
were putting in lacquered black counters, advertising overnight send-out service, playing "continuous soft hits" inside, and prettifying themselves in general: squeegeeing the windows clean every morning, hosing off the sidewalk,
repainting signs, power-washing stubborn brick.

The message there was that the renewing power of capitalism was a lot like
falling in love. No other force in the universe could have moved old man
Charlestown to run a new razor over his cheeks, close his collar with a necktie,
check his manners, splash on a little cologne. Springtime was in bloom all over
the Town, and free-market commerce was a pretty girl in a sundress and heels.

Jay's was narrow like a tobacconist's, new-Town up front—chrome fixtures
on the counter, free coffee—while still old-Town in back—corkboard walls stuck
with business cards and guitar lesson flyers, the ancient soap machine, and a
broken wooden-bead maze table for the kids. The washing machines were lined
up in back-to-back rows under a high center shelf, double-decker dryers facing
them along both long walls. The newer dollar-accepting washers were up front;
the older, thudding, coin-tray jalopies rattling in back.

Doug was positioned halfway down the left lane of washers, sitting atop the
last clean machine before the dials got crusty. He was feigning interest in the
free *Boston Phoenix,* riding out his churning clothes, with Claire Keesey's loads
tumbling almost directly behind him. She had been there a while now—long
enough for Doug to book home to grab up some dirty clothes, get back, follow
her inside. His hamper bag lay empty on the floor now, one of the few things of
his father's that Doug had held on to: a strap-tie army sack with faded black
stenciling, MACRAY, D.

Now what? He had acted on instinct, or else simple insanity, sensing opportunity but now not knowing how to follow through. He was just a few yards
away from her, and they were basically alone—the guy behind the counter rub-

bing his bald head and talking Greek into the phone—yet he could think of no good way to bridge that final gap. Borrow some soap? Be that obvious? *Hey, you wash your clothes here often?* Sure, why not just scare her off for good?

Even if she did happen to look over at him now and didn't immediately turn away—even if some small smile were to appear on her face—it was the middle of the morning: no matter what, he looked like an out-of-work Townie making a clumsy play.

Hey, haven't I seen you at the Foodmaster?

A brilliant, foolproof plan. Except for his clothes getting clean, this whole thing was a colossal waste of time. He imagined the others walking in and seeing him there trying to work up the courage to bump into the manager of the bank they had robbed.

Her first load finished while he sat there berating himself. She started pulling out warm clothes one by one, folding and packing them into a custard-yellow laundry basket. Her other dryer load was nearly done, along with a pair of tennis sneakers rumbling alone in a third machine, going *pum-pum-pum-pum* like the drumbeat of battle.

He closed the newspaper and threw it down, determined now, stand or fall. His boots hit the floor, hands vigorously rubbing his face to rouse himself from wussyland. What could he say here that didn't make him seem like a panty-cruising creep?

A relevant question. Something about separating colors from whites. No— any fucking idiot knows that. Just ask, What do I wash in cold, what do I wash in hot? Simple. Like, Feed a fever, or starve a cold?

He quickly examined this gambit for offensiveness: Maybe there was something somehow antifeminist about assuming that women knew more than men about laundry? Then he realized that, hey, that was exactly what he assumed, and if steam blew out of the top of her head when he asked, then good, he had his answer, he could head on home.

He shook his fists loose and cracked his neck—even as he felt himself pussy-ing out again. *Fuck you!* Thinking about the hours of agony his backing out here would cause him—that was the only thing that started him toward her.

He crossed the break in the rows of washers, hands stuffed unthreateningly into his pockets. She had paused in her folding, her back to him, a white blouse in her hands.

"Uh, hey, excuse me?"

She turned fast, startled to find him there.

"Hi, uh, I was wondering if you knew . . ."

So focused was he on his delivery that it took him until then to register the tears in her eyes. She swiped at them, fast and guilty, dismayed at having been discovered—then tried to brush off the whole thing with a fake smile.

Doug said, "I . . . oh."

The tears reappeared and she tried to smile him off again, then gave up, turning away. She tipped her head up to the ceiling fans in an *Oh, God* type of gesture, then resumed her folding, faster now, as though he weren't there.

"You okay?" said Doug, though it came out sounding wrong.

She turned her head in profile, blinking, waiting for peace. Then she turned all the way, glaring, her quick, harsh look imploring him, *Please go away*.

Which he should have done. His presence was only making her more upset. But he was stuck. If he stepped away now, it would be forever.

She scooped out the rest of her load with him hovering at her back, dumping her clothes unfolded into her laundry basket, a tennis sock and a pair of lilac panties dropping softly to the floor. She wanted to be done, to leave. She dragged her basket of warm clothes off the washing machine and started past him, head down, rushing toward the front door—her other load still going around the next dryer.

"Hey," he said after her, "you forgot . . ."

But she had turned out onto the sidewalk and was gone. The bald guy behind the counter craned his neck, holding the phone to his chest. A male customer balancing his checkbook looked to the door too, his girlfriend staring accusingly down the row at Doug.

Doug turned back to the spinning dryers and the sneakers bouncing *pum-pum-pum*, wondering what the hell had just happened.

NORTH OF THE TOWN, the Malden Bridge crossed the Mystic into Everett, the sky opening up over a dire patch of industry lit like a Batman movie, road signs reading Factory Street and Chemical Lane. Main Street in West Everett drew tired multifamily homes to the sidewalks like spectators waiting half a century for a promised parade.

Doug parked the Caprice outside a darkened funeral home and walked three blocks to a side street, a D'Angelo sandwich and a True Value Hardware plastic bag in one hand, a Valvoline carton the size of two VCRs under his arm.

The houses at the end of the side street were single-family, postwar Capes and cottages with square yards front and back. The door he went to was unlit, and he set his things down on the step. He knocked gently before going to work on the lamp over the door, unscrewing the glass cap, brushing out the dead bugs.

"Here I am, Douglas," sang Mrs. Seavey, unlocking the door and pulling it wide of her walker. She wore an Irish sweater buttoned over a red flannel housecoat, her gray face smiling moon-bright. She had seemed old to Doug back when she was his third-grade teacher.

"I'm a little late," said Doug, hearing the *Wheel of Fortune* theme song behind her. "How's that leg? Nurse come today?"

"Oh, yes. I think so."

"Getting around okay?"

With a mischievous, half-dreaming smile, she released the walker and shuffled back and forth in her foam slippers, arms out for balance, singing, "Da-daa-dee-da . . ."

Doug's class had been Mrs. Seavey's last before retirement. She cleaned everything out of her legendary coatroom closet during their last week of school, offering the contents to whoever wished to carry them home. Doug claimed as many workbooks, activity packs, phonics flash cards, and dried-up markers as he could get his little hands on, so anxious was he to take home pieces of her. But the Forneys—the foster family he was living with at the time—had hardly any room for him and made him throw out most of it anyway. His mother had been gone two years by then, his father away on a twenty-one-month tour at MCI Concord.

Doug opened the hardware-store bag and pulled out a package of coiled lightbulbs. "Now I bought you these fancy ones instead of the regular bulbs because they reminded me of you."

"Aha," she tee-heed. "Screwy?"

"Definitely that." He read from the package. "'Low-wattage, energy-saving, extended life.' Says right here, 'Years of continuous illumination.'"

She tittered again, then watched from inside the screen door as he traded the dead, tinkling bulb for the new coiled one. She hit the switch inside, and the light was soft but fast, riding the gas inside the tube.

"Anything else you need done tonight?" he said.

"No, bless you, Douglas. I'm all set, thanks be to God."

He opened the screen door, removing a thick roll of bills from his pocket. Nana Seavey liked fives and tens, small bills she could use at the corner store. "There's nine hundred," he said. "My next three months' rent."

She grasped his hand over the bills, shaking it softly. "God bless you, boy," she said, the bills disappearing into her sweater pocket.

"Now, I'll probably be out there late tonight."

"You stay as long as you want." She waved him on like he was being bad, and he saw the sore on her wrist, brown and blue, still unhealed. "I'm off to bed."

She gripped his fingers again, her skin papery and cool, the bones of her hand like small pencils in a bag. Doug leaned down to kiss her forehead. "You stay well, now. Be good."

"If not," she said, shuffling backward from the door with a smile, "I'll be careful."

He listened for the lock and waited until the light winked out, then started across the walkway to her garage. Mr. Seavey had worked and died making rubber for Goodyear, but on nights and weekends he and his brother had operated a private taxi and limousine service. Doug could still recall his last day of third grade, watching from the sidewalk outside school, Mrs. Seavey blowing him a small kiss from the backseat of a jewel-black Oldsmobile with silver window curtains.

Mr. Seavey had an Irishman's fondness for automobiles, like a hunter's love for his dogs, and he had built himself, with help from a few drinking buddies, a barnlike, two-car garage with swing-out doors. Doug had since, with Mrs. Seavey's blessing, knocked off the outside handles so that the broad front doors could only be opened from the inside. Entry now was through a small side door just inside the low picket fence marking the edge of Mrs. Seavey's property. By the scant blue light of a plastic Virgin Mother glowing in the next backyard, Doug unlocked the padlock and threw open the top and bottom bolts, closing the door behind him before hitting the wall switch inside.

Halogen work lights clamped to the rafters illuminated the emerald green Corvette ZR-1 in the center of the cement floor. The jewel of the price-doubling ZR-1 performance option package was its all-aluminum, 405-horse Lotus LT5 engine. Doug's was one of the last of the 448 ZR-1s built in 1995, their final production year. The car stickered at $69,553, paid in cash, papered in Krista's name in order to avoid federal tax scrutiny.

The custom emerald finish was so creamy that running a hand along the long, sloping prow, from the solar windshield down to the retractable headlamps, was like swiping frosting off cake. The car was jacked up on blocks, Doug nearly finished installing a new stainless-steel exhaust system.

He set his sandwich down next to the *Chilton's* repair manual on the workbench beneath a broad array of Mr. Seavey's old tools. The garage had been built deep to accommodate the Olds, and there was a four-foot drop in back: a dirt-floored, stone-sided storage area cluttered with ancient three-speed bicycles, push-powered grass clippers, and a monstrous electric snowblower, its rusted blades like gnashing teeth stained with dry blood.

Doug left the Valvoline box on the edge and hopped down, lifting the heavy snowblower by its handles and boosting it away from the stone wall. The rock he wanted was ostrich-egg-sized and loose, coming away from the chipped mortar and exposing a cavity. Originally Doug had found in there, behind a row of empty Dewar's flasks, a dusty airmail letter with a 1973 postmark, written in jerky English by a Frenchwoman searching for an American soldier named Seavey who had passed through her mother's village in the winter of 1945.

Doug lifted the newspaper-wrapped parcels out of the Valvoline box and added his cut from the BayBanks job to the rest of the odd-sized stacks of cash, then stared at his ditch-cold treasure. In the hole its value was zilch: a collection of numbered strips of fabric made up of 75 percent cotton and 25 percent linen, printed with green and black ink. Little rectangular rags whose unbankable mass was becoming a problem. Doug was running out of both space—the hole had been dug as wide as it could go—and time—Nana Seavey being just one stumble away from a nursing home. His garage rent payment was an offering meant to bring them both three more months of good luck, because Doug had no contingency plan, either for his stash or his Vette.

He withdrew a cold, inch-thick wad from a neat pile of already washed bills, then folded up the thick plastic wrap and fit the stone back into place, repositioning the blower and climbing back up top. The heat from the lamps was starting to warm the garage, and he unwrapped his roast beef sub and pulled a Dew out of the minifridge he kept there, switching on the portable radio. Normally the thought of grabbing tools and getting greasy underneath the ZR-1 was enough to make the anxieties of the outside world disappear. He lay back on Mr. Seavey's old "Jeepers" creeper—"Immigrant Song" on 'ZLX following him in underneath the jacked-up car—and though Doug never totally lost himself under there, at least for a few hours he got far enough away.

FROM THE STREET, DOUG heard music slamming out of Jem's. Inside, climbing the stairs, he felt the heat from the second-floor door as he passed. Inside his own apartment, the weak walls shuddered and the sagging floor thumped like drum skins. Doug's spoon quivered on his kitchen counter and one of his cabinet doors swung open on its own. That was Jem: all bass, no treble.

Doug pulled his bed out of the sofa and sat on the end, eating a bowl of Apple Jacks, debating whether to fight this barrage with his own TV noise or just ride it out. He was too tired to go pounding on Jem's door, and more than that, too wary of getting pulled inside. He figured there was an even chance the roof was going to come down on top of them all anyway.

Who is Doug MacRay? These are the questions sober people ask themselves over bowls of cereal at three in the morning.

Folding her laundry for her and leaving it at the counter: big mistake. Too feminine, too puppyish and nuzzling, tail-wagging, hand-licking, proudly-pissing-on-the-newspaper eager-to-please. It was pussy.

He lay back flat on the mattress and waited for the ceiling to fall in on him.

* * *

DOUG ENTERED JAY'S ON the Corner briskly, knocking on the counter—"Hey, Virgil"—and nodding to the bald clerk in the Rolling Stones red-tongue T-shirt, whose acquaintance Doug had since made, and whose confederacy he had purchased with a fifty-dollar bill.

Doug moved down the left lane of washers, aware of her gaze but ignoring it. He sensed her surprise at seeing him again—she was about a third of the way down on the right—and then her suspicion at the coincidence.

He opened a dryer door and lifted out a load of cool laundry. The clothes had been sitting in that machine for two days, awaiting his return, but only Virgil knew that.

Doug went about folding the clothes like he had a lot of important things on his mind, jeans first, then shirts, beginning to think she wasn't coming over—until he heard the voice, soft like a hand on his shoulder, turning him around.

"Excuse me? Hi?" A nervous smile across the central double-lane of washing machines. "Hi."

He looked blank, then let his face come to life. "Oh, hey—how are *you*?"

"Mortified." She clasped her hands together, twisting them. "In fact, I was almost too embarrassed even to come over here, but my conscience, it marched me right over to tell you thank you—"

"No no no."

"I was, I guess, having a really bad . . . well, month, actually. I don't know why, but it all kind of hit me at once. Here, unfortunately." A forced, guilty smile, as in *My bad*.

"Don't worry about it. So long as you're feeling better."

"Much, yes," she said, still mock-formal, maybe even talking down to him a bit, putting her good manners on display. "Anyway—thanks for pulling my clothes out. I can't believe I just abandoned them like that. And your folding them, Virgil told me you did that."

"Oh, yeah, Virgil. Well . . ." As though it were supposed to have been a secret between two men. "That was nothing. So long as it was all right with you, I mean. Kind of weird, you know, folding a stranger's laundry."

"Yeah." Smiling, but there was tension in her neck. "I guess so." She patted her flat hand against the washing machine lid, glancing away. "So anyway—it was really nice of you to do that, you're a nice person. And I'm sorry I ran off like that, sorry I wasn't as polite to you in return." Trailing away now, an abrupt nod punctuating her halting gratitude. "Anyway, thanks again. Thanks."

Doug watched her retreat to her machine, nodding, wanting to say something.

Nothing came out. He turned back to his open dryer with a harsh face. He had pushed it too far, scaring her off with *folding a stranger's laundry*—idiot panty-sniffer. What was he doing here anyway, taking advantage of this emotionally confused person? *Fuck.* He wanted to smack himself on the head but maybe she was watching.

He looked over and she was reading a paperback. It occurred to him then that he had *forgotten to ask her name!* Or offer his! That was some quick thinking there. No wonder she walked away.

He had blown it. He'd had his chance, and now he was in an awkward no-man's-land with her: not strangers anymore, but not acquaintances either. Running into her again somewhere else would only raise her antenna, make her skittish.

Maybe it was better this way. Over before it began. Where had he expected to go with it anyway? Ask her to drinks Upstairs at the Tap? Dinner at Olives, then on to the fucking opera?

No sparks. There it was in a nutshell. *No fireworks.*

Then he remembered her smiling. Twisting her hands anxiously. Looking at him longer than she had to. The suspense in her eyes, shining beyond politeness. This summoned the counterbalancing image of her wearing a blindfold, and Doug remembered how much he wanted that image out of his mind.

She sensed him coming, looking up from her book as he approached her across the washing machines. "Hi," he said. "Slightly creepy Laundromat guy here again."

"No-o," she laughed.

He pressed his fingertips atop the machine before him like a pianist about to launch into a solo. "I was back over there pairing off socks, and you were over here—and I knew I would never forgive myself if I didn't come over and take a shot."

Her eyebrows flinched at his poor choice of words, making him talk faster.

"Because if I don't take a shot," he said, repeating the offending phrase, pretending that it was not in fact unfortunate, "it's going to wind up haunting me for like the next four weeks at least."

She smiled, changing direction, showing lighthearted concern. "Are you really that hard on yourself?"

"You don't even know," he said, relaxing just a fraction. "It would progress from, say, smacking myself repeatedly on the forehead, to, like, stopping in here a couple of times each day, doing my laundry one sock at a time, hoping you'd come back in alone and that you'd remember me, and we'd get to talking again, and I'd have something incredibly devious to say about the weather. . . ."

She was smiling by the end of it, until some sort of protective instinct closed her lips. "Well," she said, "now that you've taken your *shot*"—she kicked the word playfully—"is that enough? Enough to keep you from hurting yourself, I mean, and spending all your quarters here?"

"No way. Not anymore. See—now we've talked. Now it's a character issue. If you were to say no to me now, then it's like—then there's something wrong with *me,* and this whole haunting thing continues, only much, much worse. Because now what it means is, I'm not fit to attract a quality person like yourself."

She squinted, still smiling but mulling this over, not knowing what to make of him. Which was okay: Doug didn't quite know what to make of him himself.

"Quality?" she said, liking the ring of it, and he felt her giving in.

"For sure," he said, dazzled by his success. "Quality."

12
CHECKING IN

HER MESSAGE ON HIS voice mail went:

"Hi—Agent Frawley? This is Claire Keesey, um, the branch manager from the robbery—the one, the BayBanks in Kenmore Square? Hi. I don't have any, this isn't—I have no pertinent information regarding the robbers or anything like that. I'm just calling to let you know that I'm normal—that I finally had a little mini-episode, my junior breakdown, and I'm feeling better now, I really am. It was at a Laundromat, and . . . I guess something made me think of my jacket, the one they cut? And it all came crashing down on me at once. I actually ran off and left my clothes there and now have to get up the nerve to go back and claim them. A total case. Anyway—I know this is a strange message and I'm probably taking up valuable crime-fighting time, but who else would understand? And I really wanted to thank you, because if you hadn't warned me that something like this might happen, well—I would think I was headed for Prozac and a group home. So—thanks. That's all. Bye."

Frawley didn't get the voice mail until a day and a half later. He tried her at the bank first, then reached her at home.

"Oh, hi. Hold on, okay?"

The call-waiting blip.

She came back in a few seconds. "Sorry about that. My overbearing mother."

"No problem, how're you doing?"

Music being turned down. "Good. Doing better. I'm doing well, actually."

"Good. I just got your message."

"Oh, God. Rambling, right? I just—after feeling so blah for so long, so walking-dead, getting that little bit of relief—it was almost the same as feeling great."

"I tried to reach you at work."

"Yeah, no, I haven't—I finally went back today. For the first time, just to look around. They redid my office. Desk, chair, ceiling. It was a little bit of a haunted house, but I'll get there. I start back full-time tomorrow."

"That's good. It's time."

"No, it is good. Otherwise I'm just sitting around here, watching way too much TV."

"You might experience a rush of anxiety or even adrenaline, seeing someone enter the bank with the same body type as the bandits', or a similar demeanor. If so, you might try to remember what it is about them that triggered that, and let me know."

A pause. "Okay. Wow, I hope not."

"Don't stress out about it. Get your clothes back?"

"Oh—from the Laundromat?" she realized. "God, it was so humiliating. Yes, I got my clothes back. Cleaned and folded."

"Nice. A little service they provide weepy customers?"

"That's right. As advertised in the window."

He could hear her smile in her voice. "You had a coupon or something?"

"A competitor's coupon, for emotional distress, which they honored. But seriously—the weirdest thing?"

"What?"

"Some guy there asked me out on a date. Another customer, the guy who pulled my clothes out. He's actually the one who folded them. It was funny—he definitely seemed not the type for folding women's clothes."

"Really," said Frawley, intrigued by the competitiveness this news triggered in him. "What did you say?"

"I actually said yes, because it was sort of in-the-moment. But I think he's like a furniture mover or something. I mean, I don't think my head's quite right yet. A guy I met in a Laundromat? I'm sure I'll just end up blowing him off."

Frawley smiled, feeling oddly energized. "You would laugh out loud if you could see me right now."

"Why? Are you undercover or something?"

"My neck and cheek, and my left hand—they're all stained red. A dye pack exploded on me."

"A *dye* pack? Get out."

"A robbery in Brookline, I chased the guy down and it went off. And of course it takes a lot longer to fade than the three days they claim. So I'm sort of out of commission here for a while, at least socially. But maybe next time we see each other I'll tell you my tale."

"Sure. That sounds good."

"Good," he said, buzzed. "And, hey, good luck tomorrow."

"Oh, yeah. Yuck. I'll be fine."

As Frawley hung up, Dino's voice surprised him from behind. "What was that?"

Dino was sitting on the edge of Flott's desk inside the Lakeville bull pen. "Branch manager from the Morning Glory."

"What's she got?"

"Nothing. Just checking in."

"Checking in, huh? Thought you cleared her."

"I did."

"Uh-huh." Dino smiled. "Okay. Just watch yourself there."

"No, no."

"They love cops in their life after something goes wrong."

Frawley shook that off. Dino was holding a legal-sized manila envelope in his hairy hands. "What's that? Congress Street subpoena already? The Nynex records?"

Dino danced it out of Frawley's grasp. "Like a kid on Christmas morning. Say *please*."

Frawley pulled his hand down contritely—then lunged and swiped the envelope out of Dino's hands, sitting back again and smiling and ripping it open. "Please."

13
AM GOLD

DOUG PLAYED A RARE street-hockey matinee up where Washington Street dead-ended beside the rink on a paved bluff. In terms of the neighborhood, this was an *event,* like if native son Howie Long had come back to play touch football over at the Barry Playground. Doug didn't skate much anymore, and never out on the streets, because the game to him was freighted now with too many negative connotations: his youth, faded dreams, his father. Pulling on the skates and pads was like climbing inside his younger self again, and that kid was a royal screwup. Doug had to be feeling good to want to play—and today he felt really, really good.

A kid from Chappie Street who fancied himself a street Gretzky faced off against Doug, and got schooled. Doug put on a clinic. Jem, who lived for this shit, was a conspicuous no-show, leaving Gloansy to dust off Doug's old high school handle, hooting, "Stick came to *play!*" as Doug finished the third game with a rising slap shot that nicked the crotch of the goalie's droopy jeans—a wannabe-black white kid from the Mishawum houses—the orange-ball puck finding a tear in the net and arcing away down the slope to the streets below. Doug skated a victory lap backward, pumping his fist under the wide blue sky.

Fast-forward to a quarter after eight that evening, Doug MacRay rearranging the appetizer card, the glass salt and pepper shakers, the purple petunia in the tiny black vase. He had sent the aproned server away twice and now felt the other Tap diners looking his way, entertaining themselves, watching some Townie bozo get stood up but good.

He tried hard to appear relaxed, not pissed, like everything was cool and going according to plan. But first of all: Why the Tap? Why pick a place where he might get made? Secondly: Why Upstairs? Who the fuck was he trying to be? These frauds he despised?

Bottom line was, he'd panicked at the Laundromat. She said yes and he blanked, because he had no strategy beyond that, the Tap Upstairs the first thing that jumped into his head.

Like a teenager, he had been idealizing their date. *She'll sit there, I'll sit here.*

I'll say this, she'll laugh. A fucking little boy. And this "oatmeal"-colored pullover tugging tight across his shoulders, that he had bought off a headless mannequin on a last-minute run to the Galleria—after spending half an hour going through his closet? Fucking God—*look at yourself.* Black pants with the crotch cut too high. A braided leather belt, soft black shoes.

Huge mistake, this whole thing. Hiding in the back of the place, taking this table because he couldn't risk being seen up front. He scanned the appetizer menu for the eighth fucking time. He watched the glass doors, the color bleeding out of his vision.

He deserved this humiliation. He deserved to be stood up. A mistake from the word go.

Five more minutes he waited. Then another five beyond that—his punishment, sticking his nose in it, forcing himself to soak in his own shame. *Learn from this.* What was it Frank G. had said? *Aside from not walking into a bar alone, this is the most important decision you're ever gonna make.* Nice work. Fucked up on both counts.

Two choices: either resume drinking, hard, and right now—piss away two goddamn years for a stuck-up yuppie bitch—or get up, walk to the door— *Maybe stop at the ladies' room on your way out*—and walk his tight-crotch pants back home.

As always, Doug fell back to the one thing he knew he could count on. The one thing Doug had that no one could take away from him. His criminal eye. Others—maybe it was a wife or kids they took shelter in. Someone or something to run to where they could feel like a success no matter how often the rest of the world humiliated them.

Double up on the armored-car surveillance. Focus on the big multiscreen movie theaters, Revere, Fresh Pond, Braintree. With the "summer" releases starting in early May, all he needed to do was zero in on a place and a time.

The front windows were darkening with night, headlights finding their way along Main. Dim enough for Doug to make a clean escape and drag his sorry ass back up the hill. He waited for his server to get busy at another table, then stood and started heavy-legged for the door, head down, his exit slowed by two chicks picking through the basket of mints at the hostess station.

That's where he was when Claire Keesey came rushing in. She gave the tight-skirted hostess a quick once-over, then looked right past Doug to the central bar.

The chicks in front of him exited, and he could smell the street and the night, and he started to follow them out, wanting to be done with it. He had already torn her down beyond repair in his mind—himself too—and the moment had passed.

"My God! You're right here!" She reached out and squeezed his elbow. "I am so late, I know. Were you leaving? My God, I'm so sorry. I don't even—but you're still here, I can't believe it."

Believe it. Or, maybe, *Hey, I don't believe it either,* cutting her dead—and then walk out on her, take his anger on home.

But she was looking up at him and smiling, catching her breath. "It's Doug, right?"

"Right."

"I didn't, when I came in . . . you look different."

"Do I, yeah."

Sizing him up. "I didn't . . . hmm." Concerned about her own clothes now, a white cotton button-up blouse fitted nicely at the waist, distressed jeans, black shoe boots. "I was running late. I thought more casual . . ."

"Doesn't matter. I think I folded those jeans."

She checked them out with a smile. "I think you did."

He started to feel good again, despite himself. "Searched the pockets for loose change and everything."

She smiled brightly, her eyes fully involved. He realized he was standing inside the entrance to the Tap, the door to the Downstairs five steps behind him. He nodded to the back of the room. "Maybe I haven't lost our table yet."

They threaded through the tabletops to the back wall. She tucked her little red key-chain purse in next to the flower vase, Doug sitting across from her on a cushioned, bar-height chair, his back to the wall. The low-watt overhead lamp sprayed soft light onto her honeyed hair, the rest of the lounge room fading from view behind her.

Doug patted the table, smiling, exhaling.

"Well," she said. She leaned forward a moment, the overhead lamp creating a mask of shadow around her eyes. Doug leaned back reflexively, not wanting her to see any masks on him. "So why am I thirty minutes late?" She looked away for the answer, but became distracted. "I'm still shocked you waited. I mean—I'm glad. And I'm sorry. But I'm also amazed."

"Well, really only about fifteen minutes of it was me waiting for you. The other fifteen was me pouting, knocking myself in the head."

"Oh, no! You warned me about that."

"It's a problem I have."

"You don't—I think I tried to tell you this at the Laundromat—but you don't strike me as the type to be so, I guess, tough on yourself."

"I'm a fragile sort."

She smiled at his arms, his shoulders. "Right. You bruise easy."

"I put too much pressure on myself, I guess. Some things I take too seriously."

"Please, you're sitting across from the original life-or-death, agonizing-over-everything girl."

She went off searching for that answer again as their server arrived, a short-haired platinum blonde with one ear rimmed with copper clips. She smiled at Claire. "You made it."

"I made it," said Claire, pleasant, appraising.

"He looked very worried," she said, hugging her leather order pad, nodding cheerily at Doug. "Actually, he looked pissed off."

Doug said, "Thought I was hiding it."

Claire said, "Was he really hitting himself in the head?"

"Close to it. My name is Drea, what can I get you?"

Claire asked for a wine recommendation and settled on something Italian called a valpolicella.

"Glass or bottle?" said Drea, looking at them both.

"Bottle," said Doug.

"Terrific." Drea started to leave.

"And I'll have a soda water, lime," said Doug.

Drea paused a second before nodding and flipping her pad back open and scribbling that in. "I'll be right back." And she was gone.

Claire looked at the table, wondering about his order.

"I'm driving," Doug told her.

She looked up at him. "Okay."

"For the rest of my life."

Claire nodding, then gesturing after Drea. "I don't even have to . . ."

"Nope," he said, rocking gently. "It's cool. Really."

"Why did you get a bottle then?"

"I don't even know," he said, his head pounding. She was looking at him differently now. Questions popping in her mind like flashbulbs. "You were saying . . ."

"I was?"

"About being . . ."

"Right, yes. About being late." She crossed her arms on the table and leaned on them, damning body language. "Well . . . the truth is, I wasn't even going to come at all."

"Ah. Okay."

"I was going to blow this off. I had decided not to come. That's why I was late."

Doug nodded, waiting. "So what was it that changed your mind?"

She took a deep breath, held it, smiled. "I guess, in a weird way—the decision *not* to come. In other words, deciding that I didn't *have* to come here tonight. Realizing that I don't *have* to do *anything* . . . sort of relieved me of any obligation. The longer part of the story is that . . . I've been through a lot of crap recently, and I'll spare you all that—but my thinking's been strange. Thinking and rethinking everything, examining my life to death, driving myself absolutely nuts. More so than usual, that is. So, fine—I'm not going to go, right? Okay, that's decided. Then eight o'clock rolls around and I'm sitting at home, deliberately doing nothing, watching eight o'clock roll around, and I was like—'Well, Claire, you don't have to *not* go either.' These are the conversations I have with myself. But it seemed like I was setting these rules, these arbitrary rules, putting up fences around my days, my nights. Following rules instead of following . . . the flow, you know? Doing what I want. Being me. So I decided—why the hell not? This is two people meeting for a drink, not life-or-death. Right?"

"Sure," he said. "No."

"People meet for drinks all the time, it's not that mind-bending. I know I'm rambling. This happens a lot."

"It's good. Saves me from coming up with a bunch of clever things to say."

"Long story short—I yanked my head out of my butt, and here I am."

The wine arrived and she grew quiet again, circumspect, Drea opening the bottle at her hip with professional flourish, pouring a taste into Claire's glass with that drip-saving twist of the wrist. Claire sipped and nodded that it was fine, and Doug drank some soda while Drea poured Claire a deep glass and said she'd be back for their food order.

At the end of this, in the background of Doug's vision, two guys entered the Tap, saluted the doorman, and disappeared downstairs. Doug had made out an oversized Bruins jersey on one of them and, with a jab of anxiety, believed it to be Jem.

"Leave the iron on?" she said.

"Huh?"

"You had this look."

"Oh." Reading her smile. "Yeah. I think I left the milk out on the counter. Hey—are you even hungry?"

"Well, considering I didn't plan on coming, I already ate."

He checked the door to the stairs again, thinking, thinking. "How about getting out of here?"

"I—what?" She looked at her glass. "And going where?"

Good question. "Someplace with a view maybe. Of the city. Unless—I don't know, your place, does it have a view?"

"I—" She stopped fast. "*My* place?"

"Whoa, no, hold up, I don't mean—I only meant, I don't want to be showing you the city if it's something you see every morning when you wake up."

"Oh." Suspicious now. He was losing her, and fast.

"See," he said with a glance at the surrounding tables, "I picked this place—I wasn't ready for you to say yes, and so I went with here because it seemed like maybe the sort of place you'd like. You, who I don't even know, right? And—*do* you even like it?"

She smiled through her confusion. "You don't even drink."

"Exactly. I lost my head. So what do you say?"

She looked at her glass again. "But what about . . . ?"

"Bring it with you." He was pulling his cash roll from his pocket.

"Bring it?"

"I'm paying for it. Take the glass too."

"I can't—the glass?"

Doug unfolded his roll, discreetly but making sure she got a look at its heft, winding the thin red rubber band around his fingers and stripping a century off the top, standing it in front of the vase, Franklin out, then snapping the band back around the roll and tucking it away.

"Just smile at the doorman," he said, lifting the bottle as she stood. "I guarantee you, he won't see a thing."

THEY MADE SMALL TALK going up the hill, walking slow, she with her arms folded, the wineglass in one hand. Their date had spilled out into the Town at large, potential complications on every block. An undercurrent of self-interrogation went on like radio chatter inside his head. *What the fuck are you doing?* And his answer became a mantra: *Just one date. Just one date.*

"So what about you?" she asked. "You've lived here—"

"All my life, yeah. You, before this?"

"I've lived all over the city, since college. Grew up in Canton."

"Canton. That's Blue Hills, right? There's a rink there, off the highway. Skated there a few times."

"Right, Ponkapoag, I think."

"So, the suburbs, huh?"

"Oh, yeah. The suburbs."

Doug plucked an overturned recycling bin out of the street, returned it to a doorway. Working hard to be smooth. "What do you do for a job?"

"I'm in banking," she said. Then: "Wow."

"What?" Doug looked around for *wow*.

"No, just that phrase. 'I'm in banking.' Not sure if that was meant to impress you or bore you. I manage a BayBanks branch. It's a lot like running a convenience store, except I move money instead of calling cards and snacks. You?"

"What do I do? Well, that depends. We still trying to impress each other?"

"Sure, go for it."

"I'm a sky-maker."

"Wow," she said again. "You win."

"I'm in demolition. Blasting rock, bringing down buildings. *Making sky,* that's from when you level a big building, opening up views. Suddenly you've made some sky."

"I like it," she decided. "Do you do those old hotels and stadiums they always show on TV, that detonate inward into their own pile of rubble?"

"No, I'm more hands-on. Basically, if you've seen *The Flintstones,* that's me. When the whistle blows, I'm surfing down the neck of a brontosaurus and outta there."

They crested on Bunker Hill Street, having climbed from about nine to almost eleven on the ticking Charlestown clock. He led her across the gas-lit thoroughfare to the mouth of Pearl Street, the outline of a plan starting to form.

Any thoughts he had of changing his clothes were dashed with one glance at Jem's mother's demo-worthy house halfway down the plunging street. The Flamer, Jem's banged-up Trans Am, blue on blue with blue flames detailed on the sides and hood, was parked there like a flare in the road warning Doug away.

His own Caprice Classic was three cars down. "Just a sec," said Doug, pulling out his keys, opening the driver's-side door.

She stayed back on the curb, looking at the dingy white four-door and its fading blue, soft-top roof. "Is this your car?"

"Oh, no," he said, reaching under the velour passenger seat, rocking the musky orange Hooters deodorizer dangling from the cigarette lighter. "I loaned this jerk I know some CDs." He felt around the blue carpeting for them, then straightened, waving two jewel cases, too fast for her to read them.

He walked her back across Bunker, hiking up three blocks west under the gas lamps to the Heights, stopping before St. Frank's steeple at the top of the hill. "Here we are."

It was a clean brownstone triple with bowfront windows and blooming flower boxes painted fireball red. The double doors were black with buffed brass knockers, handles, and kickplates. Doug stepped inside the faux-marble entrance, nudging aside a couple of FedEx boxes with his new shoes.

"You live here?" she said, cautious, remaining on the sidewalk.

"No way." He reached up, feeling along the top of the frame of the interior door. "No, friend of mine manages it." He came down with the key, showed it to her, turned it in the door. "We're just gonna use the stairs to get up top. What do you say?"

After a glance of concern up and down the sidewalk, she followed him inside.

The roof was rubber-sealed and lumpy, hedged on all four sides by two-foot brick crenellations. An abandoned wire-and-wood pigeon coop did not obstruct their postcard view of the city, Boston laid out against a silk screen of blue-black, from the financial towers to the mirrored Hancock to the dominant Prudential building, with the busy interstate a twinkling ribbon wrapping it all.

Claire stood at the southern edge, the city side, looking down at the rest of the Town like a woman on a high bridge, the now empty glass in her hand. "Wow."

"That is the word of the night," said Doug. He unfolded two lawn chairs from inside the coop, their blue-and-white nylon webbing frayed, the hollow aluminum frames predating cup holders. "Drops off pretty good down the hill, don't it."

The rooftops on either side were graded steps climbing to the sky, many with cedar decks, patio furniture, grills. Old, thorny TV antennas mixed with satellite dishes turned like hopeful faces to the southwest. To the left, looking east above Flagship Wharf in the navy yard, jet lights slid out of the sky, stars on a string. Other planes circled overhead in defined holding patterns, a swirling constellation.

The sounds of the Town rose to them as she walked back to the chair next to the wine bottle, her free hand in her pocket. "This sky—is it one of yours?"

Doug took a careful look around. "Yep, it's mine."

"I especially like what you did with these stars over here."

"We get those imported. Hey—ever ordered anything off TV? You know, late night, infomercials?"

"No. But if I did, it would be a Flowbee."

Doug held up the two CDs. "*AM Gold.* Time-Life stuff, you know, try it for thirty days, we'll send another every four to six weeks, you can cancel at any time?" The boom box, an old Sanyo missing its cassette drawer, was bike-chained to the doorpost of the coop. Doug dropped in the first CD, let it spin.

"Oh my," she said. It was the Carpenters.

"You gotta give it a little time to work on you. This is a big step for me."

"What is, coming out of the closet as a Carpenters fan?"

"Let me correct you right there. Definitely not a Carpenters *fan.* This is about the total effect of the music, the predisco seventies. I don't sanction every single track, and some of them are pretty bad. 'Muskrat Love' is on here some-where. What I like is the radio station aspect of it, like receiving a signal time-delayed twenty years."

She took the jewel case from him and sat down to look it over. "Wow," she said, amused. "My mom used to have these songs on all day."

"Sure, WHDH, right?" He sat down a respectable three feet away from her, both of them facing the city like it was the ocean.

"Every morning, getting ready for school."

"Jess Cain."

"*Yes.* Wow." The uniting power of nostalgia. "And Officer Bill in the traffic copter."

Doug's mother had kept the kitchen radio going day and night. It was one of his clearest memories of her. But sharing this fact with Claire would have invited other questions, and his past was a minefield. He had to be careful not to blow himself up here.

She handed him back the CD case. "You come up here often?"

"No. Almost never."

"This isn't where you take all your dates?"

"In fact, I should admit it now, what I said downstairs was sort of a fib. I don't actually know who manages this building. I just know where the key is."

"Oh." She thought about that, looking out at the city winking back at her.

"I wanted to get us up above the Town, you know, try to show you something."

She settled back into her chair, good for a little mischief. "Okay."

Lou Rawls started up with "Lady Love," and Doug mustered all the bass he had to say, *"Oh, yeah . . ."*

She smiled, stretching out her legs, flexing her ankles like she was lifting them dripping out of a light surf. "So where do you live?"

"Back of the hill." He thumbed behind them. "I rent. You own your place?"

"I got a great rate from my bank. Actually cheaper for me to own. Are you going to live here forever?"

"You mean, like most Townies? I can admit, until maybe a couple of years ago, I never even considered it a choice."

"Okay, you see now—I could *not* imagine living in my parents' same town. There's just no way. So what is it about this place that keeps such a tight hold on people?"

"Comfort-level thing, probably. Knowing what's around every corner."

"Okay. But even when what's around that next corner maybe isn't all that . . . good?"

"I'm giving you how it *was* more than how it *is,* because honestly, I can't say for certain how it is right now. I feel sort of apart from it, these past couple of years. But growing up, yeah, it was easy. You were known. You had a role in the Town and you played it."

"Like a big family."

"And families can be good or bad. Good *and* bad. Me, my role around

Town, I was Mac's kid. Mac was what they called my father. Everywhere I went, every corner I passed, everybody knew me. *There goes Mac's kid*—like father, like son. And you wear that around long enough, it becomes part of you. But now things are getting different. Everybody's not related to everybody else anymore. New faces on the corner, strangers, people who can't recite your entire family history, generation by generation. And there's freedom in that, at least there is for me. What you give up in comfort, in familiarity—for me it's nice not to be reminded on *every* block, 'This is who I am, I'm Mac's kid.'"

"But I would think that sort of thing would inspire people to want to get out more. To go on their own, make a clean break."

Doug shrugged. "That what you did?"

"What I tried to do. What I'm *still* trying to do."

"I think suburbs are like that. Launching pads. The Town, it's more like a factory. We're local product here, banging it out every day. There's pollution, but it's *our* damn pollution, know what I'm saying?" That didn't come out as clever as he had hoped. "It's a box, I'll give you that. It's like an island that's tough to swim off of."

She sipped her wine, having poured herself some more without his noticing. The song changed. "'Wildfire,'" she said, gazing back at the radio. "My God, I used to love this song. The horse?"

"You see?" he said, getting jazzed again.

They listened awhile, under the orbiting plane lights. "You mentioned your dad," she said.

Shit. Minefields. "Yeah."

"Your whole family live here?"

"No, actually, none of them, not anymore."

"They all left and you stayed?"

"Sort of. My parents, they're split up."

"Oh. But they live close by?"

"Not really."

"'Not really.' What does that mean?"

Boom! His leg below the knee. "My mother, she left my dad and me when I was six."

"Oh, sorry. I mean, gosh, sorry I asked."

"No, she got out while the getting was good. For her own sanity, I'd say. My father."

"You're not close with him?"

"Not anymore." Skirted that one—still hopping along one-leggedly.

"I hope I'm not asking too many questions."

"First date," said Doug. "What else are you gonna do?"

"Right, I know. Usually, guys I meet for the first time, they go on and on, packaging and selling themselves. Either that or they try to wear you down with questions, like proving how *interested* they are. Like, if I'm so involved recounting my own life story, maybe I'll lose track of how many Stoli and Sprites I've had."

As the song faded out, there was a spray of bullying laughter from the street below, then the pop and smash of a glass bottle shattering, followed by cursing, laughing, footsteps running away. "Nice," grumbled Doug.

Then the Little River Band came on, making it all right.

"I know this one," she said. "I'm realizing I've been listening to some really depressing music recently."

"Yeah? Like how bad?"

"Like college-radio bad. Like, old Cure. Smashing Pumpkins."

"Yikes. The Pumpkins. Sounds serious."

She nodded.

He went easy. "This something you want to talk about?"

She held up her glass, empty again, twirling it by the stem, examining her lipstick on the rim, the finger smudges. "I don't know. Kind of nice to get away from it."

"Good, then. We're away."

She lowered the glass. "Do you have any questions you want to ask me?"

"Oh, only about a couple of hundred or so. But like you say, this is a nice vibe right now. I figure there's time. Least, I hope there is."

That was good. Saying that did something to her—even as his mind reminded him, *Just one date*.

"Can I ask you another question then?" she said.

Doug cut her off at the pass. "I had a very misspent youth. When I drink I become a jerk, so I just don't drink anymore."

She smiled gently, almost embarrassedly. "That wasn't what I was going to ask."

"I haven't had a drink in two years. I go to meetings regularly, a few each week. I like them. I consider what I have an allergy. Someone's allergic to nuts or something, people don't hold that against them. Me, I'm allergic to alcohol. I break out in jerk hives. And this whole thing, it makes for a very bad first impression, but that's what I have to live with." He breathed. "Okay. Sorry. What were you gonna ask?"

"Whew." She undercut that with a smile. "I was going to ask why you wanted to take out someone you saw crying in a Laundromat?"

Doug nodded thoughtfully. "This is a good question."

"I know it."

Police lights crawled along the interstate, bright, pinpoint blues. "I don't have a good answer for you. I guess, sure, I am curious about that. A pretty girl with problems—that's not something you see every day."

This time he heard the wine trickling almost guiltily into her glass. "Miracles" was starting now, Jefferson Airplane, or maybe Jefferson Starship. He closed his eyes a moment and saw his mother's old black-and-silver RCA singing from the top of the refrigerator.

"Honestly," Claire said after a sip, "how much of this did you plan?"

"Not a second of it, I swear to God."

"Well, it's perfect. I mean, you can't even know how. If I could stop time right now, keep that sun from coming up tomorrow morning . . ."

"Yeah? What's the sun got on you?"

"Tomorrow morning I start back at work."

"Start back?" said Doug, mustering innocence.

The wine slowed her words down a little. "I've had sort of an extended vacation."

"That's nice."

"Not really." Another sip and she turned to him. "You've lived here all your life, right?"

"Right."

"So what do you know about bank robbers?"

He cleared his throat, letting out a long, silent exhale. "What's to know?"

"There's supposed to be a lot from here. I figured maybe you grew up with some."

"I guess—maybe I did, yeah, I guess."

"My bank, where I work . . . a couple of weeks ago, we were robbed."

"Oh. I see."

"They were hiding, waiting for us inside." ·

Stunning, how immediately shitty he felt. "And what, they tied you up?"

"Held us at gunpoint. Made us lie down. Took our shoes off." She looked at him again. "Isn't that the weirdest? Our *shoes*. I'm stuck on that, I don't know why. Belittling, you know? I have all these dreams now where I'm barefoot." She looked at her shoe boots against the rubber-coated roof. "Anyway."

"But you weren't hurt."

"Davis was—my assistant manager. They beat him. A silent alarm went off."

He had to keep it up now. "But if it was silent, then . . . ?"

"One of them had a radio wire in his ear. A police radio."

"Right. They beat this guy up because he set off the alarm."

She stared at the city as though the correct answer were out there somewhere. She never answered him. Doug pondered that.

"Police catch these guys yet?" he said.

"No."

"They're on them, though."

"I don't know. They didn't say."

"You probably had to go through, what, a whole interrogation?"

"It wasn't too bad."

He let it go. Best not to push. "And you haven't been back at work since?"

She shook her head, frowning, pensive. "They took me with them when they left."

Doug couldn't play along with her here. He couldn't say anything.

"They were worried about the alarm." She followed the jet lights in the sky to the airport off to their left. "Somewhere over there, they let me out. I was blindfolded."

It was all there in her voice, everything he never wanted to hear. "Scary?"

She took a long time to answer, so long that Doug started to wonder if he hadn't given himself away somehow. "Nothing else happened," she said.

She stared at him now, eerily intense. Doug stumbled over his words. "No, I didn't—"

"They just let me go. That's all. Once they knew they weren't being followed, they just pulled over and let me out."

"Sure," he said, nodding. "Of course."

She folded her arms against the creeping cool. "I've been in such a funk since. The FBI agent, he told me it would be like being in mourning."

Doug said, as evenly as he could, "FBI agent?"

"But I don't know. When my grandparents died, I was sad, very sad. But did I truly *mourn* . . . ?"

Doug kept nodding. "And you're working with them?"

"The FBI? Just this one agent I talk to. He's been great."

"Yeah? That's good." Waiting a patient beat. "What does he ask you, like, 'What'd they look like? What'd they say?'"

"No. At first, yes. Not anymore."

"Now what, he, like, calls you up, checks in?"

"I guess." Her little side glance informed Doug that she had noticed he was asking a lot of questions. "What?"

"No, I'm just wondering. From his point of view. Maybe he's thinking, 'Hey, inside job.'"

She stared. "Why would he think that?"

"Only because, this other guy was beat up, you were taken for a ride, let go unhurt."

"You're saying he *suspects* me?"

"How would I know? It's just a thought. You never thought that?"

She sat perfectly still, like someone hearing a strange noise at night and waiting to hear it again. "You're freaking me out a little."

"You know what? Maybe I should stick to talking about things I know something about."

"No," she decided. "No, it's impossible."

"They're probably just casting a wide net."

But he had thrown a little monkey wrench of uncertainty her way, and that was enough. Her shoulders were bunched now, arms crossed high on her chest.

"Getting cold?" he said.

"I am."

"I think 'Muskrat Love' is coming up next anyway. That's our cue."

She said she was done with the wine, so he poured the rest into the roof gutter, stowing the chairs and switching off the CD player in the middle of "Poetry Man." The wine formed a bloody stain on the sidewalk as they left the building, walking back down Bunker Hill Street to Monument Square. A handful of skateboarders hanging out around the stairs at the base of the granite obelisk put Doug in the mind of his crew, making him itchy. They came to a five-street junction in the heart of the remade section of Charlestown.

"Okay," said Doug, bringing her up short on the brick sidewalk, her door only a hundred yards around the bend.

She was surprised. "Okay . . ."

Ask for her number. It would be rude to do otherwise. Then fade away forever. For her sake as much as yours.

"So," she said, waiting.

He swiped a mustache of sweat off his upper lip. *You had your date, your flirtation with danger, you got that out of your system.* She was looking up at him, her empty glass catching some of the lamplight, holding it there.

"Look," he said. "I probably shouldn't even be here with you."

She reacted like he was making up his own language. "Why do you say that? What do you mean?"

"I don't even know." He shuffled his feet, needing to leave. "I'm all messed up recently, my mind. I'm used to order, clarity, things a certain way. Not this. Not doing things I don't understand."

"But that's—me too." A revelation, a bright smile of communion. "I'm exactly the same way right now."

"And I need to . . . I'm trying to be good in my life, you know?"

"Hey." She stepped up to him, examining his face in the light of the gas lamp. She reached for his forehead, and when he did not protest, touched the scar that split his left eyebrow. "I wanted to ask at the restaurant."

"Hockey scar. An old injury. You—you like hockey?"

Her finger came away from his face. "I hate it."

Doug nodded fast. "So what are you doing tomorrow night?"

She said, surprised, "What—tomorrow?"

"Probably have a busy day, right? Back to work, you'll be tired. How about the night after?"

"I don't . . ." She looked amazed. "I don't even know."

Doug felt like someone was trying to open up an umbrella in his chest. "Okay, here it is right here. Whatever it takes to see you again, I'll do. Would you want to see me again?"

"I . . ." Looking up at his face. "Sure."

"Great. Okay. So we're both crazy, that's good. Your turn this time. You pick the place—somewhere outside C-town. I'll pick you up right here. Give me your last four digits."

She did, and he gave her no time to ask for his, forsaking all thoughts of a parting kiss, just trying to tear himself away from her. He was acting drunker now than he ever had before.

"Good luck," he said, backing off. "With tomorrow."

"Thanks." She held up the glass as though it were a gift. "Good night, Doug."

"Wow. Hey, could you say that for me again?"

"Good night, Doug."

"Good night, Claire." He said it, and there was no lightning striking him dead in the street.

14
THE POPE OF THE FORGOTTEN VILLAGE

DEZ LIVED IN THE NECK.

As Charlestown was the orphan of Boston, so was the Neck the orphan of Charlestown. Getting there meant heading out past the Schrafft's tower at the western gate of the Town, banging a one-eighty by the MBTA rail shop in the Flat, ducking under two crumbling highway elevations, then turning past the all-cement salute to urban blight that was the Sullivan Square Station. Tucked behind there was the six-street patch of old railroad houses also known as the Forgotten Village, an outpost teetering on the edge of Charlestown and of Boston itself, the last settlement before the Brazilian food markets of Somerville's Cobble Hill.

The Neck embodied the Town's siege mentality. Dez's mother still hissed about the traitors who'd accepted the city's relo money, making way for planners and engineers to carve up the Neck. Whole streets had been bulldozed—Haverhill, Perkins Place, Sever—chopped off like arms and legs, and yet, proud old veteran that it was, the Neck survived.

Dez's mother's aluminum-sided two-story on Brighton Street was shouldered between two taller houses, its square front yard fenced with child's-height chain-link. Growing up beneath a major highway had made Desmond Elden feel isolated and marginalized—and proud. Looking up at the rusting struts—the corroding Central Artery and its crumbling chunks of concrete—Dez often thought of the view fish had, looking up at a pier.

Dez earned enough—legitimately, from his other mother, dear old Ma Bell—to move them both out of there, though he knew better than to even bring up the subject. Ma would never give up the land she had been bitching about for years. Certainly there was no leaving the parish. Dez's mother didn't drive, and her daily walks to mass were a hike: a dreary quarter mile over hot asphalt in summer, battered by whipping river winds in winter, always taking her life into her hands crossing the highway rotary. And this was just to reach the Schrafft's tower—from there she had to march all the way up Bunker Hill to the steeple at the crest of the Heights. But you'd just as soon ask her to trade in Dez for another son as leave St. Frank's. This daily odyssey was part of her experience of mass, as it was part of the experience of living in the Neck, of being Catholic, of being Irish, of being an aging widow. It was suffering made proud. There were only two ways she would leave the Neck, Ma always said, and one of them was by being bulldozed.

Dez understood her view of the world, though he no longer embraced it. Wire work had taken him high above much of Greater Boston, in a cherry picker over leafy towns like Belmont, Brookline, Arlington, neighborhoods with grass and parks and unobstructed sky, even some elbow room between houses. But the Neck was all she knew. It was like smoking to her now—gone beyond habit and addiction, a way of life.

The smoking, pursued vigorously over four decades, was finally and forever drying Ma out. Her hair—the wavy red mane she had been known for—was thinning into wisps of brown. Her skin was stiff and going gray like an old sink sponge, her eyes marbling, her lips shriveling along with her beauty, all that was supple and yielding about her evaporating away. Her wrinkled hands trembled without a butt or a soft pack or a lighter to busy them, and more and more nights she spent alone at the kitchen table under the fruit-glass lamp, listening to talk radio and filling the house with exhaust.

She put the smokes away long enough to sit down and eat the meal she had prepared. Doug's visit had brought her to life, which was nice to see. At least she could still snap-to for company: fussing about the old kitchen with a dishrag on her shoulder, humming the way she used to. Both she and Dez had needed this lift.

"Meat loaf's better than ever, Mrs. Elden," said Doug, bent over his plate, scooping it in.

Her secret was to bake a small loaf of spice bread first, then shred that and work it into the meat. Her cooking was getting spicier and spicier, the cigarettes snuffing out her taste buds one by one.

"Potatoes, too, Ma," said Dez. She whipped them with a mixer, melting in four sticks of butter.

"Yeah," said Doug. "This is a meal."

"Such manners on you two," she said, pleased. "My Desmond, of course, I expect it. Raised him that way. But, Douglas, the way you were brought up? The bad luck you seen?"

He helped himself to a little more ketchup. "Just so as I get asked back."

"Don't give me that now. You know you're welcome here, any day of the week."

Dez ate happily with his father's photograph at his elbow. It had been moved there from its customary position across the table in order to make room for their dinner guest. The picture showed two blurry nuns and most of the word *Hospital* behind a happy, surprised-looking man in shirtsleeves and thick-rimmed, black eyeglasses, holding a thin-banded summer hat. The picture had been taken on July 4, 1967, the day of Dez's birth, and the resemblance between father and son was made extraordinary by their shared pair of eyeglasses. The specs in the picture were the same ones Dez wore now. In the sixteen years since Desmond senior's murder, neither Dez nor Ma had taken a home-cooked meal without his portrait joining them at the table.

The linoleum floor was warped, and when Doug rested his arms on the table, all three glasses of Pepsi jumped. Dez said, "I gotta get that shimmed."

"How's your father doing?" Ma asked Doug. "See him much?"

"Not that often," said Doug.

"Jem says he's doing good, Ma," said Dez. "Jimmy Coughlin goes up and sees him more than Doug does."

Doug wiped his mouth, nodded. "His old man and mine ran around together, and Jem, I think he likes to hear the tales. Stories about his old man, because that's all he's got."

"Those Coughlin kids," said Ma, shaking her head—Dez tensing. "How you became who you are today, Douglas, living in that household, I'll never know. Any trouble you ever got into, I blamed that family."

"No," said Doug, aiming his fork at his own chest. "You can place all that blame right here."

"That woman and her tirades. *Mother of God.* Get herself loaded and start calling around town, ranting at her enemies. I know she took you in, Douglas, and God bless her for that. Her one and only ticket upstairs. I do wish we coulda taken you at the time, given you a proper home."

"That's beautiful of you to say, Mrs. Elden. But Jimmy's ma, you know, she did her best. Truthfully, I think she liked me better than her own kids. I know she treated me that way."

"And that daughter of hers . . ."

"Ma," said Dez.

"Desmond don't like me talking about it, but"—she put out a hand to keep Dez from cutting her off—"I am just over the moon that you two are no more."

"*Jesus,* Ma," said Dez, "I didn't tell you that so you could—"

"No, no, no," said Doug, putting out his own hand. "It's fine, really. Krista's all right, Mrs. E. She'll land on her feet. She's doing good."

His respectful lie hung in the air as the three of them chewed.

"I know the four a you were all friends in school, but that's not the kind of boy I let Desmond hang around at night." She looked over at her Dez. "But he's a man now, and he can pick his own friends. He knows right from wrong.

Knows enough to stay out of trouble."

Dez kept his head down, chewing over his plate.

Doug said, "Everybody we meet, Mrs. Elden, I tell them Dez is the best of us."

Dez frowned, looking up, pleased. "Come on."

"College-educated," said Ma, needing no encouragement, "good phone company job. Clean boy. Manners. Such a help to me all these years. And look how handsome. So why isn't he married then? The both of you's."

Dez pointed at Doug. "You walked right into that one."

"Your pal there, what's his name." She snapped her fingers dryly. "The Mead Street Magloans. Freckled kids, like a litter of toads."

"Gloansy," said Dez, sharing a grin with Doug.

"Alfred Magloan," she said, nodding. "Desmond tells me he has a boy with this girlfriend of his now. I don't know her."

"Joanie Lawler. From the houses."

"Okay, the houses, that explains some of it. But ask me and she is damn lucky to be getting *anything* out of him now, after already giving away the store. My day, we wouldn't have let a pair like you get past twenty-three. We'd've grabbed hold and held on. Those days, girls knew how to." She sat back, done with her meal though she had hardly touched it, lighting up. "I used to think the problem was you very modern men. Now, the more I see, the more I realize it's the women of the species. Too soft."

THE ODOR OF SMOKE clung to everything in the house, including Dez's bedroom upstairs. The comforter on the twin bed, the dumbbells on the floor, his work gear. All his U2 imports, rarities, and bootlegs stacked on top of the bureau. Dez put on The Alarm's *Strength,* just loud enough to give them some privacy. The Alarm had been on the same socially conscious, Catholic, protest-punk track as U2 and Simple Minds in the eighties, and Dez was doing his part to keep the music alive.

A bus moaned into Sully Square. All day and night they arrived, the subway cars and the squealing wheels of the commuter rail—never mind the trucks pounding the highway overhead. But to Dez it was all lullabies. God forbid it should ever stop some night, how would he ever get to sleep without it?

Doug sat big in the small chair at Dez's computer, his hand clumsy over the mouse, reminding Dez of old men at the library trying to work the microfilm. Dez was showing Doug the speed of his ISDN line, and how to use a search engine called Alta Vista.

Doug had entered *Corvette* and was surfing the Web pages it gave him. "All right, now what?"

"Any of those words that are a different color interest you, click on them."

The screen jumped to a site named Borla, something about exhaust systems. "Your Ma really likes Jem, huh?"

"Loves him," said Dez. "You want to know what that's about? Specifically?"

"I bet I don't."

"All these years, Jem's been inside my house exactly once, okay? Maybe a year ago now. Not ten minutes total, he's here—and he takes the biggest fucking smash of his life."

Doug cracked up laughing. "He did not."

"Doesn't even flush, just leaves it there. Kid has no respect."

Doug swiped his face with his hand, trying to control his laughter.

"Scented candles, my mother lit," said Dez. "They burned for three days straight, trying to exorcise the spirit of that kid. And this is a one-bathroom house!"

"Hey, don't tell me, I live above him."

"He should of just lit the bathroom on fire when he was done with it, saved us the trouble."

"Remind me to flush, if and when."

"Hey—you could piss on the curtains and dry-hump the sofa, Ma'd find some redeeming aspect in it."

"Well, the kid's a maniac. Always has been."

"Yeah. But getting worse. Every time he hands me a piece before a job, he says, 'I know you won't use this.'"

Doug nodded. "He says that about you. 'He'll never shoot.'"

"But if you have to shoot a gun on a job, it's because you've blown it. Right? You screwed it up. The gun is your emergency backup plan."

"You don't open up your parachute while you're still standing inside the plane."

"But to Jem—you *don't* shoot a gun on the job, you've blown it."

Doug was onto another page. "Kid's warped."

"So what are you doing about this wedding?"

"Don't know. I fucking hate weddings."

It was to be a double ceremony, Gloansy and Joanie's nuptials as well as the christening of their little freckle, Nicky. Jem was Gloansy's best man, Doug the boy's godfather. Dez was just a groomsman. He was never the type to be first or second in any group—but Gloansy rating third out of the four of them irked him. Dumb-guy Gloansy, the car booster—whereas, without Dez, they'd be pulling low-percentage strong-arm heists, risky in-through-the-front-door jobs. Dez wondered if other people spent as much time as he did worrying about his place in the hearts and minds of his friends.

They had all come up through school together, Jem joining them after being kept back a grade. Good friends right up through middle school, when Dez started drifting away. Or they drifted away from him: part of it was his college-track classes, and part of it was Ma keeping him in nights to study. Doug never became a stranger, but he wasn't exactly a buddy either. Dez followed his career the same as everyone else in Town: hockey star, destined for glory, drafted by the Bruins out of high school—then bounced out of the AHL under murky circumstances, returning to the Town, and after a few months getting pinched for armed robbery. "High School Hockey Star Arrested," sang the papers. Then back to the Town after his release, drinking and brawling, a wrong-way hood maturing into full-time criminal. Then a second short prison sentence, and back out on the streets again.

Dez played in a couple of street hockey games with him after his return, with not much more than a *Hey, what's doing?* between them. Doug's circle had always been a tough group who lived like they played—rough, loud, and cheap—and openly mocked working guys like Dez. But the Doug MacRay who had returned from prison was like a soldier home from combat overseas: a changed man, newly sober, more concerned with security and survival than being a punk.

Hockey was never Dez's game, not like baseball. But one day over on Washington Street, choosing up teams, Doug picked Dez first. Week after that, same thing—Doug even feeding him some easy assists at the net, shots Doug MacRay could have put in eyes shut, and chatting him up between points. Dez started coming around more regularly, and after one game they had a talk about their fathers, on a long walk down Main Street, which came as a revelation to Dez. As part of the old neighborhood Code of Silence, no one had ever talked to Dez about his father. All he knew was that, one night in January 1980, some three years after losing his Edison job, the man was found shirtless in the snow in the middle of Ferrin Street, shot twice in the chest at close range, once through each nipple.

No witnesses had ever come forward, and no one was ever charged. Before the casket was closed that final time, twelve-year-old Dez lifted the eyeglasses off his father's sagging face and slipped them into his pocket.

His mother only spoke of the pain of his passing, and even the priests who helped her raise Dez, keeping him on track to college, discouraged Dez's inquiries. It was Doug who told him that Dez's father had been killed on his way to deliver a "package" to one Fergus Coln: then an ex–professional wrestler doing low-level mob enforcement; now the head of the PCP ring in Town, the notorious Fergie the Florist. Whatever had happened to his father after losing his Edison job, Dez realized that this package he was delivering on Ferrin Street in the middle of a winter night—it wasn't doughnuts.

In time, as Dez and Doug's renewed friendship evolved, Doug began to ask questions about Dez's work at the phone company. Pole work and junction boxes; alarm procedures and switching stations. Doug's motivation was transparent, but rather than being disappointed, Dez was thrilled to bring something of value to their relationship.

He started on the setup end of things: half-blind advance work like line rerouting, plug-pulling, cable cutting, all the while earning Doug's trust. Doug kicked him a decent percentage, but it wasn't the money that kept Dez coming back. Half always went into St. Frank's collection box anyway, in Ma's name. It was the attention Doug paid him, this neighborhood legend, and the dividends that paid Dez around Town.

Dez started to think like a criminal, keeping his eyes open at work, feeding Doug new schemes. When Doug needed a fourth pair of hands for a job in Watertown, Dez insisted on jumping in. They wore disguises and carried guns, and Dez threw up when he got home afterward, but then he looked at himself in the mirror over the sink, righting his father's thick, black rims on his face, and it was like a switch had been thrown.

Most of all, it was the belonging: the intensity of the crew during the Watertown heist, their brotherhood, like rocking in a great band. Friendship was by nature a thing that could never be consummated—could never rise to an ultimate point of perfection—but pulling these jobs together, that was when it came closest. That was the high he kept chasing. The rest of the time, he never felt as tight with them as they seemed to be with each other. They called him the Monsignor, a tease on his devotion and his strict upbringing, but also using the elitism of the clergy as another way to set him apart.

Dez's lot in life was to be the guy behind the guy, and as such, his side friendship with Doug not only continued, but flourished, and for that he was grateful—it was worth everything—though at its root, theirs was a partnership founded upon need: Doug needing Dez's phone company knowledge, and Dez needing Doug as a friend. This particular evening was one he had been looking forward to longer than he cared to admit.

"Elisabeth Shue," said Doug. "What is that, *u, e?*"

"I think." Dez started his $275 set of four U2 bobbing-head dolls—a recent purchase via mail order from Japan—nodding. "That's who you're bringing to Gloansy's wedding?"

Doug tapped in her name two-fingeredly, results filling the screen. "Either her or Uma Thurman, I can't decide." Then he sat back, shaking his head. "Some fucking inconsiderate shit, him getting married."

Dez nodded along with his bobble heads. Screen caps from *Cocktail* came up, showing Elisabeth Shue topless under a waterfall.

"That's it," said Doug. "I gotta get me a computer."

All evening Dez had the sense that Doug had wanted to tell him something. Anything personal, besides the radio static of shit-shooting guy talk, they only discussed when they were alone like this.

"I gotta get you married now," said Doug. "Mother's orders."

"Yeah," said Dez. "Well, good luck."

An outsider watching then might have thought Doug's facial expression a goof on seriousness, his brow knit, his eyes somehow sad. But Dez knew that this was as close as the guy ever came to baring his soul.

"You ever meet somebody, Dez, and, like—you *knew* something was there, beyond the boy-girl, man-woman stuff? Something almost touchable?"

"Honestly?" said Dez. "I fall in love, like, two or three times a day. I see women all the time on the job, everywhere. Even moms are starting to look good to me now."

"I could see that. You fitting in with a ready-made family. Single mom, you move right in. . . ."

"A *hot* single mom," added Dez, throwing in a little guy talk to keep them centered.

"You're not still, you know, for Krista though, are you?"

"Nah," said Dez.

"'Cause that would be trouble."

"She's outta my league, I know that."

"No, no, no. Not what I'm saying. I'm saying you're outta hers."

Dez didn't understand that; that would not compute. "Know what she calls me? The Pope of the Forgotten Village."

"And you love it. But she's like a whirlpool, Desmond. Know anything about whirlpools?"

"Sure."

"They don't just drown you. They swallow you. They hold you down there in that swirl, going round and round, days at a time, even weeks—the force of the water sucking away your clothes, your hair, your face."

"Hey," said Dez, "Jem would never go for it anyway."

"He would freak. And your ma."

"Ho, she'd be racing around the house, hiding the silver, stashing the Hummels." Dez grinned at that image, enjoying it maybe a little too much. "Krista never came clean about who's Shyne's father, did she? After admitting it wasn't you?"

"She never even admitted that, least not to me."

Dez remembered her at the Tap the other night, coming up to him after

Doug had breezed, touching his shoulder like it was made out of mink, requesting that Cranberries song again—and the dollar bill she had pulled from her jeans, the way she offered it to him clipped between two fingers. *My treat,* he had told her, then watched the seat of her jeans as she walked back to the bar.

Doug turned in his chair. "What do you say we hit a movie theater?"

"All right," said Dez. "What's playing?"

"No, I mean—*hit* a movie theater. What would you say?"

Dez got it then. "Yeah, whatever. You think?"

"Let's go see something, take a look around."

Dez nodded, excited, reaching for his coat. They had a mission.

Downstairs, Doug said good-bye to Ma, who held her cigarette away to receive his kiss on her cheek. "Watch out for my Dezi, now."

"Always do, Mrs. E."

And so Dez had to pop in for a kiss too, still tasting the smoke on his lips as he moved to the door. "We're gonna catch a flick."

"Meet some girls," she called after them. "Preferably Catholic ones."

Dez patted his pockets as they moved through the low gate onto the sidewalk, ritually checking for his wallet. The night was cloudless and cool. He scanned the street on which he had lived his entire life, a car parked a few houses down catching his eye. Dez continued forward a few steps with Doug before tugging his leather jacket sleeve, turning him around.

"Look, this is maybe stupid, but . . . today I was out in Chestnut Hill, this neighborhood set off the parkway, family area, lotsa money? I'm up on a pole checking a reading, and I could see the whole street from up there—and I notice this red sedan, like a Chevy Cavalier, keeps cruising past. Like it's circling the block or something, every couple of minutes. As I said, it's a family area, kids roaming around. So I keep an eye out. I know he can't see me with the trees up there, my truck's parked around the corner. Then, just as I'm thinking maybe something needs to be done about this, the Cavalier stops coming around. I finish up, climb down, move on."

"Beautiful story, Desmond."

Dez pointed to his own sternum, indicating the street behind them. "Couple of houses down. Red Cavalier parked across the street. Or else I'm just paranoid."

Doug's eyes going dead gave Dez a chill.

"We can head up this way," said Dez, pointing up at Perkins Street. "Loop around, take the shortcut back to—"

Doug was out in the street, striding right out toward the dark Cavalier.

Dez hesitated, surprised, then went after him, but staying on the near sidewalk.

When Doug was more than halfway there, the Cavalier's engine gunned to life. Headlights came on and it swung out into the one-way road.

Doug stopped where he was in the street and the Cavalier had to brake, stopping just a few inches from Doug's knees. It was beaten and dull-looking, its sour headlights throwing Doug's shadow over the street.

As Doug moved around to the driver's-side window, the car peeled out, Doug thumping the side with his fist before watching it go. Brake lights reddened the intersection with Perkins, the Cavalier veering hard left.

Doug took off the other way, running fast toward Cambridge Street, and Dez followed, adrenaline surging now. They reached the corner just in time to see the Cavalier empty out one street over and rev past them, speeding under the interstate, lifting over the rise before plummeting toward Spice Street, back to the Town.

"The fuck was *that*?" said Dez, out of breath.

Doug stared after the disappeared car.

"A cop?" said Dez.

"Cop would have gotten out, badged me. Not hid. Not run."

"Then what?"

"Fuck," spat Doug, kicking at the sidewalk.

A bus hissed past them, turning into Sully Square, gassing them with a lead-colored cloud of exhaust. "But if it's the G, how'd they . . . wait, through *me*?"

"Maybe we pushed the phone stuff too hard. Motherfuck."

"You get a good look? I didn't."

"Birthmark," said Doug, waving at the side of his face. "Like a rash."

"What, one of those, a port-wine stain?"

"Yeah. His hand too." Doug squeezed his own hand into a fist. "Fuck it, Dez. I gotta pass on the movies."

"Right," said Dez. Then: "You sure?"

Doug was looking toward home, the old candy-factory tower, the hilltop steeple of St. Frank's.

"What do I do?" said Dez. "Am I made? What's it mean?"

A gleaming black Mercedes wheeled past them into Somerville, pumping bass-heavy rap. "We gotta huddle up," said Doug. "Let me talk to the others. You just keep your eyes open like you did. Making him—that was good work."

Doug held out his fist for a smack, then jogged across the street back toward the Town. Dez watched him go, wanting to run after him and help him piece this thing together, but maybe Dez was too hot now.

The G parked there on his mother's street. Dez jammed his hands deep into his pockets, spooked, watching for red Cavaliers as he walked back home.

PART II
WHEN LOVE COMES TO TOWN

15
THE MEET

THE FREEDOM TRAIL WAS a tourist thing, an inlaid-brick sidewalk trail retracing the "birth of America." It started downtown at the Boston Common training field and snaked north through the city, past the site of the Boston Massacre, past Paul Revere's House in the North End, all the way across the Charlestown Bridge to end at the 221-foot granite obelisk marking the site of the Battle of Bunker Hill.

The second-to-last stop along the trail was the oldest commissioned floating warship in the world, the USS *Constitution*, also known as *Old Ironsides* for her thick, cannonball-repelling hull. In the warming of early May, the pavilion at the southern edge of the old navy yard saw a surge in attendance from school field trips: teachers in sun visors and knee-length shorts, parent chaperones gripping huge cups of iced coffee, and fifth-graders with lunch bags and foil-wrapped cans of soda, all squinting up at the flags tracing the sail outline along the ship's three tall masts.

Doug, Jem, and Gloansy wandered around the dry dock between the ship and its museum, mixing with the school groups and the knee-socked foreign tourists, Doug hoping to confound any parabolic microphones that might be aimed their way. Jem worked the brim curve of his lucky blue Red Sox cap, which not coincidentally had the added effect of flexing his arms. He wore small, smirking, syrup-tinted sunglasses too expensive and European-looking for his bargain-bin American face. Gloansy wore yellow-tinted sport shades that made his toad eyes bulge, his freckled forearms looking like two logs of Hickory Farms cheese.

Jem spit into the ocean and said, "Fucking cunt."

Doug turned on him fast, too fast. *"What?"*

"What *what*? Fucking branch manager, who else?"

"What are you talking about?"

"It's fucking gotta be."

"How? What could she have told them?"

"I dunno. Something."

"You tell me. What could she have told them?"

Jem flipped his cap back on top of his head, the brim newly horseshoed. "Easy, kid. How would I know?"

Doug should have stopped himself, didn't. "I don't want to be throwing stuff around like it doesn't matter. Because this matters. This is important—fucking critical—and I want to be dealing in certainties. She could tell them what? That there were four of us? What, we drove a *van*?"

"Okay. Then how?"

Doug looked off across the harbor at the Coast Guard piers jutting off the North End. "Could be any number of things. Anything."

"We took a lot of precautions on that job. Fucking drove me nuts, but we did them, and it all went smooth, until the bell."

"I'm saying I don't have any answers yet, and neither do you."

"We bleached it up. I did the tool count, there was nothing left behind."

"Could be an accumulation of things. Could be they put someone on us special. We been pulling a lot recently."

Gloansy said, a one-hand-in-his-pocket shrug, "How do we even know it's anything? Could've been some guy parked on the street."

"Yeah," said Jem, pointing at Gloansy, "Banjo Boy is right. Some Peeping Tom. A Somerville hypo, shooting up. How come you're so sure of yourself here, Duggy?"

"I don't know anything," said Doug. "Except what I know."

A class shuffled past, boys smiling and pointing out Jem's *Yankees Suck!* T-shirt. When they were gone, Jem said, "Sniffing around the Monsignor, that I don't like."

"I talked to him," said Doug. "He knows how to handle it."

"*You* know how to handle it. Gloansy here, *he* knows how to handle it. The Monsignor, I don't have that kinda faith in."

"Here's the thing," said Doug, facing them. "Boozo's crew running wild—that was our cover. They took every ounce of heat that was out there because they were so fucking Cagney and greedy all the time. It was a vacation in Tahiti working in their shadow. Couldn't *buy* that kind of protection. But now they're good and gone, and the G still sees jobs being pulled. See, that machinery's all still in place. I think they're turning it on us now."

Gloansy said, "The G?"

Doug looked at him, *duh,* and went on, "It's not like they weren't *aware* of us before, but not this close. Maybe they're more focused now, because they can be. What bothers me is—why Dez? The only one of us with no record?"

Jem set one unlaced high-top sneaker on top of a piling, facing the harbor as though he owned it. "So we're the top dogs now."

Doug threw him a *duh* look too. "That's not a vacancy I'm looking to fill. We don't want to be out there in front, attracting attention. I like us running second, riding the wake of the high-stepping idiot in first place."

"Second place?" snarled Jem, as though Doug had insulted him.

"There is no finish line, kid. The trophy is this, right here, us walking around, money in our pockets, free as the breeze. This is breaking news to you?"

"I'm saying, number one is number one." Big shrug. "Sucks being the best—but there it is."

A foreign tourist with a crazy accent and his safari-hat-wearing wife approached them with a guidebook, looking for Faneuil Hall, and Jem played his favorite game, kindly directing them to Chelsea Street, up toward the projects.

Gloansy turned to Doug in private. "How bad do you think they have us?"

"Maybe not at all. Maybe they just have Dez right now. Or maybe they have all our houses and our cars, I don't know. Maybe they're up on one of these rooftops right now, watching."

"That means court orders and everything?"

"They don't need anything to start snooping on their own. No probable cause or subpoenas, they can just start tapping into us first, figuring out who's who and what's what, then once they know where to look and what to look for—then they go legal, get their papers in order, come marching into Town."

Gloansy was lost in thought a moment, a scary thing to see. He leaned closer to Doug. "What about, like, cameras in the bedroom, shit like that?"

Doug was forced to entertain a split-second image of Gloansy and Joanie grinding. "I would say, kid, these guys' jobs are tough enough."

Jem came back to them still muttering about Dez. "Fuckin' nearsighted Pope. Walking around out there with all our fates in his pockets. Makes me fucking nuts."

"I told you I talked to him," said Doug. "He's the one who made this guy in the first place."

Jem said, "This is why the movie thing is good. Changing our whole MO, if they're onto that."

Doug shrugged. "Good, maybe."

"Whoa," said Jem, protesting. "Douglas. C'mon, kid. Don't let these fuckers get you down."

"I think we gotta pull back a while."

"Fuckin'—no way."

"We gotta coast a bit."

"Why? We'll work around the Monsignor. Hijacking a can means no black-box phone shit, no tech. We'll go in the original Three Musketeers."

Gloansy said to Duggy, "For how long?"

"Listen," said Doug, "if you two've got nothing tucked away in the back of your sock drawers, I got this much sympathy for you."

"It ain't greed," said Jem. "It's knowing a good thing when I see one."

What do you see except what I show you? "Why you always in such a rush?"

A tour guide dressed as Paul Revere nodded to them as he passed.

"Why? Because I been on the losing end of things, and the one thing I promised myself when I was there was to make hay while the sun shines. Sun's shining bright here, Duggy."

"Too bright. That's not sunlight you're feeling, that's heat, that's the G, and I gotta know what we have here first."

"How you gonna do that? How you ever gonna know?"

"*And* we gotta keep our distance, starting now. Gotta stay separate, case they haven't made all of us yet. Even if they do. Avoid any criminal-conspiracy rap."

Jem shook his head like he was going to have to punch somebody. *"It was a fucking guy in a car!"*

Gloansy said, "My wedding, Duggy. Joanie will go apeshit."

Doug said, "Wedding's fine. Big group thing. So long as we skip the photos, it's fine. I'm talking about the four of us getting together for some ice cream, going out gallivanting. No."

"Fucking *cunt*," sang Jem under his breath.

Doug turned on him again. "You're making me fucking crazy with this."

"Why? What's it to you?"

Doug didn't know if what he said next was meant to put them at ease, or just to cover his own ass. "I'm going to do some looking into that."

"Looking into what? How? Tail her again?"

"Let me worry about it. I'll do my thing, you two go off and do yours. And quietlike. Be citizens. Assume they got eyes on you whenever you step out the door. Don't cross against the light and don't litter. Use the streets, use the neighborhood—they can't hide there. None of us sees anything more in a week or two, we'll get back together, think about moving ahead again."

"A week or two?" said Jem. "Jesus *fuck*."

"It's a vacation, kid. Enjoy it."

"Vacation? I'm fucking *always* on vacation."

"Duggy's right," said Gloansy, probably still worried about cameras in his bedroom. "Maybe we should cool it a whi—"

Jem flat-handed Gloansy in the chest. "That's for thinking, dumb shit. Fuck you, 'cool it.' *I* decide when to cool it."

"Fine, whatever," said Gloansy, rubbing his pec. "Jesus."

"Two fucking weeks, Duggy," pronounced Jem. "Then we'll see."

16
THE GIRL WHO GOT ROBBED

HE SAW HER WAITING for him in the lamplight of the five-street junction, wearing a shimmering black top that was either velvet or silk, a slim turquoise skirt ending in a ruffle at the knee—her legs were as blond as her hair—and low black heels, a black sweater in one hand, a small black handbag dangling on a string in the other. The taxi ahead of him slowed, trawling for an early evening fare, and she smiled and shook her head no, waving it along—and already Doug felt his reserve melting away.

He eased the Corvette's prow in along the stone curb at her knees. He was wearing Girbaud jeans, the same toe-pinching black shoes, and a white shirt under a black jacket. He stood out of the car—he always felt good rising out of the Vette—and walked around to get her door.

Her eyes broadened at the sight of the emerald green machine. "Wa-*how*," she said, her hand going to her chest. At first he thought she had expected a dusty pickup with tools rattling around in back and a pissing-Calvin sticker on the window. But as she sank into the low passenger seat, he recognized the look on her face as one of amusement. He felt a sting of foolishness then, that he wasn't prepared for. She swung her legs inside and he closed the wide door on a whiff of butterscotch, rounding the flat rear of the car, seeing himself and the city block reflected and elongated in the glassy green finish, not liking his hurt-little-boy feelings.

"So," he said, closing his door, trying to stay positive. "What do you think? Too much muscle?"

She turned to look in back. "I can't believe how clean it is."

"It's a collector's car, but not a fetish with me. Some guys, forget it. Working under the hood, that's what I like. Taking it apart and putting it back together again. I don't even drive it that much." She was exploring the upholstery with a light hand, the instrument panel with curious eyes. His plans for being so tough and crafty and inscrutable—like a magic trick, one glance from her had turned all his face cards blank. "I had it painted custom. Most collectors, stripping down and painting the exterior an off-stock color, that's ruining

a collector's item like this. Me, I kind of liked making it mine. A one-of-a-kind."
She touched the soft trim, and he couldn't take her silence any longer. "So, what? Is it ridiculous?"

"*Yes*," she said—but with a smile, not catching his meaning. "Do you race this?"

"I've taken it around a speedway in New Hampshire once or twice on my own, just to open her up."

"How fast?"

"One-sixty, sustained. I topped out at one-eighty."

"Gulp," she said. He shifted into first and pulled away from the curb, clutching into second, the engine lifting them toward City Square like a speedboat over calm water. "I feel like I'm lying down."

Doug eyed her legs extended into the deep foot well. "I think it looks good on you."

She rubbed the leather seat hips with her palms and shook out her hair a little, getting comfortable. "I think my car's going to be jealous."

"Yeah, well. Corvettes and Saturns, that's like dogs and cats."

He slowed into the traffic light onto Rutherford, feeling a little better. "Hey," she said, turning to him curiously after the stop, "how did you know I drove a Saturn?"

Doug kept his eyes hard on the red light. "Didn't you mention it? You must have mentioned it."

"Did I?" Green light, Doug gripped the wheel and gunned it out toward the bridge, and she looked ahead again. "I guess I probably did."

Shithead. "Where we going?"

"I was thinking about the Chart House? It's nice but not too nice, you know? By the Aquarium on Long Wharf, overlooking the harbor? What do you think?"

"Let's do it."

"You thought I was going to pick some place on Newbury Street, right? Sonsie, or something."

"Yeah, maybe," he said. Newbury Street, he knew of only as an avenue of art galleries and shopping boutiques; Sonsie, he had no clue.

"But—before that." She turned to him again. "I was wondering if I could ask you a huge favor."

"Sure," he said, trying to read her as they crossed the rusted bridge into the city. "Anything, what?"

"I know it's not much of a way to start the night . . . but I have a friend who's having an operation tomorrow morning, and I promised him I'd stop by and visit."

Doug nodded, thinking, *Him.* "And you wanted some company?"

"I promise it won't take too long. Cross my heart."

"No problem at all." *Him.* "Just tell me where."

When she said, "Mass. Eye and Ear," Doug realized who the friend was.

SHE WAS SOMEWHERE OTHER than inside the elevator with him, and Doug realized that she was more anxious than he was. "You seem worried about something."

She stopped nibbling her lips and switched to pulling invisible thimbles off her fingers. "Just hospitals," she said. "Give me the creeps." She watched the numbers blink. "My brother died in a hospital."

"You had a brother?"

"He had a tumor in his bladder. It wrecked my parents." She shook it off, turning to him for distraction. "You cut your hair." She reached up and rubbed the stiff bristle over the nape of his neck. Her hand was gentle, cupping, cool. "What is it about a new haircut on a man?"

He thought that nothing had ever felt so good. "I might start purring here."

The floor dinged and the doors opened, her hand falling away. Signs pointed them to a circular hospital wing where they followed the numbers to the correct room.

Doug said, "I'll wait out here."

"No," she said, thinking he was jealous. "Meet him."

She took his hand, and before he knew it she was leading him into the room.

The patient was propped up against an avalanche of pillows. He turned toward them, head and shoulders moving as one. Gauze and bandaging masked half his face, bulging thick over his right eye, but Doug saw enough to recognize the assistant branch manager of the Kenmore Square BayBanks, Davis Bearns.

Claire released Doug and crossed to Bearns, Doug remaining just a few steps inside the private room.

Bearns held out his johnny-bare arms and Claire bent into them, a gentle kiss against his unbandaged cheek. "Hey there," said Bearns, his throat and lips doing most of the work, his fixed chin giving him a Harvard lockjaw. When she was slow to pull away, he said, "I'm getting some action here."

Claire straightened and smiled, whisking away a tear. She looked back at Doug and made introductions, and Doug nodded, giving Bearns a flat wave and a *Hey*.

"Are you comfortable?" she asked. "I wish you had let me bring you something."

"I just want to be done with it—this operation, this place."

"You said they're hopeful."

"They better be. I am. If I recover fifty percent sight in this eye, it will be a roaring success. I just want to get on with it, get home, get back to work."

"Really?" she said. "Back to work?"

"Anything, God, yes. Something to focus on instead of large-print crossword puzzles. But it won't be for a while. They'll have me on this dim-light-only diet for a few weeks, at least."

She nodded, tugging on a sheet wrinkle. "I'm having trouble at work."

"Well, see, you have memories. The one inconvenience I was spared." He turned his face farther toward her for inspection. "Which would you rather?"

She shook her head at his halfhearted joke, looking away. "Someday I'll go through it all with you. I promise. But not now."

"Of course not now. Tell me your plans for tonight. Vicarious living is all I have."

Doug cut in, "I'm gonna step outside. Nice meeting you, good luck."

"I won't keep her long," said Bearns. "But we will talk about you."

"Fair enough," said Doug, turning away, remembering Jem standing over bloody Bearns with the open jug of bleach.

BEING AT THE CHART HOUSE with Claire felt nice and clean and free of deception—until Doug remembered that, in fact, their entire relationship was founded on deception. But then the conversation would continue and he would again lose himself in the flickering candle of temporary innocence. What amazed him was his sincerity. Within the overarching lie—maybe because of it—he talked freely and was more honest and open with her than he had ever been with anyone else.

She ordered a single glass of white wine without comment. They worked out three Boston College football games they had separately attended. His steak arrived, her scallops. She talked about work at the bank and how unmotivated she was, killing two-hour lunches in her garden in the Fens and then suffering from pangs of guilt. "BayBanks does this community service thing, you know, masquerading as a small bank that cares? It's mostly bullshit, but they do pay you a couple of hours each week to volunteer somewhere. I started a year ago, at the Charlestown Boys and Girls Club?"

"Sure, yeah."

"Working with kids who were about the age my brother was. Whatever that means, right?" She smiled self-consciously, shrugged. "I just chaperone trips and stuff. They're delinquents, but they're good delinquents. Funny kids. Probably like you were, I'm guessing, right?"

"Nice that you do that."

"Thing is, it's supposed to be like three hours a week, and I'm spending more time there than I am at the bank."

"They're gonna catch up with you."

She nodded. "Part of me hopes they do."

The waiter wasn't used to being paid in cash. Outside, they followed low, black iron chains slung post-to-post along the waterfront, the night surf knocking boats into docks, groaning the piers, slapping wood. Doug was hit up by a skinny extortionist hand-selling roses out of a mop bucket, and Claire stripped away the cellophane and tissue down to the dethorned stem, raising the petals to her nose, then slipping her hand around the crook of his elbow.

In Columbus Park, at a sprawling, vacant play structure, they crossed the soft wood chips to still rubber swings. She sat and twisted in circles, letting the chains twirl apart and then twisting them again. She stuck her legs straight out as she spun, flexing her smooth calves, and Doug imagined that every flight of stairs she had ever climbed was mere training for that moment in that light, in his eyes.

"Okay, getting dizzy," she said, swiveling to a rest. Doug stood near her like a bodyguard, toeing at the tamped-down mulch. She looked out at the airport, the planes coming in. "Weird, isn't it? Here we are, two people, enjoying the night—and then Davis, sitting alone in a hospital room, waiting."

Doug watched her eyes. Something was happening in them. "He got a tough break."

She tracked a seagull flying over the docks. "One little thing—that's all it takes. You turn the wrong corner one morning and suddenly—you're Davis, you're on the outside of life, looking in."

"Some terrible luck."

"No," she said, looking down now. "It's worse than that." Her arms were inside the swing chains, worrying the stem of the rose in her lap. "It's actually my fault."

Doug followed this through. "How is it your fault?"

"I was the one who set off the alarm at the robbery. Not him. They beat up the wrong person." She sighed to forestall tears. "And I watched them do it. I could have spared him, I could have told them it was me. But I just stood there and let it happen. I took the easy way out, because that's what I always do."

"But come on. You were scared."

"He's marked for life now, and he did nothing wrong—nothing to deserve it. I did this to him."

"Look," said Doug, dropping into the swing next to her. "You gotta find a way to stop thinking about this. Is it the FBI? They still coming around?"

"The agent, he assumed that it was Davis who hit the alarm. And of course I let him. Admitting otherwise wouldn't have been the easy way out." She looked up into the sky over the water. "Why am I this way? You wouldn't have lied."

"Me?" said Doug, going for it. "I wouldn't have told them anything."

"What do you mean? Anything like what?"

"Nothing beyond the basics."

She turned, confused. "Because you think the agent suspects me?"

"This is one of the differences between growing up in Canton and Charlestown, I think. People who don't deal with cops that much, such as yourself, you probably tend to believe all that stuff about the Search for the Truth. Forgetting that cops, FBI, anybody with a badge who has a lot of power—they're just people like anyone else. They have lives, they have jobs to protect. And how they do that is by clearing arrests. Getting results. Which also means, if they can't catch the one who did it, sometimes they'll settle for the one who fits. And that person is usually the one who talked the most."

She stared. "You're serious."

"How often do you hear about convictions overturned, confessions coerced? We learn early where I'm from, don't talk to the cops. Or if you do, get a lawyer present."

"You're saying I should hire a lawyer?"

"No, too late. Don't do it now. You lawyer up now, you better believe they're going to start taking an interest in your story, a very close interest."

She nodded, assailed by his logic.

"You did your civic duty," Doug told her. "And that's great. You don't know anything, right?" He pressed her. "Right?"

"No, I don't."

Doug nodded, relieved, easing off. "So leave it at that. Personally? It seems to me like you're hanging on to this robbery too tight. I think you know this. It's bad, what happened to your friend. And bad, sure, what happened to you."

She was eager to cut him off. "I know, it doesn't seem . . . a robbery, okay. Masked men, guns, the van. Other people have been through so much worse— I *know* this. But it's like I'm stuck. I thought I was going to be murdered, I was going to die on the floor of the bank . . . and my life seemed wasted." She winced, frustrated that this sounded like whining. "If only I could get that morning back. Or like Davis, have it wiped away forever."

"Here's the thing," said Doug. He had put this pain into her face, maybe he could take it away again. "I'm outta my league here, I know. But I can tell you this. For a long time in my life, I was The Kid Whose Mother Left Him. That's all I was, the sum total of my existence. And it led me into a world of trouble. Right now, I think you're The Girl Who Got Robbed."

She stared, listening hard.

"Now," he went on, "I happen to like The Girl Who Got Robbed. I don't mind her at all, she looks pretty good to me. But I think she's not all that thrilled with herself."

"You're right," she said, thinking, nodding. "You're really right."

"You can get past this."

"I have to. I know." She sat up, squaring her shoulders, a harbor breeze lifting her honey-colored hair with its fingers. "I'm sorry for getting into this with you, bringing you down. I'm going to cheer up now, I promise. Grow up too. Count to three."

"One, two, three."

"Ta-da." She smiled. "Happy face."

They sat there in swaying silence, drifting away from and back toward each other.

"You know what you are, Doug?" she said. "I just figured it out. You're decent."

"Oh." Doug gripped the swing chains. "Christ, no."

"You are, and more than that—a lot of people who are decent, they were *raised* to be decent, you know? Like me—good parenting, good manners, blah, blah, blah—which is all fine and good until a little pressure comes into your life, and then you crumble like stale bread. But you—you've made mistakes, you've said as much. You're not a saint or anything, but you know how to be good. Your decency is earned, not learned."

Doug said, "I don't know how well you know me," but she mistook his discomfort for modesty.

"Can you tell I've been thinking about you?" she said.

"Oh yeah?"

She swayed a little more, bumping her seat gently against his, eyes bright, grateful, and deep. "Yeah."

17
DEMO

THE CHARGES CRACKED LIKE a volley of gunshots from the head of the cliff, wind whisking away the smoke tails, sheets of rock dropping like a hand had opened up and let them go, sliding off the stratified face into rubble and dust.

Doug and Jem squinted at the rip and crumble, feeling the earth shudder in complaint, watching the gray dust arise. They stood near the silver-sided break wagon and the hard hats lining up for Winstons and coffees, Doug wearing a loose, long-sleeved shirt reading *Mike's Roast Beef*, Jem a white sweatshirt bearing a peeling green shamrock under the arched word *T O W N I E S*. The hood was snug over Jem's head and ears, emphasizing his small skull. Both carried their old yellow helmets under their arms, like blue-collar jet pilots.

"Look at you," Jem said.

Doug watched a hard hat cup a blue pill into his mouth like it was his morning vitamin. The break wagon also sold speed at $3 a pop. Doug remembered the jolt of a blue with a beer back, ten or ten thirty in the morning, kicking the workday into gear. "What?"

"You."

"What?"

"All the way up here, you're in fucking La-La Land. You get laid last night?"

"Yeah. I wish."

"Anybody I know? He do you right?"

Doug smiled in spite of himself, watching the dust spreading in the distance.

"What is it, then?" said Jem. "You found Jesus or something?"

"I did. In a condo over on Eden Street. Nice place."

"Yeah, I hear he's a good carpenter. I would of thought maybe you ran into him at the Tap."

Doug went cold under the white sun. "What are you talking about?"

"Splash the bartender said he thought he saw you in there, few nights before."

"That Saturday night, all of us?"

"No, fuckhead. Recent."

A dismissive shrug, a good one. "Different Doug MacRay."

"I see. Maybe the *old* Doug MacRay, come back to us like Jesus on Eden Street. All I can say is, you *better* not be drinking on the side. I been waiting too fucking long. Your first drink back, I'm there at your elbow, or else."

Relief seeping in. "Speaking of abstinence—how's that going for you?"

"I remain pure."

"Get the fuck."

"My mother's grave."

"Yikes, that's where you do it?"

"I'm pulling two full workouts a day. Check these guns."

"Hey, cowboy—all the same to you, I'm gonna take a pass on standing here, checking out your shoulder hard-ons."

Jem studied him one-eyed in the sun. "You got laid, motherfuck. Come clean."

Doug smiled big. "I always do."

The whistle blew the all clear and Jem found his hat under his arm. "Let's go see Boner and get this shit over with."

In the distance, a demo crew in hard hats, goggles, and face masks advanced on the settling dust. Doug could smell the grit from where he was, remembering the feeling of it stopping up his pores. "You ever miss this?"

Jem twirled his helmet like he used to, the *J. Coughlin* fading on the back, the head strap inside worn to the foam. "You fucking kidding me?"

"I miss it a little. Not the commute, the bullshit, eating lunch out of a truck, fucking dust in my hair."

"You like blowing shit up."

"No. I just like watching it fall."

"Well, second thought, going at a wall with a crowbar, that wasn't so bad either. The old wrecking crew, right? Hammers, sledges, and pickaxes. Walking into some condemned building in our dusted overalls like, '*Warriors, come out to play-ayy . . .*'"

Doug shrugged. "I just liked watching it fall."

Inside the construction trailer, they waited for Billy Bona, Billy saying, "Yup . . . yeah . . . sure . . . ," into the phone and strangling the cord in his hands. Ten years before, while tearing out a condemned building alongside Doug, a falling cinder block claimed the nails of the last three fingers of his left hand. Doctors told him they would grow back twice as thick, but they never grew back at all. Now Billy was the demo foreman in his father's company and only used his helmet-less fingers for pointing at guys and signing things.

He hung up and came across to shake hands. "The original thick-dick micks."

Doug said, "Billy Boner."

Jem said, "'S'up, Little Italy?"

"You know how it is," said Boner, sliding a clipboard off his desk, "this and that, that and this. I got two minutes here, literally. What's the squeal?"

Doug said, "Highway project, huh?"

Jem was twiddling Boner's Rolodex like a kid on a visit to his dad's office. "This economy, I take it where it comes," said Boner, distracted, not liking his cluttered desk touched. "What you got? Potato famine suddenly? Coming back to do some real work?"

"Never, man," said Jem. "Just wanted to go over terms of our deal."

Boner frowned, looked at Doug, concerned. "Fuck's wrong with the deal?"

Jem held up a *Bonafide Demo* paperweight showing the Leaning Tower of Pisa. "Know what I'd like to see on this instead?" he said. "That chef from the pizza boxes, twiddling his Rollie Fingers mustache, you know? That would be good."

Boner said to Doug, "What's going on here, MacRay?"

Doug had forgotten Jem's sourness toward Boner, it had been that long. "It's all good, Billy," said Doug, dropping *Boner* for the moment. "Nothing wrong with the deal. Everything's cool."

"'Cause your guard dog here is slobbering all over my desk."

Jem smiled his smile, challenge accepted, and went around to sit in Boner's big chair, putting his mud-caked boots up on the desk. "Seat's a little hard, Boner. Your ass is much more accommodating than mine."

Boner gripped his clipboard two-handedly. "If this is some fuckin' poor man's shakedown, you can both—"

"Whoa, whoa," said Doug. "Hold on. How well you know me?"

"*Used* to know you good, Duggy. Going way back. So what the fuck?"

Doug said to Jem, "Get out from behind the man's desk," just to be polite, not really expecting Jem to move, which he didn't. Doug said to Boner, "Everything with the arrangement is going great, everything's fine. We just think we might be hearing hoofbeats, so to speak, so we wanted to come up here, make sure all our bases are covered."

"A reminder," said Jem, picking up a pad of pink phone-message slips, flipping it at Boner. Boner made no move to catch it and the pad bounced off his arm, falling to the floor.

"Not a reminder," said Doug. "A courtesy call, let you know you might have visitors coming up here with badges, questions. Or maybe not, we don't know."

"Jesus," sighed Boner, not needing this hassle.

"You been making a tiny little mint off us," said Jem, sitting up behind Boner's desk. "Keeping us on the books, paying us full sal, us kicking half back to you."

"Keeping you outta *jail,* sounds like, giving you taxable income for the IRS." He looked back at Doug. "And what, an alibi?"

"Maybe," said Doug. "But mostly just gainful employ. Our good citizenship. They got nothing pinned on us, 'cept their own ambitions. So you don't have to worry about a thing. We just didn't want anyone coming up here and throwing you, catching you off guard. All you need to do is pledge us as two of your contract guys."

"Your very best contract guys," said Jem. "Good workers and nice fellows, handsome guys. Only out sick that day."

"And then let us know. That cool, Billy?"

Boner nodded. His glance at the wall clock told Doug that Boner was busy and this was no big thing to him, which was all Doug wanted to know.

Jem said, "Boner's cool. 'Course, he's got no fucking other choice anyway."

Boner wheeled and pointed with a finger off his clipboard, sputtering. "Why you so fuckin' hot all the time, Jimmy? I mean, what the *fuck*?"

Doug explained, "He gave up jerking off."

"Yeah? Traded it for *being* a jerkoff," said Boner, having had all he could stand. "You never showed my dad any respect, you fucking hump."

"Respect?" said Jem, hands folded, still seated, too calm and comfortable. "That's all you ever showed him, fuckin' daddy's little girl. Taking over the business so he can head off down to Florida."

"Seems like you inherited your daddy's business too."

Jem bounded up and around the desk, up into Boner's face with the chair back still rocking. Doug stayed where he was, so fucking tired of it all.

"You think I'm afraid of you?" said Boner, the clipboard at his hip now. "Huh? Yeah? Well you're goddamn fucking right I'm afraid of you, you half-a-psycho." Boner backed off and picked his message pad off the floor—then whipped it at the papers on his desk, slapping down his clipboard and bouncing a pen off his phone.

He stopped, facing his vacant chair, shoulders riding his anger. "You two came here to tell me something, and now you told me, and now I've got some real fucking work to do. Guys under me who actually work for their paychecks, guys with families to feed, *earning* their salaries."

He turned back looking for some trace of shame in their faces and, failing that, banged out of the thin trailer door empty-handed.

BACK INSIDE THE FLAMER, Jem's beat-up Trans Am, driving south from Billerica to the Wendy's parking lot off the highway where Doug had left his Caprice. No tail either way, and they had been super-fucking-careful—but instead of relief, this only increased Doug's paranoia. He made a mental note to

recheck his wheel wells and firewalls and poke around under the hood for tracking beacons.

Jem drove eager-eyed, tearing up the road. He tried the radio and a *Sesame Street* tune blasted out of the speakers. "Jesus *fuck*," he said, hitting Eject and tossing the tape into the backseat like it was on fire. "See that? That's why I don't fucking let her use my car. She wanted me to put a *baby* seat in back there, full-time? Yeah, like Jem's cruising around Town with that chick magnet."

He wheeled onto the highway, the white sun glaring off the gaudy blue-on-blue flame work on the hood, bouncing into Doug's eyes. Their helmets rolled around the piles of crap in back like the aggravation rattling inside Doug's head.

"So what about the Dez situation?" said Jem.

"What about it?"

"I don't like it."

"Okay."

"Of all of us, he's the weak link."

"Dez is fine, I told you."

"When's he been proven? A fucking *candy* store, even—the kid's never put gum in his pocket without paying for it. How's he gonna stand up under a grilling, told to turn us over or else? Where's his track record on that?"

Doug wasn't so annoyed that he couldn't find some truth in this.

"And what about the manager?"

"The bank manager?" said Jem.

"No, Don Zimmer. Yes, the bank manager. Said you'd have something there."

"There's nothing there. A dead end. Done."

"You think so."

"I know so. I can fucking guarantee so."

"How?"

"She checks out. Don't worry about it."

Jem switched lanes, slicing between two cars with maybe six inches to spare on either end. "So there's no need to remove her from the equation, then."

Doug turned to him, Jem's stupidity as blinding as the sun. "Are you fuck-ing *kidding* me?"

"I'm just saying."

"You're just saying what? What are you just saying? You're a fucking con-tract killer now?"

Jem shrugged, playing tough guy. "I don't like loose ends."

Doug had to take a breath and remind himself that this was all just talk, part of the movie playing twenty-four hours a day on the cable channel in Jem's head. "Listen, De Niro. You need to start jerking off again. And I mean fucking pronto, like right now, pull over, I'll wait. Fuck's gotten into you? The music all night—"

"What, is it too loud?"

"Is it too *loud*?"

"Awright, whatever, what the fuck."

"Turn down the volume in your head, kid. What is it? Vampire bite you or something?"

"Just trying to be careful."

"Let me be the paranoid one, all right? Let me do the worrying. Cool it."

"Fuckin' . . . it's cool, man. It's cool."

They were quiet for a while, Doug's head ringing, Jem rolling down his window to spit.

"So, Gloansy's wedding, huh?"

"Yeah," said Doug.

"Who you taking? Got anything set up?"

Doug shook his head. "I'm nowhere on that one."

"Yeah." Then: "Krista has no date neither."

Doug stared ahead, letting it pass.

"What else're you doing with your time?"

"Why, what the fuck? What are you poking at me for?"

"Poking at you?" said Jem. "What are you talking about?"

"I don't know—what are *you* talking about?"

"See—this is you between jobs." Jem nodded like one of them was crazy and it wasn't him. "Time off for you is no fucking good, time off for *any* of us." He palmed the wheel, pushing the car ahead. "Speaking of time. Mac, last weekend—he was asking for you."

"Yeah?" said Doug, wondering where the hell this was suddenly coming from. "Yeah, how's he been?"

"Good, good. Says he wants you to come by sometime."

"Yeah. I been meaning to."

"Says he don't like to ask, but he wants to see your face. Wants to know what's up, I guess. I said I'd tell you."

"Sure," said Doug, already angling to duck it. There was a latent smudge on his side window, brought out by the sun: a little round handprint, dead center, and Doug wondered what the fuck Shyne was doing riding around in the front seat with no belt on.

Jem said, "You know I get the fuckin' biggest kick outta your dad."

"Yeah," said Doug, thinking, *You're the only one*—his eyes staying trained on the oily ghost of a tiny little uncreased palm.

18
DATING THE VIC

"**B**UT HOW DID YOU KNOW?" asked Claire.

"Know what?" said Frawley.

"'Mortgage or sick kid,' how would you know that?"

"Ah." Frawley rubbed his cheek, a ruminative habit he had adopted since getting stained. The dye had faded to a coppery orange, like misapplied self-tanner. "The smell of coffee on the note. The way his first, failed attempt went down. And then just looking at him there, facedown in the playground. A kind of desperation I've seen before."

They were seated away from the bar inside the Warren Tavern, over low-key drinks and apps. The place was crowded on a weeknight, and Frawley wondered how a colonial-era pub suddenly got so tony.

Claire wore a cream top with the sleeves shrugged up. She sipped her white wine, concerned for the robber. "And that's five years in jail?"

"Federal sentencing guidelines are pretty strict. Between forty and fifty months for a first-time offender, then add on maybe a year and a half for the bomb threat. But I spoke with the assistant district attorney and recommended that only state charges be brought. It's not up to me, but that would be less of a smack. This yo-yo might even be able to put his life back together after that."

She said, "That's because you're a nice guy."

"No, it's because he's not the kind of bad guy I'm after. Note-passing is the dumbest of crimes. Broad daylight, plenty of witnesses, and you're photographed in the act. Hello. Fifteen hundred dollars against four or five years in prison. Banks attract dumb, desperate people." An excuse to reach across the table and touch her forearm. "Bandits, not employees."

She smiled. "Thanks for clarifying."

"A professional crew that's ready to hurt people, put them in the hospital— that's what I'm here for. Not the sad case sitting in a Dunkin' Donuts one morning, thinking his life is ending."

She noticed him rubbing his cheek again. "Does that itch?"

"Only psychologically. I'm like half-cop, half-criminal. You should see the looks I get."

She smiled and Frawley thought he was doing well. "So, why banks?" she said. "What is it about banks and you?"

"Have you seen those ads for the tornado movie coming out, *Twister*?"

"Sure, with the cow flying across the screen?"

"I grew up—well, I grew up all over. My mother had this knack for meeting men just as they were about to move out of state, and she would move with them, only to split up a few months later, leaving us out on our own again. We didn't have much and kept losing things in the breakups. She carried around with her a couple of items she called her 'treasure.' Some photographs of her as a girl, her grandmother's Bible, letters she had saved, my birth certificate, her wedding ring. So every new town we pitched a tent in, the first thing she'd do would be to go down to the bank and rent a safe-deposit box, store her treasure there. It became a routine—new town, new bank, new box. When I was eight or maybe nine, we were living in Trembull, South Dakota, and a tornado hit. Flattened the town, killed eight. We rode it out on the floor of a fruit cellar— my mother blanketing me, screaming the Lord's Prayer—and when it was over, we climbed back upstairs, and the upstairs was gone. Roof, walls, everything. The entire neighborhood, people crawling out of their cellars like worms after a hard rain. Everything gone or moved and tipped over on its side. We all just followed the path of destruction into the center of town. Only, the center was gone too. Just a war zone of cracked lumber and debris—except for one thing. The bank vault. The bank building itself was gone, but that silver vault remained standing. Like a door to another dimension."

Her frown had a smile behind it. "I hate people who know exactly who they are, and why they want what they want."

"The next day the manager came and opened it up, and there was my mother's treasure, safe and sound."

"And where's your mother now?"

"Arizona. Fourth husband, a cattle auctioneer. The guy answers the phone, I can't understand a word he says. But of the thirty-four states she's resided in, Arizona's the first she's lived in twice. So I'm thinking, this guy, maybe he's finally the one."

Claire smiled. "Explains why you're not married yet."

"I don't know. I think it's more because I've moved around so much with the Bureau. And hope to be moving again soon."

"To?"

"The top job for a bank robbery agent is Los Angeles. Boston may be the armored-car-robbery capital of the world, but L.A. is the bank-robbery capital, no contest. One out of every four bank jobs in the country goes down there.

And with the freeway system, they have to do a lot more with tracking devices, gadgets, gizmos. Charlestown here, their methods are quaint compared to those out West."

Claire nodded, swirling the last sip of wine around the bottom of her glass. He wanted her to have another. "So funny to me that you live here too."

"It's a great town. And I've lived all over. Great neighborhood, great people. It's just that there happens to be this ultrasmall faction, this subculture of banditry." He finished his Sam Adams. "Do we need another round?"

She looked from her glass to him. "I'm not clear on something. Is this work, or is this a date?"

He shrugged. "It's not work."

"So it's a date."

"It's a pre-date. It's appetizers, drinks."

"Because," she said, "and maybe this sounds crazy, but someone warned me that I shouldn't speak to you again without a lawyer."

"Wait—someone from Charlestown, right?"

"How'd you know?"

He dropped his voice a little. "Well, that's the other thing here, this 'Code of Silence.' Born out on the docks, I guess, with bootlegging and longshoremen. Something like fifty murders committed in this town over the past twenty years, many of them with witnesses, and yet only twelve have been solved. The code was, 'Talk to the cops, you're dead, your entire family is dead.' But it's all unraveling now. People testifying against each other, rushing to cut deals. Ugly."

She nodded, only half-listening. "Do you consider me a suspect?"

Who was feeding her this? "What makes you say that?"

"I don't know. The questions you asked me at my parents' house. It never occurred to me that you might think . . ."

"Well, early on, I had a kidnapping that resulted in the bank manager being released unharmed. Add to that the fact that she lived in Charlestown, and— where are you getting all this?"

"Nowhere."

Nowhere? "Would I have asked you out here if I suspected you?"

"I don't know. Maybe."

"Not if I'd wanted a conviction, evidence that would hold up in court."

That seemed to satisfy her. She sat back, distracted. "Honestly, at this point? I almost hope you never catch them. In terms of testifying and all that. I just want to put this thing behind me and move on."

"Well," Frawley told her, "I am going to catch them. Don't sweat the testimony. Even if I bagged them tomorrow, court's easily a year or two down the line. And with twenty-year federal mandies for repeat offenders using firearms in the commission of a violent felony, on top of whatever they draw for the crimes—those are tantamount to life sentences. And believe me, once you see these bozos in court, see their faces—oh, yeah, shit." He searched his jacket pockets. "Almost forgot. Just a moment of investigatory stuff here."

He handed her the color copy he had made from a beat-up library book about the history of the Boston Bruins. It showed a pair of melancholy eyes inside a goalie mask covered with hand-drawn scars.

Frawley said, "That's Gerry Cheevers. Bruins goalie from the Bobby Orr era."

She stared as though he had handed her a photograph of the bandits themselves. "Why those scars?"

Dino's explanation became his own. "Every puck shot Cheevers took off his face mask, he drew the stitch scar over the resulting dent. His trademark."

She looked a moment longer before handing it back, not relaxing until he had returned it to his pocket. "Hate hockey," she said.

"Not so loud," he joked. "Ice hockey and bank robbing are the two year-round sports here in Charlestown."

Their server returned. Claire said, "I'll take a coffee. Decaf."

Frawley held up two fingers, masking his disappointment. "So what do you say we try a real date? Go see *Twister* or something?"

She nodded agreeably. "That might be great."

"Okay." He ran that around his head again. "Might be?"

"Could be. Would be."

"Uh-huh. But?"

"But I'm seeing someone else too."

"Okay."

"I just thought it would be fair to let you know." She smiled then, looking a little giddy and perplexed. "Why am I so popular all of a sudden? It's like getting boobs again. Two interesting guys I meet, after this robbery—what happened? What changed?"

"Is this the piano mover?"

Her surprised look said that she had forgotten telling him about that.

"The guy you met in a Laundromat." Frawley smiled. "I thought you stood him up."

"What's so funny?"

"Nothing."

"You don't want to hear this, but he's helping me."

"Good. That's good."

"He's not a piano mover."

"What's wrong with piano movers?" Their coffees came, and the check.

Frawley wasn't worried. "Competition's good. Raises the bar."

She smiled at him, uncertain. "So there aren't any FBI rules about this?"

"Against dating the vic? No. Just a personal rule I abide by."

"Which is?"

"Never, ever do it," he said, laying down his credit card and a smile.

DINO DROVE A COP'D-OUT 1993 Ford Taurus, the police blues under the grille only noticeable if you were looking for them or if the sun hit them just right. It wasn't an undercover car like Frawley's staid Bureau Cavalier, but other than the whip antenna curling off the trunk, it was good enough for cruising the Town incognito.

The police radio squawked an "odor of gas" call—the attending patrolman acknowledging the 911 dispatcher not with *Affirmative* or *Roger* or the military *Over,* but rather with the distinctly Boston *I have it*—as Dino and Frawley rolled out from under the Tobin Bridge, passing two Housing Authority sedans idling driver-to-driver at the end of Bunker Hill Street.

"I've told them," said Frawley. "I've said, you know, just get me an apartment here, set it up. Nothing fancy—just let me work this square mile exclusively, give me the *time,* give me the *space.* Let me play the *part.* I'd be a yuppie Serpico, you know? A yuppie Donnie Brasco. This town, the way it is—the streets are so narrow, so tight. Any change is noticed, any deviation from the norm. You can't surv a house here, even if you have the manpower—even if there's a vacant apartment right across the street and your target's religion forbids window shades—because the people here, they're too *involved.* Crack open a beer and a guy three doors down gets thirsty. You gotta be part of the landscape."

"But they won't do it."

"Boston would okay it. The SAC could be persuaded, but not D.C. People not from around here have a hard time understanding what a fountain of banditry this zip code is."

"Fountain of banditry," chuckled Dino. "You got a way."

The markets on lower Bunker Hill Street advertised their welfare-friendliness with window signs stating EBT Accepted, WIC Accepted. Above and to the left, the tapered spike of the monument rotated as they passed, the Town slow-roasting on an enormous granite spit.

"So what do you got on this phone company guy?" said Dino.

"Elden. Desmond Elden. What have I got? I've got nothing, that's what I've got. Guy lives with his mother, holds down a steady job, pays his taxes in full and on time, and has never spent a minute of his life in a jail cell. Goes to mass three, four times a week."

"And yet you're convinced—"

"Oh, I'm absolutely fucking positive."

"No record," said Dino. "No time in double-A ball. Jumps right into the majors."

"I don't know the backstory, but it is what it is. As for getting into it later in life, I'd offer this guy's father as Exhibit A."

"Okay, go."

"He was clean too, no record, nothing, when they found him on one of those streets we just passed, early 1980, two bullet holes in the chest. Don't have the full read, but it looks like he was a bagman, not an enforcer, more like a buffer between the street and the guys he was collecting for. Arrest bait, this guy with a clean record. Fourteen years with Edison before that."

"Gotcha."

"This guy, Elden, he'd be their tech. Spotless work record, including attendance, except for a few important dates. Such as the sick day he took the Tuesday after the marathon. Your next right."

Dino flipped on the blinker. "Okay, so it's starting to come into focus."

"Thus far, I've only made him with one other guy, ID'd from the Lakeville mugs. One Douglas MacRay."

"MacRay?" said Dino.

"Yeah, ringing a bell?"

"My age, more like plinking a triangle. Bear with me. Mac MacRay's son?"

"Bingo."

Dino licked his lips, smelling something cooking. "Okay. Big Mac's gotta be a good ten or fifteen in. Walpole, I think."

"MacRay junior last saw twenty months for ag assault. Jumped a guy in a bar, no provocation, nearly killed him. *Would* have killed him if they hadn't pulled him off. Shod foot was the deadly weapon, public intox, resisting arrest. Got out about three years ago. Note that this string we're looking at now started up about six months later."

"Hockey star, wasn't he?"

"Something like that."

"Yeah, yeah, high school hockey star, Charlestown. MacRay. Drafted, I think. Christ—was it the Bruins?"

"This is Pearl Street, where he lives now."

It was a one-way street, the one way being straight down. Frawley pointed out the worst-looking house halfway down the suicide slope. With the cars parked along the right, there was barely enough room for the midsized Taurus to squeeze through.

"See what I mean about surveillance?"

Dino watched his spacing and tried to take in the house at the same time.

"Least he keeps it nice."

"Oh, it's not even his. He rents, or shares, I can't tell. The house is in two names, a sister and a brother, Kristina Coughlin and James Coughlin."

"Coughlin."

"Heard the bells that time?"

"Like Christmas morning at the Vatican. Fathers and sons, huh? What a piece of work Jackie Coughlin Sr. was. I think—I *think*—he bought it falling out of a fourth-floor window or something, a B and E. Wouldn't surprise me if he was pushed by his own partners."

Frawley remembered the bumping he had received in the cellar bar of the Tap, having matched Coughlin's foggy, more-white-than-blue eyes to his card in the Lakeville mugs. "Young Coughlin started with DUIs and race crimes in his teens and got more adventurous from there. By some miracle he's stayed clean for the past thirty months. No arrests, even served out his parole. He and MacRay went down on a bank job together in 1983, still juvees. Amateur hour, Coughlin vaulting the counter, MacRay brandishing a nail gun."

"Oh, that's nice."

"A .22-caliber construction gun loaded with staples. Guy's got a temper. Couple of months before that, he'd gotten himself drummed out of the AHL for putting another player in the hospital."

"In hockey you usually earn a bonus for that."

"Guy he fought was on his own team."

Dino snickered. "The happy-go-lucky type. What about Coughlin's sister?"

"Sister? I don't know. Haven't even looked at her."

They bottomed out on Medford and turned left. Dino said, "That makes three."

"The fourth I'm doing a little conjecture on. We know—or almost know— at least we think that they don't farm out their car jobs, because if they did, it's a good bet we'd have had a snitch by now, or at least some whispering on the wind. Coughlin was picked up on a joyriding bid in '90 or '91 with an Alfred Magloan. On his own, Magloan is a convicted car thief and a member of Local 25, does some film-crew work as a driver."

"That's pretty comprehensive work for file-checking and part-time eye-balling there, Frawl."

"I'm on them. My sense here is, they smell something. That's why they're staying clear of Elden. But I'm having enough trouble watching one, never mind all four. That's why we're in your car today."

"You think you got made?"

Frawley was reluctant to admit it. "Just being real careful. I put in for a new Bureau vehicle, but that's going to take some time."

"You want me for some weekend duty."

"Elden is the only one we've got the subpoena for, so I'm all for sticking with him. Build up some paperwork, make a case, grow it out from there."

"What about this bank Elden's been cruising? In Chestnut Hill."

"I don't know."

"Come on. Speak."

The Schrafft's building came around the corner, the firehouse, Local 25's headquarters. "Small neighborhood branch. Two exits—a busy parking lot and narrow Route 9. A small-time bank, ATM. I don't see it."

Dino signaled and turned back onto Bunker Hill Street, the opposite end, starting up toward the Heights. "So what's he doing there then?"

"I hope not distracting us."

19
SANDMAN

"**M**Y GOD!" SHE SAID, spinning around from the purple flowers she was planting in the ground.

"Hey," said Doug.

"You *scared* me! Where did you come from?" She looked around like he might have brought a surprise party with him. "What are you doing here?"

Her smile made Doug forget who and what he was, made him forget everything. "I was in the area, thought I'd take a chance."

She brushed at the browned knees of her jeans, as though he cared that they were dirty. "You spying on me?"

"Maybe just a little."

"Well, stop it and come on in here."

The gate catch was a simple wire loop. Inside, he stuck to the neat, S-shaped path of small, crunchy stones. A hello kiss would have come off too forced and awkward, too formal even. She stayed close to him as he looked around. A weathered wooden chest was open behind the bench, stocked with hand tools, fertilizer, Miracle Grow. "This is nice," he said.

"Yeah, well. . . ." She surveyed it with the backs of her wrists curled against her hips. "My perennials are perennially frustrating, and my annuals are a semi-annual disappointment. Oh, and the spearmint is strangling my phlox."

"I thought I smelled gum."

"Other than that—welcome to my little patch of heaven. I was just putting in some impatiens for color. If you want to wait, I'm almost done."

"I'll sit."

His shoulders rustled some weeping-willow tendrils—and just like that he was sitting on her stone garden bench. He was in. He tried to see across to where he used to watch her from, but couldn't make it out now.

She knelt on a foam pad, facing away from him, planting and patting the rest of the flowers in a bed of overturned dirt. The lilac band of her panties showed over the stressed belt of her jeans, panties he had once picked up off the Laundromat floor.

"This is a surprise," she said.

"Time on my hands. I was in the area, and I remembered you raving about this place at dinner."

"Right. Now—were you really in the area? Or did you sort of *put* yourself in the area?"

"I put myself here, definitely."

She looked back at him over her shoulder with a smile. "Good."

"Plus I'm a big fan of flowers."

"I could tell." She returned to them. "What's your favorite kind?"

"Oh, lilac."

She reached forward, patting the soil around a short stem in the manner of one tucking in a blanket around a baby. "You can see my underwear from there, can't you."

"It's all right. I don't mind."

She didn't straighten, didn't cover up, a very simple, sexy thing, just letting it be. She finished and splashed some hose water on the beds and her own dirty hands, then packed away her tools, smoothed her hair back into a scrunchy, and took him for a stroll through the gardens.

"I have to tell you," she said, twirling a green leaf by the stem as they walked, "I did a terrible thing yesterday."

"What was that?"

"I watched a soap opera. Used to schedule my college classes around them. Anyway, there was this typically ridiculous scene where two people stand across the room from each other and talk, talk, talk, until the woman turns to the window, gazing off for her big close-up, sighing, 'Why am I falling for you?' It was so crazy and overblown, I was smiling when I turned it off. But then I got to thinking." She glanced at him. "Why *am* I falling for you?"

"Wow," he said, the words hitting him like booze.

"You're not at all my type. My girlfriends, I've told them about you, and they think it's just, like, big rebound. And I'm like—rebound from what? The robbery? I mean—are we that different? Really? I think we have more in common than we have differences."

"Agreed."

"We both love flowers."

He laughed. "Right."

"Anyway, my friends." She shook her hands like she couldn't express herself clearly. "I feel sort of estranged from them, I think maybe that's what they're picking up on. I have changed. I can feel it. They still have this, like, carelessness about them—which I sort of envy, but at the same time, I don't really understand anymore. It's scary to think that I might be, you know, leaving them behind."

"Yeah," Doug said, following this closely. "I think I know exactly what you mean."

They turned the corner at a double-wide plot with pebble paths and a big bonsai tree. A barefoot Asian woman was practicing slow-motion, invisible-wall-pushing tai chi.

"But this, you and me—it's happening too fast," said Claire. "I don't trust it. I think about you and I feel like . . . I can picture you in my mind for a second, but then you're gone. It's like I know you really well, but almost not at all. Like you're not real—like I invented you, or you invented me, some Zen thing like that. Are you real, Doug?"

"I think so."

"Because I can't root you in anything. Charlestown, I guess, but that's too vague. I don't even have your phone number. I can't call you. Or your address—no house to drive by and torment myself and wonder, 'Is he home? Is he thinking about me?' "

"You mean you want references?"

"Yes! And a look at your driver's license and another valid form of ID. I want to stand in your bathroom. I want five minutes alone in your closet. I want to know that you're not just going to turn to smoke on me someday."

"I'm not."

"And fine, I know this is stupid, it's only been two dates. I *know* that I'm crazy, okay? But I can't help this feeling that there's something . . ." She shook her head, throwing the leaf to the dirt path. "Are you married?"

Doug sputtered. "You said *married*?"

"Can't you see—you're making me ask! *Making* me embarrass myself here."

"*Married?*" he said, wanting to scoff and laugh at the same time.

"I need to know that there's water in the pool. Even if—okay, fine, even if I've already jumped, I still want to know whether or not there's water in the pool."

"There's—there's water in the pool," he said, confused.

"We could go to your apartment. You could show me where you live."

He started to say no.

"Five minutes." She showed him that many fingers, growing frantic. "So I can *plant* you somewhere in my mind, so you're not this, this sandman. I met you in a *Laundromat*, Doug MacRay. It is Doug MacRay—right?"

He couldn't give in here, and she slowed along the path, hands falling to her sides. "See, this is—now my mind is filling with possibilities."

"Whoa, what? Like centerfolds all over the walls or something? Dirty laundry hanging from the ceiling fan?"

"That's . . . *minimum*."

"I am not married." That time he did laugh, angering her.

"Neither am I," she said. "So far as you know."

"My place—" He stopped himself. "I was going to blame it on my neighbors, but that's not true, it's me, all me. See, I'm making some changes in my life"—Doug was hearing this himself for the first time—"and my place—that's the old me. Something I'm trying to fix."

She jumped on that. "But I want to see—"

"The old me? No, you don't. Would you want me poking around your college dorm room to find out about you now?"

"But, wait—"

"Listen. I just grew up. Just a little while ago. The day I met you, maybe. Already, I've turned over so many bad cards for you."

"And I'm still here."

"And you're still here. So what I'm asking for now is, please—let me work on trying to impress you for a change. Please."

She nodded, unconvinced.

Doug made a pretend move for his wallet. "I have a license and a Blockbuster card."

"Just tell me, Doug." She reached out and gripped his wrists. "Tell me if I'm making a mistake. I will still make the mistake. That's no problem. I just want to know now."

"I'm saying there is no—"

"*Aaah!*" Her tiny scream startled a nearby family of ducks. She pulled on his arms, staring into his eyes. "Yes or no. Am I making a mistake here, or not?"

Doug looked down at her hands manacling his wrists. He knew what he wanted to say, and he knew what she was waiting for him to say. All he had to do was say it.

"No."

She stared hard, then let go of him, pointing a finger at his chest. "You promised."

Doug nodded. "Okay."

A bird fluttering to a nearby trellis caught her eye, and she watched it peck at some vines, softening her mood a bit. "So much agitation around me these days," she said. "Stuff swirling. But with you, when I'm alone with you—there's a silence, there's peace. You make all that other stuff go away." The bird disappeared to a high branch. "But again—whether any of this is real or not, I have no idea."

"Maybe if we just stop talking about it. Maybe if we just let it be."

"I'm not looking for a guarantee. Just good faith."

Doug nodded, feeling better about it now himself. "And that's what I gave you."

She relented then, turning to start back, one hand finding its way to the pocket of her jeans, the other into his hand. "Do you think that was our first fight?"

"Was it?"

"Maybe just my first freak-out."

Relief filled him like breath. "Our first *discussion,* maybe."

"That's it, a *discussion.*" She swung their joined hands a little. "I don't even think true fights are possible between a couple until sex enters the equation."

"Yeah," said Doug at first. "Wait. Is that a vote for fighting, or . . . ?"

"A relationship filled only with firsts. Wouldn't that be the best? No past, no history to worry about, things moving too fast. You and me up on the rooftop, over and over again. Everything light and new."

"We could do that."

"Could we? Every date our first?"

"Why not?" He let go of her hand. "Hey, I'm Doug."

She smiled. "Claire. Nice to meet you."

They shook hands, then Doug looked at his empty palm, shrugging. "Nah. No chemistry."

She pushed him away, laughing, then grabbed his hand again, hooking her arm around his, pulling him close.

CANESTARO'S WAS A PIZZERIA and bistro with café seating on the park end of Peterborough Street. Nice without the Chart House finery, no table linen, butter with the bread instead of oil. He was comfortable here. With the sun still peeking over the high wall of apartment buildings lining the other side of the street, they claimed one of the sidewalk tables and split a pizza, half 'roni, half chicken and broccoli. Echoes of Fenway Park reached them from two streets away, the announcer droning, "Vaughn. First base, Vaughn."

Claire was better by the time the food came, and the meal passed as the best ones do, offering few great revelations but constant little connections, two people dining on each other's character, curious and gentle as nibbling fish. Then she said something about his mother that threw him. "Just that, how, whenever you talk about your mother leaving, it's like she *escaped* from you and your father. As opposed to, well—deserting you."

"Yeah," he said, surprised both by the change in topic and the observation itself, never having thought of it that way. "Guess you're right."

"Why?"

"I guess," he said, "because it's true."

"But you were six years old. How can you blame yourself?"

"No, I hear you."

"No one ever told you what she was going through? There must have been some signs. . . ."

"No one told me anything about my mother. Not my father, that's for sure. But that's also because, pretty much, he was the problem."

"How so?"

Cars rolled past while he deliberated. "Well," he said, "you're not gonna like it."

"What do you mean, *I'm* not gonna like it?"

The strangest thing was, he wanted to tell her this. It amazed him how honest he wanted to be, how dry he felt under the broad umbrella of the lie. "You know how you asked me one time about Charlestown, bank robbers?"

She just looked at him, waiting for him to say something other than what she was thinking.

"Yeah," said Doug, unable to spare her. "I didn't say anything because . . . well, because."

"My God. I never thought . . . I'm so sorry—"

"No, no." Doug grunted a harsh laugh. "*You're* not the sorry one. Doesn't matter to me, I'm used to it. I didn't say anything because of you."

She looked off down the street, grappling with this.

"Two years after my mother left us, he drew a twenty-one-month prison sentence, meaning I drew twenty-one months in a foster home. I was eight. I'll never forget when he got out, how he made out like he was the hero, rescuing me. I was sixteen when he went up again, and that time the bank took our house. I moved in with a friend's mother who was basically raising me anyway." He shrugged and took a deep breath, looking at his pizza. "That's my tale of woe. No one ever tells me about my mother. But between my father, being who he was, living like an outlaw, and me there, a little hydrant-sized version of him—I think it was probably too much for her. Probably her or us, you know? In her mind, I think she had no choice. I always assume she went off and started up another family somewhere, and she's happier there. I don't blame her. But—I wouldn't mind talking about something else either."

It was dizzying to speak of such things. Dizzying and freeing at the same time.

"So many of my friends," said Claire, after a respectful silence. "They pick the wrong guy, again and again." A cheer from the ballpark crowd reached them like a cry of attack from a distant battlefield. "I wonder why so many girls seem dead set on picking out a guy who's bound to make them unhappy."

"I don't know," said Doug, careful here. "Is it that, or are they picking out someone they think they can help? Maybe someone they can save?"

She poked around her side salad, considering a tomato wedge. "But how often does that happen, right? What's the success rate there?" She declined the tomato, laying it back on her dish. "And why aren't there more *guys* out there looking for *women* to save?"

Doug shrugged. "Maybe there are."

Claire looked him over, his face, and she smiled. "You are helping me, you know. It's so bizarre, the random way we met. Almost like you were *sent* here to help me."

Doug nodded, sincere. "I want to help you." Then he opened his hands to indicate the pizza, the restaurant, the fading day. "I'm having a good time. A really good time."

She pulled her napkin from her lap and dropped it on the table, pushing back her chair. "Good. Then you'll miss me while I'm gone."

After some confusion at the door with an exiting waitress, Claire disappeared inside to the bathroom and Doug sat back. The sun was just slipping behind the apartment row, a wall of shadow reaching across the street. Organ music played from the ballpark, distorted and warbling with echo. He tipped his chair back until it hit the pointy tips of the wrought-iron fencing and looked up at the sky, the smoky contrail of a jet plane. He ruffled his hair with his hand and his mind unwound, following one of those hopscotching strings of reason, wondering what they would do next, anticipating the bill, thinking about how much clean cash he had left, remembering Foxwoods and how long he had to drive every time he needed to wash currency. If only there were an Indian casino someplace where he could go and wash his soul.

He set the front two feet of his chair back down on the sidewalk terrace and pulled his money roll from his jeans pocket. As he was counting it, something jabbed into the back of his neck, and at first he grinned, thinking it was Claire. Then he remembered the short fence and realized it had to be someone off the street.

"Gimme all ya money," said a low voice.

Doug tensed, his adrenaline response delayed by the friendly street setting, the other diners eating calmly, the cars rolling past.

The stickup man appeared next to him in a white nylon Red Sox jersey untucked over jeans, and small, stupid, syrup-lens sunglasses: Jem with a white-lipped smirk.

"I froze you, fothermucker."

Doug sat up with a hard glance at the pizzeria door. The adrenaline arrived and he started to stand out of his chair before stopping himself.

"What're you doing here?" said Jem, pulling off his shades to scan up and down Peterborough, then hanging them on the top button of his shirt and stepping over the fence, dropping into Claire's seat across from Doug.

"What?" said Doug, lost, another cheat at the door.

"Chicken and broccoli?" Jem scooped up the slice Claire had been eating, bit into it. "Fuck is *this*? Who you here with?" Smiling, having fun.

"No one," said Doug—the strangest, most feeble lie.

"No one, huh?" said Jem, reaching for her lemonade glass. He put his lips on her straw and sucked, and Doug's insides went icy. "'S'up with you?"

Jem looked straight enough, his eyes lacking their doomsday blur, maybe only three or four beers in. The door was still closed. Doug peeled off two twenties and spilled them on the table, making to stand. He'd explain it to her later. "Wanna get outta here?"

But Jem stayed hunkered over his slice, waving him back down. "I'm cool, take your time." He gobbled the slice up to the crust. "But who puts fuckin' broccoli on a pizza?"

The door opened and Claire stepped back outside, and Doug went deaf.

Claire slowing, strange. Smiling at Doug, but odd, walking up to the man sitting in her chair.

Jem gnawing on crust, oblivious. Looking up. Standing, not shocked.

Hi, Claire's lips say.

Hey, say Jem's, still chewing. Not much taller than her, but broad, all shoulders and arms and neck. Guess I'm in your seat.

Surrendering the chair with his jerk-gentleman flourish. Standing behind her now, grinning at Doug. The jaw of his small head, chewing.

This was no chance meeting. Suddenly Doug was no longer intimidated, only angry. The same adrenaline surge, a different state of mind.

Claire also looking at Doug, awkward. She gave up waiting for him and turned to Jem to introduce herself, offering her hand, sound roaring back into Doug's head.

"I'm Claire. Claire Keesey."

"Jem." He took her hand, a perfunctory up-and-down shake.

"Jim?"

"Jem," he said. "Just Jem."

She nodded, turning again to Doug for help.

"I'm a friend of this loser right here," Jem told her. "He lives with me. Not *with me,* domestic partners, but above me, my house."

"Oh?" she said.

A snake's grin as Jem held her chair for her. Claire sat as offered, staring across the wire table at mute Doug.

Jem retreated to a chair at the end of the table. "Yeah, I came down here to catch the ball game, and what do I see but the Shamrock parked around the corner. Thought I'd walk the block, you know, check up on this guy." Grin. "Gotta keep tabs, always."

Claire said, "The Shamrock?"

"His machine. Scoundrel, this guy is. Never breathed a word. The secrets he can keep."

Claire took them in together. "You two have been friends a long time?"

"No, only since second grade," said Jem. "Like brothers, everyone says. Huh, Duggy?"

Worlds colliding. Doug sat still, there and not there at the same time.

"I'm sorry," said Claire, "did you say your name was Jim, or Gem?"

"Ah, both actually. A combination. You might think it's because of the family jewels. These ones up here." He pointed out the grinning blue-white marbles of his eyes. "But the truth is—Duggy knows this—truth is, that's what the teachers would say when they passed me off to each other, shuttling me around by the scruff of my neck. 'Here's this one, he's a real gem.' And Jimmy, Gem, it kinda sticked."

She wore that distant smile people get when they're evaluating someone. "A troublemaker, huh?"

"Oh, the worst. What do you do for yourself there, Claire?"

It was like watching a movie—Claire taking a slow-mo sip of lemonade through the straw Jem had just sucked on.

"I work in a bank," she told him. "Just around the corner from here, one street over. Kenmore Square."

"Hey, wait. The BayBanks?" Jem pointed at Doug, then back at Claire. He even snapped his fingers. "Wasn't that the one . . . ?"

"Yes," she said. "The robbery."

"Ha. I don't know what made me remember that." He glanced at Doug. "So how'd you two kids meet?"

Claire looked to Doug to tell the tale—to say something, anything—but he could not. "A Laundromat," she said, concerned.

"Laundromat, huh? This guy stealing bras again? Seriously, your socks get mixed up? Love among the bleach, huh?"

Doug dead-staring at Jem now. Not a crack anywhere in Jem's grinning facade.

"Like I said, I was gonna go pick up some cheap seats off a scalper, root-root-root for the home team. Guys interested? Duggy? What do you say?"

Claire looked at Doug, but Doug's eyes stayed on Jem.

"No?" said Jem. "That's awright anyway. Hate being the third wheel, you know?" He smiled at them both, then formed a gun with his fingers, shooting it at Doug. "Don't trust a word he says, Claire. What kinda lies he been telling you?"

Claire watching Doug now. "Wait," she said. "Do you mean he's not really an astronaut?"

Jem pointed her out to Doug. "Hey, that's quick, that's spunk. Very good. No, but, yeah, we are both in the space program, so if you got any friends interested in that stuff, who also happen to be redheads and a little bit on the easy side . . ."

"I will let them know."

"You do that, cool. She's awright, Duggy. Oh, hey." He patted the table before he stood. "Don't get too used to this here, your leisure, loverboy. We got some more work coming our way."

Claire said, "You two work together, too?"

"Told you, we're tighter than tight. Used to tell each other *every*thing."

"You're a sky-maker too?"

"That's us. Another takedown job. My Duggy here, he loves to watch 'em fall."

The smile vanished a moment under his dead eyes, and then just as fleetly reemerged. He stepped over the fence onto the sidewalk. "You watch out for this one now, Claire. Remember what I said—pure trouble."

Jem slapped Doug hard on the shoulder and took off down the street in a bobbing saunter, replacing the shades on his face. Claire watched him go, her eyes falling to Doug, who was still staring at the empty chair.

"He seems nice," she said flatly.

"That's being polite."

"What is wrong, Doug? You were scaring me."

"I wasn't ready for you to meet him yet."

"Is that what you were talking about—the old you?"

"Yeah." Doug still staring at the empty chair. "That was some of it."

"What's up with his eyes?"

Doug could think of no way to answer that question.

"Are you okay?" she said. "Going to be?"

"Sure," he said, surfacing, looking around, seeing his twenties still on the table. Claire reached for her lemonade again, but this time Doug took the glass from her hand. She stiffened, watching him.

"You want to be alone?" she said.

He was alone. Jem had just seen to that.

20
WORKOUT

THE MORNING WAS WET, the rising sun burning off shadows and damp-ness, raising street steam. Through the cat's cradle of power and phone wires, falling to eye level as Sackville Street plunged headlong into the Mystic, a barge was being unloaded by tall, pecking cranes. Gulls coasted over-head, dipping and swirling around Doug's mother's house, threatening to shit.

When his father had first lost the house, Doug was so pissed he didn't come around for years, avoiding Sackville Street altogether. The life he was leading then, that of a drinking man, offered little solace, his mind stewing in boyhood memories and associations, rather than drawing on their strength. But during his stay at MCI Norfolk, all thoughts of home, of the Town, centered around his mother's house. Not the Monument, not Pearl Street, not the rink. Her house was the first place he visited after his release. The Town was his mother. The Town had raised him. This house was her face, watching over him. These streets were her arms, holding him close.

Acting impulsively had been the hallmark of Doug's drinking years, and never had it come to any good. He always wound up hurting people. How had he thought this was going to end any differently?

It was the lottery mentality. Something he had been working so hard to sup-press these past three years: the all-or-nothing play, going after that "marquee score." It was something else he had inherited from the Town, like his eyes and his face: a gambler's dream of that one sweet score that would change every-thing forever.

He preached this to the others about banks: Don't be greedy. Don't over-step, don't overreach. *Get in, get the money, get out.* Now he had to take his own advice.

The thought of Jem standing behind her at the pizzeria—like a flickering image-echo of the two of them at the Kenmore Square vault, a couple waiting for the elevator—gripped his heart like a fist. It crystallized the danger Doug had invited into her life, as well as his own. Staying away meant keeping Jem away from her and the G away from him. No more daydreams about healing

Claire Keesey, or magically absolving himself. The best thing he could do for her now, the only thing, as well as for himself, was to let her go.

THE GLASS PANE RATTLED in the front door as Doug entered, heading upstairs to Jem's before realizing the music he heard was pounding in the basement, not on the second floor. He turned and went outside, walking along a weedy stripe of cracked cement to the backyard bulkhead.

The stone cellar was dank, the floor moist and brown, tears of condensation glistening in the corners. The clank of steel on steel—Jem always smacked the weight plates together, he was there to make some noise—died against the damp walls, a discordant counterpoint to the soar and crash of Zep's "Kashmir."

Jem was on his back, doing presses on the old, overweighted machine. The cables squealed, the bottom rails rusty and fuzzed with mildew from cellar floodings.

He finished and sat up, fire-faced, the long veins in his forearms like blue snakes feeding under his skin. "Hey," he said, hopping off the bench, "check it out, I just picked these up." Three thumping speakers were set on shoulder-high stands around the machine like cameras on tripods. "Wireless," he said, moving his hands around one like a magician demonstrating a levitation trick. "Receives from my stereo upstairs. Three bills each, but *damn*." He cranked the volume to demonstrate, head jerking to the beat atop his thickened neck, forgetting or simply not caring that any metal inside the speakers would be oxidized within a matter of weeks. "Fuckin' *rocks,* man."

Unlike his speakers, Jem was wired. It was the buzz of lifting and maybe something more. He turned the music back down and boosted a curling bar, balancing two wide, fifty-pound plates and a couple of twenties. "Get changed and come back down, we'll hit it serious." He started a set of preacher curls, his face filling with blood.

This was not the welcome Doug had expected. Jem coming off friendly and pretending nothing was wrong was scarier than him taking a sledge to the weeping walls.

"Last night," said Doug.

"Was that a fucking outrage or what?" said Jem, breaking off his reps, bouncing the bar on the floor. "Motherfuckin' Wakefield, I hate knuckleballers. Straight-ball pitcher starts to lose his stuff in the sixth, you can see it, his speed, his control. Funny-ball pitchers lose their stuff? It's like a trapdoor opened. Ball stops moving, and now they're serving up fucking gopher balls to free-agent millionaires."

"Who you following, Jem? Me or her?"

Still the poker face. "Told you, kid, I made the Shamrock out on Boylston, parked outside 'BCN. Which is fucked-up, by the way. Somebody take that primo shit off your hands, leave a thank-you note taped to the meter."

"You got something to say, say it now."

Jem smiled past him to the near speaker. "Don't know, kid," he said, turning down the tunes. "See—I think that's *my* line here."

Doug sniffed, shifted his weight. "Told you I was working on things. Making sure we were clear."

"Yeah. And maybe it started out that way." Jem tightened the wrist straps on his lifting gloves. "Then again, you grabbed her license from me pretty fast."

"That's bullshit."

"Is it, yeah? I mean, she's awright, don't get me wrong. I had my hand on her ass too, at the vault." He looked up. "Though I guess you broke that up too, didn't you."

"The fuck are you talking about?"

"You tell me you're workin' a scam here, I'll say, 'Cool.' 'Cause that's something I *get*. That's something makes *sense* to me. But anything else, and I'd say we got us a problem here."

Doug tried going on the attack. "That was stupid, you coming around like that. A stupid play. What'd you think—you were embarrassing me or something? You could of come to talk to me alone. I was keeping her separate from you guys—but especially you, ass-grabber. She remembers anyone, it's gonna be the guy who took her for a ride."

"You always talk about Boozo's crew and how reckless they were, like maniacs, crazy for action. Then you go off making googly eyes at the one person— the *one*—who could give the G anything on us. Oh, but I'm a fucking moron." A Jem smile to go along with the Jem shrug. "Hey, thanks for your protection."

"You're welcome."

"And no, I didn't tell the others yet. Only because it would flip them the fuck out, and they're skittish enough already. Plus your boyfriend, the Monsignor, he'd be so brokenhearted jealous. Besides—there's nothing to tell, right?"

"I told you, I got from her what I wanted."

"Yeah? It any good?"

Doug frowned. "I'm saying, it's done. Over."

Jem squinted to see him better. "Hey, guess what? By the way, me and that assistant manager? We went out hankie shopping together last week. Yeah, I didn't think it was all that important to tell you."

"If that's your fucking point, then you made it."

"I'm a fucking porcupine with points. You worry me, kid. Seeing her on the side, away from us? That's like a move, brother. Says that to me. Us or her."

"Bullshit."

"I don't see any room for overlap there. Tell me I'm wrong."

Doug had always been the only one able to handle Jem. When things got tight, he could pull that brother-withholding-love shit on him and Jem would always come around, settle down. Now everything was out of balance. Now Jem was sitting on all the power.

"Awright," Jem said, flexing out his lumpy arms, nodding. "Then we can get started on this movie caper."

Too soon, but now Doug couldn't say no.

Jem read his silence with a jacked, hungry smile. "You made anybody on your tail? I haven't."

"Somebody was watching Dez's house."

"*Was*. I think we're ready to put ourselves back in play."

"Then Dez has to sit this one out."

"Fine. And actually dandy too."

"But he still gets his quarter take."

Jem eyed Doug, taking his measure. The shrug and the smile arrived together. "Fuckin' whatever. All ends up in the collection box at St. Frank's anyhow, right? Catholic charity, bring us some luck. So long as this gig comes together *quick*. That means no fucking stalling. And don't tell me you ain't been rolling this around your mind, 'cause I won't believe it. I bet you got a mark already picked out. Hell—you maybe even got a plan floating around in there."

Maybe Doug did. Maybe this was exactly what he needed right now, something to occupy his mind. Something to bring them all back together, to the way things used to be.

21
CLOCKING IT

B RAINTREE IS A SUBURB south of Boston where the Southeast Expressway out of the city splits in two: west toward the Maine-to-Florida Interstate 95, and east along Route 3, a state highway riding south to the
flexed arm of Cape Cod. Braintree's draw for city kids of the late 1970s and
1980s was the South Shore Plaza, one of the first enclosed shopping malls in
the region, a quick bus trip via the MBTA Red Line stop at Quincy Adams. A
hobby shop that sold exploding rockets, a B. Dalton that stored overstock *Play-
boy*s under tables in the back of the store, the tobacconist C. B. Perkins that also
sold lighters and knives, Recordtown, and the suburban girls that roamed the
mall in packs and pairs—plus a movie theater, a detached two-screen job next to
a Howard Johnson, known as the Braintree Cinema.

Across the street from the mall, Forbes Road was a thin thoroughfare curling wide around the castlelike Sheraton Tara Hotel and the South Shore Execu-
tive Park. The road came into view of the highway there, tailing off along the
bottom of a blasted rock cliff. A narrow, two-lane offshoot named Grandview
Road climbed steeply to the summit of the mount where, surrounded by a few
acres of blacktop parking, the old Braintree Cinema had reopened in 1993 as a
brand-new multiscreen General Cinemas complex known as The Braintree 10.

Across an eight-lane highway gorge was another cliff road, set on the edge
of the Blue Hills Reservation, studded with industrial parks and office buildings. From there the big-signed movie theater looked like a temple above a
ravine of automobiles.

An isolated mark. Easy highway access. Secluded vantage points.

The second most important part of the job, after the getaway, is target selec-
tion. Once you commit to a target, the details that follow shape themselves to
the task at hand.

YOU PARK WITH THE other nine-to-fivers in front of the faceless office building
next to the movie theater at the top of Grandview. Behind the building is a
wood that descends into a residential area across from the shopping plaza, and

there is a neglected fire road there, its entrance blocked by two craggy boulders. This will be your emergency escape route. If everything else goes to hell, you know that you can take to the trees on foot, dump your weapons and strip down to street clothes, and cross to a car parked at the mall before K-9 units and State Police helicopters hunt you down.

Your Bearcat 210 scanner crackles underneath the newspaper, jammed between the two front seats. Field glasses wait in the glove, with the bird-watching guide as their excuse, but you won't need the nocs today. Your position is too good: a side view of the movie-theater parking lot between low shrubs, the morning crows picking at pretzel bites and Raisinets.

The only two cars in the lot appear empty. A navy blue Cressida putters in after 10 A.M., parking on the side near the trash cage. The manager locks his car, uses his key in the side entrance door under swooping, popcorn-loving seagulls, and you clock it.

Seagulls and crows, that's all you have until 11:15, when a couple of rattling imports pull in: the weekday crew, mostly older people, part-timers. You clock it.

First showing of any movie that day will be at 12:20. Late-Monday-morning pickup time means no crowd control, no citizen heroes, minimal witnesses.

At 11:29, a white Plymouth Neon rolls in, parking at the wood railing along the front edge of the lot. A guy wearing sneakers and a ponytail gets out, climbs onto the roof of his car, and sits there cross-legged. He opens a sandwich and a yogurt, eating lunch while looking across the highway at the serene Blue Hills.

At 11:32, the can rolls in. You clock it, committing the time to memory but nothing to paper—no evidence in case you get pulled over.

The armored truck rumbles in steady on oversized wheels. You recognize it as a Pinnacle truck. Pinnacle's colors are blue and green.

The can rolls right up to the front and parks in the fire lane at the stairs to the lobby. Its lone rear door faces you as the truck idles.

Nothing happens for one minute.

The passenger door opens and the courier guard, also known as the messenger or hopper, steps out with the heel of his hand on the butt of his belt-holstered sidearm. He wears an open-collared, police-blue shirt with his identification hanging alligator-clipped to one of the collar points, the Pinnacle patch sewn onto his right shoulder, an oversized silver badge pinned to his breast pocket.

He is middle-aged, portly but strong, sporting a thick, white brush mustache and walking determinedly around to the rear doors. The brim of his police-style cap sits low over his eyes. No bulletproof vest. Vests are expensive and Pinnacle neither supplies nor requires them.

You pay close attention to his movements. You absorb the routine.

The courier knocks twice on the right rear door. The driver inside unlocks it with the push of a button, and the courier pulls on the handle.

Your Bearcat is silent. No radio traffic on Pinnacle's radio frequencies. This is normal.

From the cargo area, the courier pulls out a two-wheeled dolly pasted with Pinnacle stickers and stands it next to the can's broad steel bumper. He reaches into the truck again and lifts out a long-handled, blue-and-green, canvas Pinnacle delivery bag.

This is the theater's change order. You note that it looks small. He sets the bag down on the bottom of the dolly and shuts the rear door.

The courier's hand returns to the butt of his gun as he pushes the dolly up the handicap ramp along the perimeter of the outside stairs. He goes to the center doors, which are unlocked, opens them, and disappears inside.

You clock it. 11:35.

You cannot see them, yet you know that the second set of doors, the ones past the ticket windows, are certainly locked, and that the manager waits behind them with a key.

Yogurt Man finishes his lunch and lies against his windshield, his face turned to the sun, oblivious to the cash pickup far at his back. A white paper bag tumbles across the lot where the empty cars wait.

The armored truck sits tight, locked and idling.

THE TRUCK HAS FOUR doors—one driver, one passenger, two rear—and a small sixteen-by-eighteen-inch package door on the left side. An additional jump seat is in the cargo area, separated from the cab by a locked door, which sits empty on this two-man run. The doors all have special Medeco high-security key cylinders, as do the interior safes or lockboxes. The ignition key is not a special key, but a kill switch is concealed somewhere inside the front cabin, or else a series of random actions (for instance, switching on the defrost, then depressing the brake pedal, then switching on the defrost again) must be performed in sequence before the engine will turn over.

When the ignition key is turned, all doors automatically lock. When the driver's door is opened, the back doors automatically lock. If any door is unlocked, a red warning light shines over the dash and the wheels on the vehicle lock to prevent the can from moving. In addition, manual dead bolts are installed inside each door.

In a siege situation, the driver is trained to lock down and radio for help. The twelve-ton truck is a mobile bunker impervious to outside attack, its stainless steel armor designed to preserve structural integrity. Due to weight-load restrictions, the cargo area is usually armored one level lower than the cabin; for example, the cargo area might be certified to withstand an AK-47 or M14 assault, whereas the cabin could handle M16 fire. The weakest section of the cargo area, the rear door, is still three inches thick.

Windshield and window glass is a glass-clad polycarbonate, less dense than but equally effective as heavier bulletproof glass.

There is a roof-mounted beacon, a siren, and a public address system. Four eyehole gun ports are cut into the body of the truck. The heavy-duty bumpers are built to withstand a ram attack, and the tractor-size tires are puncture-resistant. The undercarriage would resemble that of any normal two-ton truck, but reinforced to carry six times that load; for example, the fifteen-inch differential unit is easily three times that of a standard vehicle.

The security and liquidity of the world's leading economy rides on these trucks, tens of thousands of them out on the streets at any hour, billions of dollars in notes and coin perpetually in transit. You know and accept that there is no practical way to compromise the hulk of an armored bank vehicle without also destroying its contents. The can is only vulnerable through its human operators.

AT 11:44, THE COURIER reappears on the front ramp, rolling the stacked dolly ahead of him, having spent nine minutes inside. You clock it.

The courier wheels the dolly to the rear of the truck. The handcart is stacked halfway up with three white canvas sacks of cash. The plastic trays below the white sacks contain rolled coins. The original blue-and-green Pinnacle canvas bag rides on top.

Inside the sacks are deposit bags containing cash and receipts. The clear plastic bags are supplied by Pinnacle and each one bears a tracking bar code. Much of the courier's nine minutes inside was spent inspecting the bags for tears, testing the seals, and reconciling the amounts printed on the deposit slips inside with the amounts on the manager's manifest.

The driver has spent this nine minutes watching the exterior perimeter. Security mirrors around the truck are specifically trained on the rear-door ambush area.

Courier and driver remain in constant audio contact, both wearing small, black wire earphones and microphones. The driver monitors the courier's conversations for warning signs and responds to his reports, such as *I'm on my way out*.

As the courier approaches the can, a small playing-card-sized parabolic mirror mounted near the door handle gives him an eye line on anyone behind him moving into the ambush zone. Two knocks and the right rear door is unlocked. He pulls it open and promptly loads the white sacks into the hold. He stows the empty dolly and shuts the door.

He walks to the passenger door, plucking out his ear wires. The side door is unlocked by the driver and the courier climbs inside. 11:46.

The truck sits for four more minutes while the driver double-checks the deposit receipts, entering bar codes into Pinnacle's tracking system.

You pull away during this time. Armored-truck guards are vigilant for tails, and a well-trained driver will spot your car driving away and make a mental note of its color and make.

You drive to the bottom of Grandview and back along Forbes to the parking lot of the Sheraton Tara. There, you and your partner switch into a work car and wait.

The can comes rolling along Forbes Road past you toward the mall. You see that the driver is a black man in his fifties. With no vehicle following him out of the parking lot of The Braintree 10, he starts to relax, falling in with the traffic, maintaining a safe and reasonable distance from the other vehicles. You pull out a few cars behind him.

The interior of the armored-truck cab is wide but unremarkable, a cross between a police cruiser and a long-haul truck. Aside from the hypnotizing drone of the engine and the occasional radio chatter, the cab is essentially soundproof. Armoring and special glass make it like driving inside a vacuum. For such a boxy, bulky, dense vehicle—armored trucks average between three and four miles to the gallon—the suspension is exceptionally smooth, and driver and courier feel no bumps.

Guards are often retirees from the MBTA or the Turnpike Authority, usually with a military background, earning between 65K and 90K per year. The shuttle between deliveries and pickups, or jumps, is the safest and least stressful part of their workday.

You remain two or three car lengths back from the truck, in a different lane when possible. When the can pulls into a parking lot for another pickup, you radio your freckled friend, who has been circling you in another stolen work car, and who then enters the lot and eyeballs the can. One of his talents is pretending to be asleep.

Then it is your turn to circle and wait. Your other partner, the one riding with you, unscrews the cap on the empty mayonnaise jar you brought for such eventualities and relieves himself into it. Part of you can't help but think how pleased he is at any excuse to whip out his dick in public, and how proud he must be at the duration of his piss, the singing sound it makes against the jar glass. You tolerate his satisfied sigh.

Your remote friend radios you in code, giving you the direction of the can, and you resume the tail as before.

Five more jumps. Some of them quick change orders, some pickups.

Another dozen jumps. Working your way through Holbrook, into Brockton.

Ten more. Almost four o'clock now. After a supermarket jump in downtown Brockton, the can rides west for a while, ten minutes without a stop, twenty. You know, because it is your job to know, that the Pinnacle armored-car facility is hidden behind double security fences in rural Easton up ahead. Your day's work is done. You pull off when the can gets close.

DEZ WASHED HIMSELF LIKE a marked bill in order to get free. He took a taxi from Sully Square out to Harvard Square in Cambridge, bought a ticket to a late-afternoon matinee at the Brattle Theater, sat for first fifteen minutes of a subtitled Hong Kong action movie, then carried his popcorn out through the curtained doorway at the front of the theater and exited into the side alley off Mifflin Place, sliding into Doug's waiting Caprice.

Doug had tailed Dez's taxi over from Charlestown himself. No one else followed. He kept his eye on his mirrors now, making switchbacks and U-turns just in case.

"Either they're off me," said Dez, "or they've got powers of invisibility."

"You just keep cruising that bank in Chestnut Hill," Doug told him. "Go in whenever you can and make change."

"I've eaten lunch in my truck across the street every day this week. How's the other thing coming?"

"Good. Trying to figure out what weekend now, pick a movie. Going over *Premiere* magazine's 'Summer Movie Preview' issue like it's the *Racing Form,* trying to pick a winner."

"*Striptease,*" said Dez.

"I know. Demi Moore. My dick already bought a ticket. But June twenty-eighth, that's not soon enough."

"*Mission: Impossible*. Theme song remade by Adam Clayton and Larry Mullen."

"Yeah, Tom Cruise got my vote. But that's Memorial Day weekend. Jem wants it now, now, now."

"You don't need to rush it."

"No. But it's coming together fast on its own."

"As good as you thought?"

"Check my math. Theater's main screens seat, say, five hundred capacity. Two good afternoon matinees, plus the seven and ten p.m. shows, that's two thousand Saturday and two thousand Sunday, plus another thou Friday night. Five thousand numb asses per theater, say there's four outta ten screens running the newest movies. Just four out of the ten screens—twenty thousand asses and mouths. Eight bucks per ass at night, five seventy-five per in the day, and then there's the food. A popcorn, Pepsi, and Goobers alone will take you up over ten dollars, but then there's a Pizzeria Uno and Taco Bell in the lobby—with no restaurants nearby. Half a mil, easy, that's our floor, Dez. With a quarter to you for just playing decoy."

JEM'S PART WAS THE supply: weapons, vests, clothes, masks.

Gloansy's was the vehicles, the work cars and the switch cars.

Doug was the planner, the architect, the author. He was also the worrier, the perfectionist, and the cautious one. The sober one, trusted for his sense of self-preservation.

The next few days found him being super careful, spying the can guards on different routes, unrelated to the movie theater, just getting the nuances of their routine down. Also, he needed to satisfy himself that they were not plants, not FBI agents playing guards, paranoid as he was that the G was onto them. He needed to be certain that these were real wage earners with families to go home to at night. So he cooped down the road from Pinnacle's vault facility—at a safe distance from their cameras and fences; it was not unknown for these depots to hold eight figures on an overnight—and eyeballed the passing cars, looking for the guards heading home. A plum Saturn coupe stopped his heart once, but it wore no *Breathe!* bumper sticker.

He spotted the guard with the white brush mustache behind the wheel of a blue Jeep Cherokee and fell in behind him, trailing the Jeep to Randolph, to a modest split-level near an elementary school. He watched the uniformed guard leaf through his mail in the driveway as a Toyota Camry pulled in behind, the wife returning home from work.

Doug watched the guy with his happy, broad-hipped wife, walking to his aging house and overgrown lawn, and saw all the things this guy had to lose. Casing a life was different now, post–Claire Keesey. But these same pangs of guilt gave him an idea, and suddenly he knew exactly how they were going to pull this job.

He got lost trying to get back out to I-93 and found himself stuck in downtown Canton, Claire Keesey's hometown. He drove past the high school, past leafy trees and widely spaced houses with pampered lawns, the evening becoming too pregnant with associations. He felt chased as he steered out fast for the highway, antsy about returning home. Instead, he detoured to The Braintree 10.

He circled the bottom of the hill first, below the complex. The twin screens of an old drive-in theater remained there, decomposing, the property now split between a driving range and the parking lot for park-and-fly shuttle service to Logan Airport. Near a row of batting cages was a road barred by steel swing gates, secured by a key lock and chain. Doug drove back up to the theater parking lot, finding the outlet there, also gated and locked, the unused road winding down the weedy hillside to the batting cages in an S. Both Forbes and Grandview were narrow, twin-lane roads, the parking lot a nightmare to get into or out of during weekend prime time, making the emergency road necessary. Its direct access set Doug's mind jumping again.

He went inside and bought a ticket like a citizen, then laid out another fin for a personal pan pizza. He killed time wandering around the wide lobby, spotting an office door marked No Admittance half-hidden behind a three-part *Independence Day* cardboard display showing the White House being blown to smithereens. On one wall was a framed portrait of the young manager, Mr. Cidro Kosario, thin-necked and smiling in an ill-fitting suit, alongside his welcome message and his signature endorsing General Cinemas' "Commitment to Theater Excellence."

An advance poster for *The Rock*—an action movie about an old man who escaped from prison—worked on Doug like an omen, scaring him into his theater. The last preview before *Mulholland Falls* was for *Twister*. When the audience cheered a cow flying across the screen and continued to chatter about it over the feature's opening credits, Doug saw a big opening weekend coming and smiled there in the dark.

NEW HAMPSHIRE WAS THE state where Massachusetts residents shopped to avoid paying a sales tax. It was also the state where Massachusetts car thieves went to steal cars.

The reason for this was LoJack, the vehicle-recovery service, a transponder unit installed inside cars that pinged its location to police once the tracking service was activated. Not a problem for joyriders and chop shops with a couple of hours' turnover time, but if you needed work vehicles for anything longer than an overnight, no good. LoJack used no window decals to warn thieves, and the transponder and its battery backup together were about the size of a sardine tin, small enough to be hidden anywhere inside the car.

Massachusetts, Rhode Island, and Connecticut all used LoJack, but not New Hampshire or Vermont. So: boost the car in nearby New Hampshire, then slap on a pair of stolen Massachusetts plates.

Doug drove Gloansy up-country. They needed three vehicles total for the job, and today's target was the work car. They were looking for a minivan with tinted windows, Gloansy favoring the Dodge Caravan, though he would settle for a Plymouth Voyager or similar. Even a Ford Windstar, though not the new 1996 model. Ford had begun embedding transponders in the plastic heads of ignition keys, meaning that, even with the steering wheel column punched, the starting system remained disabled without a corresponding key. Gloansy carried a volt meter to defeat the system, but measuring the resistance between wires under the dash and joining the matching resistors cost him an extra thirty seconds, a lifetime in daylight car theft.

"Fucking with my livelihood," said Gloansy, working the Caprice's factory radio, the stations dying one by one as they pushed farther north. "Like when robots put guys out of work at the factory—trying to make me obsolete."

Doug said, "What's a car thief with a young family to support gonna do?"

"Start *hijacking*, I guess. Keep the keys and roll the driver into the trunk. Then car owners'll be *begging* to get rid of these immobilizer systems."

"All of us," said Doug, "getting outmoded. These wires." Old telegraph poles spaced the country road, phone wires running taut. "Money juicing through them as we speak, right there over our heads. Credit card money, dollar signs flowing like electricity. Gotta be some way to tap into that. Turn all this one-zero-zero bullshit into actual cash."

Gloansy had bought a couple of sour pickles at a country store and was chomping them like bananas, wiping his fingers on the Caprice's blue velour seats. "Like how?"

"You got me. When it comes to that, then I'll know I'm done."

They found what they needed in a parking lot outside a stadium-sized Wal-Mart. A dull green Caravan with tinted back windows, parked a quarter mile from the store. The new Caravans had sliding doors on both sides, as well as removable rear seats, which was better than perfect.

A child's car seat in back was considered bad luck by many boosters, but not Gloansy. He whistled his way across the lot to the Caravan's door, working with dried Krazy Glue on his fingers to queer his prints. It was too warm for gloves. A baseball jacket in early May was suspect enough, but he needed the bulky sleeves for his tools.

Gloansy was at the door only a few seconds before popping the handle. He was a good minute behind the wheel before the engine started up, long for Gloansy, but then Doug saw him toss a red Club steering-wheel lock in back and understood. The Club itself was basically impervious, but the steering wheel owners clamped it to was made of soft rubber tubing, so Gloansy left the Club intact and cut through the wheel around it. Then he punched the ignition barrel on the steering with a slide hammer, started up the Caravan, and rolled past Doug without a wave, only the merest hint of a froglike smile.

Gloansy: A good enough guy, and yet there was something slick and sweaty about him that threatened to rub off, his surface eagerness masking something cold and reptilian beneath, an interior life just smart enough to keep itself hidden from view. It was no surprise to Doug that Gloansy had been the first of them to father a kid, but Monsignor Dez would have been Doug's money pick as the first one to get married.

DOUG STOOD TWISTED OFF the curb, leaning across Shyne's doll legs, trying to get the frayed blue Caprice seat-belt strap fed through the back of the car seat so that he could secure the clasp. He tried hard not to curse, ignoring the little girl's unwavering gaze and her sour breath, ignoring even her hand rubbing his cheek, his neck, his hair—all of it infuriating as he tried to make this fucking thing fit.

Krista turned around in the front seat. "Sometimes you gotta kneel on the thing. Kneel on it."

He was a fucking centimeter away from catching the lock when Shyne slipped her finger inside his ear, and in shaking her off, he whacked his head on the car ceiling and roared like he was going to explode. She didn't cry, nothing, her face still, her skin waxy like pesticide-glazed fruit. There was a slight odor of spoil about her, of sour juice, of urine.

Not his child. Not his problem.

He dropped all his weight on the sides of the seat and with one final effort made the clasp bite, then ducked out fast and arched his back, feeling those red arrows of pain from the TV commercials. Shyne looked at him the same way she looked at everything: as though for the first time. He swung the car door shut on her and she didn't jump.

"Hell is Jem?"

Krista looked out her open window. "No idea."

Doug went around to his side, scanning the street as he went, then climbed in, slowly rebending his back.

"I really appreciate this, Duggy," Krista said, sitting next to him like she belonged there. "Shyne's had this cough, and the only appointment they could give me was right away. I felt funny asking."

Right. "How's she doing on those other things?" he ventured, starting up the engine. "You were going to get her checked out."

"She's doing great now, she's really starting to come along. Out of her shell. She's just shy. Like her mother, right?"

Doug nodded at the attempted joke, pulling out past Jem's blue Flamer parked curbside. "There's his car."

"Yeah," she said. "I don't know. He's probably hungover anyway."

"I thought you said he wasn't home."

"If he was, I mean." She looked out her window, close-bitten fingers at her worm-thin lips. "He's not reliable. Not like you."

Doug dropped fast to Medford Street, still hoping to sit out the morning in the parking lot of The Braintree 10. Shyne watched him through his rearview with that same passive, sad-eyed gaze.

"Gloansy's wedding's coming up, huh?" said Krista.

Doug understood now the nature of this medical emergency. He turned out along the wharves, pissed, pushing the Caprice.

"Nice, you being Nicky's godfather." She flicked at the musky orange Hooters deodorizer swaying from the cigarette lighter. "Jem says you might be going alone."

"Did he."

"Joanie said we bridesmaids can wear whatever we want, except white. So I bought this new dress I saw downtown, dripping off a mannequin. Backless, black. Comes down like this." Her hands were moving low over her chest, but he didn't turn to look. "Rides up high on the sides of each leg. Like a dancing dress, but formal. Sexy."

He rolled under the highway past the Neck, crossing into Somerville toward the free clinic, trying to be impervious. *There is no way to compromise the hulk of an armored vehicle without at the same time destroying its contents.*

"A cocktail dress," she went on. "Which is funny, because I won't be drinking any cocktails in it. I gave up drinking, Duggy." She was watching him, her body shuddering with the potholes. "This time for good."

Doug thinking, *The can is only vulnerable through its human operators . . .*

22
THE VISIT

MALDEN CENTER SMELLED LIKE a village set on the shore of an ocean of hot coffee. With the coffee bean warehouse so close, sitting in Dunkin' Donuts was a little redundant, like chewing nicotine gum in a tobacco field. But that's what they were doing, Frank G. in a soft black sweatshirt, nursing a decaf, and Doug M. looking rumpled in a gray shirt with blue baseball-length sleeves, rolling a bottle of Mountain Dew between his hands.

"So," Frank G. said, "what's up, Sport? Let's have it."

Doug shrugged. "You know how it is."

"I know that I get nervous whenever a guy strings together a bunch of no-shows."

"Yeah," said Doug, admitting it, settling back into his chair. "Work's been a bitch."

"You should take on a wife, studly. And a house to keep up, and two kids who never wanna go to bed. And yet and still, I find the time to make it down here three or four nights a week."

"Right," said Doug, nodding, agreeing.

"It the romance?"

"Nah, no."

"She have a problem with you not drinking?"

"What? No, nothing like that."

Frank nodded. "So it's over already."

"Over?" Doug had blabbed way too much last time. "It's not *over* over."

"What is it then?"

"Guess it's on hold."

"She's done with it, but you're still into her."

"No." Doug shook his head. "Wrong-o. Other way around."

"Okay. My concern is you trading one addiction for another. Like an even exchange, going up to the counter at Jordan Marsh with your receipt. *This booze thing isn't working out for me so well. I want to trade it in for a pretty girl.* And they initial your receipt and off you go. Then the new one—the *positive* one, right?

'Cause it's *love,* man. This *new* one up and dumps you, and what you're left with then is a garage-sized hole in your daily life."

"Christ, Frank—I skipped a couple of meetings. My bad. I been real busy."

"Busy, bullshit. This is the heart and soul of your week right here. This is the oil that greases the engine. Without this you have nothing, and you should know that by now. Everything else will just go away."

"This is like friggin' high school. You show up on Tuesday, they yell at you for skipping Monday."

"This isn't anything like school." Frank G.'s anger surprised Doug. "I look like your truant officer? You don't go to meetings—that means I get to bust you up about it. That's how this works."

Doug looked at the table and nodded. He waited.

And waited.

"Fine." Frank G. checked his watch. "Let's cut this short then."

Doug looked up. "What?"

"You come and make time for me at meetings, I'll make time for you. As it is, if I hustle, I can make it home for my kids' bedtime, read them a story for a change."

Doug shrugged, hands high. "Frank, I missed some fucking meetings here and there—"

"Do the work, then you get the perks."

"Perks? Did you say perks? Sitting in a Dunkin' Donuts in Malden Center at eight thirty at night, this is a perk?"

Which was stupid, stupid. Frank G. stared at Doug, then reached for his yellow windbreaker, starting to stand.

"Frank," said Doug. "Frank, look, man, I was kidding. That didn't come out the way it sounded."

"See you in church." Frank G. was checking his pockets for keys. "Maybe."

Frank was walking past him. Doug had fucked up. "I'm going to see my old man tomorrow," he blurted.

Frank G. weighed his keys in his hand as though they were Doug himself, a fish he might throw back. All Frank knew about Mac was that he was in jail. "How long's it been?"

"Good long time. He asked me to come in, see him about something."

"Uh-huh. And how's it gonna go?"

"Power of positive thinking, right?"

"A lot of it's up to you."

"Then it's gonna go splendid. And he'll go back into his cell, and I'm good for another year or so. That's how it's gonna go."

Frank G. nodded and started for the door. "See you 'round."

* * *

THE NAME MCI CEDAR JUNCTION sounded like one of those corporate-brand stadiums, with naming rights purchased by a long distance phone company or a logging concern. MCI stood for Massachusetts Correctional Institution. When Doug's father started his tour there, the place was called MCI Walpole, after its host town, but at some point during the mid-1980s, Walpole's residents realized that sharing their name with the state's toughest prison—it was also home to the DDU, the Departmental Disciplinary Unit, known as The Pit—placed a slight drag on property values and sued successfully to have it renamed after a long-abandoned railroad station.

The complex was originally constructed in the 1950s to replace the old Charlestown Prison. Entering it brought all sorts of associations flooding into Doug's mind, first and foremost his stay at MCI Norfolk, a prison still named after its host town just a couple of miles away. Norfolk was medium security, Level 4, with 80 percent of its inmates serving time for violent crimes. Cedar Junction was Level 6.

He paced in the waiting room ahead of his scheduled meet, the only male in a group of six visitors. The combined smell of their perfumes reminded him of the Haymarket on a hot, late Saturday, produce fallen between the carts, spoiling and trampled underfoot. Three black women sat heavily, depressedly, with blood-threaded eyes and bruised stares. The two white women looked hard, worn down to the core. Blue denim, sweatshirts, and bralessness were on the Prohibited Clothing List. Evidently stretch pants and cleavage-canoeing knit tops were not.

Wall postings warned against physical contact, and a brand-new sign on the door, UNDERPANTS MUST BE WORN, made Doug's arms itch.

Only one person visited Doug while he was in stir, and that had been Krista, every third weekend. How grateful he had been—though he never admitted it—for those brief conversations, at least at first. But once he started getting into AA inside and taking the program seriously—how she had changed in his eyes.

They were called inside and Doug sat alone in his partition, getting his head together. It was almost worth the visit just for the leaving, being able to walk back out of the prison again, getting into his car, driving away. Stopping at a gas station for a soda on the way home: simple freedom, an impossible dream within these walls.

Visiting Mac was like a dentist appointment and license renewal at the RMV all wrapped up in one. A trial. Something to dread, something to endure. Though in truth Doug had a good setup here, and he knew it. He controlled the contact, having Mac brought to him like a damaged library book pulled from general circulation.

Mac's shadow fell over him, and there was always that little kick when Doug saw the old crook again, always a ripple in his fabric of the hero he once knew, the strong man who used to call him Little Partner. Not the selfish *me* machine who had gone down sixteen years ago and lived mainly as a voice in Doug's head ever since.

Mac sat in his chair with a smart smile, a rooster sucking all his strength into his chest. But things were settling in him, Doug noticed: the middle getting thicker, the neck loosening up, his face sinking deeper into his skull. The casino-dice eyes that dared you to trust them, telling you straight out, *Play with me long enough and you'll lose*. The smile that was always more for him than for you. And his big Irish gourd, the shiny scalp oranged with freckles, now scored with pink treatment scars.

Mac straddled the chair, his proud, strawberry arm hair lighter now, nearly invisible. He always acted as though they were meeting on equal terms—as though their relationship had some balance—and Doug felt as sorry for him as he did for any trapped thing, having been there himself. Seeing Mac once a year was like flipping through a scrapbook, watching hair go, the features fading, blemishes rising. The resemblance between father and son, always remarkable, haunted Doug now more than ever. Looking into that partition was like look-ing into a mirror twenty years deep. The traces of his mother that Doug used to find in himself—that he once took great pains to seek out—were long disap-peared.

"Look at you." This was what Mac always said.

"Dad," said Doug, that word he got to use for about twenty minutes each year. "How's it going?"

"How ya been?"

Doug nodded. "Good. You?"

Mac shrugged. "Still here."

"Looks that way. Been getting the money?"

"Money's good. Makes things easier. Though it ain't that bad in here nei-ther. You know how we got things arranged."

The hive of Cedar Junction was home to a colony of Townies who, with the assistance of a few friendly guards, got most of what they needed. There were good and bad assignments in the prison industries program, like laundry or making license plates, whatever they did for their seventy-three cents an hour.

Doug nodded to him, pointed to his own head. "That it?"

Mac touched it like it was hot. "The skin cancer, yeah. They just keep burn-ing off bits of it. Gets me into the infirmary now and then, which is good. Passes the time."

"Where you getting all this sun?"

"This is pre-1980 damage. Shoulda worn my scally cap more, I guess. It's not the bad cancer, now. This is just freckles on a mutiny. I'm still as strong as the stink in Chelsea." He inhaled like he could smell it now. "So, Jem talked to you?"

"Jem told me this, yeah."

"Never get lonely with him around. In here all the time. Funny kid when he gets going. Excitable like his dad. What you gotta do with a Coughlin is, you gotta keep that carrot hanging out in front of his beady eyes. 'Cause the stick in back, it don't register."

"Got it," said Doug.

Mac pretended to work on some food in his teeth, studying Doug, his only child. Whatever he saw, he kept his observations to himself.

"I should have come to see you more," Doug said, having to say something.

"Well, it's a long trip, coming out here to the country."

"Been doing things, you know. This and that. Time goes by."

"Hey. You're talking to a clock here." Still looking at Doug, one year older. "I didn't blow it with you, Duggy. What I hear, you're doing awright."

Doug shrugged. "Day to day."

"Older I get, the more I think about the years I missed. Fuckin' shame."

"Yeah." Doug tugged at the shelf, wondering how much longer.

"I think I know why you're pissed at me all the time."

Doug sat up a little. "Yeah? Am I?"

Mac crossed his arms over his blue scrub shirt, his chest now sagged back into his midsection. "Me losing your mother's house."

Doug rubbed the back of his head. "Nah. I don't care about that no more."

"Those legal bills, Duggy. Fuck. I had a shot at staying out—some nervous witnesses, a few changed stories—but you know no court-assigned PD could do it. You claim indigence, you might as well drive yourself to prison the day the trial starts."

"It's just that—you never had anything solid put away. With all you took. It's like you never imagined a rainy day."

Mac absorbed this criticism along with whatever else he was drawing off Doug. "I heard some knucklehead crew took a hostage in that Kenmore Square thing."

Doug said, "Yeah. I read that too."

"Bonehead play. Hostages bring a lot of heat. Better to take the pinch, should it come. Less of a bill to pay, and you earn your stripes, you come out stronger."

Doug looked at the patches taken out of Mac's head, thinking, *Are you coming out stronger?* "Well," Doug said, vigilant for guards within listening range, "like I said, I read about it."

"Seemed like a good haul, though."

"I suppose it might have been."

"And how's about old Boozo and his crew?"

"Gone away forever. Boozo's on a shelf in some federal pen in Kentucky or somewheres. Not like here. No connections. No home away from home."

"His kid, what's his name?"

"Jackie."

"There's a fuckup. Not like my boy."

"Jackie's gone too, and he's not missed."

"RICO, huh? That racketeering stuff?"

"RICO was twenty years ago. G's got a bigger stick now, a much heavier stick. Called the Hobbs Act. Anything interstate, interfering with any commerce like that. They don't need to prove conspiracy now."

"Getting tough out there."

"I guess. But when was it easy, right?"

Mac smiled. He was trying to read Doug's face like words might appear. "Jem says he's worried about you."

Doug was beginning to understand the eyeballing. "Is he."

"Says you're doing some things, acting some ways . . . he's concerned."

"Uh-huh. Was it his idea for us to meet again, or yours?"

"Both."

Doug crossed his arms, unused to getting played by Jem. "So here I am then. Presenting myself for inspection to show you everything's fine, thanks for asking. Next topic?"

"He's worried about you not having your eye on the ball."

"I'm gonna tell you something. Him looking after me? That's like you looking after me, okay? You wanna push it, that's what you're gonna hear. You mentioned something, I think, about a hostage, earlier? Who do you think was *solely* responsible for that little fiasco?"

"You still keeping dry?"

"Fuckin' . . . next topic. How was your Christmas?"

Mac scratched the back of his neck, looking lazily at the guards on either end, then leaning closer to the glass. "Sixteen months."

Doug nodded, waiting for more. "And? What? Sixteen months, what?"

"Sixteen more months for me, here. I'm getting out."

"Out? Out of what?" Doug was sitting up now. "What do you mean, *out?*"

"Out, Little Partner." Mac nodding, smiling. "Gonna be you and me again."

All feeling flushed from Doug's face. "What are you talking about?"

Big, satisfied shrug. "Been in the works for a while. Parole board's under pressure to free up room for all the young shoot-firsts coming up. Either that or build a new prison, you know? Old outta-step bank robber, never even seen an ATM—what's he gonna do, right?" Big grin. "Hey, I didn't even tell Jem. Didn't want to jinx it. Would of kept you updated, I'd seen you more."

He was getting out. Mac was getting out.

"The neighborhood, Dad—it's all gone. The Town. There's nothing left."

"You trying to talk me into staying? We'll get it back."

"Get back what? There's nothing . . . it's all changed, understand? It's *gone*."

"You've been doing good, I can see that. Some bumps in the road, but okay. Now we're gonna take things to the next level."

Doug's chair was no good for him anymore. He needed to stand, to move, but the room rules kept him low and squirming—panicking like the old man was walking out *right now*.

"I'm gonna get back your mother's house, Duggy."

Doug shook his head, hot. "You don't even know, Dad. You couldn't even begin to afford it."

Mac smiled his smile. "I'll get it back."

"What you think, you're gonna walk in, have one of your famous sit-downs? Like you're still the king thief? Nobody's afraid of you there, Dad. Nobody even knows you anymore. A few old guys, sitting outside the Foodmaster— they might shake your hand. They might doff the cap. It's not like it was. The code is gone. The old ways, all of it. Gone."

"Ain't gonna be just like it was, Duggy," said Mac, the old *ka-ching* returning to his eyes, popping up like dollar-sign tabs on an old-fashioned cash register. "Gonna be better. Let the G bring their big sticks. You two, you and Jem, working under me . . . ?"

Doug stared. Mac was getting out.

DOUG DROVE HARD INTO the night, turning out the ZR-1 along the 95-to-93 interstate circuit, doing ninety-mile-an-hour doughnuts around the city. Sometimes he imagined he had taken all the bad energy of his youth and harnessed it in that 405-horse, all-aluminum V-8. He watched the lights in his rearview mirror, thinking about the G following him, or even Jem, when in reality it was the ghost of his father. The old crook had been chasing him all along.

Mac and all the old-school armored-car guys and stickup men—they were the neighborhood Evel Knievels. Daredevils who went after cans instead of strapping rocket packs to their backs. Winding up short of the mark was just another part of the job—a prison hitch their equivalent of a hospital stay. That was what was coming Doug's way: Mac's jailbird disease. The years being burned off him like cancer. Doug's father was hard time incarnate.

Sixteen months. For Doug, it might as well have been sixteen days.

* * *

HE RETURNED TO THE city in the Caprice, parking it illegally in the alley behind Peterborough. Streetlights and the glow of the city were just enough to help him find his way to Claire Keesey's garden, hop her fence, open her unlocked wooden chest.

With a short-handled spade he dug into the overturned soil. Four feet deep seemed good enough for short-term storage.

The walk back from the trunk of the Caprice with the few hundred thou packed in auto parts boxes inside thick plastic sheeting—that was the only really chancy part. The Fens was home to a lot of unsavories on warm nights, and his digging had made noise. But the traffic on Boylston Street provided adequate cover, masking the thump of the heavy boxes at the bottom of the hole. He looked at his small fortune a moment before covering it over with dirt and felt like he should be saying a prayer. He couldn't see the one-to-one between visiting his father and moving his stash from Nana Seavey's garage to Claire Keesey's garden, but where money was concerned, Doug listened to his instincts. Things were changing. That was all he knew for sure.

Call her.

He longed to. This, here—the treasure he was stashing in her garden— seemed like a commitment. He patted his pockets for coins, even thinking what he might say into a pay phone, inviting her to the wedding tomorrow. Showing up with her on his arm. It was pleasing to think about as he drove away. Almost like he could go through with it.

23
RECEPTION

DOUG SAT HUNCHED OVER his soda water lime, his bow tie undone, watching Gloansy and Joanie, groom and bride, work the far end of the VFW hall together. The new Mrs. Joanie Magloan was squeezing and smooching everyone in sight, a Bud Light in her hand, while Gloansy got his palm pumped by every wisecracking husband and father in the place, laughing too empty, too hard. Meanwhile, little Nicky Magloan was over at his grandma's table, his freckled face and nonstop hands coated with wedding-slash-baptism cake frosting.

The Monsignor yanked out a chair next to Doug and dropped into it. "Well," he said, "the music sucks."

"Desmond," welcomed Doug, rousing out of his pissy mood.

Monkey-suited Dez looked bleary behind his trademark rims. Jem had been treating the rest of the wedding party to rounds of Car Bombs: a half-pint of Guinness with a shot of Baileys and Jameson dropped in.

The girl Dez had brought with him, Denise or Patrice or something, a thin-faced but flabby-armed 411 operator, rose from her seat across the dance floor and started toward the bathroom. Doug said, "You left her alone over there."

"Because she won't mix! She doesn't know anybody, and this group—how can you introduce outsiders? And fucking Jem—thinks he's funny, working 'bat wings' into the conversation, like she doesn't already know she has heavy arms. Asshole." Dez wrapped himself in the flaps of his tuxedo jacket like a cold boy inside a black blanket. "It's my own fault for trying to bring someone. I see *you* came stag."

Doug shrugged and sat back. He tried to imagine himself there with Claire—huddled together at the rear of the room, happily making fun of other people.

"Smarter than I am anyway," said Dez. "She's miserable, I'm miserable. I already called her a cab."

Doug said, "Here comes the happy couple."

"Yeah, how about that dress?"

"Nice. If you like mosquito netting."

"I was talking about the neckline, the lack thereof."

Joanie was the type of girl who never missed a chance to show off the twins. "She's sturdy," Doug said, "and this is her big day."

She bustled over and Doug stood for a kiss, going cheek to cheek against her red-veined rosacea and getting a generous chest press for his trouble. One or two beers in, Joanie was always good for a ten-dollar hello. He received a chin squeeze on top of that, as thanks for being Nicky's godfather.

"Joanie, I don't know," said Doug, nodding over at the cake-smeared kid. "I'm not sure that baptism took. Little freckle's still got the devil in him."

She pretended to smack him, then put Dez on the receiving end of another friendly tit rub. "Great dress," he said, fixing his glasses as though they were steamed. "Lots of fluff on there."

"Itches like a fuckin' disease," she confided, scanning the room as she shimmied up the twins before taking another swallow and hustling on. "Don't you guys lose those jackets or wander off nowheres. Pictures in a little while."

Gloansy stepped up in her place, rapping fists, looking foggy and dazed. "Fuckin' shoot me now," he said.

Doug said, "She mentioned pictures."

"I know, I know. But it's her wedding, man. I'm already ducking out on my own honeymoon, ain't I? Your wife gonna let you do that?"

Dez set him straight. "Elisabeth Shue will have absolutely no say in the matter."

Doug said, "Okay, Dez is blotto, but you better not be. Where's Jem?"

"Fuck knows. Lighting fires somewhere."

"Try to keep him cool too, all right?"

Doug smacked fists with Gloansy and watched him slink away after his wife. He never liked that Joanie knew about their exploits—assuming she knew at least as much as Krista learned from Jem, which was much too much. Doug never understood that, telling your girlfriend, your wife, your Irish twin. At times he wondered how much his mother must have known—how much had been enough for her to leave. This was another reason they were so tough on outsiders. Heisting was the sort of thing you had to be born into.

Dez said, "I better go check on Patrice," and started toward the doors, walking chair back to chair back. Doug sat down again and watched an old couple dancing alone out on the parquet floor, cheek to cheek, the photographer shadowing them, flashing away. The shutterbug wore a cheap magician's tux, his gold hair slicked back, something iffy about him in general. He was also the videographer, whose prying lens Doug had spent half the afternoon avoiding.

"This seat taken?"

Another prying lens he had been avoiding. Krista sat down and Doug focused on the clumsy dancers, clapping politely when the swing tune ended.

She sipped her soda water lime, making certain he saw her do so. "Any idea why Dez's date is crying in the bathroom?"

Doug shook his head. "I don't think she feels welcome."

"You haven't said anything about my dress."

"It's nice," he said, not having looked at her since she sat down. He was in a cruel mood. That usually warned people away, but not Krista.

"They say it's good luck at a wedding if a bridesmaid and a groomsman hook up."

A new tune started quietly, the annoying DJ saying something about a special request. "Well, your girl Joanie needs all the good luck she can get."

She toasted that, drinking again, then leaning closer. "You know, I don't think we ever did it straight. Sober, I mean. Think about it. Even once, all those years, I don't think we just looked each other in the eye and went at it."

He heard, from the direction of the bar, voices cheering his name now and saw bottles and pint glasses going up in salute. He recognized the song then, "With or Without You," the tune Doug had sung at Dearden's wedding.

More cheers and catcalls followed, and Doug nodded through his anger, glowering at the crumbs and gravy stains on the tablecloth.

Krista touched his elbow with hers. "Dance with me?"

"I don't think I'm in a dancing mood."

"It's a slow one. I bet I could change your mood. We don't even have to *dance* dance, just stand together."

He looked up halfway, saw a few couples out there moving slow. He felt sluggish, like a candle burning down, the flame winking out.

She laid her hand over his, rubbing the raised veins there. "You know you sang this song to me?"

She turned his hand over, revealing its softer palm, nestling hers inside. Doug went blank for a while, determinedly so, until her hand slipped away again. She sat back.

"Maybe I should ask Dez then."

Doug shrugged, feeling snuffed out. "Maybe you should."

Dez was cutting back across the room now, as though summoned by the music. He smiled their way, then in response to some motion of Krista's, pointed to his own ruffled chest and changed course, heading over.

"Hey," he said, checking Doug, uncertain of what he was stepping into.

"She leave?" asked Krista.

"Yep," Dez sighed. "She's gone."

Krista swung her legs out from beneath the table, the dress falling off them.

"Doug won't dance with me. I need to dance."

It took Dez a moment to realize he was being asked. He checked Doug to see if it was okay. All Doug did was drink his drink.

"Don't look at him like he's your boss," she said, getting to her feet. "If you want to dance with me, take me out there."

"Sure," said Dez, emboldened, seizing her offered hand. She finished her drink, pointedly setting the empty glass back down next to Doug's. He was certain she had a look for him as she started away, but Doug wouldn't give her the satisfaction of a glance. This was what happened when people break up but don't leave each other, he thought. Scars itch and get picked at. Scabs form but never heal.

Jem came up along the edge of the dance floor—he the solar center of this never-leaving, the rest of them spinning in his orbit of nostalgia, his scarred-knuckle sentimentality, his bullying and unweaned devotion to the old ways of the Town. He was jacketless, half his shirttail hanging out, a High Life tangled in his fingers. Psycho glee in his face, white fire in his eyes. "Hey, to the bar. Toast to Gloansy."

Dez and Krista hadn't gotten far, and Doug saw Dez let go of her hand. "You already made your toast," said Doug.

"That was for the corpses here, you know." He came around and pulled Doug's underarm, lifting him out of the chair, Doug smelling adrenaline on him as they moved. "How we lookin', huh? Everything cool?"

"Everything's cool."

"I got the pieces, I got the vests." He was close, talking in Doug's ear as he pulled him along. "Got jumpsuits from this air-conditioning repair company outta Arlington—fucking perfect."

"We got a lot of work to do tonight. Cutting the fence, finding a truck to boost. Said you'd go easy, right?"

"Ah, sleep—fuck needs it?"

Alarming, the blue-white snap in Jem's naturally fucked-up eyes. It was raining outside, but there was no mist in Jem's penny-brown hair. "Where you been? What you been doing?"

The grin. "It's a party, man. Great occasion." He pointed out the World War II medals under glass behind the bar. "Ever tell you my gramps was a war hero?"

"Only every time you drink Car Bombs."

The laugh. "Hey—am I fuckin' crazy, or what the hell was the Monsignor doing holding my sister's hand?"

The others assembled around Gloansy now, the commotion drawing in more guests and even a few ladies. "Just cool it," said Doug, "all right?"

Jem snarled a laugh—then broke from Doug's side to rush up on Gloansy, fist cocked, following through with a fake sucker punch in slow, hard motion. Gloansy's head snapped back, his toad lips spraying beer over their audience, with Jem's cackle leading the dowsed guys' laughter, the routine succeeding in scattering all the ladies except Krista. She remained close to Dez, trying to throw Doug looks.

"Here we go," said Jem, parting the group, revealing a cluster of a dozen or so High Life longnecks, uncapped and waiting.

They went fast in the confusion, passed around like rifles during an ambush. Doug found one in his hand, cold and smooth. Jem said into his ear, "Gloansy's big day, don't be a fag."

Doug looked at the bottle in his hand, its grip familiar and icily sure. He missed most of the ribald toast, the bottle sweating cold into his hand—Jem saying something to the effect that while marriage and fatherhood were known to change a man, he was confident that Gloansy would always remain faithfully, resolutely, 100 percent gay. It ended with another explosion of drunken laughter and the old Irish salute: *Here's how*.

Doug's bottle got clinked hard by Jem, who then turned his up to the ceiling and opened his throat to drain it at a swallow. Every bottle went up and empty around him.

Doug's life now: a drink he couldn't swallow; a fortune he couldn't spend; a girl he couldn't date.

It wasn't the thirst that shook loose the first few boulders of the cave-in: it was this self-disgust. This worthlessness. And the feverishness of his friends, the box they had him trapped and suffocating in.

Then the bottle was gone from his hand—Dez at his elbow, draining Doug's beer with a wet-eyed wink of confederacy. Krista wiped her lips behind him, an empty in her hand. When she was drunk, she wanted to be sober; sober, she wanted to be drunk.

Doug was halfway across School Street outside when Jem's voice turned him around. "Yo!" he heard through the rain, Jem holding the door to the VFW post open at the top of the brick steps. "'S'up? Where you headed?"

"Nowhere," Doug told him, moving on. "That's my problem. See you at midnight."

THE NAME NEXT TO the doorbell, hand-printed in all capitals, read KEESEY, C. The door opened wide, and her eyes followed suit.

"Hey," Doug said, breathing mist into the rain. "Wanna go for a walk?"

She looked him over, his soaked tuxedo. She was barefoot with rosy pink toenails, wearing loose, maroon shorts and a soft gray T-shirt, warm and dry. She checked the street behind him, as though for an idling limousine. "What are you doing?"

"I was just in the neighborhood."

She stepped aside. "Come in here."

He moved onto her white-tile landing, arms held away from his trunk like sopping branches. "Kick off the shoes," she said, all business, pointing him ahead. "Hang your jacket in the shower."

In damp socks he padded over a lemon-carpeted living room to a bathroom of old black tile. He peeled off his jacket and draped it over the curtain rod, the pale pink shower curtain billowing, the sash of the frosted-glass window raised a few inches on the rain-swept back alley.

Back out in the living room, clothes clinging, he took a good look around. Prints on the wall, the Maxell-tape guy being blown back into his chair, a couple kissing on a street in Paris. Her diplomas, high school and college. She had a decent Sony stereo set on a steel-wire hardware-store shelf unit, some CDs spilled around it. A cozy breakfast table stood outside the kitchenette, half of it taken up by mail, a checkbook, and statements in sliced envelopes, banded together. The centerpiece was a large wineglass with a small pink flower floating in it, which Doug looked at twice, believing it to be the glass from their night in and out of the Tap.

She returned from her bedroom and made to toss him a clean, mocha towel—then pulled it back, holding it hostage. "Why haven't you called me?"

He was seeping into her carpet. "Because I'm an idiot. Because I'm a jerk."

"You *are* a jerk." She tossed him the towel.

He buried his face in it, hiding a moment, then went to work on his hair. He blotted uselessly at his pants, water running off him. "I probably shouldn't have come."

"Unannounced? Dripping rain all over my place? No, probably not. Now sit down."

"You sure?"

"Sit."

He eased down into the soft tan leather sofa, trying to minimize the damage. She sat on the coffee table opposite him, gripping its edge, bare knees facing him.

"Are you coming from a wedding or something?"

"I am."

"Yours?"

He smiled only at the thought of it. "No."

"Your date dumped you?"

"She sure would have, if I'd've brought one."

She studied his eyes, finding no lie in them, then wondering about the accuracy of her own internal polygraph. "Look at my hectic Sunday afternoon.

What are you doing going to weddings alone? Why haven't you *called*?"

But before he could answer, she got to her feet and thrust out her hands, stopping everything. "You know what? Don't even answer. It doesn't matter. Because I'm past all this. I am past the dating games, the waiting games."

"I'm not playing games—"

"I finally figured out that the reason my life feels so out of my control is because I haven't *taken* control. Of it. And that is something I have to change."

"Look, don't—can I tell you something? This is how messed up I am. Waiting outside your door just now—every time I'm about to see you, I tell myself, 'She's not going to be as pretty as you remember her. She's not going to be as sweet. She's not going to be as great.' And every time I'm wrong."

She looked at the floor and blew a strand of hair out of her eyes. "I guess you're entitled to your opinion," she said, showing some game.

"I try to tear you down in my head. Nothing against you—just reducing my expectations. Suffering through the breakup without even . . . is that crazy?"

"No," she said. "No, I know all about that."

He felt himself puddling on the sofa. "I'm sorry for showing up like this. It's stupid. I'll leave whenever you want me to."

She thought about that, then held out her hand for the towel as though the time to go was now—then threw the towel over his head and went at his hair vigorously with both hands. When she was done, she dropped down onto the sofa next to him, him pulling the towel down around his neck.

She said, "I saw your picture yesterday."

That stopped him cold. The light smile on her face baffled him.

"God, you look stricken," she said. "It wasn't *that* bad of a picture. On the wall at the Boys and Girls Club. You playing hockey."

Doug had imagined mug shots, surveillance photos. "Jesus. Right."

"A local hall of fame they have there."

Now he was squirming. "Please."

"It was a Bruins uniform you had on."

"Providence Bruins. Like minor leagues."

"You were drafted? You played professional hockey?"

"There was a time, yes."

She waited. "And?"

He was feeling her air-conditioning now, his shirt and pants going cold. "It didn't work out."

She read the disappointment on his face. "Well—you gave it your all, right?"

"Actually, it was worse than that. I got kicked out. I got into a fight with another guy on my own team."

She was almost smiling. "On your own team?"

"This guy was better than me. I can say that now. Not much better . . . but I had never faced that before, someone with stronger natural skills. He was a shooter, all finesse, and sort of expected me to run interference for him. Me to take the hits and the penalties, him to get the shots on goal and the glory. And the coach supported this, everything about the team geared toward grooming this guy for his pro debut. What ignited me that day, I don't remember. An accumulation of things. Both teams tried to pull me off him. I don't even think he'd ever been in a hockey fight before in his life. The only shot he got in on me was as they were dragging me back. Kicked me with his skate."

She reached for the scar that split his left eyebrow. "Is that how you got . . . ?"

"Yeah. Marked for life."

He remembered showing up hungover for practice the next day, and the coach coming up to him in the locker room, telling him not to lace up. Then the long walk upstairs to the general manager's office, his agent waiting inside. The office windows looked down over the ice, and Doug watched the team practice as the GM waved around an unlit Tiparillo and berated him. Dollars and sense—how much Doug had cost the franchise, how little sense he had shown. And still, they weren't shit-canning him completely. *Take some time off, get your fucking head on straight, kid. Keep up with your workouts and stay out of trouble.* They would have taken him back in a couple of months. But Doug returned home pissed off, back in the Town with a will to self-destruct. Getting loaded with Jem, pulling the nail-gun job. His agent wrote him a letter, something about the possibility of starting over in Hungary or Poland or somewhere. Doug never even called the guy back.

Good, he thought, all this flashing through his head with Claire sitting right there next to him. *Remember it all.* Don't blow this shot too.

"You know," she said, "when I first opened the door, I thought you'd been drinking."

Doug smiled, sad but determined, thinking of the wedding toast near-miss and shaking his head. "Not drinking. Thinking."

"I thought maybe you thought you were showing up here for a booty call."

"Ha!" he snorted. "How could you even . . . oh, man. No. I mean, unless you're into it."

Not even a courtesy chuckle. He was only 70 percent joking, but her eyes effectively told the other 30 percent to take a hike. "What *did* you come here for?" she asked.

The difficulty of that question sat Doug back. "This wedding reception I left? It was more like a farewell party. My own."

She nodded without understanding, needing more.

"Let me ask you this," he said. "Am I your boyfriend?"

She smiled at the word. "'Boyfriend?' I haven't had a boyfriend since sixth grade."

"Am I your guy? Could I be?"

"I don't know." She didn't flinch, eyes near and unblinking. "Could you?"

The question hung in the air between them, her eyes inviting him to close the gap. He did—kissing her for as long as he could hold his breath—then he sat back, his question answered. "That's what I came here for."

24
THE SURV

O N A SURV, MURPHY'S LAW reigns: forgetting your camera is the only way to guarantee that something photo-worthy will happen.

Tailing Desmond Elden that drizzling Sunday afternoon brought them to St. Francis de Sales at the top of the real Bunker Hill (the famous monument actually stood atop Breed's Hill; Dino assured Frawley it was a long story) for a May wedding, with Magloan, the car thief, apparently the groom. Frawley decided against risking entry, waiting curbside with Dino until it was over, then falling in with the attendees making their way down to the Joseph P. Kennedy Post of the Veterans of Foreign Wars, a stand-alone brick building located at the foot of the hill, behind the Foodmaster.

Dino stayed parked out on School Street until the last of the stragglers arrived, then crept into the parking lot, tucking his Taurus in deep next to a pale blue Escort with a photographer's name spelled out in gold stickers on the side window. From there they had a decent side view of the entrance, wipers clearing away the drizzle once every fifteen seconds or so. Beyond the VFW post, the city stood high and wide, looming like a wall.

Dino said, "They say rain is good luck for a wedding."

"You had hail, I take it."

"Worst drought in fifty years. When are you gonna get busy, get yourself some wedded bliss?"

"When I can afford it."

Frawley had spoken to Claire Keesey a few times since their pre-date, once setting plans, to meet for drinks at the Rattlesnake, but the late-afternoon robbing of an Abington bank—a crackhead counter-jumper so junkie-sick and nervous he'd puked on his own gun—forced Frawley to cancel on her at the last minute. Judging by her remarks, it seemed that the piano mover was out of the picture.

The wipers slicked the rain-smeared windshield clean, Frawley watching a guy in black exit the post, jogging down the front steps to the street without umbrella or coat.

"Your generation," said Dino, smiling. "So cautious. So afraid of marriage. But then somebody suggests skydiving, and everyone's fighting over parachutes."

Frawley said, "Dean, hit these wipers again."

Dino did. Frawley saw the guy in the tuxedo, now halfway across the street, turned and talking to a jacketless guy standing outside the door.

"That's MacRay," said Frawley.

"Which? On the road?"

"I think. And the other one, that's Coughlin."

Dino rolled down his window but the rain drowned out the conversation. It didn't look like an argument, but it didn't look like *See ya soon* either. MacRay continued away across the street, Coughlin watching him a few moments before ducking back inside.

"What do you think?" said Dino.

Frawley watched MacRay cut into the mall parking lot outside the 99 Restaurant, shoulders hunched against the rain. "Don't know. Home is that way." He pointed to the hill behind them.

"Could be just ducking out for a Certs. What are we doing here, anyway? It's not like they're gonna knock over their own wedding reception."

Frawley was pulling on his red rain shell. "You take off, Dean. I'll jump here."

"Sure now?"

"Navy yard's in that general direction anyway, so I'll see where he goes, then get home myself."

"No argument from me," said Dino.

Frawley stood out of the Taurus—rain always looks harder than it feels—and jogged toward the mall parking lot, wishing it was Coughlin he was following, reading the pale-eyed bumper as the likely ringleader. MacRay was hard to miss in his tuxedo, and Frawley stayed well back, following him across the lot to the next street, climbing a side road past the skating rink.

Near the five-street junction, Frawley felt something happening. He sensed a convergence but pushed it aside until he neared Packard Street and alarms started ringing in his head. Still it was too much to accept, even as MacRay stopped outside one of the doors. Frawley watched from the corner, unable to tell from that angle which building was Claire Keesey's.

He felt a lift when MacRay changed his mind, starting away—but MacRay was only pacing, and Frawley watched from the corner, standing under a downspout, roof runoff pattering his shoulders.

MacRay ran up the stoop again and pressed the bell. The door opened. Words were exchanged, MacRay was invited inside, and the door closed.

Frawley splashed up the sidewalk and climbed the same three stone steps, finding the bell buttons, noticing immediately the one that was wet. The name next to it read KEESEY, C.

He went blind for a minute, standing there. She had invited MacRay inside—one of the thieves who had knocked over her bank and taken her for a ride. And Frawley had cleared her. He had excluded her, beyond a doubt. He had been trying to *date* her.

Had they scammed him? Was he being outfoxed by these scumbags? Had she—of all of them—fucked him over good?

The piano mover.

If the door opened now, they would see him there, standing before them. And he wanted that. He wanted them to see him, wanted them to know that *he knew*, that he had seen them together. And then—

And then he didn't want that at all.

THE GOLD ALPHABET STICKERS applied to the second-story window of the Brighton row-house apartment read GARY GEORGE PHOTOGRAPHY, and below that, smaller, PROFESSIONAL PORTRAITS—HEADSHOTS—GLAMOUR.

Frawley reached inside the wrought-iron cage over the basement apartment window to rap on the glass. Through it, he had an odd, God's-eye perspective looking down into a living room, where an Indian guy was curled up on a sofa in lounging pants and a T-shirt, cuddling with his lady friend in front of a soccer match on TV. They spooked at Frawley's badge, the guy leaping off the sofa and buzzing Frawley inside.

The tile floor of the lobby was cracked but clean. The soccer fan padded up the stairs alone, barefoot, nervous. "You're all set, I just needed a buzz in," Frawley told him, displaying the creds again and shooing him back downstairs.

Frawley climbed to the second floor, finding the door with the business name on it, again in mailbox letter stickers unevenly spaced. He knocked and heard soft footsteps coming up on the other side.

Frawley held his credentials over the peephole. "FBI, open up."

The door yielded two inches, the length of a security chain. The photographer's skin was shiny and buffed, like he'd been scrubbing it all evening. "Is this a joke—"

Frawley shoved open the door, shoulder lowered, the chain snapping, the doorknob banging, the links *ching*ing across hardwood like spilled dimes.

The photographer staggered backward, stunned. He wore a short, blue, terry-cloth bathrobe with nothing underneath it. Frawley knew there was nothing underneath it because the shock of jerking back from the door had caused the robe to fall open.

Frawley straightened, the door having suffered for his anger. "Close your robe, Gary."

Gary George closed his robe. "You can't come in here without a search warrant."

"I can't collect evidence without a search warrant," said Frawley, closing the door. "But generally all I need to get in anywhere is this"—he showed him his creds—"and this"—he flapped open his jacket to show him the SIG-Sauer shoulder piece. "That's usually enough."

Gold hair slicked back with mousse during the day now flopped dryly around Gary George's face, drooping weedily to his cheeks. He double-knotted his robe. Frawley smelled incense.

"I'm having a bad day today, Gary," Frawley told him, "a real bad day. I'm warning you in advance so that you know not to make it any worse. You worked a wedding in Charlestown this afternoon. How did you know those people?"

"I don't."

"Who hired you?"

"I came with the flowers."

"You came with the flowers."

"Mainly as a favor to someone."

Frawley's realization nearly made him step back. "Fergie the Florist?"

Gary George's silence was a yes.

"Fergus Coln, Charlestown gangster and drug dealer? Hell of a guy to be doing favors for, Gary." Frawley stepped close, checking Gary George's pupils. "You loaded right now?"

He was too stoned to be properly defiant. "I might be."

"The photographs you took today—I want them. Group shots of the wedding party. Anybody in a tuxedo. I will pay you for the prints, maybe even throw in a buck or two for the busted door chain if things go smoothly. Do we have a deal?"

Gary George thought about it, nodded.

"Excellent decision, Gary. So far, so good. What do you have, one of those bathroom darkrooms?"

Frawley paced among the mood lighting and beaded doorways and velvet slipcovers, waiting while Gary George worked. On one wall was a giant studio portrait of a model wearing a bobbed black wig, long beads, and a flapper dress, and, of course, the model was Gary George himself. Frawley found four sticks of incense smoldering in the kitchen and threw one after another out of the window into the rain. His anger built again as he thought of MacRay lounging at Claire Keesey's, while Frawley waited on a doped cross-dresser in a ladies' beach cover-up.

"What?" asked Frawley, when Gary George emerged from the bathroom at the half-hour mark, empty-handed.

"Taking a little cigarette break."

Frawley shoved him back inside the bathroom and shut the door.

When it opened again, Gary George held dripping prints with rubber-thumbed tongs. Frawley studied one group shot posed around a table, the bride and groom in back, the wedding party in chairs before them. He recognized Elden on the far right, and beady-eyed Coughlin near the middle, a beer bottle half-hidden next to his leg. But no MacRay. Nor was he in any of the others.

"The big guy," said Frawley. "Kind of thick-nosed, buzzed hair."

"This is it for tuxedos. They weren't very into the whole portrait thing."

Frawley checked the image again. The woman in a slinky black dress, darkly blond, bad-girl hot, had to be Coughlin's sister, the one living in the house with him and MacRay. She had Coughlin eyes.

"Maybe he's on the video," suggested Gary George.

Frawley turned and stared until Gary George started moving.

Back through the doorway beads, out in the main room, Frawley snatched the videocamera out of Gary George's hand, ejecting the unlabeled VHS tape himself.

"I'll need that back," said Gary George.

Frawley kept a twenty and threw down the rest of his wallet money on a lace-draped sewing table. "Tell anyone about this, Gary, and I will return with a narcotics warrant and a thick pair of gloves and tear this place apart. Understood?"

Gary George picked through the bills. "This is only like thirty-seven dollars."

But Frawley was already through the door and moving down the hall to the cracked stairs, thinking only, *MacRay, MacRay, MacRay* . . .

PART III
BAD

25
POPCORN

THE MANAGER, CIDRO KOSARIO, drove a dusty blue Cressida with a failing muffler. He parked in his usual spot on the west side of The Braintree
10, unfolding reflective silver sun shields over his dash and rear ledge
before locking the car and twirling his keys around his finger as he ambled to
the side door. He slid the key into the lock, and Doug stepped out from behind
the trash pen.

"Morning, Cidro."

Cidro startled. He saw their fucked-up faces and the guns pointed at him
and his Monday-morning eyes died like stabbed yolks.

Jem was at Doug's elbow. "We're here for the popcorn."

Doug told Cidro, "Inside."

Cidro unlocked the door, Doug's gloved hand pushing him through. The
warning tone was shrill, the alarm keypad flashing on the wall. Jem shut the
door on the daylight behind them and got right up in Cidro's face. "Bet you
couldn't even *remember* the panic code right now, if you wanted to."

Doug said, "And you don't."

Cidro looked incapable of much of anything at the moment. He took one
more quick glance at their faces—*yes,* this was happening—then turned his eyes
to the geometric pattern of the dark carpet, barely looking up again for the next
two hours.

Growing up, Halloween had always been Doug's and his friends' number
one holiday. Christmas brought presents, Independence Day bottle rockets and
cherry bombs, but only Halloween allowed them to be criminals: wearing
masks, roaming the night, marauding.

Gloansy, in his legit life as a sometime union driver for local movie produc-
tions, was always nicking stuff off sets. Props, cable, snacks—anything he could
eat or move. Off an Alec Baldwin movie called *Malice* he had taken a makeup
kit that looked like a big fishing tackle box, to which Doug had since added
clearance rack Halloween disguises.

Doug and Jem had used the mirrors inside the stolen Caravan to apply their faces in the hour before Cidro pulled up. The point was to intimidate as well as disguise. Jem wore a gargoyle application over his nose and cheeks, an old man's chin, some Frankenstein-style ridging over his eyebrows, and a clown's red mustache. He looked like sort of a dog-man, a human mutt, and when he had turned to Doug for a quick check, Doug said from the backseat, "Christ, that's fugly. Take my money too."

Doug had made himself look like a cross between a burn victim and an ugly man with a creeping skin disease. They wore vests underneath the blue repair-man jumpsuits and matching service caps, with pale blue latex gloves and wide, mirrored sunglasses. Doug carried a Beretta, Jem a Glock 9.

"Key in the disarm," said Doug, his hand squeezing Cidro's shoulder. "Go."

The theater manager did, five digits, the aliens' tune from *Close Encounters of the Third Kind*. The warning tone ended on two beeps, the keypad lights blinking out.

Cidro Kosario was a mix of Portuguese and black, a dark-eyed, mournful young man with short, kinky hair and an eagle beak, his flesh nearly silver. The two types of citizens who got hurt in heists were assholes and superhero-in-waiting movie fans. Accordingly, Doug had tailed Cidro. "What's your baby, Cidro, boy or girl?"

"She's a . . . huh?" He almost looked up at them again.

After seeing Cidro and his short wife walking their baby stroller outside a Quincy apartment building, Doug knew the manager would give them no trouble. "A girl, that's nice." Doug kept his hand heavy on the skinny man's shoulder. "So this is a robbery, okay? Everything's gonna go smooth, and then we're out of your life for good. Nothing's gonna happen to you—*or* them—so long as you follow along and do as you're told."

Doug felt the guy starting to shake.

Jem took Cidro's keys from him and said, into the crew's walkie-talkie, "We're in."

"*Yah,*" came back Gloansy's voice.

They started past the individual theater doors toward the brighter light of the central lobby. Being in a quiet theater in daytime reminded Doug of matinees, and how going to them had always felt like playing hooky—before he went into playing hooky full-time.

Doug asked, "How long until the armored truck comes for the money?"

Cidro was sagging, twisting a little, buckling into a standing squat.

Doug said, "About an hour and a half or so, am I right?"

Cidro tried to nod, breathing funny.

Doug said, "You're gonna take a shit, aren't you."

Cidro froze, his face a mask of pain.

"Lucky for you, we got time. Can you still walk?"

DOUG WAITED AGAINST THE wall across the handicapped stall, his gun on Cidro, the guy's pants around his ankles, hugging his bare knees as he exploded himself into the toilet. "Yeah, go ahead, wipe," said Doug. The humiliation on Cidro's face was genuine, boylike. "Okay? Let's see the office."

Jem staggered away from the draft caused by the opening restroom door. "Ho! Armed robbery *enema*."

They walked Cidro behind the triple-wide *Independence Day* cardboard display into the locked manager's office. It was a drop safe, a small manhole in the floor with twin locks like eyes over the flat grin of a one-way deposit slot.

Doug said, "Why don't we get your safe key now, so we're ready."

Cidro pulled it from a cash box full of stamps and gift certificates at the back of a desk drawer. That weekend's deposit receipts were paper-clipped to a cash sheet on the calendar blotter, waiting to be tallied and phoned in. Doug glanced at the slips and liked what he saw.

Jem yanked the phone lines out of the wall, cutting them while Doug scanned the room for potential weapons. "What time does your day shift arrive?"

Cidro glanced at the wall clock, stalling. Doug decided not to give him the opportunity to lie.

"About eleven fifteen, right?" said Doug, collecting *Edward Scissorhands* scissors, an *American Me* letter-opener shiv, and a heavy *Jurassic Park* paperweight. "All right, back out. Lie down here on the carpet, on your stomach. We're gonna chill for a while."

Cidro did as he was told, lying on the floor of the lobby with his face turned away from them, his wrists bound with a plastic tie.

Jem's impatience allowed Doug to hang cool at the end of the candy counter, watching him pace. Jem wandered around the lobby inspecting the posters and the freestanding cardboard displays, studying the stars' faces up close as though trying to see what they had that he hadn't. Later he opened up a $2.50 box of Goobers on the glass counter, popping one after another into his mouth.

Gloansy's voice squawked on the radio, "First one's on the way."

Doug's watch read 11:12. "Cidro," he said, using his Leatherman to cut the manager's hands free. "You're gonna stand up now and let in the first of your day shift. You've had a lot of time to think, lying there, and I hope it was all about your family, your home in unit eleven on the fourth floor of the Livermore Arms, and not about alerting your employees or trying to bolt on us once you open up that side door."

Cidro let in the first worker, the second, the third, fourth, and fifth—all without incident. The old projectionist held his chest after seeing mutt-face Jem, but he seemed okay once they laid him down and cuffed him with the others. Jem yelled out, "Stop fucking trying to look over here!" every few minutes, just to keep them properly terrorized. Doug brought Cidro to the front to unlock the outside doors as usual, then re-locked the inside ones and brought him back to the lobby, laying him down to wait.

Jem was popping Sour Patch Kids now. *Too fucking easy, man,*" he hissed, resuming his pacing. He didn't mean that something seemed wrong. He meant that he wasn't having any fun. It was all going too smoothly and he wasn't enjoying himself.

The radio squawked again at 11:27. "Yogurt Man."

Doug stepped to the tinted lobby doors and saw, way out at the far edge of the parking lot, the white Neon, Yogurt Man climbing onto the hood with his lunch.

Gloansy's voice: "It's on. Heading your way."

Doug yawned, pulling oxygen into his lungs, enriching the blood feed to his heart, his brain. The old fear rising nicely. Jem waited back with the prone workers as Doug pulled Cidro to his feet and at gunpoint told him how it was going to go.

They heard the can pull up outside, the squawk of the heavy brakes, a fart-like sigh.

Gloansy's voice was different now: juiced, in motion. "Road's set. Good to go."

This meant that Gloansy had blocked off Forbes Road, the only way in, with the boxy green *Boston Globe* delivery truck he had boosted from South Boston that morning—in the early hours of what was supposed to be the frogman's honeymoon.

Doug returned the keys to Cidro, then stood behind a *Striptease* standee.

A shadow moved to the doors. The click-clack of a key tapping against glass.

"Go," whispered Doug, and Cidro went, fumbling the key into the lock and admitting the white-brush-mustached courier, pulling the handcart behind him. ID card on the collar, patch on the shoulder, big badge on the pocket, gun in holster, black wire earphones.

"And how're you today, sir?" said the courier, blustery, efficient.

"Good," said Cidro, a blank.

"Good, good."

Cidro stared at him a moment, then the courier moved to the side, waiting for Cidro to lock the door. Cidro did.

"Inside, and all clear," said the courier aloud. Then, less automately, he said to Cidro, "Rough weekend?"

Cidro was staring at him again.

"Or is that new baby of yours keeping you up? Yep—*been* there, *done* that."

Cidro nodded. "Okay," he said, then started them toward the office.

Doug stepped out from behind the cardboard Demi Moore with his Beretta up, moving straight at the courier. The courier halted, seeing everything at once, the gun, the cap, the shades, the face—his mind waking up to *ROBBERY!*—but before he could speak or even let go of the cart, the Beretta's muzzle was in his face like a bee on his nose.

Doug unsnapped the guard's sidearm, tugging the .38 free of his belt. Jem appeared and pulled Cidro away, then Doug traded Jem the guard's gun for the walkie-talkie and Cidro's keys.

Adrenaline made Doug's voice loud and strange. "Arnold Washton," he said in the direction of the microphone in the courier's chest, "driver of the truck. You have a wife named Linda. You live at 311 Hazer Street, Quincy, with three small dogs. *Do not* make the distress call. I repeat—do *not* make that call. Morton, tell him."

The courier stared, dumbfounded.

Doug said, "Morton Harford, 27 Counting Lane, Randolph. Wife also named Linda. Two grown children. Tell him, Morton."

"There's . . . two of them," said Morton, the good-natured bluster evaporated from his voice. "Two I see, Arnie. Masks. Guns."

Doug said, "Arnold, do not make that call. The two Lindas join me in telling you that you are to sit tight in the truck and do nothing. There is a van pulling up next to you now, the driver wearing a dinosaur mask. He is monitoring a police radio and will overhear any dispatches. If you understand and agree with me, raise both hands off the wheel now so that the driver of the van can see them."

They waited, Doug holding up his radio. Gloansy's voice squawked, mask-distorted. "Hands are up."

"Good." Doug took one step back from Morton the courier. "Open your shirt, Morton. I want your radio and earphones."

Morton did, but slowly, as though stalling were the same as resisting. He lifted the microphone off the V-neck collar of his undershirt and, with Jem holding Morton's own gun on him, surrendered the wires and the black box to Doug.

Jem patted Morton down for an ankle holster while Doug miked himself, hanging the wires inside his ears. "Arnold," he said, "say something to me."

No static over the two-way channel, Arnold's voice entering his head crystal clear. "Look here, no money's worth anybody getting—"

"That's fine. Turn off the engine using one hand, then raise them both up again."

Jem was getting goosey, holding the guard's gun on him palm-down like they do in gang movies. It occurred to Doug only then that maybe he hadn't given Jem enough to do.

Outside, the rumble died. Gloansy said, "It's off."

Doug told him, via radio, "We're good." Then to the truck, via the microphone now clipped to his jumpsuit collar, Doug said, "Sit tight, Arnold. We won't be long."

He motioned Cidro and the open-shirted courier toward the office. Cidro entered first, then Morton pushing his hand truck. Doug remained in the doorway.

"Empty the bag on the desk."

The courier lifted the blue-and-green canvas bag off the tray of rolled coins at the bottom of the dolly. He opened the bag and pulled out a standard-sized bundle of currency, ten packs of one hundred fresh-cut one-dollar bills banded in blue Federal Reserve Bank straps. Then he lowered the handles of the sagging bag, facing Doug with an *If it weren't for that gun* expression.

"Is that it?" said Doug.

Morton did not respond. Doug cocked his head at Morton, then pulled the first safe key from his pocket. He tossed it to Cidro.

Cidro caught it and looked at Morton. "C'mon, man, just do what they say."

The mustached courier's scowl intensified. He reached back into the canvas sack and pulled out Pinnacle's safe key.

"Down on your knees," Doug said. "Take the coin tray off the cart, open the safe, and start stacking bags."

They were bringing deposit bags out of the floor well when gunshots cracked in the lobby. Doug ducked automatically, wheeling and pointing his Beretta out the office door, seeing nothing. He didn't know where Jem was— stopping himself from calling out his name. He turned back the other way and put his gun on Morton and Cidro, who had both dropped facedown onto the floor.

Then another smattering of gunshots. Doug was wild with incomprehension, yelling *"Fuck!"* as Arnold's voice in his head said, "Dear God, *no*."

Doug backed through the doorframe, low, still seeing nothing. Glass cracked and tinkled, the employees screaming, Arnold yelling in Doug's head, "Morty? *Mort!*"

Doug backed straight out of the office, crouching, keeping Morton and Cidro in sight as he scanned the lobby, smelling cordite, searching for Jem. Then another crack and thump—this time followed by Jem's voice: "Goddamn! That's a pretty fuckin' good milk shake!"

"THE FUCK!" bellowed Doug at him, backing into a fake ficus tree.

Jem moved into view, the guard's .38 at his side. He spun and brought the gun around fast, firing twice, *crack-crack,* shootout-style, shuddering Bruce Willis on a cardboard standee for *Last Man Standing,* singing, "Yippee-ki-yay, motherfucker!" Then a shot—"Ain't gonna *be* no rematch!"—into Stallone's chin, on a standee for *Daylight.* "Say hello to my leettle—" Pacino got one in the gut, a promo for *City Hall.*

The gun clicked twice, finally dry, sparing the animated stars of *Beavis and Butt-head Do America.* Jem tossed the piece aside, slipping his Glock back into his right hand and then seeing Doug crouched beneath the plastic tree. Jem's vested chest was heaving, his face a slicing, fucked-up smile.

Arnold screaming, *"Morty!"*

Gloansy shouting from Doug's hip radio, *"Fuck is that?"*

"Arnold!" Doug said, rising to full height, elbowing the tree out of his way and checking Morton and Cidro again. "Arnold, everything is fine."

"What in fucking hell—!"

"Do not make that call, Arnold. Your partner is fine, everyone is fine—no one has been hurt. Here—" His body pounding, Doug returned to the office and pulled the mustached courier to his knees. "Talk to him, Morton. Speak, tell him."

Morton said slowly, "I'm okay, Arnie. I think."

"He's not hurt," said Doug.

"I'm not hurt," said Morton, checking himself over, making sure it was true.

"Mort, what they shooting at?" said Arnold—confused, thinking his partner could still hear him.

"Do not make that call, Arnold," said Doug, getting his breath back now, grabbing Cidro by his shoulder and hauling him to his feet. "Here is the manager." Doug pulled Cidro out of the office and showed him his employees: still lying on the carpet, hands covering their heads. "Tell him, Cidro."

Cidro looked around at the target practice Jem had made of the lobby. "I don't—"

"Just tell him!"

"No one is hurt!"

"No one is hurt, Arnold," said Doug, shoving Cidro back into the office.

Gloansy said from his hip, *"Fuck is going on, man?"*

Doug grabbed the radio. "We're cool, everything's cool."

Gloansy said, *"Everything's cool?"*

"Yogurt Man, what's he doing?"

"Nothing. No movement."

"All right. Sit tight. Almost fucking there."

WHEN THE SAFE WAS empty, Doug had Morton wheel the cart out into the smoke-hazed lobby. Jem got the employees up, hustling them into the windowless office—"Let's *go*, fucking *move* it, *go, go!*"—putting them in there with Cidro. "Now if you're thinking about opening this door, I am going to be standing right fucking here." He slammed it shut and hustled away.

Morton pushed the hand truck ahead of him to the lobby doors, looking a little hinky, his head not moving as he walked, his mind working hard. Doug came up abreast of him and caught Morton's eyes searching the lobby for something, anything.

"You're thinking too much, Morton."

Morton stiffened, slowing down even more. His mustache rippled as he said, "No one calls me Morton."

"I do, Morton," said Doug, reacquainting him with the Beretta. "You're rip-shit at me right now, Morton, I understand that. Because I brought your family into this thing, you're super-fucking-pissed." *Reservoir Dogs* suddenly coming out of Doug. "Remember this isn't your money, Morton, and how nice it will be tonight to get home. You too, Arnold," continued Doug, into his own collar. "We're coming out now and you're not gonna do a damn thing but sit tight and still. Tell me you will, Arnold."

Arnold's voice in his ears said, "This ain't right."

"Tell me you will, Arnold."

"Lord Jesus been listening in on you just like I have."

"Arnold, tell me you fucking will."

"I will," said Arnold. "I have done my job here. I will leave the rest to Him."

Into his hip radio, Doug told Gloansy, "We're coming out."

Doug unlocked the glass door with Cidro's keys. They passed the imitation velvet rope and the ticket booths on either side, Doug stopping at the unlocked outside doors.

"Okay, Morton?" said Doug.

Morton just started straight ahead.

They exited onto the cement landing atop the stairs, Arnold sitting inside the driver's window of the Pinnacle can, hands above the steering wheel, watching them.

Doug and Jem followed Morton and the cash cart down the ramp to the sidewalk, then over the fire lane markings and around the rear of the can to where the Caravan was idling. Gloansy sat there in his dinosaur mask, eyes trained on Arnold.

Jem threw open the rear hatch of the van and tossed the bags inside, Morton standing there, his unbuttoned shirt flapping in the breeze. Doug stood behind Morton, scanning the sunny sky for helicopters.

"Arnold," said Doug, "the dinosaur's gonna keep monitoring the police radio, and I'm gonna stay in touch with you until we're outside broadcast range, understand? You don't make a call until then."

Doug yanked down his earphones without waiting for Arnold's answer. Jem slammed the hatchback shut and Doug walked Morton around to the passenger side of the van where Jem pulled open the sliding door for Doug, then climbed into the front passenger seat. Jem covered Morton from the open window while Doug backed inside and shut the sliding door on Morton's scowling eyes.

Gloansy floored it. They screeched through the empty parking lot toward the cliff edge. As Doug pulled a seat belt across his chest, Jem stuck his gun arm out his window, drawing a bead on sun-worshipping Yogurt Man.

Jem did not shoot. Gloansy turned hard toward the emergency access road, banging through the gate—they had cut the lock and chain overnight—and plunging down the road. It was no steeper than Pearl Street, and Gloansy banked hard at the end, slapping through the second cut gate and bottoming out hard next to the batting cages and the driving range.

Gloansy yanked off his mask and pushed the van for all it had, driving hard across the cracked parking lot and straight at the chain fence separating lower Forbes Road from the broad, busy highway. The fence had also been precut overnight, links snipped up the middle so that when the van bumped the curb, it smashed clean through.

They rattled over a stripe of high grass before jumping out onto 93 at the mouth of Exit 6, cutting off another minivan and veering across the breakdown lane into the traffic flow, throwing off a pair of hubcaps like wheeling quarters. Other cars braked and honked their disapproval, Gloansy punching the horn to scare off the panicked midday commuters, zooming ahead, falling in with the traffic and running south through the highway split, toward the rail station and the switch—with the cash-filled deposit bags sliding around in back, Jem howling like a madman in front, and Doug furiously stripping off his face.

26
INSIDE THE TAPE

FRAWLEY STOOD AND WATCHED the highway traffic zipping past him as though the green minivan might come around again, hours after the fact, MacRay and his crew in their ugly-face masks hooting at him out of the windows, waving fistfuls of cash.

The tire tracks, twin stripes of churned soil cut into the high grass, drove right through the precut six-foot chain-link fence and out onto the highway. The highway split offered them a variety of escape routes . . . and blah blah blah blah blah.

Thwock! Behind Frawley, the lone driving-range employee teed off again, eyeing the cops and the evidence van as he reloaded between drives. Frawley envied the guy's bystander status, tired of cop-think, and nearly on autopilot here, having trouble finding a reason to care about this particular crime—while at the same time feeling a mounting sense of fury toward the bandits.

The photographer was done, the tire tracks measured and cast, a fireman now cutting out that section of fence for crime lab comparison, in the event the offending tool were to be found. But it would not be found. It had certainly been chopped into several pieces and disposed of in various trash receptacles between here and Charlestown.

Dino was saying something about estimating the time of the fence snip and the cut gate chains. He was still working the crime; Frawley was working the criminals.

The van offered a glimmer of hope. Frawley had a BOLO out on suspicious green vans, with special attention to handicapped plates. None of the witnesses had said anything about handicapped plates, but Frawley and Dino both knew that armored-car guys loved the tags for their access, letting them park closest to business doors without attracting attention.

None of the highway drivers who dialed 911 could pinpoint where the getaway van had pulled off the highway. Frawley guessed they had skipped the split in order to put some distance between them and the looky-loos who saw them bang through the fence—but they wouldn't have gone too far before making their switch, not with the new highway-overpass traffic cameras.

Now the TV news helicopter was making another pass overhead. A hot, muggy June afternoon, thunderstorms due to crack the heat. Frawley's boxers clung to him like wet swim trunks he had pulled pants on over. Leaving his necktie on in this humidity had been a form of self-punishment, but now he ripped open the knot and yanked it out of his collar, stuffing it into his pocket as, with Dino, he turned back toward the access road. The heat was one more obstacle the robbers had left him in their wake, one more taunting F.U.

"It's them," Frawley said.

Dino nodded, saying, "Okay," not doubting or disbelieving Frawley, only wanting to make him work for it. Dino's shirtsleeves were sopping, rolled up past his hairy gray forearms. "The guards, the manager, everyone says only three doers."

"Could have been one more in the back of the van. Or maybe one of them was an extra pair of eyeballs out on the mall side, watching for cop patrols."

"But no tech whatsoever. Not one clipped wire. All manpower and coercion."

"None of the armored-car jobs have used tech. There can *be* no tech on an armored. This is them shaking it up. Knowing they're being sniffed at."

"Okay. But Magloan—he goes out robbing the morning after his wedding?"

"That's the first thing their lawyers will proclaim in court. It's perfect."

"And if it turns out Elden's been at work all day?"

Frawley shook his head, adamant. "It's *them*."

A Braintree cop stood by the dented gates, waiting for someone to collect the green-van-paint transfer. The cut chain lay there like a dead snake. Frawley and Dino walked the hooked road back up to the parking lot. "Some big movie, I guess, this weekend?" said Dino. "*Twister*? That the movie of the game?" He was trying to pull Frawley out of his funk. "'*Huge* opening,' said the manager. What my last partner used to say about his wife, '*Huge* opening.'"

Frawley nodded, stubborn, nursing his bad mood. The wind up at the top was the stale gust of heat that comes at you when you open an oven. The broken chain there was being bagged, print dust smoking off it like gray pollen. The *Globe* truck stolen out of South Boston, which they had used to block off the roads leading in, sat on slashed tires atop a flatbed trailer, its green sides dusted as though it had been driven through a sandstorm.

Frawley stood at the knee-high wooden railing around the parking lot and looked across the highway canyon to the facing road of industry set atop a cliff of blasted stone. A dozen different angles for casing the theater from there.

They crossed the lot to the armored truck, still parked in the fire lane outside the theater entrance. Something about the yellow police tape offended Frawley and he tore it down himself, saying, "They never even touched the truck."

"Went backdoor. Like at Kenmore."

"Going out of their way to get the drop on the mark. They could have come at the truck head-on. It's isolated enough up here—doesn't get much more isolated. Doable, though messy."

Dino patted the can's side reassuringly as he might a spooked elephant. "They knew better."

Frawley watched the police tape slithering across the baking lot. "These guys knew there was more money in the can, had complete control of the situation, *and they let it go.* Add in the days and weeks of prep, casing the job, following all the players? Decidedly risk-averse. Being super careful."

Dino said, "That's another kind of good for us. They get too careful, too tricky, they'll screw themselves up."

"Yeah," said Frawley, starting up the stairs to the lobby. "Except, I am through waiting for them to screw up."

Entering the theater lobby was a jump from the oven into a refrigerator. The manager had set out bottled water and tubs of popcorn for the cops. They were hoping to reopen in time for the seven-o'clock shows.

"That older guy, the projectionist, he okay?" asked Frawley.

"No chest pains," said Dino. "Just gas."

The two guards were sitting on folding chairs with their caps in their hands, going over forms with a rep from Pinnacle. Their fuzzy descriptions told Frawley that the bandits' intimidation—their knowledge of the men's home lives—was still working. Neither Harford, who had spent time in both gunmen's company, nor Washton, into whose ears the radio gunman had issued his instructions, said they would be able to identify the bad guys. The only useful thing Frawley had gleaned from their accounts was the fright makeup, similar to an earlier job he suspected these Brown Bag Bandits of, a co-op bank in Watertown.

The guards acted like they knew their interview with the boss from Pinnacle was a formality. Both men had allowed themselves to be tailed on the job and followed home after work, enough to get them fired for cause.

The smell of gunfire lingered in the chilled air. Little numbered orange evidence triangles stood on the carpeted floor, marking where brass cartridge casings from Harford's gun had been collected. Frawley stood by a *Barb Wire* cardboard display, looking at the bullet-hole nipples in Pamela Anderson Lee's vinyl-corseted tits, contrasting that act with the discipline of leaving $1,000 in new, traceable bills sitting on the manager's desk. It was like the kidnapping after the Morning Glory job: schizo.

Maybe they'd start spending their money now. Their take was all clean, circulated cash. Frawley turned to remind Dino of this, but Dino was gone. Frawley wondered how long he had been standing there alone, ruminating.

He saw the manager down by the side door where the robbers had first jumped him. Mr. Kosario was rocking a baby, his wife's arms tight around his waist. She was a small Latina with straightened, blond hair, wearing a silky blouse and a red leather skirt with a tight hem. A skinny movie-theater manager with a hot little wife, and there stood Special Agent Adam Frawley, still trying to pimp his gold shield to get laid.

He ducked into one of the empty theaters and took a seat in the dark back row. When he first received the call that afternoon, he hadn't wanted to report. He wanted to ignore it altogether. *I am tired,* he told himself, *of chasing bank robbers and bad men.*

Now this heist vexed him. Viewed one way, it was a step forward for this crew: a takeover robbery, a broad move beyond banks. Viewed another way, it was a step back: a safe play, shying away from financial institutions. He feared it might be evidence of them cycling down—until he remembered that bad guys like these almost never quit until they're caught.

Either way, Frawley needed to move fast.

He kept going back and forth on Claire Keesey, between raging contempt and white-knight longing. Was she knowingly sleeping with the enemy, or just an unwitting damsel in distress? He stood and faced the blank screen, but try as he might to make a blank screen of his mind, the movie that kept playing there was Claire Keesey inviting MacRay into her home, into her bedroom, in between her legs.

In the lobby he found Dino looking for him, pointing with his clipboard. "Van on fire, about a mile away. Hosing it off now. Might not be a total loss."

FRAWLEY RAN OFF HIS excess adrenaline that night, doing intervals through Charlestown, down the suspects' streets and past their doors—even all the way out to Elden's house, in the area they called the Neck. The black-and-orange Monte Carlo SS outside Magloan's wooden row house on the downslope of Auburn Street still had beer cans tied to the bumper, JUST MARRY'D spelled out in Silly String on the rear window.

He needed to remind himself how close he was to them. He ran past the Tap on Main Street and thought about getting cleaned up and dropping back Downstairs for a beer. Instead he turned onto Packard Street, past Claire Keesey's and through the alley behind, looking for inspiration and also MacRay's beat-to-shit Caprice.

At home he made a protein shake and microwaved some chicken, eating in front of the Bulls-Sonics NBA Finals. Then he showered, put away some laundry he had stacked up, opened his mail. All of which was a prelude to the night's main event.

A pot stash, junkie works, porn mags, fishnets and garters—the sneaker box on the floor of his closet could have held any old shameful fetish, but Frawley's kick was minicassette-tape dubs of old crime-scene interviews. He wired his Olympus recorder through his stereo receiver, first warming up with a few older teller debriefings from past cases, some Greatest Hits—tellers weeping, reaching out to him for answers, *Why me?*—just to get his mind in that place. Then with the lights off and the shades down, he lay on the floor and listened as Claire Keesey's voice filled his room, transporting him back to the Kenmore vault and his desire for justice for her on that day . . .

   . . . The one who was sitting next to me. Not next to me . . . but in the same seat, the same bench, the two of us. The one who blindfolded me. I could tell somehow . . . he was looking at me . . .

27
NEXT MORNING

HE HAD PUT UP with the blaring music all night. On his way out of the house, pissed-off first thing in the morning, Doug came down banging on Jem's door like a cop.

Nothing. No response. Doug's pounding was just more bass in the mix.

He was near the bottom of the stairs when two guys unlocked the inside door. Young guys with clipper haircuts, thick with new muscle, sporting different T-shirts but matching fatigue pants and paratrooper boots. Camo kids who looked like they'd walked straight off the rack of the Somerville Army/Navy Surplus store.

They entered like they belonged there, the loose pane of glass rattling in the door. Doug thought he recognized them, maybe just from around the Town. Then he remembered—the Tap that night, the two younger guys Jem was talking to in the corner.

They nodded at him—not friendly, more out of respect of Doug's size coming off the steps. "Hey, man, 's'up?" Something like that.

Said Doug, "Who're you?"

"Aw, we're going up to see—"

"How the hell'd you get a key?" He was on the landing now, facing them.

"Jem, man. He gave it to us." They said it as though Jem's magic name solved everything.

"What's that mean? You live here or something?"

"Naw, man." Now they looked at each other like cats, sensing trouble, wondering what to do. "Yo, we got some business with him."

"Yo, no you don't. Not in this house."

Another look between them. "Look, man," said one, coming on confidential, "hey, we know who you are. We know—"

Doug was on him fast, grabbing him by his T-shirt collar and driving him back up against the door. "Who am I? Huh? What do you know?"

The loose pane of door glass popped out, shattering on the floor of the dingy vestibule. Doug hadn't meant to do it, but he didn't care much either. He shoved the camo kid halfway through the empty frame.

"Take it easy, man, we just—"

Krista's door flew open behind Doug. She came out barefoot in a short black silk Victoria's Secret robe that was familiar to him. "What the—?" she started to say, but seeing Doug there with the camo kid silenced her.

Dez appeared behind Krista, rushing to the noise, pulling on a shirt. He saw Doug and paused a moment—then stepped out onto the threshold, ready to back him up.

The music grew suddenly louder upstairs. "Hey!" Jem was over the railing, looking down at the broken door. He turned and came down a step, wearing a ratty white hotel bathrobe open over smiley-face boxers and sweat socks, coffee mug in hand.

Krista's hand pressed against Dez's chest, and he stepped back against her door.

"Duggy," said Jem, coming down two more steps, "what the fuck?"

Doug released the glaring kid. They went around him to the stairs, seething, starting up toward Jem.

Doug looked for some explanation, but Jem made a *Later* face and waved him on with his coffee mug. He started up ahead of the camo kids, then turned and came back down a few steps, seeing the light coming out of Krista's door. "If that's my sister, tell her I'm out of underwear here, she could throw in a wash."

He turned and followed his pets up onto the landing, the door closing on the music.

Krista sulked, Dez looking apologetically at Doug.

Doug turned and walked out the front door, boots crunching glass, getting the fuck away.

28
LEADS

NSIDE THE HANGAR GARAGE of the South Quincy wreck yard, Frawley and Dino examined the charred corpse of a 1995 Dodge Caravan. The heat had blown out all the glass. The rear and middle were hopelessly charred, the front hood buckled up over the fused metal of the engine, but the dash had survived. The steering wheel was warped silly but remained whole.

"They made some mods to the vehicle," said Dino, pointing out a blackened strap attached to a clip soldered to the frame along the driver's door. "Racing harness, in case of a chase. They also replaced the steering wheel—the original had a Club on it and must have got cut. The accelerants were in freezer bags duct-taped to the floor in the rear, which is why the bad burn there."

Frawley leaned inside the driver's window frame. The melted upholstery gave the stinking heap its extra-toxic stench. The steering wheel was plain black with grip grooves and an illegal "suicide" knob clamped on for fast steering.

"No prints," said Dino. "The driver guard, Washton, said he saw driving gloves on dinosaur man."

Magloan. Frawley fit Coughlin for the quiet one with the clown mustache who shot up the inside of the lobby, MacRay for the talker, the earphone man with the cosmetic burns. "Stolen out of New Hampshire?"

"Wal-Mart parking lot, week ago Monday."

"Handicap plates?"

"Off a customized Astrovan outside a medical building in Concord, the day after."

Frawley went around to the blackened rear of the still-warm car.

"Little spots of latex there from the disguises, and some shreds of incinerated clothing," said Dino. "That would be the uniforms, stolen out of a dry cleaner's in Arlington. That melted box there, that's the guard's radio unit."

Frawley returned to the front. Something about the warped steering wheel bugged him. "Wheel wasn't stolen though."

"No. Probably new. Pick up a wheel at any auto store anywhere."

"You say the dinosaur wore driving gloves?"

"Right."

"The kind with the holes in the knuckles?"

"Probably so."

Frawley pointed. "They print the entire wheel, or just the grips?"

Dino shrugged. "Long shot, with the flame heat—but good question."

"One of the 911 callers from the highway—you remember?"

"She said they were hitting the horn, getting stragglers out of their way."

Frawley mimed it. "He's fired up, strapped in with a racing harness and a suicide knob, just pulled off a big job, speeding down the highway, hitting his horn . . ."

Frawley punched the center of his pretend steering wheel with his fist.

THEY TURNED IN THEIR loaner hard hats and stood in conference outside the Billerica work site, having just been lied to, lavishly, by Billy Bona. The double whistle went off, which, according to warning signs on the fence, meant a blast was imminent.

"These guys used a shape charge in the Weymouth armored job, one of the early ones."

Dino nodded, crossing his arms and sitting back against the Taurus's trunk. "Wonder what the arrangement is here. Maybe they got something on this Bona."

Frawley squinted up into the sun, promising himself that when this all came down, he would personally deliver Bona his subpoena for aiding and abetting.

"Problem is," said Dino, "on paper they were here yesterday."

"Yeah. He happened to have their time cards right there with him."

"We could go man-to-man here, break down every hard hat on this job, waste a day or two trying to find one who's ever worked with these two goofs—"

"Funny how they're not here today. 'First day they've missed, I can remember,' Bona says. Lying to a federal agent. The *balls* on that guy."

"Then there's Elden too, at work all day yesterday, and that one's verified—"

"Yup. Boss says yesterday Elden checks in with him before getting in his truck—says he remembers this because the guy's never *once* before stopped in to shoot the shit, ask how the kids are, the whole production."

"Means he knew it was going down. Maybe there was no falling-out. Not if he's part of their alibi. And Magloan—let's face it, he'll have somebody swearing up and down he was otherwise occupied the whole day. Bottom line is, bogus or not—we got nothing. Not enough to bring anybody in on."

"I'm not talking about putting them in a lineup."

"It's not even enough to go around shaking trees," said Dino. "We start turning the Town upside down over this—even if we ignore Elden and his squeaky-clean record—lawyers will be leaping out of their wing tips crying witch hunt. We don't have it."

"We can get it."

"Not enough to haul in these jokers. DA's office would ball this up and throw it right back at us, and we'd be poisoned for the next time. Where'd you get the authority to check their tax returns for employment anyway?"

"This MacRay has no credit cards, nothing in his name. His ride, this '86 Caprice Classic piece of crap, it's registered to the Coughlin sister who lives on the first floor of their house. I run her—it turns out she's got seven different cars reg'd to her name, her insurance. One of them's a high-line Corvette. Fifty dollars says she doesn't know about any of them."

There was a hot crack of thunder, a cannon shot, and Frawley felt the pulse in the ground like a shudder. They could not see the blast but heard the echo riding out, fading away.

Dino said, "I think we need to go full-court press on this. Bring on some assistance."

Frawley watched for rising dust. "No need."

"If these tea-pissers are feeling our heat, then we need to go broader, push them harder. Farm out some of this work."

"We can push them ourselves."

Dino said nothing, meaning Frawley had to turn back to face him.

"Okay," said Dino. "Now tell me what the hell is going on here."

"What's going on is, I'm trying to catch some bad guys."

"No, I think what's happening is, you're taking this thing personally. I can't figure why, but that is the numskull approach and you're too clever for that. This is how mistakes get made."

"I want to bring this one home ourselves."

"Look, Frawl—I can play hard. I've been a detective seventeen years, I know how. I don't particularly mind going to war. All I need is a good reason."

"This is no war," said Frawley, backing off. "Boozo and his crew, they were like a big rock we flipped over, all these other little bottom-feeders wriggling out into the light. MacRay and company, we know who they are and we know where they are. Them squeaking by has gone on long enough."

"MacRay?" said Dino. "I thought you liked Coughlin as honcho."

"I'm thinking now it's MacRay."

Dino frowned impatiently. "And this is based on?"

"Call it a hunch."

Which Frawley regretted saying as soon as it left his lips. Dino slow-crossed his arms, leaning against his car, Frawley waiting for it. "What is this you're giving me now? Bullshit *hunches?*"

"Dino, look. These guys, they're an insult, an affront. Laughing at us. Now it's our turn to make them sweat a little. Let's take a bite out of *their* day for a change, just to let *them* know *we* are but a matter of time."

Dino's cell phone rang. "We get one chance," he told Frawley. "One." He went into his car for the phone and stood there with his elbow high, talking fast. He hung up and turned back to Frawley almost disappointed. "Your steering wheel," he said. "It's dirty."

29
ROUNDUP

DOUG STEPPED OUT OF Lori-Ann's coffee shop and saw two uniformed patrolmen waiting at the curb. Only a split-second reluctance to spill the large tea in his hand saved him from obeying his first, immediate, and not entirely irrational impulse, which was to take off running. Illness rose in his chest, a gut reaction to these two uniforms and the death of freedom they represented. But running would have been a huge mistake, and this near catastrophe was a second cup of ice water down his back.

Everything else looked normal for 7:30 A.M. on lower Bunker Hill Street: cars moving, civilians waiting for the 93 bus into the city, two project kids sitting on basketballs at the corner. For the arrest of an armed-robbery suspect, the G would have shut down the street like it was parade day, or else dispatched plainclothes federal marshals to serve the warrant.

The cops stepped up to him. "Douglas MacRay?"

He elected to go with them rather than follow in his own car. That they gave him the choice after patting him down was another good sign. The backseat of the cruiser was torn up and cramped, with the usual foot or so of legroom. Nice to be in there without handcuffs for a change.

He set his copy of the subpoena down on the duct-taped vinyl next to him and pulled out a glazed doughnut and bit in, relaxing. "Might want to go Prison Point instead of the C-town bridge," he told them through the plastic partition, "unless you're gonna light up your roof."

Instead they sat for minutes on the groaning iron skeleton of the Charlestown Bridge. Doug finished his second doughnut, a Boston crème, while reading through his subpoena.

United States District Court, it headlined. *SUBPOENA TO TESTIFY BEFORE GRAND JURY,* below that. Under *SUBPOENA FOR,* there were check boxes, and an X was drawn through the box next to *DOCUMENTS OR OBJECT(S),* leaving the box for *PERSON* unchecked.

Area A-1 was the police district that covered Downtown Boston and Charlestown. The station was a big brick box around the corner from City Hall

Plaza. They parked between two other blue-and-whites angled along Sudbury Street and led Doug down the steps to the glass doors and the lobby. It was a shift change, the halls crowded as they moved left past the women's detention room to the booking area, in sight of the holding cells and the slumbering prisoners.

The cop opened the ink pad and Doug licked sugar off his fingers. "What happened, you guys lose the prints you had?"

They printed his palm also, and the soft side of his hand opposite his thumb, then they had him make fists and printed each of his bottom knuckles before handing him a tissue. This was strange and worrisome, though Doug went along like he was enjoying the tour.

They took photographs with the height marker, front and profile, no booking number around his neck. Doug didn't smile, but he didn't not smile either, going for a borderline-amused *Sure, why not?*

They took a DNA swab from the pockets of his cheeks with a double-sized Q-tip that screwed into a plastic tube. Then they plucked eleven strands of hair from his scalp. "You want some piss too, I drank a large tea on the way over."

They declined his offer, handing him a script instead and making him recite witness-remembered sentences into a digital recorder:

Arnold Washton, 311 Hazer Street, Quincy.
Morton Harford, 27 Counting Lane, Randolph.
Take the coin tray off the cart, open up the safe, and start stacking bags.
Remember this ain't your money and how nice it's gonna be to get back home.
Ain't gonna be no rematch. Say hello to my little friend.
We're here for the popcorn, Mugsy. Yeaaahh, see?

They made him do the last line three times over until he read it straight, then allowed him into the bathroom for his unwanted piss before shutting him inside an interrogation room and leaving him alone for the better part of an hour. Soft carpeting covered the soundproof walls. Doug got up once to check the thermostat—he had heard this was how interrogators turned on hidden microphones—but couldn't tell anything without lifting off the box. Instead he dropped a little whistling on his imagined audience, "The Rose of Tralee," and hoped they liked it.

The one who came in introduced himself as a detective lieutenant assigned to the Bank Robbery Task Force, name of Drysler. He was long-armed and walked with the stoop of a tall man getting older. He set down a clipboard with Doug's print card on top and pulled off a pair of reading glasses, folding his long arms like someone collapsing the legs of a card table.

"One chance," he told Doug. "I'm giving you one shot, and this is it."

Doug nodded like he was interested.

"You're the first one brought in," said Drysler. "So lucky you gets first crack at setting up a deal."

Doug nodded and leaned close to him. "Okay, I did it," he confessed. "Tell O.J. the search is over. I killed Nicole Brown Simpson and Ron Goldman."

Drysler stared, too old and too pro to get pissy. "Did you like prison, MacRay?"

"To that I'd have to answer no."

"They say life is full of choices, MacRay, but it's not. Life is lived choice by choice by choice. What you eat, what you wear, when you sleep, who you sleep with. You choose wrong here, MacRay, and you may never get the opportunity to choose anything again. That's what life in prison means—the death of choice."

Doug swallowed, the older detective's words going down like razors, but he smiled through his pain. "If you got that printed on a bumper sticker or something, I'll take one home with me."

Drysler nodded after a long moment of consideration. "Okay, you can go."

On his way out to the lobby, Doug passed a guy standing near the water-cooler, jacketless like Drysler, a simple blue tie on a long-sleeved white shirt tucked deep into tan dress pants, shoulder rig prominent beneath his left arm. He was drinking water from a cone paper cup, watching Doug over the rim, and Doug found something in the guy's eyes that was familiar.

The cup came down and the guy looked at Doug as he swallowed, showing attitude. Doug was past him before he realized who it was and stopped, turning back.

"Hey," said Doug with a nod. "Rash cleared up, huh?"

The G-man just kept looking, wearing the same I'm-smarter-than-you face as do all the true believers in the Cult of the Gold Badge. The only thing different about this one was his hair, not straight and tight like a boy's regular but a tawny morass of rings and tangles. Doug had two or three good inches on him, and at least forty pounds.

Doug said, "What, a little penicillin from the clinic took care of that?"

The look became a stare. Drysler came up on them to shoo Doug along, and Doug should probably have kept going to the lobby and out the door, but he couldn't resist. He stopped again and snapped his fingers, pointing back at the G-man and his professionally insolent face.

"Red Cavalier, right?"

No answer, the G's hand a tight fist at his side, trying to compress the paper cup into a diamond. Doug grinned, then turned and walked through the lobby, though by the time he hit the outside steps rising to the sidewalk, his grin was well gone.

* * *

SPENCER GIFTS SOLD ASS-SHAPED beer mugs that farted when tipped to drink. The mall store was deep, dark, and disorientingly loud, the clerk behind the counter—looking like a cross between an Orthodox rabbi and the Red Hot Chili Peppers' Flea—mouthing the anguished lyrics of a screeching Nine Inch Nails song like a man mumbling prayers at work.

Doug felt ridiculous himself, having outgrown this place ten years ago, but the store was G-proof and the music made it virtually unsnoopable.

Dez arrived late, his black eyeglass rims achieving a kind of retro rightness as he passed a jewelry counter of body art and skull rings. He was all worked up, Doug holding out a hand to slow him down, giving him a quick fist-rap of reassurance.

"They picked me up in the parking lot at work," said Dez. "This is after paying my boss a visit, checking on my story."

Doug nodded, keeping an eye on the store entrance. "Easy, kid. Take a breath."

"Trying to make me lose my *job*." Dez brought his voice down. "This is a *federal grand jury*."

"Relax. All that means is a roomful of citizens sitting around deciding if evidence is evidence."

"Oh? That's all?" Wild sarcasm didn't look good on Dez.

"The cops. What'd you tell them?"

"What'd I tell them? I didn't tell them anything! They didn't even *ask* me anything, just, 'Smile for the camera, open your mouth.' I don't even know if it was for the"—Dez looked back cautiously at two kids looking through Tupac and marijuana-leaf posters—"the most recent thing, or what. They didn't say *anything*."

"And neither did you."

"*Christ*, of course not. *Jesus*. They take that swab thing of your mouth?"

"Yep. Your palm, knuckles?"

"Sure. That's not normal?"

Maybe the van didn't burn right. Maybe Jem did something asinine, like taking off a glove while eating candy at the glass counter. Or maybe it was nothing. "They're just shaking the trees, trying to get lucky. Stirring us up."

"Well—it fucking worked!"

Doug nodded, shushing him. "Newspaper said they brought in some fifteen other Town guys. A dragnet, all of them players—except you. Calling you in with no armed-robbery record, that shows they're onto the other capers."

"But how? How do they know?"

"*Knowing* means nothing more than a hassle. It's what they can or cannot *prove*."

Dez looked at a disco ball twirling on the ceiling. "Trying to make me lose my *job*. . . ."

Doug shook his head, amazed that Dez was worried about his job here. Two people walked in the front, just girls, not thirty years between them, with skunked hair and pierced ears more metal than flesh.

"Jem thinks it's the branch manager from the Kenmore thing," said Dez.

Doug looked hard at him. "Where's that coming from? You talk to him?"

"No, not recently. This is from before."

"When before? What'd he say?"

Dez shrugged. "Just that. That she told them something, or she knew something—I couldn't really follow him. She's bad luck anyway, you gotta admit."

"How's that?"

"Ever since then, you know? It's been one thing after another."

Doug looked away to hide his annoyance, his eyes falling on a Jenny McCarthy poster, the topless blonde clutching her tits like she was going to rip them off her chest and chuck them at his head. "Jem's fucking up all over the place," said Doug. "He went *Full Metal Jacket* in the movie theater lobby. Shot it up with one of the guard's guns—for no sane reason."

"He say anything about me?"

"About you? What, like you blabbed?"

"No. Wait—he thinks that?"

"Whoa, I don't know what the hell Jem thinks, I haven't seen him. What are you talking about?"

Dez tried to say it once, failed, exhaled, tried again. "Krista."

Doug stared. With everything else he had completely forgotten about that. "Aw, for Christ," he said in semidisgust.

"I ran into her at the Tap, the night of you guys' thing." Dez assessed Doug, wondering whether he should say anything more. "We hung out awhile, then she wanted to go back, watch the robbery coverage on the late news."

Doug knew how Krista got when she drank. So did a lot of other guys. And so, now, did Dez.

"Kid, I'm gonna say this just once. You're being played. She's putting you in the middle of what she thinks is this epic tug-of-war battle between her and me, not understanding that that's a rope I let go of a long time ago."

"Duggy—"

"On top of that . . ." A guy in a polo shirt and a ballcap passed the entrance without looking in, Doug getting antsy, starting to feel trapped. "On top of all that, she's running all over town doing errands for the guy who killed your dad."

"Her uncle. She works for him, does his books."

"A distant, *distant* cousin at best. And Krista's not known for her algebra, Dezi."

"What are you saying? About what she does for him?"

So idiotic, Dez getting all twisted up over Krista with these bombs going off around them. "Christ, will you cool it? What I'm saying is, she helps out Fergie the Florist from time to time, and I know what the Florist peddles and so do you. Clean those specs of yours."

"My specs are clean, Doug."

"Fucking fantastic for you. Oh, and one last little thing."

Sour now, pissed. "What?"

"That guy in the Cavalier outside your ma's house? He was at the police station when I was there."

Dez's face breaking, getting nervous again. "No."

"And no rash disguise this time. He is the G, and he's coming after all of us." Doug thumped Dez in the chest with his finger. "You want something to worry about, kid, start worrying about that."

30
BUY YOU SOMETHING

H E WATCHED HER THERE a moment, kneeling and working in her garden, before making his presence known. The riot of color and life that surrounded her was at its peak, this long late week in June. Though gardening in general struck Doug as the ultimate in futility—bringing a plot of land to life only to watch it die again, a chore doomed from the beginning—something in the way she threw everything she had into it, regardless of the outcome, was lovable.

All this passed through him in the instant before she saw him: Doug watching her kneeling on the dark rug of soil that held his treasure, in the thin, sidelong light of the setting sun, her shadow reaching across her garden sanctuary.

"I WANT TO BUY you something," he said.

They were in the plaza outside Trinity Church, part of an early-evening crowd surrounding a street performer juggling two bowling pins, a bowling ball, and a pair of bowling shoes. Only Claire watched the juggler—Doug watched the amusement in her face. The act ended to applause, Claire clapping prayer-handed under her chin.

"What do you want to buy me?"

"What do you want?"

"Hmm." She retook his hand, twisting slightly on her heels. "How about a new car?"

"What kind?"

"I was kidding. I don't want a car."

He said nothing, waiting.

"You're serious," she said.

"It's the first thing that came into your mind."

"That's because I was *joking*."

"If we trade in your Saturn on top of it, you could do pretty well."

She smiled, mystified by him. "I don't. Want. A new car."

"What do you want then?"

She laughed. "I don't want anything."

"Think. Something you wouldn't buy for yourself."

She made a thinking face, playing along. "Got it. Frozen yogurt at Emack's."

"Not bad. But I was thinking more along the lines of jewelry."

"Oh?" She smiled at the sidewalk ahead of them. "Yogurt or jewelry. I could be up all night wrestling with *that* choice."

Earrings didn't excite him. He looked at her neck: graceful, bare. "How about a chain? Where would we go to look for something like that?"

She put her free hand to her throat. "Why—Tiffany, of course."

"Okay. Tiffany it is."

"You know I'm still joking."

"I know you were joking before, when we were talking about a car. But once the topic of jewelry came up—I think you got a tiny bit serious."

She laughed like she should have been insulted and hit him lightly in the chest. Then she looked at him more closely. "What's gotten into you tonight?"

"I want to do this," he said. "Let me."

THE BROAD-HIPPED SALESWOMAN with the jailer's ring of cabinet keys waited as Claire turned and gathered up her hair. The woman worked the clasp and Claire turned to the framed mirror on the counter, opening her eyes and fixing on the diamond pebble glittering in the freckled scoop of her neck. Ringed in gold, the solitaire rode out a deep swallow.

"This is crazy," she breathed.

"It looks good on you."

"How can you . . . you can't afford this."

"It's cheaper than a car."

"Lasts longer too," said the saleswoman, smiling.

Claire's eyes never left the diamond. "I almost wish you wouldn't." She turned her head and watched it sparkle. "I did say *almost,* didn't I?"

The saleswoman nodded. "Will that be credit, or do you need to finance?"

"Cash," said Doug, reaching for his pocket.

CLAIRE STOPPED BEFORE A window a few shops away, checking her reflection again, this time over a display of fountain pens and sport knives. She touched her collarbone in exactly the same manner as the women in diamond advertisements. "I have to buy a whole new wardrobe now, just based around this."

Doug noticed her bare wrist. "There was a matching bracelet too, you play your cards right."

She admired it a few more moments before her hand fell away. "I should never have let you buy me this."

"Why not?"

"Because. Because the intent on your part was enough. The impulse you felt—I love it, whatever prompted it. That was the magic. A stronger person maybe, she would have told you that—and meant it—and let it go right there. A more secure person, maybe. But you didn't have to do this."

"The guilt," marveled Doug. "It's immediate."

"It is, isn't it?" she admitted, smiling a moment. Then she turned toward him, the smile gone. "Doug—I did something today, I have news."

A little heat came into his forehead. "What's that?"

"I quit my job."

Doug nodded slowly. "The bank."

"I had to. And really it was only a matter of time before they fired my ass." A flash of a smile at her slang, again quickly replaced by earnestness. "I was slacking off so much, I was no use to them anyway. Ever since the robbery . . . I won't bore you with that again, but I just couldn't do it anymore. Not because of what happened there. Because of me. I needed to make a clean break. I just— I can't believe I actually did it."

"It's sort of sudden, though, isn't it?"

"I guess. Why?"

"I'm just thinking about the police. A few weeks after the robbery . . . and now you're quitting the bank."

Her hand went to her open mouth. "Oh."

"I mean, maybe they won't . . ."

"That never even occurred to me. You don't think . . ."

He did. This was sure to bring renewed attention from the FBI. And if they started watching her, how could he keep seeing her and stay out of their crosshairs? And then, if they ever put him and Claire together . . .

That made him think. "You still talk to that FBI agent?"

Her hand came away from her mouth. "You think he'll be talking to me again?"

Doug felt icy suddenly. He wondered why he hadn't thought of this before. "What's he look like? Anything like on TV?"

They were moving again, through the Copley Mall toward the escalators, the Tiffany & Company bag dangling in Claire's hand. "He said he's a bank robbery agent, that's all he does."

"What's he like, a haircut in a suit?"

"Not hardly. He actually lives in the navy yard somewhere."

"The yard, huh?"

"Like my height, maybe an inch taller. Thick brown hair, kind of wavy-curly, all over the place. In fact—it's probably gone now, but he had this reddish sort of stain on his skin from this guy he was chasing, a bank robber who got a dye pack. Do you know what a dye pack is?"

They were on an elevator going down, which was lucky, because Doug could barely move.

Too convoluted, the whole thing. Too massive, he couldn't break it down. Had he fucked up? Had this bank sleuth somehow been feeding off him through Claire?

He watched her at the revolving doors, pausing in her story about the bank robbery agent getting stained in order to eye her necklace again in the reflective chrome.

She knew nothing. Maybe the sleuth knew nothing either. Maybe.

Outside, they crossed a brick-and-stone plaza, commuters flooding the street from the Back Bay station, jumping curbs and chasing down taxis. Claire took his hand. "Delayed sticker shock?"

"No," he said, coming back around. "What are you going to do now?"

"Right now? I don't—"

"No, I mean—now that you're out of a job."

"Oh. I've got some money saved, I have a cushion. What do I *want* to do?" She looked up at the tops of the skyscrapers. "Stay out of banking, that's for sure. My parents are going to freak out. I thought about teaching, but—what I do with the kids at the Boys and Girls Club, that's not really teaching. It's not social work either. It's nothing you can make a living at. Though I did talk to the director over there, in case a paid position opens up."

Thoughts came to him as fast as the commuters swarming around them. "What would you think," said Doug, "if I quit my job too?"

She laughed a little. "I guess then I'd have company. But why?"

"I got some money saved too. My own cushion. Hell, I got a whole sofa stashed away."

They walked a few more steps against the crowd, then she looked up at him, remembering the necklace. "A whole sofa, huh?"

"Matching love seat, even."

Everything seemed threatened now, everything converging. Like his old life had suddenly been condemned, explosive charges being laid on all the load-bearing beams, a crew of badass demo hard hats advancing on it with crowbars and sledges.

"You know how everybody's always got that place they want to go—their *if-only* place? You know, *If only I had the money,* or, *If only I had the chance.*"

Claire nodded. "Sure."

"I never had a place like that. I bet you do."

"Only about half a dozen."

"The problem is—no one ever goes to their if-only place."

"No, they never do."

"Well, why not? Why couldn't we be the first?"

She smiled, finding a different angle on his face, discovering something there. "Know what, Doug? You're a romantic. I think I knew it all along, only you hide it so well."

"Things are changing for me, Claire. Changing fast, like hour to hour."

"There's one small problem I foresee with your if-only plan."

"What's that?"

She smiled. "There's no Charlestown anywhere else in the world."

"Yeah," he said. "Yeah, that is a snag."

And he left it floating there like that: mere talk. Twenty-six years ago his mother had walked away from the Town. Maybe now it was his time to follow.

31
KEYED

CLARK MAYORS WAS A locksmith with a small key-making shop on Bromfield Street, one of the narrow lanes off the cobblestone boulevard of Downtown Crossing. The night-duty agent had given Frawley Clark's pager number, the Boston FO being without a good lockpick and contracting the sixty-year-old keymaker for side gigs, both on and off paper. Clark was a careful, square-faced, solidly built black man with a pleasant, home-cooked smell and half-glasses over snowy cheek stubble. His no-questions fee of a hundred an hour was coming straight out of Frawley's own linty pocket.

Just a few hours before, Frawley had been sitting in the backseat of his new Bureau car, a banged-up, navy blue Ford Tempo, trying to stay awake half a block down from Claire Keesey's door. The muscular growl of a Corvette engine roused him in time to see the two of them nuzzling in the front seat, then her getting out and going into her place alone. Frawley put off his plan to drop in on her then, instead rolling out after MacRay.

The bold green sports car seemed headed for the interstate, in which case Frawley wouldn't bother trying to keep up, but then MacRay cut sharply toward the Schrafft's tower at the last moment, crossing the Mystic north into Everett. He turned off Main Street down a dim residential road, Frawley thinking MacRay had made him, only to see the Corvette's round brake lights turn into a driveway. Frawley backed off and waited, parked up on Main trying to figure out his next move, when just in time he recognized MacRay's second car, the dumpy white Caprice Classic, parked right in front of him. Frawley took off and made a slow loop past a funeral home, and by the time he returned, the Caprice was gone.

Frawley's adrenaline had hardly subsided from then until now, watching Clark work on the side door of a broad garage. The only light source was a pale blue spritz coming off the next-door neighbor's backyard Madonna.

Clark first snaked a worm scope under the door, previewing the interior bolts and checking for alarms. His handheld, gray-and-white monitor showed no booby traps, nothing tricky. Then he hiked up his pants and knelt before the padlock, a folded rag under his knee, an old black curtain draped over his shoulders and head to swallow his working light. Frawley kept an eye on the street—the neighborhood struck him as one likely to mete out swift street justice to housebreakers—listening to Clark's patient click-scratches.

The cloak was whisked away and Clark straightened with a soft grunt, lifting his Klein Tools bag off the ground and nodding to Frawley. Frawley gripped the knob with his break-in gloves and it turned easily, no creaks or whines to worry the night. Clark followed him inside, Frawley quickly shutting the door.

Clark turned his flashlight back on—a white spray off a wire hooked to his half-glasses—and found a wall switch screwed to an unfinished beam by the door. He gave the exposed box the once-over, fingering each electrical connection, and then with the aid of Frawley's stronger Maglite, followed the stapled wires up to the ceiling rafters and the lamps clamped overhead.

Clark hit the switch and the lamps came on loud, the halogens blazing up the old garage. The muscle car glowed dead center, emerald against cement, a long, low, lustrous jewel resting on five-spoke, star-rimmed wheels.

Against the near wall was a red tool cart on casters and a built-in workbench under particleboard shelves of small parts, accessories, and tools ancient and new.

"Pretty thing," said Clark, snapping off his spy light.

Frawley walked to the car and rested his gloved hand on the glass-smooth hood, expecting a pulse. It must have had half a dozen coats of paint. He slipped his fingers underneath the handle of the driver's-side door and opened it wide.

The interior was black leather, still smelling like a new baseball glove. He lowered himself into the driver's seat, the upholstery moaning but not protesting. He reached for the stick and toed the pedals, touching the leather-wrapped wheel. He would have needed to inch the seat forward to operate it comfortably.

"Dope dealer, huh?" said Clark, eyeing the finish, tool bag in hand.

Armor All slicked the dash. Frawley reached across the passenger seat for the glove compartment, and suddenly smelled Claire Keesey there, that butterscotch hair product she used. The car was registered to Kristina Coughlin of Pearl Street, Charlestown, Massachusetts. Underneath the registration card was a CD jewel case labeled *AM Gold*.

Frawley climbed out, shut the door. He moved to the workbench, sliding open each drawer of the tool cart, then checked the minifridge, pulling out a one-liter bottle of Mountain Dew. He cracked the cap and drank down half of it at a gulp. He peered into a cardboard-box trash can, but it was just empty Dew bottles and shop rags.

In the rear of the garage, the cement floor ended over the old wood framing, dropping down four feet or so to packed dirt. Frawley trained his flashlight on the yard tools rotting there, the bicycles and sleds, a limp tetherball game. The soil looked hard and unlikely to preserve his shoe tread, so he hopped down, exciting dust in his flashlight beam. Decades of oxidation gave the dark trench a metallic tang. He looked around but it was all just junk, and Frawley wondered what the homeowner's relationship was to MacRay, making a mental note to run the address in the morning.

He was on his way back up when his beam found a head-sized stone loose from the rocky subfoundation. Its shadow moved when he did, betraying a hollow inside. Frawley shoved an ancient snowblower out of the way and crouched down before the stone and the scooped-smooth hole, like an eyeball tumbled out of its socket. The cavity was empty but for a few silica-gel packets, the Do Not Eat kind packed inside sneaker boxes to absorb moisture. Frawley put his face to the opening. The smell he got was the unmistakable old-linen odor of stored cash.

He stood, downing more Mountain Dew. MacRay had just recently moved his stash. If only he knew how close on his heels Frawley was.

Clark yawned up top, reminding Frawley that the meter was running. He climbed back to the cement floor, the Corvette gleaming proud. He tried to envision it torched. "You can lock it back up again from the outside?" asked Frawley. "Make it look like no one's been in here?"

Clark nodded, his voice rug-soft and shag-smooth. "No time at all."

"Go ahead and kill the light then, get set up outside. I'll be right there."

Clark switched off the rafter lamps and exited, leaving Frawley with his Maglite beam and the car. Frawley dug out his ring of keys, comparing them in the heat of his flashlight, the new Tempo key having the sharpest teeth. He walked to the long front fender of the Corvette and dug the key into the soft finish, gouging it across the driver's-side door and all the way to the rear, then stepped back to admire his work.

There were some exceptionally handsome front doors in Charlestown, but Claire Keesey's was not one of them. Around Monument Square and the nearby John Harvard Mall, the European-style entrances compared favorably to those in Beacon Hill and the lower Back Bay, but hers was entirely ordinary: no brass, no stained glass, no bold color, just a drab brown door, the weathered varnish flaking off the grain.

She opened it wearing gray gym shorts and a ribbed, black tank shirt, braless and barefoot, her hair wet but combed out, falling straight. Surprise in her eyes when she recognized him behind the sunglasses—though Frawley noted disappointment as well.

"Hi," she said, as in *What are you doing here?*

"This a bad time? Were you expecting someone else?"

"No. No—come in."

He moved past her across the white-tile threshold, down the short hallway into the living room. Against the widest wall, a wire shelving unit and a bamboo hutch were paired off in a feng shui tug-of-war. The leather sofa was a plump, safe tan straight out of Jennifer Convertibles. There were other staples—the rattan CD tower from Pier One, the Pottery Barn slab rug—as well as some out-of-place wall prints left over since college. It was all mishmash, the product of a decade of gradual accumulation.

The coffee table was cluttered with clothing catalogs and issues of *Shape* and *Marie Claire*. He peeked into her bedroom, the comforter rumpled, the bed unmade, then cut back to the kitchen, looking out the window to the buildings across the alley.

"You want to blow-dry, I can wait."

"No," she said, put off by his wandering around. "That's okay."

He looked at her a long moment. He carried MacRay's mug shots in a manila envelope tucked under his arm. "So you quit the bank."

A tiny bloom of panic in her eyes. "Yes, it just—it got to be too much."

He had tried to give her the benefit of the doubt. To view her as an unsuspecting pawn, as the victim of an ex-con's con. Along with needing to determine how much she knew about MacRay, Frawley had gone there that morning in the hope of working up some sympathy for her.

But any chance of that went away when he saw the flat-shell jewelry case on her kitchenette table, classic Tiffany & Company blue. He laid the manila envelope down on the table and opened the hinged case, lifting out a thread-thin necklace, dangling it between his hands, the solitaire quivering like a tiny crystal eye.

"Lovely," he said.

"That—it was a gift."

"Not from the piano mover?"

She did not answer. Frawley kept himself in check. He was holding a chunk of MacRay's movie money in his hand. The crook was buying her jewelry with it. "May I see it on you?"

Her hand went protectively to her neck. "I'm not really dressed for . . ."

He was already bringing it to her, undoing the delicate clasp and waiting for her to turn. She did so, reluctantly, sweeping the hair off the back of her neck, and Frawley clasped the necklace beneath her darker roots, waiting for her to turn back around.

She kept her eyes low, self-conscious, trying not to be. The diamond winked above the scoop neck of her tank top, her breasts pressing against the black fabric. Her nipples were erect and she crossed her arms guiltily.

Frawley said, "Did you hear about that movie theater in Braintree?"

She blinked at this abrupt change of subject. "Yes, sure, the holdup."

Frawley nodded, backing away. "The same guys. We're pretty certain."

"The same?" Her surprise was authentic.

"It was an armored-car pickup. We also now know they're all Charlestown guys."

Again, her shock. "For sure?"

"In fact we're watching a couple of jokers now. Getting close."

She looked down, nodding like she was trying to figure out something. Maybe some ghostly concern that had been tugging at the edge of her consciousness for a while. Frawley talked to keep her off-balance.

"These Townie guys, they love armoreds. Banks and armoreds, that's always been their thing. Rite-of-passage stuff, them getting dusted and pulling stickups. Boston cops used to respond to bank alarms by shutting down the Charlestown Bridge and waiting for the dopes to try to cross back over with their loot. Especially in winter—they love the snow, the havoc it wreaks, pulling on ski masks and going robbing. But some of these kids, a select few, after bouncing around the system a little—something kicks in and they start getting smart. Those are the ones who grow into professionals. The ones for whom robbing banks becomes a career, a vocation, their life's work. See, the prison theory, that's always seemed a little too pat to me."

She shook her head, trying to follow him. "Prison theory?"

"The community college, under the highway? Used to be *the* prison in Boston. Sacco and Vanzetti, Malcolm X. Theory goes that the inmates' families settled here to be near them, breeding successive generations of crooks and bandits. But I think it's simpler than that. My own theory is that bank robbing is just a trade here, the way villages in old America and Europe used to be known for a particular craft. Like glassblowing or bootmaking or silversmithing. Here it's bank robbing and armored-car heists. Techniques developed and refined over time, talents passed down through generations. You know, father to son."

Claire looked pale now, staring into the middle distance, reaching for the sofa corner with one hand and absently touching her necklace with the other.

"And then there's this Revolutionary War mentality," Frawley went on. "They've taken that mythology and perverted it. The fuck-the-invaders tradition—appropriated it for their own criminal means. The bank robber as folk hero, all that nonsense. Like I'm the enemy here, right? The law is the bad guy." He picked up a CD from the top of her stereo, turned to her. "Huh. *AM Gold*. Any good?"

She didn't hear him. She was somewhere else now.

Frawley replaced the case and moved on. "But, no, don't worry. These guys always find a way to screw up, even the smart ones. Things like talking too much about banks. Or asking too many questions of people, trying to learn things about the FBI. Or flashing lots of cash around. These are things people notice."

Claire's hand came away from her necklace.

"And on top of all that," said Frawley, returning to the table to pick up his manila envelope, "on top of all that, we've got ourselves a partial handprint."

This roused her from her trance. "I thought you weren't able to talk about things like that."

"Well . . ." He showed her a big smile and a shrug. "Who are you going to tell, right?"

She nodded without meeting his eye. The necklace was starting to choke her now, and Frawley found that he could pity her ignorance, but not her fate: she had invited aboard this shipwreck of her life the very pirate who had scuttled and looted it in the first place. Frawley could have protected her if she had let him. He could have spared her all this. But now she was his advantage over MacRay, and as such, a thing to exploit. He tucked the sealed envelope back under his arm. Catching bank robbers was his job, not rescuing branch managers from themselves.

"Sure you're okay?" he said.

She crossed her arms again, nodding, standing almost on one leg. She could see dark clouds massing on the horizon, but refused to acknowledge the storm they forecast.

"Yeah," said Frawley. She was waiting for him to leave now, and he let her wait. "Yeah," he said again. "Well." Then he fit his sunglasses back on his face and started for the door, stopping next to her, again struck by the necklace. He pressed the tip of his forefinger lightly against the pocket of flesh between her clavicles, touching the starry little pill, absorbing her discomfort, her distress. "Okay," he said, and left.

32
RINK

FOUR GUYS IN KNEE-LENGTH denim shorts and T-shirts, black skates over heavy cotton socks pushed down under meaty calves, eating lunch on the indoor ice in the middle of June. They had the rink to themselves, refrigerator fans rattle-roaring like truck engines outside the boards as they circled around two Papa Gino's pizza cartons set upon milk-crate pedestals.

"So," Jem said, swigging a Heineken, calling the summit to order. "Somebody fucked up somewhere."

Doug dropped his crust into the open box, curling effortlessly around Jem's back and plucking his bottle of Dew off the ice floor, gliding backward.

"And we still don't know how," said Jem. "I don't even know yet who the fuck to dock."

Dez drifted away from the pizza without meaning to, better on Rollerblades than he was on ice.

Jem said, "That ride better have burned."

Gloansy finished a Heineken and stooped to return the bottle to the six-pack carton, saying, "Fuck you, you were there."

Doug looked up at the rafters. He remembered the cheering and the bleacher-stomping and the way his last name rhymed with *Hurray!* and also how it always seemed that a win for the home team was never enough—how it seemed that nothing short of the entire building going up in a ball of flame would satisfy the bloodlust of that crowd.

He could still see the Bruins scout, the guy in the Bear Bryant hat and fingerless wool gloves sitting in the last spot on the fifth riser, center ice, making frantic marks in his spiral notebook as the Martin sisters next to him kept screaming Doug's name. His summary report, showed to Doug after the draft, described MacRay as "a thug player with a touch of class," a high-scoring, high-potential defenseman blending the goon tradition of the seventies with the new eighties finesse.

But it was all just echoes now. He found himself touching his split eyebrow and pulled his hand away, angry. This was why he didn't like being out on this ice anymore.

"There were no obvious problems on the job," Jem continued, "least none nobody admits to. So how come we each spent half our morning making sure we were clean of the G, getting here? How come all of a sudden we're earning so much heat?"

No cops were waiting for Doug when he carried his tea out of Lori-Ann's that morning—yet everything seemed changed. It was like a protective seal on the Town had been broken, and now there could be cops waiting for him anywhere: his car, his home, his mother's house.

"Simple," said Doug, coming back around for another slice, spraying some shavings against the stacked crates with a sharp stop. "They were onto us from before. And we went ahead and rushed it anyway."

"Rushed, nothing," said Jem. "But we didn't sit around neither, let 'em shut us down."

"No," said Doug. "No, that would have been foolhardy."

"Aha, a little attitude from the mastermind here. Okay, genius. Tell us, then. Where and when did all this shit go wrong?"

"For that I'd have to take us all back to a bitter-cold day in early December 1963."

Jem frowned off the reference to his birthday. He turned to Dez, the only one of them who hadn't been at the movie theater. "Duggy's pissed 'cause I went and had a little fun."

"That what that was?" said Doug. "That was fun?"

Jem smiled his angry smile. "That job was the driest fucking job. It was *nothing*."

"Nothing," said Doug.

"Truth be told, Douglas—it was pansy-ass. It was pussy. Hadda be said."

Doug slowed and drifted back toward the crates. "So let me get this straight. The job went *too* smooth for you. Not enough fucking up, far as you're concerned, your usual quotient."

"It wasn't no heist. It was a friggin' lemonade stand we knocked over. We could of been three *girls* in there, pulling that off."

"It was a sweet score, and it fell like a feather."

"Awright, assholes, enough," said Gloansy, looking to douse the flames.

But Jem wasn't interested. "It's not the paycheck, kid," he said, gliding away from the pizza podium to engage Doug. "It's how you bring it home."

"It's *that* you bring it home—*period*," said Doug. "You're too old to die young, Jemmer. That time is passed."

"Fuckin' Johnny Philosopher here. What've you got to lose all of a sudden?"

The leer in Jem's face was for Claire Keesey, but Doug was in no mood. "This is about being a pro and acting like one. About doing it good and right. That's the thing."

"No, Duggy, see, that's *your* thing. *You* plan it, no one else. And then what—I gotta follow your rules and regulations? I'm your employee here?" Jem's slow trajectory brought him closer to Doug, his hands resting on his hips. "See, my thing is getting into it on the job, mixing it up. 'Cause I'm a motherfucking *outlaw*."

Doug let Jem drift past, the smell of beer trailing him like a cloud of flies.

Dez and Gloansy had stopped chewing, waiting on opposite sides of the pizza pedestal like kids watching their parents fight. Doug said to them, "You guys on board with that? You want me keeping you *out* of danger, or putting you *in* some?"

Jem circled back, speedy but measured, lifting skate over skate. "And what is this with playing it safe? We are *bank robbers,* man. Stickup men, we go in packing, balls to the wall. It's a gun in our hand, not a fuckin' briefcase. There is nothing *safe* about this." He spun around so he could face them all, gliding backward. "The hell happened to you, Duggy?"

Gloansy said, "Can we all fucking forget this, please?"

Dez said, "Yeah. Frigging boring."

Gloansy put down his beer. "Give us our magic number and let's call it a day."

Jem started back at a decent clip, looking to do a breeze-by. "Like your trick there with the guards. Holding their families over them, immobilizing them with that. So *safe*. So fucking *clever*. Know what?" He zipped past Doug, spinning, heavy-legged but clean. "I fucking *hate* safe and clever."

Doug said, "This is why you beat on the assistant manager at the Kenmore thing. Why you had to go and grab the bank manager. Stealing's not enough for you anymore. That won't get you caught fast enough."

"This is what I'm talking about," Jem said, talking to Doug but playing to the jury. "Since when did you let the people in our way *get* in our way?"

"You tuned up that guy for no reason. Other than to bring the heat down on us, which we are now enjoying this very fucking day."

"Did you forget that that motherfucking brown hound hit the bell?"

"No, he didn't."

"No, he didn't," scoffed Jem. "Yes, he very well fucking—"

"He didn't," said Doug. "She did."

Jem just drifted past, staring.

Gloansy checked Dez, then Doug. "How do you know, Duggy?"

"How do I know?" Doug watched Jem curling around them, Doug saying, *Shall I?*

You don't have the onions, said Jem's white-eyed challenge.

Doug said, "I know this because she told me."

Jem still stared, trying to figure Doug out, Doug saying, *You got nothing on me now.*

Dez said, "What do you mean, she told you?"

"Checking her out after the job—I met her. We talked a couple of times."

Jem said, "He's fucking going steady with her."

Doug kept talking. "And now Jem has her as an undercover FBI agent or something. All sorts of conspiracy theories, probably. When she's just someone trying to put her life back together, simple as that. There. Now everybody's caught up."

Jem said, "You're still seeing her."

"Am I? What, you gonna follow me some more? Follow the G following me? We'll do the motherfucking parade down Bunker Hill Street, how about that? Streamers, silly hats, everything." Doug kicked away then, rounding the three of them in a tight, slow circle.

Gloansy turned, tracking Doug. "Who's following *who*? Fuck's going on?"

Jem said, "What is it you're not getting? Our Duggy here's been dating that cooze from the Kenmore job. The one who rode with us. Oh, wait—but *I'm* the one that wants to get caught."

Dez said, stunned, "How long, Duggy?"

"Not long."

"Well—you still seeing her?"

Jem said, "How about it, Romeo? When you gonna bring her around, meet your buds?"

Doug said, "She doesn't know anything."

Gloansy said, "Well, Duggy, for Christ—she *better* not."

"She doesn't."

Jem said, "And I bet he hasn't even lit her lamp yet." He mimed a slap-shot goal. "Hasn't slipped one in between the pads."

Doug threw Jem a look saying, *Enough.*

"You know," said Jem, blowing through that stop sign, "me and the assistant manager, we danced that one time. Whyn't I call him up, we'll double-date? Go out for milk shakes or something. Can he drink through a straw yet? Or wait— what kind of milk shake did I mean?"

"All right, Jem," said Doug, throwing down the gloves. "Here's the deal. And this is as un*safe* and as un*clever* as I can make it. Okay? You ready?"

Jem's waiting smile was full of dragon steam.

Doug said, "I am not with your sister anymore. And I won't be, and I never will be, and that's the end of that. Krista and me—we are not getting married. Never. We are not all going to live in your house, the three of us and Shyne, happily ever after. Not gonna happen."

Jem's wild smile became a hot, dark slice in his face. A Jem-o'-lantern with the candle blown out, smoking. He stood perfectly still on the ice. "She's got you wrapped so motherfucking tight."

"That's right," said Doug.

"You fucking whip-ass pussy."

"Man," said Doug, swinging at the chilled air, amazed that it had gone this far, and at the same time not surprised. They were grappling on the edge of a cliff here, this close to going over together for good.

"You're turning into fucking tapioca right in front of me. What's she got on you, man? Or are you so fucking blind you can't see?"

"What is it I can't see, Jem?"

"You can't see what she's doing."

"Tell me, Jem. Tell me what she's doing."

Jem's head shook in disgust. "If we can't trust her, kid—how we gonna trust you?"

Doug smiled. So much coming out of him, a riot of pent-up thought and anger. "You are so fucked in the head, Jem boy. You don't trust me? No? Then find yourself someone else to set your scores. No—better than that, *you* do it. Yourself. *You* map it out. And I'll sit back until game time, then show up and shoot the place up from under you, just for fucking *fun.*"

"There's always Fergie, man."

Doug's head jerked back like Jem had taken a jab at him. "Don't fucking even."

Jem's eyes were bright and daring. "He's got some real scores lined up. Big hits for big hitters. He's said as much."

"Excellent. Then you're all set, kid. You don't even need me here. 'Cause I will *never* work for that psycho piece of shit." Doug glided backward on the strength of his own outburst. He looked to Dez. "How about you, Monsignor? Wanna go work for the guy who gunned down your dad?"

Dez exhaled a stream of determination and shook his head.

Doug shrugged back at Jem. They were paired off now, Doug and Dez versus Jem and Gloansy. A lot of silence, everyone's breath billowing out fast.

Doug said finally, "So is this how it ends?"

Gloansy put out his hands as though elevator doors were closing. "Hey, okay, hold on, just hold on."

Jem shook his little head. "Nothing's ending, man."

"No?" said Doug. "Only because you don't have the *sense*. Gloansy too, the both of you—you're gonna keep taking jobs until you get grabbed."

Fury twisted at Jem, his frown warping, jumping. "I ain't never getting grabbed."

"Always, I knew this, but I never saw it as clear as right now. The movie theater score—that was our biggest ever. Not enough. Nothing ever will be."

Jem looked at him in white-eyed amazement, slow-drifting toward him. "You talking about money? When's it ever been about money? This has always been about *us*. The four musketeers here, taking on the fucking world. About being outlaws, man. I don't know when you forgot that, Duggy. I don't know when you forgot that."

"All right then. For kicks, since no one here really cares—what's our split?"

Jem still drifting forward, eyes locked on Doug, a collision course. "One-fourteen, three oh two. Per."

Dez said, next to Doug, "Holy shit."

Gloansy laughed out a tension-breaking gasp. "And that's all clean? Spendable, like right fucking *now*?"

Dez said, "Holy fucking *shit*."

Jem remained staring at Doug, Doug at him.

Gloansy said, "Lemonade stand, whatever—that's fucking *genius*!" Cackling now, shouting at the ceiling. *"Aaawooo!"*

Doug said evenly, "The split is light."

Jem stopped drifting.

Doug angled his blades on the ice, setting himself. "Even with your ten percent ass-kiss to Uncle Fergus, it's light. That's a soft split."

Gloansy stopped his celebrating. Dez looked at Jem. No breath came from anyone's mouth now.

"I saw the receipts," said Doug. "But, hey, right? I mean—it's not about the *money*."

Jem started for Doug, and Doug started for Jem, Gloansy and Dez lunging after their respective teammates, wrapping them up to prevent a brawl. Gloansy was just strong enough to keep Jem off Doug, and though Dez was overmatched by Doug, Doug didn't really want a fight here. He wanted to win the argument, then leave.

"Every split you ever did was soft," said Doug. "And why did we let you handle the cash? Because we trusted you? No—because you're Jem. Because that's the cost of being fucking friends with you."

Jem lunged again, Gloansy digging his skates into the ice and fighting hard to hold him, swinging Jem around, taking some of his blows.

Doug went on, shouting, "'Cause you're a thief with a petty fucking heart. Little rip-offs, ever since I known you. A Wiffle bat here, a comic book there. Things of mine that would vanish."

Another swipe missed, Jem getting closer, saliva slicking his chin. Doug kept himself back just enough to deny Jem contact.

"That Phil Esposito photo card you needed to complete your set, that I wouldn't trade you? What—you thought I never knew? But that's the kid you were, and that's the kid you are still. Funny-guy Jem, the cutup—that's what's carried you through. But it's not funny anymore. This is the last split of mine you are gonna handle, and I mean *ever*. Always gotta have more than the rest, always gotta be in charge."

"I *am* in charge, you mother—"

"No." Doug used his skating advantage to muscle Dez off him. "You keep your skim, and when you're using it to buy your next pair of fucking speakers or whatever, just remember how, yeah, it did all used to be all about us, four kids from the Town. How, yeah, we did have something once."

He looped around past Jem, just beyond his reach, bringing Jem tumbling down on top of Gloansy. Doug curled to scoop his Dew back up off the ice, then skated for the doors, Jem's vulgarities bouncing off his back like boos.

His skates were off, socks stuffed inside them, by the time Dez came out, looking more anguished than usual, a guy full of questions, forever quizzing the world about himself and his place in it. Doug stopped him before he could say word one. "You cut loose of Krista, you understand me? Now you know for sure that I got no stake in it. You had your thing with her, now get out. These Coughlins'll kill you. You hear me?"

Dez nodded, shocked.

Gloansy came out skate-walking over the hard rubber flooring to where Doug sat lacing his Vans. It surprised Doug that Gloansy, of all of them, was the one most desperate to keep the crew together. "Duggy, hey—you're gonna cool this down, right? And so's he? You guys, huh?"

Doug could already hear the dominoes clicking, tiles spilling from the end all the way back to the beginning, spelling out his flight. But there was no point trying to explain this to Gloansy. Doug stood and carried his skates to the door.

33
BILLY T.

FRANK G. LOOKED GRAY under the yellow doughnut-shop lights. He hadn't shaved in two or three days, and kept running his hand across his bristly lips like a rummy. His eyes were tea-bagged and his shoulders flat under a *Malden Little League Coach* shirt.

"Well, that's good to hear," said Frank G., distracted. "Yeah, you been needing to break with them for a long time."

Doug waited, shrugged. "That's all I get? No trumpets, no angels singing?"

Frank G. squirmed in his seat. "So—we get this call at the station last week."

Doug was startled. Mr. Anonymous made a point of never talking about himself or his work. "The station," said Doug, alerting Frank G. to his slip.

"Guy's hit by a truck on the Fellsway. Okay, no big deal, we suit up and head out to assist EMS, it's routine. Then, big commotion as we arrive on the scene. Something's up. Middle of the road is this huge dump truck with a haul full of sand, engine still running. They tell us there's an elderly man pinned underneath it. Truck's got four twin sets of wheels, big mothers, and I'm thinking, mashed foot, some poor jaywalker's looking at a wheelchair for the rest of his days. So my guys are getting out the equipment, and I go round this truck, find the driver sitting on the curb median, bawling into his hands. A big guy, and he's falling apart, sobbing, asking for a priest. So I know it's gonna be bad.

"I go round to look, and my eyes, it takes a second to process this. The tire, the outside one, is right on top of this guy's pelvis. Flattening it. Inside tire has his legs crushed at the knees. EMTs and a young lady cop are crouching by this guy, attending to him, and my mind's telling me it's fake, it's a movie, guy lying in a hole in the road, dummy legs set on the other side of the tires.

"And then the old guy's head turns. I can't even believe he's still moving. His head turns and his eyes find me, his mouth open like a baby's. And now I *really* can't believe it. Because I fucking know this guy. It's Billy T."

Doug said, "Whoa, whoa. Billy T.? Sad-sack Billy T.?"

"From the meetings. The scally cap he always wore, that moth-bitten thing, it's lying next to the EMT's medical case. And then I see in his eyes, his wet, little wooden eyes—he recognizes me. He's trying to place me—I'm in uniform, red helmet, jacket, reflective stripes—but he knows the face. Probably thought I was an angel or something, you know? The body like that, the brain releasing those, whatever they're called, hormones, opiates, whatever. Least I hope that's what it does, when you wake up under a dump truck."

Frank G. watched steam escape from the triangle torn out of his cup cover.

"'Billy,' I says to him. The people attending to him, they look up at me like he's my dad or something, I know this guy's name. One EMT jumps up, takes my arm, handles me like I'm next of kin, tells me Billy was crossing the street against the traffic, truck knocked him down, rolled over him, stopped. Billy T. should be dead, he tells me. Any other way this had happened, he would be gone already. But the truck was like a giant tourniquet, cutting off the bleeding, keeping him alive.

"Meantime, my crew is scrambling to slide a twenty-five-ton hydraulic jack under the dumper, setting up these two big seventy-ton air bags. They see me huddled with the EMT and think Billy's my wife's uncle or something, so they're working double-time for me, and I'm like, Whoa, whoa, *whoa!* We raise this thing off him and Billy dies. We leave it where it is, Billy dies too—only more slowly.

"So now I've got the EMT in my face, he's flipping out on me, talking about surgeons and field amputations and such, and I'm no doctor, but I can see there's nothing to amputate here. A magician, maybe, could saw Billy T. in two, pull him out, then wave his hand and put him back together again. So I become the point guy on this. I want to go off, sit down with the truck driver, wait for the priest—but I'm the guy now. I have to make the call.

"So I kneel in the road next to Billy. They'd cut his shirt off and I can see his little heart beating through his old dishrag of a chest, but real slow. He moves his arm—guy's moving still—reaching for me, so I take his hand. His little fingers are hot, he's burning up. And the look on his face. But I see his lips are working, so I get down low. Both feet in the grave and he's still able to whisper to me. 'Frank,' he's says. I yell back to someone to turn off the truck so I can hear, and then the engine goes silent, the whole world goes silent.

" 'Billy,' I says to him. 'My friend.' All of a sudden this weepy old man's my friend, like we're soldiers on a battlefield somewhere, the same unit. I take off my helmet. 'We gotta lift this truck, Billy. We gotta get it off you. Anything you want to say?' I don't know if he's got kids, what. 'Any message for anybody, something I can do for you, my friend?' I keep calling him my friend, over and over. 'Anything you want to tell me, Billy, anything to say?'

"And his hand, there's like this little squeeze of pressure, and I get in tight. I'm right there, him breathing on me, this half-ghost, looking me square in the eye. 'Frank,' he whispers. 'Frank.'

"I say, 'What is it, Billy, anything at all.'

" 'A drink, Frank. Get me a drink.'

"The EMT next to me, he jumps up again, calling for bottled water, a dying man's last request. Me, I'm kneeling there as cold as a fish on ice. Because I know Billy T. I know this weepy old, bandy-legged Irish punter with bologna on his breath. He didn't want any *water* to drink just then. He didn't want fucking *water*."

Doug shared Frank G.'s chill, but not his anger. Frank left it hanging there, until Doug finally had to ask, "So what happened?"

Frank G. looked at him like Doug hadn't heard a word he'd said. *"That's* what happened. *That's* the story."

"No, what happened to Billy T.?"

Frank shrugged, pissed. "My guys did the best they could for him. We shimmed some timber cribbing around the wheels to cut down on the vibration, we raised the truck. What happened to Billy T.? They put a sheet over his face and took him away. We hosed off the road and went back to the station."

A gust of laughter from the clerk and an Indian customer at the counter— Doug and Frank G. sitting there like two guys who had just donated blood.

"Okay," Doug said.

Frank G. looked up from the study he was making of his coffee cup. "Okay, what?"

"Okay, so I'm waiting for you to drop some wisdom on me."

"Wisdom? I got nothing for you, buddy. I'm fresh out here. Billy T., he was a royal pain in the ass at meeting—but the guy did good work. He was dry some twelve fucking years. I can't get my mind around this thing."

"What, that he—"

"That with all the work he did, *twelve long years*—every single day of it he was just marking time until he could take a drink again. Waiting for that day. Like someday he'd hit all nines on the odometer and it would roll over to zero again and he'd get to start fresh. A life with no restrictions on it. And what *I* want to know is—is that all of us? Just marking time here, waiting? Thinking someday, some miracle's gonna happen, and we're going to be free again?"

Doug nodded. "Maybe, yeah."

"Christ, don't agree with me, Doug. I'm fighting for my life here. What was he thinking, what? That heaven is an open bar? Jesus wiping out pint glasses, setting out a coaster, *What'll you have?* That's what we're being good for here?"

"The guy was dying, Frank."

"Fuck him." Frank sat back. "Fuck Billy T."

"All right, Frank. Hey."

"Fuck you, *hey*. You weren't there. How would you like it if I was going down, you holding my hand, and I asked you for a quick pop? Huh? I *begged* you?"

"I wouldn't like it at all."

"You'd be sick. Fucking repulsed. All my words here? You'd tell me I was full of shit, and you'd be right." He dropped his hands on the table. "I am, anyway."

"Frank, man," said Doug, looking around for something to say to him. "I don't wanna see you like this."

"Listen, Doug, you're still my obligation, you got my number. But I can't do this anymore. Least not right now."

"Whoa, hold up. What are you—"

"I'm saying maybe you ought to be in the market for another sponsor."

"Frank—no fucking way, Frank. No way. You can't."

"Can. Am."

Doug stared. "Frank—you would never let me."

"No? How would I stop you? Huh? How you gonna stop me?"

Doug rubbed his face hard in a panic. Up popped a memory from a long-ago meeting, one Jem had appeared at—uninvited, twenty minutes late, and stinking drunk. He had dropped into a folding chair two rows behind Doug and, in the middle of Billy T.'s lament, started humming "The Star-Spangled Banner." When someone finally asked him to leave, Jem burst out crying and started talking about his father and how he never really knew the guy, and all he ever wanted was his love. Two people slid down the row to comfort him, at which point Jem jumped up and cackled, *Suckaz!*—knocking over chairs and lurching toward the door. *Duggy,* he had said, *c'mon, man, lezz go!* And it was Frank who came over to Doug later, telling him, *Your friends are afraid of you getting healthy. They want to keep you sick.*

"Frank," said Doug, still searching for some angle to play, some lever to pull—but all he could summon was unreasonable anger. "Don't walk out on me now. I *need* this."

"Hey. Sorry if my little crisis of faith is inconvenient for you. Sorry if I'm the one maybe needs a little counseling now."

"I—I can't fucking counsel you. I wouldn't know the first—"

"Then respect my decision and leave it at that, for Christ's sake." Frank picked up his keys and started to stand, then sat back down again. Something else was tugging at him. "I wasn't going to tell you this. But this guy came to see me about you."

Doug froze. "What guy?"

"Other day, over at the station house. Showed me an FBI badge, asked if I knew someone named Doug MacRay. We went back and forth on that one a little while, me trying to go the priest-doctor-lawyer route, confidentiality. He wouldn't have it. Kind of a prick. So I basically told him what I knew. That this Doug M. reminded me of myself some fifteen years ago, and that I was trying to be a sort of priest to him, the way I wish someone'd been a priest to me. I asked this guy, I said to him, 'You got a priest?' And he says, 'Yeah. Me.' So I tell him, 'No, then you're lost. Gotta answer to someone.' He says, 'I do answer to someone. The archdiocese of the FBI.'"

Frawley. What had he told Frank G.? Frank, who had always praised him. Frank, who thought Doug was something.

"You probably . . . maybe you heard some things," Doug said. "About me— did you hear some things?"

Frank ignored that like he hadn't heard Doug. "So then this guy, he says to me, 'Priests don't hit their wives.'"

Doug got lost on that one.

"Yeah," said Frank, nodding his way through this. "I hope you're hearing this first from me. I am a shitbag wife-beater. That was my drunk, getting pissed off and slapping around my first wife. Great guy, huh? Good sponsor. Finally she had me arrested one night, but jail time would have meant no fire-fighting job, no salary, and as she was now fixing to divorce me, no alimony. So she dropped the charges. I have her greed to thank for my life now." Frank smiled bitterly, blowing out a long breath. "So much pride I had. That I'd turned everything around since then. That I'd put down this asshole living inside me." He shook his head. "Fucking Billy T.," he mumbled, pulling himself to his feet. "You got my pager if you need it."

Doug stood with him, in shock. "Frank . . ."

Frank shook his head, unable to look Doug in the face. "Careful crossing that street," he said, and then he was out the door.

34
DEFINITELY GOOD NIGHT

DOUG TURNED IN HIS seat again, scanning the faces behind him, fans carrying beer caddies up the aisles behind home plate, leaning on the back rail with their scorecards and their ballpark food. The wires in their ears were just radio earphones, and Doug told himself to relax.

"What are you looking for?" asked Claire, next to him.

"Nothing," he said, turning back. He had bought her an official Red Sox dugout jacket after the weather turned chilly in the fifth inning. The cuffs were empty, her hands tucked inside the leather sleeves. Her necklace hung below her throat. "Just taking in the crowd. The Fenway experience. Getting my money's worth."

He looked out past the plate umpire's broad back to Roger Clemens on the mound, the ace, ten years off his rookie season. Clemens hid his grip behind his glove and stared in, shaking off a sign. He went into his motion, delivered, and the pitch sliced flat off the bat, fouled straight back against the screen—the first ten rows jumping like heads on springs.

"Are we hiding?" she said.

Doug turned to her. "What?"

She shrugged under the bulky jacket, curious. "I don't know."

She had picked up on his sleuth paranoia. A yellow-shirted hawker appeared in the aisle and Doug waved him up, as though a box of Cracker Jack was what he had been looking for all along. "Here we go."

"I guess I thought the secretive stuff would go away after a while," she said, softening her words with a smile. "You being so hard to get hold of. I mean—it's romantic and all, you leaving me a Red Sox ticket on my garden seat. Just not normal."

"It bothers you, yeah? I can give you my phone number, no problem. Just that I'm never home, and I don't have an answering machine."

She shook her head, denying making any demands on him. The kid with the $2.25 price button on his cap came with a rack of oversized Cracker Jack boxes, and Doug busied himself paying for one. The kid was slow making change, his leafy roll of cash drawing Doug's roving criminal eye. Maybe someday that would go away, he thought. Maybe he could train himself not to watch for these things, not to compulsively puzzle out ways to relieve cash businesses of their profits.

For the first time in a long time, certainly since he got sober, Doug had nothing lined up. Nothing else he was working on, no jobs, nothing in prep. Frank G.'s defection weighed on him as one more reason to move on. All he had to do now was devise some sort of graceful exit strategy from the Town, some way to tell the others good-bye.

Claire eyed him as he rose half out of his seat to stuff his cash roll back into his jeans. He remembered how she had fallen silent when he'd pulled it out to pay for her jacket.

He ripped open the box of caramel popcorn and offered her some, which she declined. "Do you ever see your father much?" she asked.

Doug looked out to the left-field wall, which was where this question seemed to come from. "I see him once in a while. Why?"

"What sort of things do you two talk about?"

"I don't know. Not much." He dug down to the bottom of the box for the prize. "Hey, flag tattoo," he said, making to hand it to her, but with her hands pulled into her cuffs, he tucked it into her jacket pocket.

"I guess I'm just imagining my father in prison. . . ."

Why was she pawing him with questions? "I'm not my father," he told her. "Maybe that's what you're asking. It took a while, because as a kid I idolized him—it was just him and me, after all. Took a while for me to get a good look at him and start working hard at being everything he's not."

She nodded, liking what she heard. Still, something in her eyes wanted more.

Doug looked down. This seemed as good a time as any. He prefaced his story with "Seems like I'm always doing this with you."

"Doing what?"

He took a breath before launching into it. "I was at this bar once. Five years ago now. Bully's, a Townie tavern. Doing my thing, bunch of us, drinking pitchers, carousing. I don't remember much of this firsthand. I know a guy came in, older than us, getting his drink on. He's looking at me, and I'm getting annoyed. Some point he comes over, asks am I Mac MacRay's son. Tells me he knew my dad years ago, worked with him close, and I'm like, whatever. Until he tells me how he recognized me. Smiles and says I look exactly the way my dad looked when he got drunk."

The wave came around, everyone jumping to their feet and throwing their hands in the air except Doug and Claire.

"And I guess I attacked the guy. I have almost no memory of this. But if they hadn't pulled me off him, it would have been bad. Hospital he went to got the law involved, and the guy fingered me. And I'm grateful now. I am."

She watched him closely. Almost like she knew this already or suspected something like it.

"I did some prison time for that. Hated it, and I will never go back. Only thing to come of it was, I started on the program while I was in there. Changed my life. Cleared probation a year ago, now I'm free and clear. And I *feel* free and clear." All of this was the truth. He'd only left out his earlier stint inside.

"Wow," she said.

"Yeah, I know. It's like a knife in my eye, every time I have to tell you these things." He ticked them off on his fingers. "Alcoholic. Broken family. Ex-con. Not much to take home to your parents, huh?"

She absorbed all this, turning back to the field. "I told my parents I quit," she said. "They want me to go see a psychiatrist. Which I actually had been considering on my own—but now, forget it."

"You don't need one."

"No?" she said, shooting him a quick, angry look she seemed to regret.

Doug felt the chill. "You're full of questions tonight."

"Am I?"

"Something on your mind?"

She shook her head, hesitant, as though easing her way into this. "Agent Frawley came to see me again and I guess it shook me up a little."

Doug stared at the mound to control his reaction. "Yeah? How so?"

She was looking at him now. Fucking *looking* at him, and Doug made a study of the Milwaukee pitcher checking the runner on first. He would not look back at her.

"He said they were sure now that the bank robbers are from Charlestown."

Doug nodded. "Yeah?"

"He said they're watching some people. Getting close."

Did she know? Would she be telling him this if she knew anything? Was she testing him? Feeling him out? Trying to *help* him?

"I guess I'm worried," she said.

Maybe she did know. Maybe she knew and she accepted it and she was only waiting for him to come clean to her. Clear the air. Put all this behind them.

A fantasy. He turned slowly, giving her plenty of time to break off her scrutiny of him. "What are you worried about?"

She shrugged inside the dugout jacket. "Testifying, I guess. Living in the same town as these people. Things like that."

She looked back at him on *Things like that,* searching him—was she?—and

Doug held his expression, nearly impossible, looking into her eyes, wondering suddenly who was lying to whom.

Had Frawley put her up to questioning him? This was Jem's voice inside his head, he knew that, and it twisted his stomach.

Would she wear a wire for Frawley?

"He told me there were some developments in the case," she said.

Don't ask.

Doug nodded, checking the game, keeping his eye on the ball. *Developments? Don't. Let it go.*

"Must be a long process," he said, "an investigation like that." He had hardly felt the words leaving his throat. "Probably still a long ways off."

Why was she nodding? Was she waiting for more from him? Baiting him here?

Don't.

Going crazy. "Maybe if you just don't think about it," he said. Were they communicating in code now? *Don't think about me that way—think about me the way I am now.* "Put it out of your mind. Don't deal with it unless you have to."

Her eyes were on him again, and he tried to guess her emotion. Relief? Surprise? Was she hearing this other thing in his words?

Do not ask.

Developments.

He had to know. Maybe she wanted to tell him—maybe she was trying to warn him here.

Or maybe she didn't know anything. His head was pounding like his heart had traded places with his brain.

Don't.

His words caught her just as she was looking away in relief. "Why?" He shrugged it, like he didn't have a care in the world. "What are these developments?"

And she came back to look at him—they were searching each other—and he could tell by her eyes that he had made a disastrous mistake.

She turned away first, looking down at the ballcap of the boy sleeping against his father's shoulder in the seat before her. Doug had been found out.

"Fingerprints," she told him.

Doug nodded, frantic to unmake his mistake, trying to swamp her doubts with forced enthusiasm. "Fingerprints, wow." *Whose?* "I didn't even know they still solved crimes that way."

She shrugged.

"Anyway," he went on, headlong, "you definitely shouldn't worry. Not about your role in it. There's really nothing to worry about, that I can see."

The silence that came over them was charged, the game going on before their eyes and not mattering. Nothing mattered suddenly. The wave swept past and again failed to lift them. Then another sort of commotion—someone slapped Doug hard on the shoulder, and he turned fast, expecting Adam Frawley and federal badges and guns.

It was Wally the Green Monster, Fenway Park's furry green mascot, demanding a high five.

People around them pointed to the electronic scoreboard over the center-field bleachers, the seat numbers flashing there. Claire was one of four lucky winners of a free pancake breakfast at Bickford's.

The guy inside Wally said, "Jesus, man, lighten up," and Doug stuck out his hand, accepting the Green Monster's salute and watching him dance away.

Claire looked bewildered.

"Free pancakes," Doug said, riding the interruption. "Not bad."

"Sure," she said.

If he had any chance of salvaging things with her, it would have to be away from the ballpark crowd, alone. "You okay here right now, or . . . ?"

She turned and looked straight into his eyes. "Let's go back to my place."

Doug blinked. "Your place?"

Her hand came out of its sleeve and took his. "On one condition."

"Okay, sure."

"You can't stay over."

"Okay," he agreed. He would have agreed to almost anything.

Only after driving back to the Town in near silence—his hand leaving hers only to shift gears—as he neared Packard Street, did he ask:

"Why can't I stay over?"

She turned toward him. "'Mornings after' are so excruciating, and I don't want that with you. Morning only raises questions. I'm tired of questions."

He eased down her block, pulling up outside her door, shifting into neutral. He idled there, not turning off the engine.

"You're not parking?" she said.

Doug looked over at the light shining above her front door. "Oh, man."

"What?"

He couldn't go in there. Not this way. There was no future in sleeping with her without telling her everything first.

Her hand went slack in his but he would not release it. All the cars parked up and down the block—the sleuth could have been watching from any one of them. "How about I come back first thing in the morning instead? We'll make breakfast, we'll do the whole 'morning after' thing first, get that out of the way. All those questions. What do you say?"

Disbelief in her eyes, but also concern. The dash vent fans floated the edges of her hair.

The urge was powerful, and for a moment he relented. "Oh, fuck it, no. Christ, what am I . . ."

But then he remembered the ballpark and how it had felt sitting there, thinking he had lost her. He still had a chance here. *Don't blow this too.*

"No," he made himself say. "I can't."

She yielded a little. "If it's about leaving . . ."

He saw it in her eyes then: she was afraid it was ending. All she was doing here was trying to hold on to him a little while longer.

"Look," he said, "there's plenty of time, right? Tell me there is. Because I have a long night of second-guessing ahead of me."

"What about work tomorrow morning?"

What was she asking him? Was she asking him something?

"I quit that," he said. "I told you, I'm ready for a life change. I'm committed to it. What about you?"

"Me?"

"Your if-only place. Us blowing this town. Together."

She searched his face, reaching for his eyebrow, touching the smooth scar. "I don't know."

Yet her indecision lifted Doug's heart. Whatever she knew or had figured out about him—she did not tell him no.

"Pancakes, maybe," said Doug. "You like bacon? Sausage or bacon?"

She looked at their intertwined fingers, then pulled her hand free. She opened her door, swinging one leg out, looking back for him.

"If I walk you up there," he said, "if I get anywhere near your door . . ."

With the interior light on now, he felt anxious, exposed. She read more into it than that. "Is this good night or good-bye?"

He reached for her, pulling her back inside. The kiss was deep and all-encompassing, and she surrendered to it, gripping him tight. She didn't want to let him go. Maybe never, and maybe no matter what.

"Good night," he told her, stroking her hair. "Definitely good night."

35
DUST

JEM, IN MOTION.

On foot patrol in the Town, feeling the air currents curl around him as he walked. If it had been foggy, moisture giving character to the air, then others would have witnessed the slipstream in his wake, would have stared in awe at this native son trailing a flowing cloak of smoke. Then they would have understood.

Some knew already, a respect he felt but never deigned to acknowledge. Their hesitant glances, the quick look-aways. It hurt their eyes to stare. But their esteem for him was evident in their silence, the hush that fell over people and children as he passed.

He was carrying this Town on his back. All his concentration, all his brainpower was focused on remembering the Town as it had once been, and returning it to glory.

Fucking Duggy.

Jem fingered the tea bag in his pocket, the smooth plastic packet. As he walked, he envisioned the Town in flames. Cleansing flames, flames that built, destroying the unworthy, flames that cauterized and forged. The row houses and triple-deckers burning clean and new.

At the corner of Trenton and Bunker Hill, another new dry cleaner's. Yuppies passing him unaware. In a purging fire the dry cleaners with their chemicals would be the first to go up. Then back across the bridge would go the yuppies, ants fleeing a burning log. On paper, they owned the properties, but Jem still owned the streets. In the way that animals own the forest, he owned the Town.

He felt the itchy flecks of Colonial brick flowing in his blood.

Fergie. Jem could listen to him talk about the old Town for hours, having just left the wise man sitting in his flower shop walk-in cooler. The Florist knew about tenacity, about pride. The ex-wrestler and ex-boxer wore it on his face, the defiance of a window all cracked up but unbroken. Fergie knew how to win and win ugly.

Fucking Duggy. Treason and betrayal all around Jem. Everyone weakening and succumbing to change, to *progress,* and Jem, the glue, single-handedly holding everything together. Patching up the cracks. After Fergie it would all be up to him.

On the fucked-up clock face of the Town—as off-kilter as Fergie's—Pearl Street ticked up toward midnight. The witching hour was where Jem was born, lived, and would die. He was proud of the house's disrepair, the way it taunted the refurbished triples up and down the street, houses that had gone condo like whores transformed into virgins. All the sellouts who bailed: the Kenneys, Hayeses, Phalons, O'Briens. If it had been firstborns the yuppies were paying top dollar for, these traitorous fucks would have placed their kids' school portraits in the classifieds section of *The Charlestown Patriot*. Moving out ain't moving up—it's giving up, it's pussy.

Where the sidewalk plummeted like the first drop on the old Nantasket Beach roller coaster, Jem walked in the door. He had duct-taped an old cardboard box where Duggy had busted out the glass—solved that window rattle anyway. At the bottom step, he stopped and looked at Krista's door. Thinking about the next generation produced in him a powerful urge to see Shyne. His eye fell upon the old pictures standing on the hall table: the house as it had been in the sixties; an old jalopy parked on the slant with his dad unloading something—swag, most likely—from the trunk; his parents' wedding-party photo, Kennedy/Johnson campaign buttons under each groomsman's rose boutonniere; him and Krista in rompers, sitting on a blanket out on the back lot when it was grass.

He walked in without knocking, down the dark-wood hall, finding Shyne in her high chair as usual, abandoned in front of the tube. Her hands, face, and hair were smeared with bloodlike ravioli sauce while she zoned out on the goddamn purple dinosaur hopping around on a pogo stick. Sauce in her ears too.

"Hey, kid," he said. She did not turn. He touched the back of her neck, a clean spot there, but he might just as well have been touching a Shyne doll. "Uh-oh!" sang the purple dinosaur, and she stared like she was receiving some coded message, unable to look away.

The toilet flushed and Krista came out of the bathroom wearing a Daisy Duck T-shirt and saggy-ass bikini underwear.

"You didn't cook nothing, did you?" He didn't even want dinner, only to point out one more thing at which she had failed.

"The fuck do I know when you're gonna be home anymore?" she said.

But he had neither the time for nor the interest in fighting—and this, she noticed. A weird little moment of mind reading between the calendar twins, and suddenly she knew exactly where he had come from, whom he had met, what he had in his pocket. Almost like she could see inside his shorts to the little tea bag nestled there. A look crossed her face—hunger, want—and Jem saw it. She knew he saw it.

"What?" he said, more taunting than angry—another chance to punch home his authority.

She used to say, after every slow, smoky exhale, *Don't tell him, Jem.* Every single hit. Stronger than her taste for dust was her fear that she would be found out by Duggy. Everybody needed a parent or a spouse to run around behind. Come to think of it, Jem spent a lot of his time running around behind Duggy's back too.

He stared at his sister, the failure. To be a slut was one thing, but a failed slut? That took something almost like talent.

Now he is as disgusted by you as I am.

Jem almost said this. Yet even he held out hope for a turnaround from Duggy. It had happened before. The kernel of a plan was already forming in Jem's head.

Maybe, Kris, I can save even you.

Anything was within his power. But now he was furious again, staring her down, hating the thing that he loved. He bent down and kissed the top of Shyne's stained head and tasted sauce. The kiss said, *She will not be a fuckup like you,* and at the same time, *I alone can save us all.*

"I'll be upstairs," he said—knowing that she knew what that meant, knowing that she would sit down here in her saggy-ass panties and stare up at the water-stained ceiling knowing he was up there getting high without her. *Because you couldn't hold up your end of the deal. Because you couldn't hold on to Duggy, and now it falls to me.*

Upstairs in the cramped air of his hi-fi room, he dialed up the Sox on his stolen cable, his big-ass TV, and drew the tea bag from his pocket. He got his stuff from the cabinet over the kitchen sink and set it all out on the coffee table, slicing open the tea bag with the tip of his X-Acto knife. In a shot glass nicked from Tully's years before, he mixed the milligrams of magic with an equal pinch of dry Kool-Aid powder. Then he worked up a little saliva, drooled it into the glass, and watched the dust take to the spit and fade, becoming one.

He thought of that dude at the halfway house those years ago, the four-eyed former CVS pharmacist who in his spare time made lung-busting bongs out of bicycle pumps, and who was eventually bounced back into lockup for cooking speed in his room. He had told Jem that dust was medically not a hallucinogen but in fact classified as a "deliriant." Jem had never forgotten that. A *deliriant.* That was the fucking balls.

He swirled the glass, the mix turning cherry red. Then he tapped out a Camel unfiltered and dipped the tip into the scooped bottom of the shot glass, soaking up paste. His thumb came down on his Irish-flag Zippo, the bloody tip flaring as he inhaled.

He took it all in, so deep he thought he might never send it back out again, his chest expanding like the universe.

The atmosphere in the room depressurized as his head sank back and sighed. Things changed. Sounds—the TV, his heartbeat—separated from their sources, jettisoned like escape pods from the mother ship, tumbling free. Time stopped for him and he drifted out of it, watching it slide greasily by. The play-by-play man called a home run, and minutes later Jem watched the ball sail into the bleachers.

Wind back the clock. His words, speaking about the Town. *Wind back the clock.*

A Texas voice talked to him out of the TV, Roger Clemens yelling at him from the mound between pitches. "She's the G, you stupid fucking dicksuck!"

Jem said, *Fuck, Rocket—you think I don't know that?*

"The hell is Duggy? Where *is* he?"

What do I look like, his goddamn keeper?

"Fuckin' A, man, you do. Don't shake me off here. I will plunk you in the ass."

You couldn't plunk fucking Mo Vaughn's fat ass, you washed-up has-been.

"Don't Buckner this, bitch!"

Well, fuck you, you fat fucking . . . oh, shit . . .

Clemens was now a big, soft purple dinosaur in a Red Sox cap, singing, "Uh-oh!"

Jem's jellyfish brain glowed in the room. The transformation had already begun, his blood turning into mercury. Jem stripped to boxers and flip-flops and flapped down to the basement.

He hit it hard, chest presses and forty-pound curls, heart thumping like a body falling down an endless flight of stairs. The dank basement smelled of the sea, the iron weights clanking like anchor chains.

The camo kids. His foot soldiers. It would start with them, this rebel army he was putting together. Roving bands of Townie kids taking back their streets. Patriots planning for the second Battle of Bunker Hill, winding back the clock. The red, white, and blue of their bloodshot eyes.

He finished with power squats and climbed back up the stairs, his legs and arms aching the way bent steel aches. He shut his door on the world and stood there as the hallway wavered at either end. Jem the deliriant.

He flipped on the hanging lamp over the mirror, his body so pumped that there was no longer any distinction between flexing and not flexing. Jem was flexed. Every part of him blood-tanned and tumescent.

Every part.

The shorts came off. Facing himself in the mirror under the swinging lamp, he gripped his ass with his other hand, and his third hand—had to be—pulled back on the bank manager's hair, making her want it, making her work for it. The purple dinosaur pounding at the door threw him off, the bank manager momentarily becoming Krista, but he concentrated hard, and by the time he corrected himself he was too close for Kleenex.

His acid spew scorched the vanity in the shape of a question mark, Jem finishing and stepping back, decreeing, "That shit is fucked-up."

In the hot shower, his pig's dick hung swollen and pink between his legs. He gave the nozzle his back, shutting his eyes—the water jet turning to fire on his shoulders, the nozzle like a welder's torch spewing flame. Sparks danced off his body like spray, the blue flame fashioning something of him, forging a new being, a man of iron transformed in a baptism of fire.

He knew now what he had to do. What the Man of Iron—formerly the Man of Glue—must do.

He dressed in black and returned to the basement, to his grandfather's old steamer trunk under the stairs. He worked the combination on the lock, and the hinges—arthritic from the dankness—groaned as the trunk opened its mouth. He lifted his gramps's uniform off the weapons and trophies the old man had brought back from the Pacific—his rifle, the swords, the half-dozen grenades cling-wrapped in an oversized egg carton—along with some other small arms he had tucked away, and some cash, that was the seed out of which the great rebellion would soon grow. From the bottom of this trunk, he pulled out the Foodmaster bag, then closed and relocked his treasure chest.

This was what brothers did. They watched each other's back.

In darkness he set out on his mission, soldiering through the night Town with the bag tucked under his arm. Crows and keening pterodactyls swooped down from the Heights, screaming over Bunker Hill Street. Voices spoke at him from doorways, alleys, corners. An impossibly ancient woman, older than the sidewalk, whispered to him, *Take care of her for us,* to which Jem replied telepathically, *Ma'am, I will.*

Through Monument Square under the granite spike. Night creatures sailed around it on robe wings—the spirits of altar boys loosed from church attics—drawn to the heaven finger that was a radio tower broadcasting WTOWN, all day and all night, the reception strong and clear inside Jem's head.

Doug was getting ready to fly. Jem picked up his pace, the ocean roaring in his ears.

Packard Street was the heart of the disease. The G was a cancer in the Town, Jem the fucking deliriant chemo. Jem, the sin eater, the avenging archangel.

In the alley behind Packard he saw her glazed bathroom window, pushed open a few inches for him, just enough. Jem pulled on gloves, and with a glance up and down the alley, tucked the bag into his belt.

He asked for invisibility. It was granted.

Up onto her purple car without a sound, from its roof to the top of the dividing brick wall. He found a hand grip on the brick face of the sleeping building, the window within his reach now. It was old, like those in his mother's house, hanging on clothesline pulleys, needing only a shove to rise.

He asked for, and received, stealth, night vision, and cloaking silence. For a moment he hung two-handedly from the wooden sill—then he raised himself over it, crawling inside headfirst, being born into the room, coming to rest on the cold tile floor.

The bathroom—the crotch in the body of the home. The kitchen was the heart; the bedroom the brain; the dining room the stomach; the living room the lungs. The front door its face; the garage its ass.

The crotch was dark and cool. A steady dripping inside the porcelain bowl at his shoulder. The flower smells of night creams.

His vision was good, and he untucked the paper bag from his waist, controlling the wrinkling noise. He pulled out the mask by its oval eye sockets, standing, fitting the black strap over the back of his head.

So long as you ditched the masks, she's got nothing.

Course I ditched the masks.

Well, you seemed pretty fond of your artwork, I want to be sure.

Fuck you, Duggy. So fucking clever.

In the sink mirror, the white Cheevers mask floated against the blackness of its eyes and graffiti scars.

He emerged from the crotch into the lungs. Green digits of a stereo clock pulsing against the wall. A nightlight showing him the way.

The door to the sleeping brain was closed. He gripped the knob with his gloved hand and entered.

Streetlights gave him the room. Red clock digits quivering near the bed where she awaited him.

His knee touched the side of the mattress as he stood over her, listening to her breathe.

She sensed his presence. Her legs moved beneath the sheets. Her head turned under spilled hair, first finding the opened door. She brushed the hair back off her eyes. Then she saw.

The face of the deliriant. She opened her mouth to scream.

36
WIRE

DOUG SHOWED UP ON her doorstep with a plastic Foodmaster bag of groceries, feeling pretty good. There was a peculiar morning-after pleasure in having refused immediate gratification, in resisting his craving with an eye toward a greater design. This was the bedrock of Alcoholics Anonymous, and it occurred to him that this was also how religions were born.

He found her door open a crack and felt a moment of concern, quickly mastered by rationalization. Lots of people in Town left their doors half-shut while running out for a quick errand. There would be a note on the table telling him that she had gone for more eggs, and to make himself at home.

"Hey?" he said with a knock on the open door, moving inside. "It's me."

Nothing. He moved down the hallway, telling himself it wasn't danger he was sensing.

"Claire?"

She was standing in the living room, on the other side of the sofa between the coffee table and the stereo, wearing faded blue jeans and an untucked yellow T-shirt, a cordless telephone in her hand at her side.

"Hey," Doug said, stopping, feeling something in the air. "You know your door was open?"

The way she was staring told him that she knew.

"Why?" she said.

Doug went numb. He set the grocery bag on the floor. "Why what?"

"Is this a thing you do?"

Something in him believed he could bluff his way out of this, even as it was all slipping away. "You talking about breakfast, or . . . ?"

"Tearing women down and building them back up again?"

The side of the sofa was as near to her as he dared move. His talk was pointless, but he wanted to keep on believing. "I brought bacon, I . . . ."

"Or was I some sort of bet? A contest maybe?"

Something had happened since last night. Somehow she knew things now, and his instinct for self-preservation kicked in. The way she was standing at the back of the room with the phone. "Who else is here?"

Her eyes filled with tears. "No one," she snapped. "Not anymore."

Frawley. The kitchen was empty. Doug stepped to her bathroom, sweeping aside the shower curtain on the wide open window. He crossed to her bedroom, also empty.

Doug's defeat found an outlet in fury. "What did you tell him?"

She hadn't moved, watching him. "I didn't tell *him* anything."

A trap. The plan was to draw him into apologizing his way through a confession, him explaining himself right back into prison. The microphones could be anywhere.

He reached for her stereo, the CD player, turning it up loud. Smashing Pumpkins music filled her condo, all gunning guitar and bald-boy thrashing.

Her eyes went dark as he advanced. "Stay away from me," she said, backing up a step, raising the phone antenna-first. "I'll call the police."

Doug lunged for her and grabbed the phone, ripping it out of her hand, whipping it across the room at the sofa.

She froze, stunned.

With the music blasting, he pushed her up against the wall and shut his hand over her mouth, his calloused palm catching her scream. He felt down both sides of her chest, her belly and her waist, groping her through her shirt.

Her voice was smothered, eyes wide. She tried to fend him off but he pinned her near arm to the wall with his elbow, working fast.

He reached beneath her shirt, sliding his fingers around the waist of her jeans. Then up her abdomen to the satin band linking the cups of her bra. Her free hand gripped his wrist, trying to stop him from going there. He pushed his fingers underneath the center strap, exploring her cleavage, finding no wires.

His hand came out of her shirt with Claire still gripping his wrist. He was too strong for her, reaching around for the small of her back, feeling nothing through her jeans there, then sliding his hand along the insides of both thighs, feeling up her inseam to her crotch.

Nothing. No battery pack, no wire.

She stared into his face, her hand still fighting his wrist. Then he eased off, realizing what he had just done. "I had to see if you were wired," he told her. "I had to—"

She jerked her knee up, hitting him in the thigh, just missing his balls. She went at him, slapping and whacking, and he let her. Her barefoot kicking didn't have much behind it, but the cracks across his face hurt. He defended himself without fighting back, eventually retreating a few steps.

She screamed, "You go to fucking *hell*!"

"It's not what you think." What could he say to her? "Whatever he told you—"

"I fucking *hate* you!"

"No." He shook that off, he refused it.

She looked for something to throw at him, found the *AM Gold* disc he had loaned her, cracked it off his elbow. Then she struck out at her blaring stereo, shoving it twice before it crashed to the floor—and even then, the music still played. Not until she ripped the plug out of the wall did the tune die.

Doug talked fast. "The robbery—whatever you know is true. But since then—I don't know what happened. All I can think about is you."

"You Townie gym-head . . . asshole . . . convict . . . fucking street *trash* . . ."

He stood up to all of this.

"What?" she said, wild-eyed, fixing her bra through her shirt. "Did you think you were going to come over here this morning and make me breakfast and *fuck me*? Tell all your *friends*?"

He shook his head, mouth closed tight.

"Making me feel sorry for you," she said.

He exploded. "*Sorry* for me?"

His rage shocked her. A long moment of brittle defiance, then she cried like she was vomiting tears into her hands. "Why would you do this to me?" she wailed. "Why would you do this to anybody?"

What could he tell her? *I am in love with you? I want to go away with you?*

"You knew last night," he said. "At the ballpark—*you knew*. Yet it was all right. You wanted me back here." He opened his hands down at his sides. "Why not now?"

She caught her breath, sniffling, bringing her hands away from her raw face. Defiant again. "I guess your friend refreshed my memory."

Doug's blood rose again. "Is that what Agent fucking Frawley calls me? His *friend*?"

She stood still, breathing. "What?"

Doug could not disguise the look of murder on his face. "What else did he say?"

"Frawley? It wasn't Frawley." She smiled crazy. "It was your friend in the hockey mask."

Hockey mask. Doug stared at her, confused. *"What?"*

Claire crossed the room to retrieve her phone from the sofa.

Doug shook his head but couldn't feel anything. He looked to her bathroom, the window she kept open. He looked at her open bedroom door. "He what?"

Hockey mask. Open window.

"I want you to go," she said.

Jem. Doug looked her up and down. "Did he touch you?"

She held the phone poised to dial. "He warned me not to go to the police, but so help me God, if you don't *get the hell out* . . ."

Doug shook his head, staving off hysteria. Jem's lips on her lemonade straw. *"Did he touch you?"*

She had tears again, and Doug stared, looming before her, fists at his side. "Out," she told him. "Of my house. Of my life."

Her words drove him back a step. "Claire. Wait—"

"Don't you *ever* fucking speak my name again." She held out the phone with her thumb over the numbers. "If you make me call, I will tell them everything."

He stepped back again, the phone like a gun in her hand. "All I ever wanted—"

She pressed her thumb down. *"Nine."*

"Don't do this."

"You better run now." She pressed again. *"One."*

He was going to stay. He was going to face whatever came.

Then she lost it, screaming at him, *"Get out!"*—backing him down the hall to the front door by the sheer force of her emotion—*"Get out!"*—shaming him down the steps and out alone onto Packard Street.

37
A BEATING AND A MEETING

THE OLD DOOR GAVE in like it had been waiting years for someone to put a good shoulder to it. Doug brushed past the cardinal's picture and the holy-water bowl to Jem's game room, where the stereo was on, the CD long over, the volume turned way up on nothing, speakers emitting a dry auditorium PA hum. The couch of green leather was empty.

Seeing the plastic tea bag underneath the glass coffee table was like finding the last piece to a jigsaw puzzle Doug didn't even know he was working on. If he had been paying closer attention, he wouldn't have needed that one final piece to make out the complete image.

The late-night music. Jem's disappearances, his raccoon life. The camo kids. His dukes to Fergie.

Doug tore back down the hall, banging open Jem's bedroom door along the way and whipping blankets off the heap of cushions Jem called a bed. Then into the front parlor and its bow windows with torn screens overlooking Pearl Street. Jem's woodworking tools were laid out on sheets of newspaper, and there, atop an old end table, stood a nearly completed dollhouse. It was a scale replica of that very same triple-decker, all three stories with the western wall cut away. Doug lifted his boot to crush it, but some small voice of mercy told him the house was a gift meant for Shyne. Instead he kicked over a standing lamp and stomped in its head.

Then he heard the familiar revving of the overtuned engine and went to the center window. The Flamer was pulling up curbside on the street below. Doug was downstairs and outside in a flash.

Jem smiled his broad, Joker-faced grin as Doug strode toward him, the grin fading just as he saw Doug's fist coming around—no telegraphing it, no buddy-boy slo-mo—Doug tagging his chin with a "Fucking mother*fuck*!" and Jem banging off the trunk of his car and rolling into the gutter. A shopping bag spilled out of Jem's hand, little paintbrushes and tubes of modeling paint and wood glue tumbling into the street.

"*Chrissst!*" said Jem, getting up on his knees and touching his mouth, his fingers coming away bloody.

"You kept your mask, you fucking *psycho*—" Doug kicked him under his shoulder, high on his ribs, bouncing him against the bumper of his car.

"Wait. What?" Jem was back up on one knee. "Hold it. Duggy. Hold it."

Then Jem sprang at him from a crouch, burying his neck and shoulder in Doug's midsection and running him back across the sidewalk, slamming him hard against the clapboard siding of the house.

Doug took a fist to the hip. He hammered Jem's back, trying to throw him off, but Jem anticipated this and shifted his weight as Doug tried to muscle him around, Doug falling ass-first to the slanting sidewalk.

Jem was on top of him now, head still buried in Doug's gut, arms swinging strong. A hockey fight, Doug with Jem's shirt almost up over his head, the freckled spray of his back exposed.

"Fucking duster!" shouted Doug. "How you stayed up all night after the wedding, huh? Why you shot up the place? I pulled a job with a fuhhh—"

Jem landed a shot on Doug's kidney. He was working hard, wrestling his way up Doug's chest, a lot bigger and stronger than he used to be. With just a little more leverage, Jem would have him pinned.

Doug was losing this fight. If Jem got up onto his chest, Jem would hammer him into the sidewalk.

Doug reached under him and grabbed Jem's belt with one hand, his shoulder with another. In a burst of righteous fury, Doug used all his strength to lift Jem off his chest, the dust-head's work boots kicking in the air as Doug boosted him up and over, Jem coming down hard on his shoulders and back, Doug rolling away free.

Jem scrabbled to stand but Doug was up and running at him, grabbing shirt and shorts and ramming him headfirst into a neighbor's pickup. Dented and dazed, Jem tried to kick backward at Doug's balls, but Doug caught the boot and spun him around, grabbing him up and teeing off, landing a good hard punch, undeflected, in Jem's face.

His nose burst its blood and Jem crashed back onto the hood of a car, sliding down off the corner headlamp and dumping onto the street in a heap.

There he lay, squirming on his belly, holding his face with both hands. Doug stood over him, head roaring from the madness of savagery and the earlier fall to the sidewalk. The wet things in his eyes: they were tears.

"Get up."

Jem rolled over, curling in pain. Blood hung in snotty ribbons from his chin and a gash had opened over his nose, street sand matted in the bloodstain on his cheek. "Did it few, man," he said.

"Get up."

"I did it few." His words came out in gobs of bloody drool. "Did it fuss. Why her, man? All udder chicks in a world. Why?"

"Get up, Jem, so as I can *knock you the fuck down again!*"

"Fuckin' who you better 'an? You better 'an me?"

Onto his knees. Far enough. Doug tagged him in the chin and Jem dropped back, sprawling.

Jem smiled now, bloody-toothed, lying there in the street. "Din't even touch'er, man. Jest a warning. I true her back. Small fiss."

"Good for you. Then you'll live."

Jem wanted to sit up but his ribs wouldn't let him. He rolled to his side but couldn't get up that way either, so he gave up and lay back, grinning up at the sky.

It wasn't enough for Doug. He bent down and grabbed Jem's bloody shirt, lifting him off the road. Jem's white eyes lolled as he smiled at Doug's fist.

"Why 'on't you hit yousself," said Jem. "Jest fucking hit yousself."

Doug wanted one more. He wanted it bad. But he feigned it first, and Jem didn't flinch, his eyes cloudy like dishwater.

Doug let him drop. Jem coughed, giggling as he bled. "'Appily ever after," he muttered.

Doug walked away unsatisfied, a dark cloud carrying a massive electrical charge, still needing release.

Krista was out on the sidewalk. She had stood there and watched her brother get the Irish kicked out of him—and remained there still as he lay muttering and giggling in the street. She looked at Doug, taking a step toward him—but Doug was already starting away up the slope, hands aching, ears roaring, half-blind with despair.

FRAWLEY'S SUBLET CAME WITH a parking space in a low-ceilinged garage just off First Avenue, the main road bisecting the decommissioned Charlestown Navy Yard. On the land side of First stood the old brick shipbuilding factories, including an obsolete ropewalk building a quarter mile long. On the water side stood the redesigned wharves, brick foundries that had been carved into waterfront two-bedrooms. The redeveloped yard was more campus than neighborhood, skewing predominantly toward successful single professionals. Frawley imagined the old dockworkers and longshoremen coming back from the grave to find their stomping grounds turned into a community of high-rent condos populated by the young, the clever, the uncallused.

The ninety-minute commute home from Lakeville had nested in Frawley's lower back, and he stood out of the dread Tempo, both hands on its roof, stretching the pain away. He was examining the car's fading blue finish—gray spots spreading across the roof like mold—when he heard footsteps coming up behind him, hard and thudding, like boots. Frawley instinctively reached inside his jacket before turning.

MacRay was empty-handed, unshaved, and hungover-looking in a faded gray T-shirt and jeans, moving fast through the sulfurous light.

Frawley gripped the butt of his SIG-Sauer 9mm but did not draw, and MacRay stopped within an arm's reach, breathing hard, homicide in his eyes.

Frawley was shocked and trying to conceal it. Pulling his gun would have been prideless. He slid his creds out of his breast pocket instead, folded them open.

"Special Agent Frawley, FB—"

MacRay swatted the billfold out of Frawley's hand. It fluttered like a wounded bird and dropped to the concrete a few feet away.

Frawley's heart fell just as fast. The rudeness of the act, its near childishness, settled on his face like a dark pair of sunglasses, helping him move past fear.

"Don't make a mistake here, MacRay," said Frawley. "I want to take you down, but not for this."

MacRay stared, more controlled than Frawley had first thought. He looked past Frawley with expert distaste. "Upgraded to the Tempo, huh? Nice ride."

Frawley fought off questions: How long had MacRay been on him? How had MacRay known he would be here?

MacRay said, "Know what happened to me? Some fucking douche bag keyed my Vette. You believe that shit?"

Frawley saw the emerald green car parked along the wall, saw its long silver scar.

"Fucking with a man's ride, that's some cowardly-ass shit, don't you think?" MacRay went on. "I mean, what do you call someone who would do a thing like that, huh? A punk? A pussy?"

Frawley said, "I take it she dumped you."

"Hey, *fuck* you."

Frawley worked up a smile. "How long did you think that was going to last? What was your play there, MacRay?"

"You don't know nothing about it."

"Reminds me of smokehead ATM jumpers. Password thieves, they get the secret code, they think they can ride that card forever." Frawley then noticed MacRay's open, anxious hands—the crook's knuckles cut, swollen like walnuts. Frawley said, "If you laid a hand on her—"

"Fuck you," said MacRay, dismissing him with a wave. It was convincing, but Frawley would have to check on Claire Keesey himself to be sure.

MacRay backed off a little, walking in a tight, agitated circle like a dog in a cage, while Frawley stood in repose.

"Like your sponsor there," said Frawley, pushing back at him now. "Fire-fighter Frank Geary. The wife-beater, trying to school me. You reformed drinkers, you're the worst."

MacRay came back at him hard, pointing. "Listen to me. You stay the fuck away from him, got that? Who's this between? You want to know something about me? Here I am. What?"

Frawley held his composure. "I have nothing to say to you."

"'Course not. You'd rather go slinking around, talking to everybody else *but* me. Who had the balls to face who? Fucking little dink."

"You came here to call me names, MacRay?"

"Just thought I'd swing by, introduce myself personally."

"Damn neighborly of you."

"Strip away some of this bullshit between us. This dance."

Frawley said, "I'm not dancing."

"Yeah? Me either." MacRay looked out through the open walls of the garage to the lights along First Avenue. "What you think, you're undercover here? You think you live in Charlestown? The yard ain't Charlestown. You got no idea what's going on."

"I know plenty."

MacRay squinted, taking Frawley's measure. "So what is this? This about her?"

Frawley frowned him a *fuck you*. "This is about a bank."

"Yeah." MacRay turned away, his circular pacing again. "Sure it is."

"About a movie theater too."

"Movie theater?" MacRay cocked his head like he might not have heard that right.

"You fucked up, MacRay. You and your crew."

MacRay continued his circuit. "You lost me back at the movie theater thing."

"Surprised me, that. Armored-truck heisting with the crusts cut off. A soft job. Maybe you're gun-shy. Maybe you're a little more afraid of me catching up with you than you'd like to admit."

Frawley was inside his head with a bullhorn, MacRay walking faster, mad.

"Struck me that maybe," Frawley went on, "maybe this was a job pulled by someone thinking about getting out. Even hanging it up for good. For the love of a good woman, perhaps. I'm thinking it's fifty-fifty you came here tonight to tell me good-bye."

MacRay slowed then, denying Frawley the explosion he expected. "She doesn't want you, man," MacRay told him. "Nothing you can do will change that."

Frawley grinned away a chill. "Yeah, she's Helen of Troy. She's the Mona Lisa. I mean, she's nice, MacRay, she's all right. Got all her teeth. But why her? Careful guy like you. A vic from one of your own jobs? What made you cross that line?"

MacRay stared.

"Wait—was it love? That it, MacRay?" Frawley's taunting smile bloomed and died. "What made you think it would ever work?"

"Who's saying it's over?"

Frawley smiled wide at his bluff. "Oh, it's not?"

MacRay said, "Nothing is."

Frawley grinned, stopping himself from saying *Good*.

"What's so funny, sleuth?"

"Funny?" Frawley shrugged. "Us standing here. Chatting."

It had gone on too long, them standing there together, Frawley's anxiety building.

MacRay said, "You know how in movies, cop and robber, they spend the whole picture matching wits and end up with this grudging respect for each other? You got any grudging respect for me?"

Frawley said, "I have not one ounce."

"Good. Me fucking either. I just didn't want you to think we'd be holding hands at the end of this."

Frawley shook his head. "Not unless you count handcuffs."

MacRay took his measure once again. "If you did get a fingerprint—it wasn't mine."

She had warned him. Frawley burned. "You're a dead end, MacRay. Maybe you *should* just walk away for good, you're so afraid to go up against me."

MacRay came close to a smirk then, and Frawley *knew* he had him locked in—then MacRay started back to his car, and Frawley wasn't so sure.

"I'll see you around then," Frawley called after him.

"Yeah," said MacRay, opening his car door and climbing inside. "Yeah, maybe."

PART IV
A SORT OF HOMECOMING

38
EXCALIBUR STREET

MRS. KEESEY ANSWERED THE front door in a designer running suit, the Round Table Estates' version of the 1950s housecoat. Theirs was one of the few screen doors in the world that did not squeal when opened. "Thank you, Mrs. Keesey, for letting me stop by in the middle of the day," said Frawley, stepping inside the chilly foyer.

"Quite welcome," said Mrs. Keesey, looking out at his moldy Tempo cluttering up Excalibur Street, then closing the heavy door. She stepped to the balustrade, where bank statements and investment prospectuses in sliced envelopes were filed between egg-white banister spindles. "Claire!" she sang out, then looked at Frawley with a nonsmile. "She's back with us again. I don't know what brought this on."

She eyed the manila envelope in his hand suspiciously, as though it contained information on her. The odor of whiskey on her breath was like a premonition of early death.

"Can I offer you some spring water?" she said, studied and formal, an actress bored in her long-running role as wife and housemother.

"No, thank you. I'm fine."

Claire Keesey came down the stairs in a white T-shirt and even whiter sweatpants, greeting Frawley without expression—Mrs. Keesey already withdrawing to the kitchen.

Claire took him the other way, her white socks whispering across a smooth maple floor, through French doors into her father's home office, just as before. This time Claire sat behind the desk, puffy-eyed from crying, but not bruised or battered. MacRay's swollen hands had beat up somebody, but not her.

Frawley sat in the college rocking chair, eyeing her, harboring feelings he was not proud of. Triumph. Satisfaction. Also pity.

"You made a mistake," he said, magnanimous in victory. "A misjudgment."

She picked at her fingers, ashamed, sullen.

"I wish you hadn't gone through this," he said, and meant it. "And I wish we didn't have to do this now."

Frawley opened the envelope flap and slid out four photographs, playing the mugs out on the desk blotter like a winning hand. MacRay's cocky black-and-white was top right. She locked on it, her eyes showing hurt.

"Okay," said Frawley. "Know any of the others?"

She took in each, lingering an extra moment on nasty-eyed Coughlin and his jerk smirk.

"No?" said Frawley. He pulled another photograph from his envelope and placed it down in front of her. It was a still developed from Gary George's wedding video: an off-angle image of Kristina Coughlin in a black dress, sitting next to MacRay in a tuxedo at an otherwise empty table, drinks before them. "What about her?"

Claire stared, confusion giving way to a defiant blankness. She asked no questions. She didn't even shake her head.

Frawley was just trying things here. He laid down a blurry, retouched, six-year-old surv photograph of the reclusive Fergus Coln, the Florist wearing a dark sweatshirt hood and apparently pointing out the telephoto lens. "What about this man?"

She squinted at the murky image, rejecting it immediately.

"Have you ever been inside MacRay's place?" Frawley asked.

No answer, but it didn't look like she had.

"Ever seen him handling large amounts of cash? Or talking about a particular hiding place? Ask you to hold or hide anything for him?"

Her silence answered no.

"Did he ever admit anything to you or implicate himself in any way? How did you finally find out about him?"

Now her silence seemed like something greater than mere recalcitrance.

"Look," said Frawley. Her hand was on the desk and he reached out and squeezed it reassuringly. "I'm sure your sense of trust is pretty tender right now."

She looked at his hand on hers, pulled away. "How long did you know?"

Frawley withdrew his empty hand. "Not long."

"But long enough," she said. "When you came to see me that day—you were carrying that same envelope."

Frawley shrugged. "I might have been carrying *an* envelope."

"Were you . . . punishing me?"

"Don't be ridiculous."

"Did you want me humiliated? Because I chose him and not you? Is that why you didn't tell me?"

Frawley shook his head adamantly, not in answer but in retaliation. "You don't get to do this. Don't look at me like I'm the one who seduced and betrayed you. Like I'm the one who made you a fool."

She went silent, and Frawley knew he had been too harsh. He eased off.

"You're angry," he said. "You're feeling betrayed. I understand these things. But don't take it out on me. I wanted to help you. No big deal, but I was here for you. And you chose badly. It happens, people make mistakes. And now you know."

She was looking down—not at the photos, not at him.

"What you need to do now," he went on, "is turn your anger where it belongs—on them." He knocked on the blotter of pictures. "With your help we can put these assholes away for a long time."

She went into her sweatpants pocket and brought out a business card, handing it to him. The first thing Frawley noticed was the icon of the scales of justice printed in the lower-left corner.

"This is my lawyer," Claire said. "If you want to talk to me again, you do it through her."

Claire punched the *her*. Frawley read and reread the card, the saliva in his mouth turning bitter.

"Lucky," he told her, slowly collecting his photographs from the desk blotter. "Lucky for you I don't need you much anymore, or else this would get very unpleasant." He took MacRay's mug last, reviewing the cocksure face once more himself before returning it to the envelope. "Why didn't I tell you you were being sweet-talked by the guy who kidnapped you? Because I needed to keep MacRay close. Because this is a federal criminal investigation, not fucking *Love Connection*."

"You can go now."

"Here's the deal, Ms. Keesey. MacRay is going to come back to see you again."

"No, he's not—"

"And when he does," Frawley talked over her, "and when he does—any contact you have with him, any conversation *whatsoever,* you will report it to me. Either yourself or through your *lawyer*"—he flicked at the business card—"or else you will be looking at a criminal prosecution yourself. That is not a threat, that is a promise. This is a felony case I am investigating, and any unreported contact between yourself and the suspect will be prosecuted."

He stood, pocketing her lawyer's card, still pissed.

"You think you feel humiliated now? How about going on trial for aiding and abetting an armed felon? How about putting this whole affair out there for the entire world to see? 'Bank Manager Falls for Armed Robber'—how's that sound? You like reading tabloids? Want to be in one?"

He stopped himself there, opening the French doors.

"Yeah, it's rough, but you brought this on yourself. I can't help you if you won't let me. MacRay *will* come to you again. And when he does, you will tell me."

39
LINGER

WHAT IT FEELS LIKE, being underwater.

Krista was there, finally. Submerged. The Tap Downstairs a brick aquarium tank now, the bourbon in her system giving her gills.

Everything slower. Sounds reaching her late, stretched out so that she could mull them over or just let them pass her by. Life becoming fluid, languid. She reached her hand to the bar and met the resistance of the water, the push starting a ripple. Every movement began a current and left a wake. A twist of her head tipped the balance of the room, everything lifting then settling back into place again, the sounds lagging behind, a moment or two before finding her ears in their new position. One thing flowing beautifully into the next.

Alone at the bar in the center of the liquid universe. *Fuck you, Mrs. Joanie Magloan.* The former Joanie Lawler always used to love to say, *Shit, what you think, I'm gonna be one of those married girls who stops going out?* This was before she kissed the freckled frog prince Magloan and got turned magically into a housewife. Two nights ago Krista called her—*Sorry, Kris, can't make it.* So tonight, Krista didn't even bother trying her. She'll put in a call to her tomorrow—you bet—letting it slip out that she hit the Tap without her, because that was psychology. Making her think she's missing out was what would get her ass in gear next time. Not Krista being the single girl, begging.

The music was a pleasant warble. No U2 without the Monsignor there tonight—her Pope, her grateful Pope. His cock crowed three times—so gratefully—each crow a stab of betrayal at Duggy, and now she couldn't get him on the phone. Hiding away in the Forgotten Village, his Vatican City.

A dollar bill from her jeans pocket—her last. Undulating in her hand like a waving fern. Her shoes touched the floor, a swimmer walking across colored rocks on the bottom of the night-lit Tap aquarium, toward the wall of brick coral, the jukebox a treasure chest opening and releasing bubbles. Three bubbles for a dollar. She punched in the same code three times, The Cranberries, "Linger."

Swimming back, she pretended to snub the guy who had been checking her out all evening. *So check this out,* she thought, moving slow, giving him the full view.

Splashy was always good for one on the house, but she liked to know she still had the power, especially now as she felt it starting to fade. They say the day your baby starts living is the day you start dying, and if they were right, then she had been wasting away for twenty-one months now.

Twenty-one months was the average life span (she remembered Duggy telling her this once—she remembered everything he told her) of a one-dollar bill in circulation. Fifties and hundreds, they lasted the longest.

I am wanted. I have currency. She was a clean, firm bill, no longer quite so crisp, but still negotiable legal tender. Maybe not a C-note anymore, but definitely a fifty.

She regained her seat and waited for the ripples to subside and her vision to clear. He was stirring now. Hooking his Bud bottle by the neck and walking it over, pulled by the tide.

I am a fifty you want in your pocket.

The swell and sway of displacement as he mounted the empty stool to her right. Sitting open-legged, aggressive, waiting for her to look his way. His words swam to her.

"Seemed like we were having a bit of a staring contest over there."

"Yeah?" said Krista, the word a soft bubble escaping from her mouth. She could tell immediately he wasn't Town. She didn't trust his face. A sea horse with barracuda eyes.

"I think I was winning," he said.

She nodded. "I think you were."

"This your song?"

It took a while for the music to reach her. "It's mine. All mine."

"Kind of sad, no?"

She finished her drink in front of him. "Only if you let it be."

Like he was studying her. A little creepy, but she hung in there. The bourbon dose reached her gills and in rushed more equalizing water.

"One night at a bar," he said, leaning closer, "this guy was going around to ladies telling them he was judging a Hugging Contest, and would they like to enter. And most of the time, believe it or not, they fell for it, and he would hold them and rub their backs, all smarmy and shit. I finally got so sick of watching this guy that I took him outside. I told him I was judging a Face-Punching Contest."

Krista smiled, drifting. "Anyone tried that shit on me, I'd do the punching myself."

He toasted her with his Bud, draining it, returning it empty on the bar. "Oh, by the way," he said. "I'm here tonight judging a Fucking Contest."

Water rushing around them, the undertow of the late hour washing bodies from the bar, Krista smiling, licking her lips. *Okay, sport.* "Why don't you buy me a drink."

He produced a twenty from his pocket and laid it Jackson-up on top of the bar. *Here I am,* she thought. *Here I float.*

He ordered two of what she was having and hopefully didn't catch the knowing wink Splashy gave her. The guy talked and he was all right. Cute guy, just not her type. Her type was Duggy. He was another in a long line of not-Duggys.

Something about kids, did he say? "I have a daughter."

It was an excuse for him to look her over again. "That you gave birth to?" he said. "Yourself?"

"Twenty-one months ago."

Only thing that bothered her was him not checking her hands for rings. *What, like there's no way I could catch a husband?*

Early on, he had said his name. She had missed it because it wasn't Doug. He had nice, strong hands. The nice, strong hands ordered two more drinks.

He said something about the price of real estate in the Town. "I own," she told him.

"You own your own condo?"

"My own *house,*" she said, his disbelief both annoying and flattering. "A triple. Left to me by my mother."

"Wow. Just you?"

"That's right." It was easy, as well as nice, to pretend she had no brother.

"I have to ask. A woman with her own house. Sitting here with an ass making the rest of the barstools crazy with envy. What are you doing down here alone on a weeknight?"

She nodded Indian-like, like she had the answer but wasn't telling. "Getting wet," she said, dancing her drink on the waves. "Drifting with the tide."

He toasted her. "Bon voyage."

"You live in the yard, huh?"

"Is it that obvious?"

"Always. What you doing down here? Slumming?"

"That's right."

"Looking for an easy pickup? A tasty little slice of Town pie?"

"Mostly just trying to do my job."

"Your job? Oh, right. I forgot. The Fucking Contest."

"Basically correct. I work for the FBI."

She threw back her head, laughing, starting to like him more now. "That was the first good giggle I've had in a month."

"Yeah?"

"You're awright. Doesn't mean I'm going home with you or anything. Don't think I'm looking to do you on your balcony, cooing over the view."

"I don't have a balcony."

"No? That's too bad."

"I'm in a shitty sublet, and out on my ass in like six weeks. A toast, Krista. Let's drink to balconyless me."

"Fair enough." She figured she must have told him her name when—

"I don't see your brother around tonight."

"My brother?" Who is this guy? "You know Jem?"

"We bump into each other now and then."

Thought he wasn't Town. "I had a higher opinion of you."

"You and Doug MacRay used to run around, right?"

Now she stared. "How you know Duggy?"

"We sorta work together."

"Ah," she says, feeling tested. "Demolition."

A smirk in this guy's eyes. "Nooo."

Things changing now. Water temperature falling a few degrees. She tightened up, a reflex around people she didn't know.

The guy pulled out one, two, three, four, five more twenties, stacking them on the bar. "You a pretty decent judge of size?"

"Depends," she said. "Size of what?"

He held up a single twenty. "How big would you say this is?"

"If this is a bar game, I'm not much of a—"

"How long? Six inches? In your estimation. Over or under?"

She squinted. "Under."

"Wrong. Six point one four inches exactly. Now the width."

"You're turning into kind of a weird guy."

"The girth. Some claim it's more important. Give a guess."

She just looked at him.

"Two point six one inches. I know everything there is to know about money. Thickness of a bill? Point oh oh four three inches. Not much to excite you there. Weight? About one gram. That makes a twenty almost worth its weight in, say, dust."

Staring at him now. Him staring at her. The water stopped dead.

"So how's it work?" he said. "Bartender takes a call, gives you an address? You pick up a package at Point A, deliver it to Point B, and for that the Florist pays you a C? That right? Easy as A-B-C?"

Water starting to drain, the stopper pulled and that sucking sound going.

"You're thinking about walking out on me," he said. "See, it's not that simple, though. I start waving this gold badge around"—he opened it on the bar next to the twenties, briefly—"lots of questions then, for you. So here's how we'll do. I'll buy you another drink, and you and I will repair to the back of the room there, a table away from everyone, have a little talk."

The door was near, but it was a long walk up those crooked rubber steps, and she didn't have her land legs yet. *Don't be stupid here.* "I don't want another drink."

He took her hand, gripping it, leaning in close. Smiling his government eyes. "Fine. We'll do this right here, nice and intimate. Like lovers." He pressed the five crumpled twenties into her hand like a wad of trash. "I'm paying you a C-note right now, to deliver a package to me. And that package is information."

No need to bother looking around to see who might overhear them because all she was going to tell this asshole was to go fuck himself. "I don't know—"

"You don't know anything, sure. I understand. Only one problem with that. I *know* that you do know things, okay? A-B-C. That's as simple as one two three. You and me."

So cold once the water runs out. When the dry air attacks you like your conscience. She looked for Splashy's help, but he was gone.

"I'm really not an asshole, all right?" the guy said, his hand squeezing her hand holding the cash. His humid cologne. "Lucky for you, I'm not the kind of cop who's going to come down hard, threaten you with losing your daughter, talking foster homes and all that dreadful, dreadful shit. Not me."

Her mind was shivering.

"And I don't even care about your messengering for Fergie. Drug dealing, racketeering, criminal conspiracy—you're just a cog in that machine. A go-between. But a good broom sweeps clean, and I'm riding a good broom here. A dynamite fucking broom. I'm not asking you to wear a wire. I'm not looking to *use* you like that, *endanger* you, no. I'm going totally positive on this. How many cars you own, Krista?"

"What?" His face was close enough to spit at. "None."

"Seven. You own seven vehicles. You didn't pay for any of them, but they're all registered in your name. Doug MacRay and your brother did that, to shield their assets. Ever seen Doug's Corvette, his green machine? You like that ride? That car is yours, Krista. Legally. He had you sign some papers for him once, go to the registry, right? Something happens to Doug—that car cannot be attached to any penalties he might have to pay, any restitution for, oh, let's just say, bank robbing. And I bet you don't even know where he garages it."

Say nothing. Show nothing.

"And here you are messengering dust for scratch money. *Scratch* money. For your daughter, right? Of course. But living like this? Do you have *any* idea how much money they pulled down on that movie theater thing? Every cent of it untraceable. Immediately spendable."

"I don't know what you're—"

"Talking about, sure. You're loyal, of course you're loyal. It's family. But listen. They are all going down. It's going to happen, and soon—that's a fact. That's what I'm here to tell you. Now you seem like a practical girl, resourceful. You must have considered this day would come. They go down—what happens to you? You don't want to be the one left behind. The cars are in your name— that's good and fine, that's safe. But hold on. Your house. Now I happen to know that your brother's name is on it too, you share it. And we will take that away, his half of your house. And if you don't get practical and resourceful with me here, the fact is that you could be going up for aiding and abetting—and this is above and beyond any drug charges—in which case we take *everything*, and you will move into a new home, called MCI Framingham. Your little girl?" Frawley shook his head. "But that's worst-case scenario. That's *if*. And I don't even like to talk about *if*. Not when there's so many things actually going in your favor. Primarily, this house of yours that we need to save. You know how much a stand-alone on Pearl Street is worth in today's market? A ready-to-renovate triple-decker in Charlestown? You're sitting on a small fortune—all legit—and yet, here you are, waiting for a call to deal dust, flirting with strangers for drinks. The sale of that house would set you and your daughter up pretty good. But for that, we need a working arrangement, you and I. I need a good reason to protect your *ass*et."

Only the stink remains, once the water is gone. Musty emptiness. "Bullshit, trying to scare me. I want a lawyer."

"Good, do that. Get one. Because all this is about protecting yourself. No— not even yourself. Your daughter. Think, Krista."

"You leave her out."

"I can't, and neither can you. They've been shafting you for years. Keeping you on this leash—and why? To hold you down. Keep you dependent, like a junkie for their goodwill. Keep you close. The right thing would have been to pay you generously for all the secrets you so faithfully keep." He ducked low to see up into her eyes. "And look, your brother? Hey. He's not even the one I'm really after."

"No?"

He picked up on the thing in her eyes. He watched her and absorbed it. "Unless, that is, you want me to be."

Duggy. He was after Duggy.

"This MacRay," the FBI man went on. "How long you put up with him?"

Hearing his name out of the G's mouth was like hearing that Duggy was dead, and her heart fell.

"The hoops he made you jump through? And if I heard about it, you know everybody in Town knows."

Elbow on the bar, she grabbed a handful of her own hair, twisting it.

"This sad song," he said, thumbing back at the jukebox. "You gonna listen to this over and over again, the rest of your life?"

Go right home and tell Duggy about this guy. Straight to his door. He would be so grateful.

"One more question. You were with him how long?"

Krista's nose was almost touching the bar. "All my life."

"Let me ask you this. In all those years you were together—how many diamond necklaces he buy you from Tiffany?"

All the water out of the air now, the dry world dripping loud. "What are you talking about, diamond necklaces?"

The FBI man said, "Answer my question, then I'll answer yours."

40
MAC'S LETTER

June 1996

Little Partner,

What a shock you just got. Finding this with my riteing and the Walpole return adress in your mailbox. Wish I could of seen your face. Whats the old crook up to now? Im not riteing to ask you anything. You no thats not my style. I never ask for anything from anyone in my life. What I wanted I took and what I needed done I did myself. I no your the same Duggy.

I do'nt rite much and I no I never rote you before. Hard to get you out here tho and after last time I felt like we were'nt done. Whenever it comes time to see you theres so much to say that it never all gets said. So much saved up in my mind. Then your gone and I got another year to puzzle you over.

When I get out theres no way I can make up for the things I owe you. Your a man you understand this. Misstakes take 2x as long to fix as they do to make. Thats why you never look back. OK you look back but never go back Duggy. You keep going on.

About your mothers house. I met your mother at the Monumint in November of 63. Kennedy had just died—shot in the head—and the town was in morning and Coffy and me and the rest of us were sick of moping so we went out to find trouble. We were kicking around the steps there and this little gide comes out—this little tour gide with copper red hair—she was younger but she bitched us out like somebodys mother. A little pint glass with a black band on her school uniform giving us all kinds of shit till she started crying her eyes out for Kennedy. We had our fun but next day I came back alone. I listened to her school speech to the torists and she saw me. Her name tag was Pam. I came back 6 days in a row before I got a smile. I do'nt no what she saw in me. I did'nt no what I wanted exept to take her out. 1 nite she snuck away from her frends and came bowling.

We had to get marryed Duggy. Her parents new I was Bottom Of The Hill. A Slope Kid and they never liked me but they never gave up on her ether. They gave us the downpayment for the house on Sackville when you came along. But I always payed the moregage. The house was mine.

What I promised her on that day we bowled was that Id never make her cry again and I broke that promise a thousand times. She did things because she was angry at me. I was away a lot and she left you at her mothers to much. The $$ I gave her for food she took down to the corner. I scared off all her hippy friends, but from then on she just did these things alone.

I am not telling you this because I am a prick. I am telling you this because I am not a prick.

She did'nt do it on purpose. The thing of the time in the 60s was to push bowndrys and walk on the moon and free your mind. Her mind just got to free. You were asleep in front of the tv when I came home and found her in the bathroom and the needle. I got you to the naybors 1st thing. When you woke up in the morning and started asking for her what coud I say? What do you tell a 6 year old kid? Your mother went away. Shes gone. I do'nt think shes coming back.

You wanted to go out looking for her so we looked. Her parents had a private funeral and insted I took you out walking the nayborhood looking for her until you cried so hard you coud'nt walk. You saw a tv show about a missing dog and wanted to put up posters on telephone polls so we put up posters. You wanted the light on over the front door for her so I change that bulb every month. You woud'nt sleep if you coud'nt see the light from your bed.

I said she went away and so who else in Town would say other wise. My truth was truer than truth. But what I did'nt plan for was that she would become this bigger than life thing and I would go from Daddy to no one. A lot of you you made yourself. I give you that. I always see her in you. But I did what I could. I teached you the things I new.

Bottom line is I will be out soon. Then it will be the 2 of us again. You had trouble with Gem but patch it up. Loyalty is what we need now. You cant buy that.

Maybe you always new about her or gessed or never wanted to ask. If you do'nt want to talk about this again I would not mind.

This is the longest letter Ive ever ritten.

By the way. Old Uncle G came to see me. But I did'nt see him.

Do'nt no how to end this Duggy. Do'nt even no if Ill mail it.

Mac.

PS. Your mother never came back, Duggy. I am.

41
BIRTHDAY

OUG ROLLED DOWN A lane of tidy homes, checking addresses, coming up on a line of parked cars and an inflatable castle in a driveway. The bladder castle jerked and jiggled like a stomach full of screaming, indigestible kids. Doug slowed at the silver mailbox festooned with birthday balloons. The house number matched.

He pulled over at the end of the row of cars and stood out of the Caprice. The house was a gray Cape, kids chasing each other around the front yard with squirt guns, parents chatting in the driveway. Doug was about to get back in his car when he saw Frank G. step away from a small group near the castle's generator and wave him up. Frank wore a collared, short-sleeved shirt, long shorts, and Converse flats, walking down the driveway to meet him. "You found it."

Doug pulled off his shades, looking at the party. "Frank, man—you should have told me."

"You said you needed a few minutes, right? C'mon."

Frank walked him past the screaming castle toward an open garage full of chairs and folding tables of food. Twin girls in matching pink eyeglasses sat hip to hip on the front lawn, eating melting blocks of ice cream cake, and three plastic paratroopers came swaying down to earth out of a bedroom window, followed by a balsa wood airplane in a tailspin. Then a kid with his arm in a blue cast came racing past, nailing them each in the gut with water out of a tiny green pistol, taunting, "Ha-ha, Uncle Frank!"

Frank pulled a pastel pink Saturday night special out of his pocket and turned on the kid, blasting him, the kid running off squealing in a war-movie zigzag as Frank's piece ran dry. "Inside," he said. "Gotta reload."

He did so at the sink, the kitchen bustling with women wrapping to-go plates of ziti and lasagna and cold cuts. Frank led Doug past two dads talking business in the hallway, past a cooing woman changing a sleepy baby on the dining room floor, past the Sox game in the family room. A ruckus up on the second floor made Frank reverse direction, taking Doug to a side door, down wooden steps into a cool basement.

Half of it was finished, the paneled walls papered with Michael Jordan, Ray Bourque, and Mo Vaughn posters. There were Koosh balls everywhere, old U-Haul boxes overflowing with sporting equipment, and an elaborate Matchbox racetrack setup in the back. In the center of the room stood an air hockey table under a billiards lamp.

"So what's doing?" said Frank.

Doug shrugged. The birthday party had thrown him, he didn't know where to start. "How *you* doing?"

"Me?" Frank walked around to the other end of the table rink. "Much better. You caught me at a bad moment last time. I let that little old guy get to me, I don't know why. He doesn't stand for everybody. I know he doesn't stand for me."

"Good. Good to hear." Doug prowled back and forth, uncomfortable, as though asking for money.

Frank switched on the game table, the jets pushing air through the perforated playing surface. "I'm back at meetings, been to a few." The puck stirred, a red plastic disk drifting to the side as though by an invisible hand. Frank flicked it back to the opposite boards—just diddling, not an invitation to play. "What about you?"

Doug ran his hand briskly through his chopped hair. "Meetings? Nah. Not since before we talked."

A herd of elephants went trampling overhead. "Big mistake," said Frank. "You got crisis written all over your face, I can see it. Beeping me was the right thing to do. Listen to me now. She's not worth it."

"Who? Not worth what?"

"That drink you haven't taken yet. Your girl isn't worth it."

"Nah, Frank—"

"'I think I met someone . . .' You remember that?" Frank pushed the wafer puck harder now, sending it clicking off the boards, coasting on the low-friction surface. "The way you first told me about her—I knew. This girl is your disease, Doug."

Doug held out his hands. "Frank—and I never said this to you before—but you're dead wrong here. This girl . . . if *anything,* she's my sobriety."

"And she's gone now."

Doug admitted, "Yeah."

"And you're thirsty. It's right there on your face. But if you can somehow get her back—that'll cure everything, right?"

"Frank, look. This other girl, my *old* girlfriend—*she's* my alcoholism. Fucking haunting me every good step I try to take. But this girl—no. She's *too* good for me. She's—"

"Everything you want but can't have. You've poured all your hopes into this person who can't be with you—am I right? *She's too good.* Can you hear it? You set up this unattainable thing."

"You're reading me wrong."

"Set it all up maybe even since the beginning. A long, slow slide into you giving yourself the okay to drink again, with her as your excuse. *With all I'm going through, who wouldn't slip just a little?*" The disk click-clanked into one of the slot goals like a coin dropping into a bank. "That's the bullshit you have to fight here. That's the demon."

Doug paced with his hands folded behind his head. "How did it get so complicated?" he said. "It's a beer. You drink it, or you don't."

"It *used* to be a beer," said Frank, switching off the table, coming out from behind it. "Face that, Doug. You got to eat what's eating you. You can't drown it. You tried that already. Didn't work."

Doug wondered what it would taste like, this thing that was eating him.

The door opened on the party above them, a woman's voice: "Frank?"

"Yeah, down here, hon."

Toeless summer sandals stopped two steps down. "Steve and Pauline just left, they couldn't find you."

"I'm sniffing glue with a friend. Hold on."

Frank trotted up the steps for a whispered conversation. Then the sandals flapped down ahead of Frank.

"I'm Nancy Geary," she said, offering her small hand for a quick, purposeful shake; not unfriendly, but not sweetly fake either. He was a guest in her house and she was presenting herself to greet him.

"You have a beautiful home here," said Doug, because he was supposed to, and because it was true.

She was small, a tough city girl. "You get anything to eat yet?"

"I'm a gate-crasher. Frank didn't tell me you were . . ." He waved at the thumping upstairs.

"Take some sandwiches home with you, okay?"

"I will. Thank you."

She was already starting back up the stairs. Probably never beautiful, but steady, no more attractive with makeup than without. A constant. Not trying to impress anybody, she had a house and a family and a birthday party to run.

The door closed, and Doug looked at Frank. "You wanted me here for this," he said. "Wanted me to see the house, the wife, the kids."

"It's not unattainable. All you gotta do is get lucky. This girl, Doug—people come and go. There're reasons. That's what life is. It doesn't mean anything about you yourself."

Doug shook his head at how wrong Frank was. "'Course it does."

Frank studied him. "What's this do to you moving on from your friends?"

Doug felt the suffocation again. "No, that's still on."

"You've been saying that."

"Frank, look, I'm committed. There's nothing left here for me now. I'm setting it up so that there's no turning back. But I gotta . . . I gotta take care of things first."

"That I don't like the sound of. You trying to save people who don't want to be saved."

"It's not that. Truly. It's knowing what will happen to them after I'm gone, and trying to give them, at least, one good last chance."

"Chance at what?"

Doug shrugged. "I guess, life."

"You really think that? Think you're the only thing kept them safe all these years? The designated driver for everyone?"

Doug considered this. "Yeah. I have to say—it's exactly that."

They went back up the stairs together. In the hallway a kid went racing past waving a plastic sword, and Frank stopped him with a shoulder squeeze. "Mikey, where's Kev?"

"Right here, Dad," said a shorter, tow-haired boy in the kitchen doorway, holding a hockey stick with a big blue bow on it.

"C'mere, Roscoe," said Frank, steering the two boys across into the dining room, past a supermarket tray of cookie crumbs. Frank stood with one hand on the swordsman's shoulder and the other on the shorter boy's blond head. "Michael, Kevin, this is the guy I was telling you about. This is Doug MacRay."

Doug looked at Frank, surprised but getting it now. Frank G. had had his number the whole time.

Frank said, "This guy was the fastest backward skater I ever saw, including pro."

Doug stood before the boys, feeling like he was the kid and they were the adults.

"Kev turned seven today," said Frank, roughing up his boy's hair, pride and love coming off him like heat.

"*Yesterday,*" corrected Kevin.

"Right. Sorry. Birthday yesterday, party today."

Brown-haired Michael looked up at Doug with his mother's no-nonsense eyes. "You were drafted by the Bruins?"

Doug said, "I was."

They looked him over closely, this stranger in their dining room, this former hockey star, mysteriously a friend of their father's.

The birthday boy, Kevin, shrugged. "So what happened?"

Doug nodded, unable to meet their young eyes, almost unable to say the words. "I blew it."

42
THE LAST BREAKFAST

BREAKFAST AT HIS MOTHER'S house, without the breakfast. He hadn't eaten anything in a couple of days, and thought he might never eat again.

My mother is a house.

Why come here now? To mourn her? Hadn't he always come here to mourn her?

My mother is dead.

No. He had always come here to mourn himself. His motherless self.

Gone now was his fantasy of her brave midnight flight from the Town, winning her freedom from his father and living reinvented and happy somewhere in the outside world, yet with a tender spot in her heart for the son she hated to leave behind.

All the baths he had taken in that porcelain tub, emerging barefoot and shivering and dripping tears of bathwater onto the tile floor where she last lay.

He wanted to believe in her sickness, her suffering. Her passionate, epic torment. Anything but the banality of a junkie fixing to self-destruct.

That night he had dreamed that the one-way streets of the Town were lined not with houses but with heads, the giant, weathered faces of old mothers talking at him as he hurried past them toward the empty lot on Sackville Street, the mouths on either side of it going *tsk-tsk.*

The Town kept its secrets close, raising them like its children. Thinking this brought on an absurd surge of panic for Krista and for Shyne, one he fought down.

Doug hadn't seen the guy exit the house. He was so lost in thought, he didn't notice the owner of the bottom-floor condo walking to his red Saab, keys in hand. Dark-haired, compact in an unbuttoned suit jacket, long tie, tasseled shoes. The guy saw Doug and slowed, and Doug couldn't even work up the energy to pretend to be doing anything other than what he was doing: sitting against this low brick hedge wall, watching the guy's house.

The guy tossed his underarm portfolio into the backseat of the car, then shut the door, considering heading over and saying something to Doug.

"Hi," the guy said, doing just that, slowly crossing the one-way street. "I notice you sit out here some mornings. Most mornings."

"Yeah?" Doug said, low-energy, off his guard. "I'm just waiting for a ride."

The guy nodded, stopping at the front bumper of the Caprice. "We—I see you out here a lot." He glanced back at the house. "You seem to be watching our house, or something. Unless I'm . . ."

"I used to live here a long time ago," said Doug, surprised by his tired candor. "That's all."

"Ah." The guy was still confused.

"It's cool, don't worry," said Doug. "After today I won't be coming around anymore."

The guy nodded, trying to think of something else to say, then turned and started back. Then he stopped, something nagging at him.

"Say—you want to step inside? I don't know, see it again, one last time?"

Doug never expected the guy to be decent. Doug could see the lady of the house now, peeking out at them from behind the parlor-window curtain. He pictured them all inside together, a pair of wary yuppies watching 210 pounds of Grade-A Townie getting misty in their bathroom.

The offer was tantalizing, but the house was his mother, and his mother was long dead.

Doug said, "You got a little girl there, huh?"

"Yes," the guy said, at first brightening, then suspicious.

"Sleeps in that corner room?"

The guy looked at the window where the faded ghost of a TOT ALERT! fire-safety sticker remained—not knowing how or whether to answer.

"Those dolphin curtains there," said Doug, pointing them out. "You want to draw those every night. Headlights come by on the street, they reflect off the ceiling and look like ghosts flying past. Scary for a kid lying there alone."

The guy nodded, mouth hanging open. "I will certainly do that."

Doug slid into the Caprice and pulled away down the steep decline.

THE KNOCK ON KRISTA's door brought her answering it in a tank shirt, nylon workout pants, and Tweety slippers. She straightened with surprise, looking past Doug as though he might not be alone. "What's up?"

Doug shrugged, uncertain himself. "Nothing really."

She moved aside, and he entered. Shyne was trapped in her sticky high chair in the dying parlor, shredding a cord of string cheese into white threads. A crushed butt in the table ashtray was still smoking.

"I think I'm hungry," said Doug.

Krista disappeared into the kitchen and Doug dropped into a chair at the table, exhausted at 9 A.M. He watched Shyne's wormy fingers working at the cheese, the dull concentration in her close-set eyes, her lips lax along the flat line of her mouth. He heard the microwave hum for about a minute, then beep and stop.

He said, toward the kitchen, "I'm going away."

Silence, then Krista's padding slipper-steps resumed, the microwave door opened and shut. "You in some kind of trouble?"

Doug shook his head, though she couldn't see him. "No more than usual."

A drawer opened, silverware rustling. "Is it the heat in Town?"

Her insider status grated on him as she reentered the room. Jem told her too much. "What do you know about it?"

She set down a steaming plate of chicken à la king in front of him with a fork and knife. Thick cream sauce studded with chunks of white meat. Anything would have looked good to him then.

Krista lifted a strand of cheese off Shyne's tray and dangled it before her daughter's mouth like a mother bird with a white worm. When Shyne didn't bite, Krista pressed the cheese in between the girl's lips, only to have it fall back onto the tray. She gave up and sat across from him on a folded knee. "When are you coming back?"

Steam from his plate rose between them. Doug shook his head.

She studied him, doubtful. "This have to do with you and Jem?"

Behind her, Shyne almost made a word then, a sound like *Shemmm*.

Doug said, "In a way."

"Does he know?"

"Probably." Doug picked up the fork, checking that it was clean. "I'm gonna do this one last thing he wants. You can tell him that for me."

She nodded. "And afterward?"

The thin wood handle of the knife was cracked, the blade rusted and wobbly. "You know I've always looked out for him."

"You were the only one who could."

"Well, this is it for me. He wants a chance at one big score, I'm gonna give it to him. It's up to him whether he makes it his last or not."

Her eyes tightened, seeing that he was serious now. "Where are you gonna go?"

"I don't know yet."

"Is she going with you?"

Doug had a forkful almost to his mouth. He set the fork back down and absorbed her blunt stare. As Shyne dropped the threads of cheese to the dusty floor, one by one, Krista's glare became full of violence, a scorned lover's inward scream.

43
THE FLORIST

GLOANSY REALIZED WHAT THE Florist's walk-in cooler reminded him of: a vault. The small-room-within-a-room thing, and the thick butcher door with the locking clasp, and the quiet inside. But with flowers in bunches on the shelves instead of stacks of bundled cash.

Why a flower shop? Gloansy wondered that now for the first time. Why not a smoke shop or a deli or something? The Main Street shop had always been there, with Fergie always running it. Probably he had taken the store from someone as part of a long-ago debt, and then—maybe with just the touch of his hand—transformed it into the ugliest flower shop ever. Petals had to be brown and wrinkled like bottom-of-the-bag potato chips before he would yank a $2 rose from a display pot. The vase water was never freshened, scummy and black-green like the harbor, and it was the only flower shop anywhere with plastic vines and silk plants in the display window.

Fergie did good parade business around Bunker Hill Day. He did some winner's circles on featured horse races over at Suffolk Downs, the wreaths they used for big-purse runs. It was bragged around that sometimes Fergie mailed the bill to the winning horse's owner the day before the race. Funerals, he did a lot of. Death, Fergie had a knack for. It followed him around in place of his lost conscience, his two sons gone, one of them a casualty of the dust he peddled, and his daughter gunned down in an ambush meant for the other. And always Fergie survived, coming back here to his workroom and wiring up his wreaths. Spools of ribbon hung in tongues of black and gold off his workbench: DAUGHTER; MOTHER; WIFE; SON.

They sat on small folding chairs with padded seats like mourners at a graveside burial, the four of them facing Fergie. Rare to get within spitting distance of Fergus Coln. He was mostly a recluse now, either bona fide paranoid or maybe just letting the legend that was The Florist feed on itself. The Code of Silence trials had all but wiped out every one of his contemporaries, but still he soldiered on. He lived somewhere near the old armory, but supposedly kept crash pads all over Town, constantly moving, like a fugitive king.

He was also known as Fucked-Up Fergie, because that's what his face was, to-tally fucked-up, thanks to early careers as both a wrestler—some of his bouts were televised in the late 1950s—and as a prizefighter on the Revere and Brockton cir-cuits. His nose was wrong, his eyes doggy and tired, his skin waxy like fake fruit. His lips were so thin they were nonexistent, and his tiny cauliflower ears were things a child would draw in crayon. As they used to say about him, in his days as a mob enforcer: some hearts he stopped with just his reputation and his face. His hands were messed up too, crooked fingers looking like each row of knuckles had been separately slammed in a drawer, his nails flat and silver like coins.

Always there was this guy with him, keg-chested Rusty, supposedly an IRA or ex-IRA gunner who couldn't go back home. Rusty had fading white hair, pale Irish skin, and liked to wear dark running suits like he was on vacation. In other words, there was nothing red about Rusty, nothing to support the name. Unless he was "rusty" because he was a little slow. Guy never talked. A zombie following Fergie everywhere—except inside the cooler on that warm afternoon, a big nod of respect to the crew. Paranoid Fergie never met with anybody alone.

He sat before them in his little chair like a fighter in the corner between late-round bells. His legs were fanned wide, as though daring somebody to kick him in the balls. He wore a grease-stained white tank, black uniform-type pants, and a scally cap turned backward over his rearranged face.

Usually if you did see Fergie around Town, you recognized him first by the tight sweatshirts he always wore, the hood string drawn around his head, shad-owing his face. It was no coincidence that Jem had cribbed Fergie's look that day. Jem also flattered Fergie in the fucked-up-face department, his nose and cheek still pasted in gauze, his left eye full of blood, lips cut and swollen.

Duggy sat on the other side of Gloansy, silent. He had been so sullen since their fight, you would have thought he had been the one who took the beating.

It was Doug's pride getting pummeled here. Gloansy knew how Doug was about the Florist. Fergie had some young muscle in the store when they came in, project kids in camo pants, and Doug had almost gotten into it with them too.

But being all together again, that was what counted. Doug and Jem had reached a sort of unspoken cease-fire. In fact, the one to watch here was Dez: sitting on the other side of Duggy, staring full-out at warlord Fergie, the guy who maybe—"maybe" in the Town sense—offed his father. Gloansy had to hand it to him. He couldn't believe that Dez had come at all.

"He looks like me now," said Fergie, nodding at Jem. His voice was clipped and raspy. "A little rumpus, eh?" He looked back and forth between Jem and Duggy, aging muscle hanging off his arms like rope. "Coupla stitches between brothers, it's good. Healthy. Clears the air."

Jem shrugged. Doug had no reaction that Gloansy could see.

"This room is clean, by the way, and that's guaranteed. Nobody comes in here without me, ever, and I got one of them mercury switch things to tell me if anyone tampers with the lock. So we can all talk free."

He reached for a cut daffodil, twirling it in his hand, then dipped the rounded pads of his fingertips into the petals and brought pollen to his nostrils, leaving a smear on his upper lip the color of sulfur. Guy was some kind of pervert of nature.

"This's been a long time coming," he said. "Wondered when you boys were finally gonna come round."

"Yeah," said Jem out of the side of his mouth. "Well, we been working hard. Sorta proving ourselves worthy."

A lift of Fergie's mangled chin passed for a smile. "I see your fathers' faces in each and every one a you." He ended with a look at Dez, Dez staring back hard. "Reminds me I'm still in the ring after all these years. Still on my feet. Gloves up, taking on all comers. And still ahead on points."

Jem said, "We're guys you want in your corner. Old enough to know the Town as it was, young enough to do something about putting it back that way."

Gloansy stayed attentive but blank-faced, the kid who didn't want to get called on.

"You're good thieves," said Fergie. "But these ten percent tributes to me." He shrugged like it pained him. "Ten percent is what you throw after a waiter you don't like. What is that? I'm not liked?"

Funny to see Jem squirm. Doug had his arms crossed now and Gloansy didn't think he was going to speak at all. He was going to let Jem do all the work.

Fergie went on, "But I been tracking you four. You've put together a good little run here. And I like your style. You're quiet, you keep your business close. Last crew I had got careless. Fucked up a good thing. You four, you're a crew that's been together awhile. What are you looking for from me?"

"We're looking to make a mark," said Jem. "We think we earned our shot at something big."

Fergie laid the stem across his lap and patted clean his hands. "Funny thing, fate. Because as long as it took you boys to hitch up your pants and come knocking at my door like men—this turns out to be good timing. Very good timing. Because I happen to be sitting on something here, something that's got to fall soon. And big it is. Big enough only for the best. I got someone on the inside, someone who owes me something."

Jem nodded. "We're interested."

"'Course you are. Who's not interested in something like that? But are you committed? Because you got to pay to play here, that is how we work. Blueprint fee just for me talking about things. That's on top of my percent of the take, and it's a big bite. But this is nothing you could get anywhere near without my inside. Do it right and there'll be plenty left over."

"What's the buy-in?"

"Normal job, average weight—between fifty and seventy-five large, up front."

Jem nodded, waiting. "And for this one?"

"This one is twice as much, easy."

Gloansy tried not to react, sitting up and mashing his hands together. One-fifty? Had he heard that right? Divided by four?

Fergie said, "Yo-yo's looking at me like you ain't got the money. Don't forget my little ten percent duke tells me what you been taking these years. And don't think I farm these out 'cause I can't do them myself. I put on guys like you because it's your specialty. I hire *professionals*. Because I'm generous, I like to spread it around Town for the good of all. You come here telling me you're ready for the big time? Well, this thing is bigger than Boozo ever saw from me, and it's all right here, right now, this moment."

Gloansy glanced at Jem, then at Doug, who hadn't moved, and then at Dez, who hadn't moved either. Then Gloansy regretted having moved himself.

"Who knows?" said Fergie to all this silence and not moving. "Maybe you're not as ready as you think you are." He picked the daffodil up off his lap again and Gloansy wondered how his touch alone hadn't shriveled the thing already. "This flower. Who owns it? Me, right? No. I don't own it. It's not *mine,* I didn't *create* it. Somebody somewhere, who knows who, pulled it outta the ground. Those who *take.* Versus those who can't *hold.* Someone tries to take this flower from me without payment, they're gonna get the ultimate lesson in this. 'Cause I will catch them and take something from them instead. A hand. A foot. Your hand, your foot—you think it *belongs* to you, think you *own* it? Your *life*?" He waited, though they all knew better than to answer. "Not if I can take it away. Not if you can't hold on to it." He twirled the flower in his fingers, then tossed it to the floor between them. "I'm a *taker,* that's my thing. Why else you come to me, right? Not cause I'm so pretty. You boys need to figure this out. Are you wanters or are you takers?"

It was Duggy who said, "We'll buy the job."

Gloansy turned to look at him, as did Dez. A shock, hearing him speak—never mind him saying yes to the Florist. Jem, Gloansy noticed, didn't look at all.

"For a hundred large, even," added Doug, cutting short Fergie's approving nod. "Twenty-five each. If it's as good as you say, and you haven't thrown it to nobody else yet, that means you got nobody else to throw it to."

Fergie's stare reminded Gloansy of his late father—God rest—and the looks the man could give, eyes that said, *Remember that you are here before me today only because I did not kill you yesterday—and that what you do right now will determine whether you will be here before me again tomorrow.*

But Fergie had met his match, or at least the first mirror he had ever faced that didn't automatically crack. No one could reach Doug now, and a shadow of nervousness flashed across Fergie's mangled face like that of a passing crow.

"With the balls of his father," Fergie said ultimately, reasserting himself with a kinglike nod. "I'm gonna make a present of this and give you your price. A onetime introductory offer."

He sat back grandly, but it was in the air now like the steam of their breath: Fergie the Florist had bent to the will of another.

"We won't let you down," said Jem.

"No, you won't," said Fergie. "Till now, you been like altar boys dipping into the Sunday collection. But this thing I'm talking about here, this ain't no parish church, boyos. This is a fucking Roman cathedral."

44
DEPOT

FRAWLEY AND DINO STALLED for time at the water bubbler until the fat black kid lugged his backpack into the classroom and the last hallway door closed. They were on the top floor of one of the buildings of Bunker Hill Community College, erected on the site of the long-closed prison.

The door at the end of the hall read: Radiation Lab Do Not Enter.

A guy dressed like a graduate student answered Frawley's knock, opening the door just wide enough to show his eyeglasses and the soul patch clinging to his bottom lip. "Hey," said Agent Grantin, recognizing Frawley, admitting him and Dino and shutting the door.

A second agent was under headphones near the windows. Dino put his fist to his own nose and said, "Whoa, Mary."

Grantin nodded. "One of you guys please tell my partner, Billy Drift, here, not to eat falafel during a surv in a room with *no working windows*."

Agent Drift pulled his headphones down and sheepishly stood out of one of the student desks. "I *said* I was sorry, man. It just didn't agree with me."

The room was tight and empty except for scattered student desks and a blond wood table. On the table was a Nagra tape recorder, a computer and a color printer, a cell phone charging, and a video monitor wired to a tripod camera aimed out of an east-facing window. The hi-res monitor showed people crossing in front of the Florist's Main Street shop.

Frawley looked out the window, taking a moment to orient himself and locate the camera's line of sight, finding the Bunker Hill Mall and the cemetery and looking west from there. He introduced Dino to the Organized Crime agents.

"We're running twelve-hour revolving shifts here with a pair from the DEA," said Grantin, pulling off the glasses and the soul patch, his masterful disguise. "I was going through some of their cuts from the past few days—and that time you came down to ask about the Florist, those pictures you brought, your bank jackers? I think we got them."

He handed over four time-coded video captures printed on photo paper.

The first one Frawley recognized immediately as Magloan, in profile, entering the front door with a second man wearing a hooded sweatshirt, his face bandaged.

"It's them," Frawley said, passing the picture to Dino.

The next image was from two minutes later: Elden wearing a ballcap, one hand in his pocket, the other on the doorknob, turning to check the street behind him.

The last one was of MacRay, six minutes after Elden, a one-quarter profile of him entering the store. Just enough of his face was visible for grand jury identification.

"A sit with the Florist," said Frawley. "For how long?"

"Twenty minutes or so. They all left separately—it's on tape somewhere but I didn't have time to hard-copy it."

Dino handed the cuts back to Frawley. "Bandage man?" Dino said.

"Coughlin, must be," said Frawley, remembering MacRay's swollen hands, but unable to share this insight with Dino. He sorted through some other captures of unsuspecting shoppers. "How well are you guys in his shop?"

"Not good. We're there, but he runs this Irish music nonstop. Picked up nothing on your team but the bell jingling over the door and *Heyhowyadoing*. I was hoping maybe you were on them better, could help us."

Frawley nodded. "We're on their vehicles. Eyes, but not ears. This town— it's impossible."

"Yeah," said Drift, motioning to the window and their panorama of the Boston face of Charlestown. "Look at us up here."

"We got bumper beacons on all four of their cars, sparing the special-ops guys tails and survs. We did manage to wire up a T-4 in Magloan's car, but he rides alone and plays that JAM'N 94.5 crap all day."

"Worse than that," said Dino, "he sings along."

"We're on their phones, but they don't use them for anything. They're wise because one of them works for Nynex—though we did stick a transponder beacon on his phone company truck."

"Well," said Grantin, looking out over the Town, "something's up."

Frawley pulled out a cut showing Krista Coughlin in shorts, a strap-shouldered tank, and flip-flops, pushing her canopied stroller into the shop. "What's the Florist been up to recently?"

"The usual. He keeps hanging in there. The whole diva gangster thing."

"When are you guys going to take him down?"

Grantin shrugged. "When someone in his organization cracks. He's the only one of the old guard left. Guy's a full-time freak. DEA wants him even worse than we do."

Frawley held up the photos. "Can I keep these?"

"Hey, with our compliments."

FRAWLEY HAD TO GO to the Boston Field Office at One Center Plaza to find out that the judge had thrown out his second request, made through the U.S. attorney's Major Crime Unit, for Title Three taps and surv warrants on Claire Keesey's Charlestown condominium. The judge cited insufficient evidence, ruling again that she could not be reasonably considered a suspect in the Kenmore Square armed robbery.

Back inside the tech room, Frawley waited with Dino while a computer program swallowed up longitude and latitude GPS coordinates from the bumper beacon transponders and spit the information back out to them in the form of street addresses and connect-the-dots grid maps.

"What's this?" said Dino. "MacRay actually went to work two days ago?"

At least he had driven up to the Bonafide Demolition site in Billerica and parked there for eight hours. Then that night, and the next morning and again in the evening, he did circuits around the shark fin of Allston, parking for long stretches in the vicinity of Cambridge Street, near the Conrail yards. Cross-checking showed Magloan spending time in that area as well, and Elden's work truck cooping there for an hour or so at midday.

Dino said, "Cambridge Street? Christ. What is that, Dunbar?"

"Nope," said Frawley, reaching for his jacket. "Magellan."

WHERE DO ARMORED TRUCKS go at night, and where do they issue from in the morning? Unassuming buildings tucked behind high-security fences and electronic gates, deep inside industrial parks or hidden among office-building complexes—the locations of which are the most closely guarded secrets in the armored-carrier industry. Inside, under video-surveillance systems that rival those of most casinos, cashiers in pocketless smocks work in glass-walled counting rooms, tallying, sorting by denomination, stacking, and strapping hundreds of thousands of dollars each night, in currency notes and coins.

For example, on December 27, 1992, thieves looted a windowless office building in an industrial section of Brooklyn, New York, making off with $8.2 million—and leaving behind $24 million they were physically unable to carry.

Set back from the southern side of Cambridge Street before the road crossed the Charles River into Cambridge, in the shadow of the elevated Mass Turnpike, stood a two-story building with no name, surrounded by twin twelve-foot-high chain-link fences topped with concertina wire. That side of the road was barren, lacking even a sidewalk, and the building looked like a modest storage facility gone belly-up.

The electronic gate at the rear of the armored-truck depot was hidden from the street. Frawley could just see it from the dusty lot, holding down his tie as cars whipped past.

"Not one exit," said Dino, pointing his clipboard at the Pike. "Not two exits. Three big exits, all within an eighth of a mile of where we stand."

Frawley squinted, blasted by sand and grit. "Firepower needed for this. Stepping out of profile."

"So is going to the Florist though. Must have somebody on the inside."

"That's an angle for us. But I don't want to tip our hand either." Frawley looked at the cameras on the corners of the roof. "You said MacRay went to work, right?"

"You think explosives? Think they're going to blow their way in?"

"Or else put up a hell of a diversion."

Frawley had not filed a 302 summarizing his meeting with MacRay. He didn't want that part of the official record, at least not yet. He had, however, filed a Confidential Informant report, Form 209, on Krista Coughlin, getting her assigned a six-digit snitch code in order to cover himself and the investigation, in case she did come through with anything. Such as, when exactly MacRay and company were planning on taking down the Magellan Armored Depot.

A black 4X4 ran up on the shoulder, Frawley and Dino stepping back, squinting into the dust cloud as a cop-type in a security uniform climbed out. He wore a badge and an ID tag, but nothing that read Magellan.

"Guys lost?" he said, coming up on them cordial but firm. "Help you with something?"

Frawley didn't badge him. He had no way of knowing who might be the inside man. "No thanks," he said. "We were just on our way."

45
BALLPARK FIGURE

MOST PEOPLE—INCLUDING MOST bank robbers—think that getting at the money is the toughest part of heisting, when in fact it is the getaway that separates the pros from the cons.

Doug climbed inside the Nynex truck at the corner of Boylston and Park, wearing a work shirt of Dez's, rapping fists with the Monsignor.

"Got the hotel room?" said Dez.

"It's a palace."

"How long you gonna stay?"

"Long as it takes. Registered under 'Charles.'"

"'Charles?'"

"As in 'Charles Town' "

"Ah."

Doug checked the mirrors for tails. "You put in for next Tuesday off?"

"Personal day, all set. But this decoy shit's a lot of work."

"Tell that to the G. You switched trucks, I hope."

"Bleeding radiator—damn the luck. Here. Buckle this on."

Doug clasped around his waist a leather lineman's belt just like Dez's, with a red-orange plastic phone-company handset on a wire holster loop.

Dez double-parked prominently on Yawkey Way, right across from the Gate D entrance, stepping out with his work-order clipboard and yanking open the back of the truck. He loaded Doug up with a pile of equipment, then they crossed the road and commiserated with the red-shirted gate girl about the heat. She consulted her clipboard. "Are you on the work list?"

"Should be," said Dez. "I know you're on mine. I just go where I'm told."

Her red shirt meant ballpark staff, not security. "This is about the . . . ?"

"System upgrades. All I'm here for now is to check things out, save us time on job day by making sure we bring everything we need. Something about everything having to be done over the next West Coast road trip. Twenty minutes, tops."

"Could I just see your work ID?"

Dez showed her. She looked it over and filled out a work pass for him.

Doug made a show of struggling under his load as she finished. "My trainee," said Dez.

"That's okay," she said, filling out a second pass without asking for Doug's ID.

The caves and tunnels beneath the Fenway stands, the concession area, was where the oldest park in Major League Baseball showed its age. Food-service workers wheeled racks of bagged hot-dog rolls to the stalls, already loading up for that night's game. A blue shirt met them at the doors to an elevator, a recent college graduate, his security ID hanging on a shoelace around his neck, handset radio on his belt. He was short, wide with machine-pumped muscle, and Dez flashed him the passes.

"Where to, guys?"

Dez said, "Ah, press box, I'm told."

The blue shirt stepped aboard the elevator and pressed five. Doug stood between black-and-white photographs of prewar Ted Williams leaning on a bat and a beaming, Triple Crown–winning Carl Yastrzemski.

Dez said, "Guess this ain't gonna be the year, huh?"

Blue shirt said, "Nope, doesn't look like it."

When the elevator stopped, Dez said, "Anyone ever ridden in this thing with you and not said those basic words?"

Blue shirt said, "You pretty much nailed it."

The doors opened on the sunny flat of an outdoor pedestrian ramp, the blue shirt leading them inside glass doors past an unmanned security desk, past back-to-back cafeterias—one for park employees, one for media—and down along a white hallway of doors open to broadcast booths. The end of the hall doglegged wide into two tiers of long counters, both of them print-media booths, resembling nothing so much as the old grandstand at Suffolk Downs. The glass wall looked out from just left of home plate, over the infield diamond of June-green grass, the cocoa base paths and warning track, thirty-four thousand tiny-ass seats, and the city of glass and steel beyond.

"Field of screams," said Dez, unloading Doug.

They made a show of walking around and plugging things in, thumping on walls, the blue shirt lasting maybe three minutes. "Say, you guys good here for a while?"

"Yeah, sure," said Dez, busy.

"I'll be back, couple of minutes."

Dez waved without looking. "Take your time."

When the footsteps faded, Dez slipped a radio wire into his ear, scanning for ballpark security frequencies. Doug affixed his work pass to his sweat-dampened shirt and nodded to Dez, starting quickly back out to the hallway, holding down his flopping telephone handset as he returned to the outdoor ramp.

Doug walked down one floor, nodding to the white-aproned food service workers on their break, entering the first open door and finding himself inside the glass-enclosed 600 Club. He strode through it like he owned the place, passing only a carpet cleaner and a bar back, crossing behind the stadium seats and their fishbowl view of the park. An escalator brought him down one more floor to a concourse running high above the third-base seats, and he made his way down through the grandstand and loge boxes, ducking into the first ramp.

Busy red-shirted Fenway employees passed him underneath the stands without much of a look. With the ballpark quiet and the concessions shuttered, Doug felt like he was back in his demo crew days—doing a basement sweep of a condemned building ahead of the wrecking ball. The angled stone floor was a skateboarder's wet dream, the iron stanchions hoisting up the park like the corroding girders boosting the interstate over the Town.

Doug passed behind Gate D, the red-shirted gate girl sitting out on the sidewalk, drinking from a bottle of water with her back to him. He passed a broad souvenir booth locked up like an old newspaper stand, eyeing the open red door beyond it. A sign on the inside face said Employees Only. Doug passed it with a long, careful glance, seeing a short hallway inside, leading to a second door with a square, one-way window.

This was the money room. Game time always found a member of Boston's finest working a detail outside it, but right now there were only cameras. According to the Florist's inside squeal, the security work scheduled for the long road trip included surveillance upgrades, meaning the park's central monitoring network would be dark for a few days. This was the reason for the job's narrow timeline.

The money room door was protected by an electronic keypad lock. Doug had the combination, but no intention of using it. He meant to grab the haul while it was on its way from the money room to the can, all packaged and ready to go.

The snag there was that the cash pickup went down inside the closed park. The can was admitted through the ambulance bay door on Van Ness Street and loaded inside at the first aid station. That meant the job had to fall right there underneath the stands.

He walked the tunnel between the money room door and the first aid station—park-wise, it matched up parallel with the distance between home plate and the edge of the outfield grass beyond first base—a brick-walled,

advertisement-filled passageway with a low, slanting roof. Along this route the
couriers wheeled the cash on a motorized handcart. Once loaded, the ambulance bay door opened again and the truck departed, making no other jumps
before returning to the Provident Armored depot in Kendall Square.

Doug lingered at the empty first aid area—just a kiosk inside the bay—
eyeing the distance between iron girders, seeing how much floor space they'd
have. Then he doubled back to the money room, checking the sight lines. He
was stalling there, worrying about them becoming trapped inside the park,
when the door opened.

Doug turned and started away fast, back down the low tunnel toward the
first aid station, making like he'd taken a wrong turn. A voice called to him, but
he did not stop, fiddling busily with the handset on his belt.

The voice called to him again, loud in the tunnel, enough to attract more
attention. Doug stopped just a few paces from the first aid station, half-turning,
still trying to shield his face from view.

"Help you?" said the man, coming along behind him. A blue-shirt security
guy, thin-haired and well-tanned, his radio still on his belt.

"Nope, all set," said Doug, still fooling with his handset. "Little lost in
here."

"Hold up a minute."

The security guy came up, looked Doug over, his pass, his lineman's belt and
boots. The guy was older, in his fifties. Maybe head of security. "Come on with
me."

He continued past Doug, and Doug followed, weighing his options. They
turned left through the first ramp, out into the open air, walking along the field
boxes in the lower stands down to the Red Sox dugout behind first base. Next
to the dugout was a short door open to the field. The grounds crew was in the
outfield spraying down grass and raking the warning track.

"This what you were looking for?" said the security guy.

He wore a knowing smile, and Doug realized then this guy was trying to do
him a solid. Give him a thrill, one working man to another. At Doug's hesita-
tion, the guy said, "Unless you throw a baseball ninety miles an hour, or hit one
thrown that fast, this is your only chance to get out there."

Doug started onto the foul-territory dirt with the cautious first step of a
ship passenger arriving on land. He crossed the grass, avoiding the freshly laid
foul line as superstitious managers do, moving onto the infield. He paused before the pitcher's mound, then walked up onto it, standing just shy of the rubber.

He looked toward home plate with a bolt of fan vertigo. He found the press
box high to his right, Dez standing in the wide viewing window, watching him,

smiling in tribute, probably thinking, *Duggy working the old magic, talking his way out onto the field*.

Doug looked out at the dinged tin of the Green Monster, then over it to the Citgo sign looming above Kenmore Square. The sight of that sign would forever kick him with a sense of failure, and of loss—the bank job, Claire—the city a boneyard of memories to him now, another good reason to walk away.

He crossed back to the home team's dugout like a pitcher headed for the showers. The security guy was leaning against the backs of the first row of seats, arms crossed, enjoying the gift more than the recipient had. "Still remember my first step out there."

"Hey, thanks," mumbled Doug, concerned about the guy remembering his face now. Doug watched him close the little door to the field, saw the guy's small, jeweled pinkie ring. He noticed the care the guy put into his fingernails, and the warm Florida vacation tan of his skin. *Head of security*, thought Doug, putting it together.

"You like to gamble?" Doug asked him.

The guy shrugged, a personal question but not too intrusive. "Here and there. Ponies mostly. Why?"

"How much you into the Florist for?"

The crash of the guy's face. From lighthearted generosity to dead-eyed fear. He looked around, said quietly, "You're not supposed to have any contact with me."

"Don't vary your routine next Monday morning," Doug told him. "Not one iota."

The guy glanced at the grounds crew, the empty stands behind him. "I was not to be approached."

"The cops're going to approach you. They'll be approaching everyone, after. You ready to sit for a lie detector?"

The guy stared at Doug: a proud man in a panic, in deep debt to the Florist, nothing left to bargain with except his life. He turned and walked off underneath the stands, and Doug saw, as clear as the seams on a Wakefield knuckler, that the Florist would off this guy as soon as the job was done.

ROOM 224 WAS IN the rear center of the block-deep, two-story Howard Johnson Hotel. With no direct sun and no cheerful amenities—just a humming TV, a mismatched chair and table, a stiff, yarny rug, a phone-booth shower, and a creaky double bed—the second-floor room was a suicide's dream. Doug drew open the stiff, ratty curtain on a patchwork window with one pane tinted rose—and looked out across Van Ness Street to the southern exterior brick wall of Fenway Park.

Fenway resembled a factory on that side, a long block of red brick and steel with small square windows made of glass as opaque as blocks of ice. Six old bay doors were widely spaced along the length of the wall, each painted green, all unlabeled except the one directly across the street from Doug's window, the last before the canvas-lined fence of the players' parking lot. Beneath a candle lamp with a red warning bulb, small, stenciled white letters on the green door read AMBULANCE.

Doug changed out of Dez's shirt and went right back outside again, crossing Boylston Street against the traffic, the hotel equidistant between the ballpark and the Fenway Gardens.

He walked slowly to her gate. The vitality of the summer flowers stood in stark contrast to the cut stems that littered the Florist's cooler tomb. Weeds were beginning to sprout in the neglected flower beds. Doug looked at the impatiens planted near his buried stash, ragged and thirsty and threatened by encroaching spearmint, wondering when she would return.

DOUG SPENT THE EVENING in the suicide room, watching the park's comings and goings before game time. The red bulb lit up two hours before the first pitch, the door rising and the ambulance backing carefully inside. Every bay door lifted in the eighth inning, the crowd soon flooding out onto Van Ness after a satisfying win, slow to disperse. The ambulance pulled away around the same time as the last of the players drove off in their Blazers and Infinitis, the red lamp going dark. The light towers above the park faded out a half hour later, and then it was just the homeless trawling for cans, pushing their shopping carts to nowhere.

THAT NIGHT HE DREAMED he was crushed beneath the rear wheels of an armored truck, twelve tons cutting him in half. But it was not Frank G. removing his fireman's helmet to take Doug's hand—it was the bank sleuth, Frawley, his federal eyes smiling.

A HORN BLAST FROM a passing truck woke him that morning—lying across the made bed, still wearing yesterday's clothes. He checked the clock, got up to take a piss, then pulled a chair to the window and waited.

At 9:17 the red lamp went bright. The ambulance door opened as a silver Provident Armored can with twin rear doors pulled up, turning toward Doug before stopping and backing into the narrow bay. Doug saw the two guards in the cab, and knew that, given the size of the haul, a third had to be riding the jump seat inside the locked cargo hold. He noticed one other critical detail, getting a clear look down at their faces, shoulders, and chests from his second-floor window: neither guard wore ear wires. No need, he reasoned, given that the exchange took place behind locked doors.

The can backed inside and the bay door closed. The red light above the closed door remained on.

A second car, a black Suburban, pulled up onto the curb on Van Ness, stopping just to the right of the closed door and idling there. Doug watched the driver, apparently the only occupant, speaking into a handheld radio.

A tail car. This complicated things.

At 9:31 the ambulance door lifted again and the can rolled out, turning toward Yawkey and pulling away. As the bay door started to close, the black Suburban eased off the curb, following the truck, and Doug curled farther back from the window as it passed. The red lamp over the closed bay door went dark just as the lamp inside Doug's criminal mind clicked on, suddenly illuminating the job before him.

46
THIRST

DOUG TOOK THE ORANGE line out to the Community College stop and walked up the hill toward Pearl. The dilapidated house leaning on the slant looked a hundred years older since he'd last seen it. His Caprice and Jem's blue Flamer were parked in front.

He slipped inside through the unrepaired front door. Above all else he wanted to avoid seeing Krista. Up in his apartment, he went around filling his father's old army sack with clothes. The only black shoes he owned were the pinching pair he had bought for his date with Claire, so he threw them in. When he realized he would never again return to the house, he made another quick, final pass. A convict's personal possessions—few in number, weighted with significance—took on a totemic quality, and Doug had, over time, winnowed his meaningful totems down to exactly one. From the bottom drawer of his bureau, he pulled out his original draft letter, typed on Boston Bruins letterhead stationery and pressed in a clear plastic sleeve, slipping it into the bag.

On his way back out, Doug paused on the steps below the second-floor landing. Jem's door lock and frame remained busted. Doug walked back up, set his laundry bag down in the hall, and rapped a knuckle on Jem's door.

"It's open," he heard, and stepped inside. He started toward the game room, but Jem's voice—"Down here"—turned him around, brought him into the bright front parlor.

Jem wore a pit-stained, V-neck undershirt and black-and-gold, smiley-face boxers as he worked on the triple-decker dollhouse. He was interior-decorating it now, having pasted in old wallpaper swatches and tiny curtains, furnishing it in miniature, even sitting a thin wooden Krista doll at the bottom-floor dining room table. Except for the empty third floor, the dollhouse was room-for-room an exact replica, inside and out.

Jem had just finished his stereo and speakers—meticulous, down to the brand names, equalizer bars, tiny knobs—and was at work on his entertainment-center TV. "Heard you walking around up there," he said without turning.

"Yeah," said Doug. "Clothes."

A bottle of Budweiser stood open on the table, soaking another ring into the ruined oak. "Where you been?"

"Working this thing," said Doug, pulling his eyes away from the Bud. "It's coming together."

"Good to hear. You walking the can guards home at night?"

"No," said Doug. "I don't do that anymore."

Jem put the tiny TV down to dry. "Tools are set," he said, making a gun of his thumb and forefinger. "Got our armor. No masks needed with the uniforms."

"Gloansy get Joanie to clean those yet?"

In the summer of 1993, Gloansy had worked as a driver on the set of one of the all-time worst motion pictures ever made, a Boston bomb-squad movie called *Blown Away*. The klepto had come through big time on that production, nabbing four cop uniforms out of a dressing room trailer, complete with badges, belts, and hats. Everything but the shoes. The costumes were so authentic that the theft was reported in the papers the next day, and Gloansy was questioned along with the rest of the film crew. He stashed the uniforms in his mother-in-law's attic, where they had been cooling until that week.

"I got yours here," said Jem. "He had his bride do a little tailoring on them, so make sure your pants don't have three legs. And he still needs to know what we want for a work car."

"Tell him I got that covered. Built into the gig."

Jem nodded without questioning it. They were quiet then, each pondering their uneasy truce. "Heard you're thinking about leaving."

"Maybe. Yeah."

Jem nodded. "Only asking 'cause I need to know whether I should put you in on the third floor here or not. Shyne, you know—I don't want her wondering who that guy's supposed to be up there, if there's no Uncle Duggy living upstairs anymore."

Jem had even included the roof wires he used to steal his cable. "I'm done," Doug told him. "And if this job falls the way it should, it's your time to step away too. A walk-off home run."

Jem considered this, eyeing his house. "Yeah, maybe you're right."

"Things do change, man. Nothing wrong with that."

"No, sure."

"We had a fucking amazing run. By any standard."

"Yo, we *set* the standard."

"The Florist, if you keep going back to him—kid, the guy's a pimp like that. He'll keep turning you out till you get bounced for good."

Jem scowled, and Doug saw that Jem was just shining him on.

"Other thing I have to say to you is, the weight of this take, all the variables involved—you should pack a parachute. We all should. In case things don't go smooth."

"Nah," Jem said. "It's gonna go great."

"It is. But in *case*."

Jem shook his head. "I don't see me running. If I have to stay away a little while, let things cool down, whatever—yeah, fine. But I don't see it."

Doug turned to the windows, chilled by Jem's faith in an unchanging future. He'd build the entire Town in miniature if he could, and sit in this same room, playing the pieces forever.

"Still out there?" said Jem.

Doug looked down to the gray van with twin antennas and tinted windows parked a few houses down the slope. "Still there."

"Dumb fucks," snorted Jem, reaching for his beer and taking a hard swig. "It's gonna go awesome, man. Fucking awesome."

THE AREA SURROUNDING A Major League ballpark is a minefield for a recovering alcoholic. Doug's own hotel had a baseball-themed lounge out front, and he sat there now, alone at a small table by the darkened windows, two hours before game time, watching fellow ticket-holders tanking up. On the wall near him hung an unlit Bud Man sign, the red-masked "super-beer-o" of the 1970s. When the waitress came by, Doug said, "Bud draft," and it was like flexing his muscles at the beach. *Let's see how strong I am.*

Frank G. always said, *Never walk into a tavern or a liquor store, especially alone.* But sometimes fate had to be tempted. Sometimes you had to walk right back up to the edge of that cliff, just to remind yourself what it had felt like lying at the bottom.

The beer arrived in a short glass, set upon a cocktail napkin like a supplicant on a prayer mat. Doug looked down at the thin brew, held a little powwow with it, then rejected it as unworthy. A vow was only as strong as its greatest temptation, and this was not enough. He threw three crumpled dollar bills at the table and emerged sinless into the all-knowing, all-seeing light of day.

He crossed the street again to the gardens. He walked to her gate and saw that she had still not been back. A few fallen leaves lay around her beds now, like dead thoughts in an idle mind. Something small-mouthed and busy had been chewing on her herbs.

After leaving Jem that morning, he had humped his laundry sack over the hill to the Boys and Girls Club, just to give fate a chance. But he didn't see her there and didn't go inside. Instead, he hailed a cab and directed it up Packard Street and the alley behind there one last time. The purple Saturn with the

Breathe! bumper sticker was back in its parking space. When the cab drove out of City Square, Doug looked back one last time, determined never to return to the Town again.

FRIDAY NIGHT, THEY STROLLED the caves of iron and stone beneath the stands, Doug and Dez, now in the company of packs of hungry, bladder-heavy fans.

The bored detail cop stood inside the short hallway between the open Employees Only door and the heavier door to the money room. Doug and Dez cruised it five or six times in the anonymity of the grazing crowd, getting familiar with the layout but learning nothing new.

The ambulance sat inside the closed bay door at the first aid station, a pair of EMTs sitting on the metal backstep, chatting up two girls. Doug's eye followed the tracks the door rose on, finding the manual on/off switch for the outside red lamp.

Concession lines ran ten and twelve deep, stretching back to the relish bowls and squirt tubs, condiment droppings spotting the stone floor like bat shit. Money was changing hands everywhere and Doug should have been thrilled. Red-visored girls tissuing out pretzels and milking soft-serve vanilla into collectible batting-helmet cups, kids jumping up and down with their pennants and posters and machine-signed team pictures, hassled dads pulling green from their wallets. Yellow-shirted snack hawkers humping empty drink racks and metal hot-dog boxes to a busy side room near Gate D, emerging moments later with a full whack and marching back out to the stands. And it was hot that night, nineties and humidity predicted all weekend, what Red Sox Nation called a *scawcha,* perfect for moving ice cream bars and Cokes.

But all this chewing and spending he viewed through a filter of disgust. The swine and their swill. He sidestepped a lump of cheesy nachos on the floor that looked like someone had shat them there and kept on moving, then ducked into the men's room to take a leak at the trough. The ballpark seemed to him a factory of shit and piss and cash. At root, the business of baseball was no better or different from the movies or from church: put on a show, promise people something transcendent, and then bleed the suckers dry.

They took their seats again in the sixth, just back of the right-field pole. A foul ball arced high over their heads, slowing at the top of its ascent like a firework shell about to explode, bloom, and twinkle away, then drifted back over the roof boxes out onto Van Ness. The fans groaned and sat back down, except for Doug and Dez, who had never stood.

Doug was hunched over a bag of peanuts, shelling one after another. Some asshole had kicked over a beer two rows back, the stain spreading like urine under Doug's seat. He dropped the cracked shells down there to soak up the spill, the same way the peanuts absorbed the saliva flooding Doug's mouth. He would never give in for a Fenway beer.

Thinking about drinking now was like fantasizing about the perfect crime. How he would do it—*if* he were going to do it.

A halfhearted wave came by, fans rising and falling in a ripple around them, Dez and Doug again keeping their seats. Dez said, "And I used to think the beach-ball thing was annoying."

Doug muttered, "Fucking retards."

Dez checked him. "What's up? You been pissed all night."

Doug frowned, shook it off. "Thought I could lose myself in the prep, but it's not happening. I'm like borderline okay when I'm focused on the job."

"Otherwise?"

Doug cracked another peanut shell. "This thing can't happen fast enough for me."

"You always said, Duggy—no marquee scores."

Doug nodded. "That is what I always said."

"And never be greedy."

"Right."

Dez looked him over. "Is it the girl?"

Doug shook his head. "Girl's gone, man."

"That's what I'm talking about."

"It's the Florist, it's the G—it's fucking everything."

Dez watched him working the peanuts. "They don't bake fortunes in those things, you know."

Doug spread his hands and saw the heap of cracked shells between his work boots, kicking it over like the mound of trash that was his life. The smell of piss-water beer assailed him from all sides, but especially from the guy in the brand-new Red Sox ballcap sitting next to him.

"Dezi, man, listen. I've been thinking it over, and this one's not for you. There's no tech on this job, nothing cute. It's us walking in the front door with guns in our hands. Something goes wrong, it could get messy. I'm serious."

Dez looked at him. "You think I can't—"

"The other two, I couldn't talk them off it if I tried. Wouldn't waste my breath. I told Jem this morning to pack a bag just in case, he didn't even hear me. But you. You know better. And I'm the one who got you into this thing. Dez—you know I used you, right? I mean, in the beginning."

"I—sure."

"'Cause I'm a piece of shit that way. 'Cause it was all about the job then, and nothing else. But now you're my responsibility, and I can't have that on me, okay? Because things are ending. You don't wanna be in business with the Florist anyway. Think of your dad."

Dez looked out at the field. "I *been* thinking about him. Probably too much."

"Fuck the Florist. Guy's a relic. Once he goes down, the whole Town goes. All the old ways."

Dez said, staring out at the field, "Someone's got to get him."

"Forget about that. Hey." Doug punched him in the shoulder. "I don't even want to hear that from you."

Dez shook his head. "I'm not backing out now, Duggy. Even if I wanted to, see? Which I don't. And besides—you couldn't pull this off with just three guys."

"Easily."

"You lie. You're full of bullshit, and I don't like this, Duggy. You look desperate. And everything you taught me, everything you're about, says that's the wrong way to go into this."

"Then gimme your out. Steer clear."

"Fine, I'll walk. When you do."

"Cut that shit out now." Doug cracked his last peanut shell, then crumpled the bag and threw it to the floor. "See, I am desperate. My life right now—fuck it. Two or three weeks ago, I could have walked away, come out way ahead. Now, I need this. Makes me sick, this whole thing—Fergie, the G—fuck them all. But I'm not leaving here without nothing. I thought one big final stake would free everybody, but Jem's not gonna stop. Gloansy, neither. It was just my fantasy. But you—you got your thing going, you got your job, your ma to take care of."

"Is there something about this job you're not telling me?"

"What I'm telling you is that you should walk. You're clear right now. Me? I'm a point down, I got no choice but to pull my goalie from the net, go for a last-minute score. I gotta finance my walkaway. This is the only way I know how."

The crowd surged around them again, jumping up—then diving out of the way of a screaming foul ball.

"The fuck—!"

A splash of wet into Doug's lap. Coldness soaking his chest through his shirt, running down his arms.

The guy next to him righted himself, standing, his beer cup dripping empty in his hand.

"Oh, Christ!" he said, the MLB hologram-logo tag dangling off his ballcap. "*Shit,* I'm sorry about that. Let me get some napkins, let me buy you something—"

Doug got to his feet and slammed the guy in the face. The guy went over backward into the row behind them, his brand-new hat popping off his head.

Doug continued to whale on him until someone hooked up Doug's arms— Dez—practically climbing onto Doug's back to stop him. Everyone shouting, no one making sense, Doug ready to turn and start fighting Dez.

Only the sight of the kid made him stop. Eight years old, sitting in the next seat over, frozen in fear. Also wearing a new ballcap. The guy's son.

Doug shook off Dez and slid past the cowering kid into the aisle, ducking quickly down the ramp into the caves just as blue security shirts arrived on the scene. He walked out the first open gate he could find and started running when he hit the street—trying to escape the odor of piss-beer rising off him, the stink watering his eyes.

47
GETAWAY

AFTER THE GAME, THERE was a party two doors down from his, and Doug lay across his bed, hearing the music, the laughter in the hallway, the late-night splashing in the hotel pool. He busied his mind by cooking up a grand scheme to implicate the Florist in the heist, while at the same time cutting him out of the split—with the double cross forcing the four of them into permanent exile from the Town, thereby saving them all. It was a plan both vengeful and heroic, but he grew tired working out the particulars, falling asleep happy. When he woke up Saturday morning, the scheme's logic fell apart like wet tissue in his hands.

The one dream he remembered was him watching the lottery drawing on his hotel-room TV, Claire Keesey in a sparkling lottery-girl gown pulling four zeros in a row from the ball machine, matching the ticket in Doug's hand.

He paced, trying to keep himself holed up inside the room and away from trouble. All the time now he was thinking about that crappy baseball lounge in front of the hotel. Everything still so open-ended. The getaway he had set up for the job was a good one, maybe even a great one—but he still had no getaway plan for himself. No getaway from the Town.

He slipped out the rear hotel entrance at the end of the hall and did a circuit around the park's perimeter. He told himself it was just light recon, passing Boston Beer Works, Uno's, Bill's Bar, Jillian's. Anything could be endured, he thought, so long as it had a foreseeable end. What he needed now, and what he did not have, was a future worth being strong for. Suddenly it was obvious to him why he had been so reluctant to plan his getaway.

Doug heard the players being announced over the Fenway PA system as he returned to the gardens on his third or fourth pass in as many days. Her plot looked empty, and it was almost with relief that he turned away, only to catch a flicker of movement out of the corner of his eye. He looked back and there she was, standing in the middle of her garden.

He gave himself no time to think or chicken out. His chest was a beehive as he walked to her gate, trampling his better judgment on the way, his mind telling him not to do this, his heart telling him he must.

She turned when the latch clinked. A floppy straw sun hat veiled her shocked expression, her bare limbs glowing in the afternoon sun. White T-shirt and jeans shorts, a pair of pruning shears in her gloved hands. Her knees smudged with dirt.

"Just let me say this."

She took one step backward, the pruning shears falling from her grip. She looked pained, scared—this was what seeing him did to her now.

"I am hanging by a thread here," he said.

She looked at him as though he were a man she had murdered, returned from the grave.

"We can do this," he said. "We can, I know we can. We can make this work. If you want to. Do you want to?"

"Just please go."

"We met in a Laundromat. You were crying—"

"We met inside the bank you were robbing—"

"We met in a Laundromat. It's true if you believe it. *I* believe it. The rooftop, that first night? We are still those same two people."

"No, we're not."

"I took advantage of you. I admit that. And I would do it all over again, exactly the same, if it were my only chance to get close to you. Telling you I'm sorry for it now—that would be a lie."

She was shaking her head.

"You want control over your life. You said that. You want to be in charge. I want to give you control over both our destinies. Everything about us, all in your hands."

The words were tumbling out. She was listening. Doug pointed to the light towers above Fenway Park, behind her.

"Monday," he said. "Two days from now. An armored truck will enter the ballpark to pick up receipts from this weekend's games. I'm going to be there."

She stared. Frozen. Appalled.

"I don't care anymore," said Doug. "About anything, except you. After this job, I am done. I am gone."

"Why tell me this?" She made fists of her hands at her sides. "Why are you *doing* this to me?"

"Frawley probably told you, what—to report anything I say? Okay. What I just told you—you could send me away forever. If you hate me, if you want me gotten rid of, that's the easiest way."

She shook her head, hard. He couldn't tell whether that meant she wouldn't report him, or didn't want the choice, or didn't want to hear any more.

"But if you don't," he said, "then come away with me. After. That's what I came here to ask you to do."

She was too shocked to speak.

"We'll ride out the statute of limitations together. Anywhere you want to go. Your 'if only.'"

A horse's snort interrupted. Doug heard hooves clopping and saw Claire's eyes track left and widen. A mounted policeman was trotting down the path toward them.

"You decide," Doug said, backing to the gate. "My future, our future—it's all up to you."

He was outside her gate now, surging with devotion, the horse hooves clopping near.

"Doug—" she started, but he cut her off.

"I'm at the Howard Johnson down the street." He told her the room number and the name. "Either turn me in or come away with me," he said, then started back toward the ballpark, back toward the job.

48
NIGHT CRAWLERS

SATURDAY NIGHT FOUND FRAWLEY in a surv van down the block from the Magellan Armored Depot with a young agent on loan from the fraud squad named Cray. Dino had knocked off after the depot went dark at seven, the turnpike traffic overhead the slowest it had been in Frawley's week of watching, Cambridge Street giving over to the night crawlers shuttling back and forth between Allston and Cambridge, from bar to party to club. Cray, single like Frawley—family men usually caught a break on weekends—ran the radio awhile, a show called *X Night,* broadcast live and commercial-free from one of the dance factories on Landsdowne Street. A taste of what they were missing.

The crew's activity around the depot had slowed to a trickle. Magloan was there yesterday for two hours with dark sunglasses on, the bug in his car picking up snoring. Coughlin had cruised the depot exactly once, though the Pearl Street detail reported a lot of activity in and out of his house. Elden was the only constant, parking there for lunch every day—even that day when he had switched work trucks, ditching their bug.

But most troubling to Frawley was that MacRay had all but fallen off the face of the earth. He hadn't been sighted near the depot in days, and his Caprice hadn't budged from its resident space on Pearl Street in a week. Frawley had raced to Charlestown when the Pearl Street surv spotted MacRay leaving the house, carrying what looked like laundry, but MacRay vanished again before Frawley arrived.

He had expected the crew to keep their distance from each other in the run-up to the heist, but he should have been seeing a lot more prep activity in and around the target—especially with Elden's day off from work just three days away.

Krista Coughlin had hung up on Frawley twice. He worried that he had overplayed his hand with her, that she had gone to MacRay after Frawley's initial contact, maybe scared him off this mark.

Cray tapped a pencil against the dash in time with the techno music, using the passenger seat as a desk upon which to read the case file. "Explosives, huh?"

"It's a theory," said Frawley.

"Three turnpike exits. This thing was made-to-order."

Frawley nodded, then sat back against the van wall, thinking. He was quiet and still so long that Cray stopped tapping and looked over. "Ever play any hockey?" Frawley asked him.

"You kidding? I grew up in northern Minnesota, closer to Winnipeg than Minneapolis. You?"

"I ran track. Played a little basketball. Not being six-six, I used to have to fake a lot. Do you fake much in hockey?"

"Sure, all the time." Cray moved his pencil over the file like a hockey stick. "You're on a breakaway, say. You and the goalie, one-on-one. You're charging in hard, he centers himself, stick down, elbows out. You draw back on a slap shot, bring the blade hard on a fake. The goalie commits. You've frozen him. You flip a little wrist shot past his skate—and the hometown crowd goes wild."

Frawley nodded, buzzing. After a moment he pushed open the back doors of the van and stood out on the dirt shoulder of the road. He looked at the double-fenced Magellan Armored Depot, and then to the turnpike overhead, the cars shooting into the city, thinking, *And the hometown crowd goes wild.*

49
THE SUICIDE ROOM

THIRTY-FOUR THOUSAND SEATS. Times three sold-out games.

Equals one hundred thousand mouths.

Saturday and Sunday matinees, loads of kids in attendance: multiple Cokes, beers, ice cream; on top of programs, T-shirts, caps, souvenirs.

Round it off. Say $25 average per mouth. Times one hundred thousand. $2.5 million.

Adjust up for day-of-game cash ticket sales, down for coins—call it even.

Subtract Fergie's greedy 40 percent, then divide by four.

Seven minutes of work = approximately $400K.

AROUND NOON WAS THE only time he left the room on Sunday. Walking the perimeter of the park before the game was the bare minimum of what he needed to do in terms of prep, and he kept his eyes off the taverns, cutting it short at the end to hustle back to 224, convinced that Claire would be there waiting for him. At the very least, there would be a message from her flashing on his phone.

Nothing. He went through the whole lifting-the-receiver thing, making sure the telephone was working, then walked to the front desk to double-check that no messages had been left, then raced back to the room hoping the phone hadn't rung in the meantime.

Around about the third inning he started to pretend he wasn't nervous. He opened the only hinged pane on his window and listened to the crowd noise across Van Ness, the game playing on his TV with the sound down. He paced. At one point he saw a female beat cop out on the sidewalk, and Doug pulled the shades, watching out of the window edge as the cop passed under the red light over the closed ambulance door. She turned the corner and never came back, and Doug told himself that it was exactly what it had looked like: a cop walking a beat. Not a uniform scouting out his room.

Claire would never dime him out to the G. He had offered her the chance to put him away only because he knew she couldn't do it.

It was the room that doubted her. The squalid little suicide room telling him that opening himself wide to Claire had been a mistake. Doug telling the room, *Fuck you*.

Again and again he reviewed their encounter in her garden. If only she had told him to stop. *Stop, for me*. And he would have. He would have called off this job and walked away without a regret. He had come too far to risk their future together on one final score. Claire Keesey was his one final score. All she had to do was come to him now.

He clung tight to this ideal of her, but as the hours passed, his faith began to pale.

A burst of noise and movement outside his window brought him back to the sash, crouching. But it was only the game letting out. He stood like the fool that he was and walked the room, pacing back and forth past the telephone, the afternoon growing short.

AROUND SIX, DOUG TRIED on the uniform in front of the bathroom door mirror. With his size and haircut, he made a good cop. Too good—the mirror cop looking at him like this was a big mistake Doug was making.

Doug took the uniform off and walked the room in his underwear. Had Claire forgotten the name on the register? Somehow confused hotels?

The impulse to call her was strong and wrong. Not even from a phone booth; they had her tapped for sure.

He checked the view hole in his door for the umpteenth time, imagining Frawley and a SWAT team of federal agents setting up around the hotel, evacuating it room by room.

He thought food might make him feel better, but by the time the Domino's guy arrived after eight, Doug was crackling with paranoia, studying the guy for cop traits, paying him quick and getting him out of there. He set the pizza box on top of the TV and never even raised the lid.

TEN O'CLOCK, HE WAS under a burning-hot shower trying to chase the crawlies away when he thought he heard knocking. He shut off the water and stood there listening to his dripping for a few, precious seconds, then grabbed a towel and walked damp to the door, opening it to the hallway.

A woman stood in the middle of the corridor three doors down, turning fast to the sound of the opening door. It was Krista, not Claire, with Shyne a dead weight on her hip.

Doug was too empty to say anything. He didn't move from the doorway, Krista coming before him, looking past his shoulder into the room, Shyne blinking slow-eyed against her chest. "Have any juice or milk or anything?" She held up Shyne's empty bottle. "I'm out."

He backed away, moving into the bathroom to pull on pants. When he came out, Shyne was sitting straight-legged on the floor, sucking on a big, pink-handled face plug and hugging her bubba full of green Mountain Dew, staring at whatever was on HBO. Krista stood at the foot of the bed, looking at the cop uniform hanging on the door.

"Dez told me you were staying here."

"What do you want, Kris?"

"To see you before you go."

Doug raised his bare arms and let them fall again. "Seen."

"To give you one last chance."

"Kris," he said. He saw it all unfolding: Claire arriving late at his room, bags packed, only to find Krista and Shyne there.

She sat down on the end of the bed. "Do you know my prick brother wouldn't even let me use his car?"

"You can't stay. We're grouping up here in a couple of hours."

"Like I'm his slave. Him and his bullshit, I've *had* it."

"We're not using the cars, you know that. How'd you get here?"

She shrugged. "I had no other choice."

Doug moved to the window, seeing his Caprice parked at a slant in the lot below. Now the G would have his car at Fenway the night before the job. "You stole my car."

"The registration says I borrowed *my* car."

He looked back at her. "Where is this coming from?"

"I'm ready to go away too. I've decided. I need the change, like you. Away from the Town, I think I can be a different person. Away from *him*." She glanced at the mayhem on TV, people running out of a burning building. "You know he's pissed at you leaving. Thinks you're hiding from him here. I said you're hiding from me." She looked back at Doug. "Which one of us are you hiding from?"

"I'm not hiding."

"He smoked tonight. He's dusted. Thought you'd want to know that."

Doug rocked on his feet, squeezing his fists.

"You know what's going to happen to him after you leave. Without you here, he's going to fuck up, and they're gonna come after his half of the house, and then where am I?"

"They can't take the house."

"Like hell they can't. Where's my security? Why am I still asking guys for rides, and washing Jem's frigging underwear?"

"That's between you and—"

"It's not because of him that I've waited. That I've been so fucking patient all these years. I took Jem's shit only because I always believed my time was coming. My time with you. My whole *life* I've lived in terms of you, Duggy. What—have I not been *loyal*?"

"What does loyalty got to do with—"

"It has to do with *fairness*. It has to do with me being treated the way I *deserve*. I have been here since the beginning—before Dez, and *waaay* before Joanie. I've been loyal and I've been patient. But I will not be left behind. I *deserve* not to be left behind."

"Kris—" he said, but had nothing to follow it up with, having no idea where all this was coming from. "Fuck is going on here? You want to go? Then go, same as me. There is no chain on any of us, holding us to the Town. Just the same, there's no chain holding us to each other, either."

"You're wrong there." Her smile was out of place. "You're wrong."

"You gotta give this up. Every day of your life, living in that same house, walking those same streets, looking up and always seeing the same patch of sky—this is the result. Hanging on too tight, thinking that things can stay the same forever."

"Just because we've been having some trouble, and you've been going through this thing—"

"It's not a *thing*," Doug said, needing to end this. "I am leaving. Leaving with someone else."

He felt like shit saying it because he wanted so hard to believe it himself. Not because it hurt Krista. Krista had come there to be hurt. To make him hurt her, then use his pity to make him stay. That was why she came toting Shyne.

"Kris," said Doug, glancing again at the mute phone. "We grew up together, you and me. Like brother and sister—"

"Don't fucking sugar me off."

"—and it should have stayed that way. I wish it had. We were too close. It wasn't right."

She stood and came to him. She reached out to his bare stomach, and his gut rippled, but he was backed up against the window. Her hands crept around his sides and she leaned into him, holding him. There was no way out of this clinch without getting rough. He let her hold him but did not return the embrace. He felt nothing for her. He watched Shyne flashing blue-green in the light of the TV, her body casting a small, flickering shadow. Then he looked at the door that Claire was going to knock on, knowing that Krista would ruin him if she had the chance.

She released him, her earlier smugness returned to her face. "You can't wait for me to leave, can you?"

"You picked up on that."

"Why isn't she here now? If she's going with you." Krista looked at the room. "And such a trashy little fuck pad. After a Tiffany necklace, I'd've thought a room at the Ritz or something."

"What did you say?" Doug went to her, fast. "Who told you about that?"

She was smiling now, having drawn him to her. "A little bird."

Doug grabbed her arms. "Who told you?"

She smiled more fiercely in his grip. He shook her but he couldn't shake away the smile. "You always did like it rough."

"What do you know about a necklace?"

"I know I don't see one around my neck. I know you'd rather see a rope there than jewels."

"You don't know what you're talking about," he said, pushing her away to keep from smacking her.

"You better be more careful. Pushing around a pregnant woman like that."

Doug froze. She looked down at her flat belly, regarding it as though it were some new part of her body, laying a proud hand over it the way pregnant women do.

"It's Dez's," she said.

Doug's hands came up to his forehead. He mashed his eyes with the heels.

"Ah," she said. "So broken up for a friend. Most people offer congratulations."

Doug raised his face to the ceiling, eyes still covered, elbows pointing at the corners of the room. He pressed until he saw stars. *Dez.*

"You think the Monsignor will do the right thing?"

"Make an honest woman of you?" Doug said. Then he dropped his hands, his vision clearing around her defiant face. "You Coughlins."

Her eyes were fierce, teasing. "I don't think his mother likes me."

"What do you want? What is this? If I agree to stay, you'll set Dez free?"

She stepped before him, her hands resting against his pecs, fingertips light as flies. "Take me with you. I'll get an abortion—I'll go to hell for you, Duggy." Her palm settled over his heart. "But do not leave me behind."

Doug stared at her with the disgust he normally reserved for his morning mirror. "Probably we deserve each other," he said, pulling her hands off his chest and throwing them back at her. "But I'm not doing this anymore. No more fixing things, me smoothing it over for everybody. Babysitting Jem. I told Dez to stay away, I *warned* him."

He moved past Krista, scooping up Shyne and her bubba, the girl's eyes still glued to the set as he carried her away.

"The fucking problem here," he went on, "is me. I'm the enabler. I'm the guy helping everything hold together, when it's all screaming to break apart." He marched to the door with Shyne under his arm, opened it, turned. "Everybody will be better off once I'm gone."

Krista followed him only as far as the corner of the bed. "Duggy. Do not do this."

"Or what? You'll have the kid? Just like you had this one?" Sad Shyne sagged under his arm, hanging from his side. "Who's her father, Krista? Huh? Since we're letting in a little truth here. Who was it? Was it Jem?"

She recoiled in disgust. *"Jem?"*

"Who, then?"

Her "Fuck you, Duggy" seemed heartfelt, but he couldn't trust anything she said now. And anyway the point was moot.

"You know what?" he said. "If I was going to take anyone with me, it would be her." Doug set Shyne gently down on the floor of the empty hall, then stepped back into the room.

Krista was not budging. "We're coming with you."

"You're getting out of here. Now."

"Duggy. Don't you say no to me. You *think* about this, Douglas MacRay. I want you to *think* about what you're doing—"

He grabbed her arm. She fought him—*"No!"*—pounding his chest, pushing up at his chin, digging her nails into his windpipe, while inexorably he maneuvered her toward the door. With a final kicking yell, she shook herself free, then walking the few remaining steps into the hallway, as though she had some last shred of pride to preserve.

Outside, she turned, alternately cool and smiling furiously. "You don't know what you just—"

Doug closed the door, threw the lock. He expected banging, screaming, and knew that she could outlast him, this woman without shame, and that he would be forced to readmit her before guests complained and police were called.

But there was nothing. When he looked through the spyglass later, fully expecting to see her still standing there with Shyne, she was gone.

50
THE DIME

FRAWLEY'S TELEPHONE RANG AS he was sprinkling shredded cheese over his scrambled eggs. Ocean-driven rain whipped his window overlooking the toll bridge. His microwave clock read 7:45.

A Sergeant Somebody, calling from the emergency room at Mass General. "Yeah, Agent Frawley? Hey, we got a DWI here, banged up in a one-car in the Charlestown Navy Yard? Kissed a big anchor on display in front of one of the dry docks."

Frawley's first thought was Claire Keesey. "I need a name."

"Coughlin, Kristina. Got that off the auto reg. A white Caprice Classic. Had a kid with her. Little girl's fine, but the mother is banged up and belligerent. Claims she's working with you, which seems specious, but she did have your card, this phone number written on the back. DSS came already and took away the little girl. Ms. Coughlin is under arrest, but she says we need to get you involved first."

Frawley dumped his hot eggs into the garbage. "I'm leaving now."

The walk to his car, the rain, the rush hour cost him thirty minutes. He walked the halls of Mass General in wet shoes, his creds getting him thumbed inside the ER to a wide room like a voting hall under morgue light, rimmed with curtained bays.

"Hi," he said, stopping at the nurses' station, "I'm looking for . . ."

Then he heard her voice cutting across the room—"How 'bout you put on that assless smock first, Denzel, then I will"—and started in that direction. A good-looking, flustered black doctor shrugged aside a pale yellow curtain.

"Coughlin?" said Frawley, heading past him.

But the harried doctor slowed him up. "Listen. She needs to be seen by our plastic surgeon. If you have any influence over her, please stress that. Laceration's too deep for simple stitching, she'll be scarred for life."

"Yeah—okay." Frawley tried to get past, but the doctor had a hand on his arm now.

"She claims she was pregnant," he said. "But the blood test was negative, and no signs of miscarriage."

Frawley took his arm back. "Hey, I'm not family or anything, I don't need to know." He walked to her bay, pushed the curtain aside.

Krista was sitting in the padded visitor's chair, a gauze wrap around her forehead with a bright red bloom over her left eye, blood spatter on her sweatshirt and her jeans. "Here's handsome," she said.

Frawley nodded to Sergeant Somebody, the older cop rolling his eyes at her and moving to the break in the curtain. "Five minutes," Frawley told him.

Krista called after him, "I take mine milk, three sugars!" She smiled over tightly folded arms as Frawley closed the curtain. His card rested on the bed, on top of the folded johnny she had refused to wear. She flicked her fingernails and bobbed her crossed foot—a black shoe with a broken heel—restlessly. "I was on my way to see you."

"That's interesting," said Frawley. "Considering you don't have my address."

"You're in the yard." She shrugged. "I would of found you."

One look at her eyes told Frawley she was good and dusted. Recognizing this slowed him down a bit. "What happened?"

"I don't know. Guess someone left an anchor in the middle of the road." She shrugged the grin of someone for whom life was such a daily absurdity in and of itself that a car accident made for a welcome start to the week. In that grin Frawley discerned the bullying contempt of her brother.

He saw the empty car seat in the corner—blue plaid fabric crumb-dusted and milk-stained—its vacancy like a mouth opened to scream.

Krista saw him looking, sucked in her smile, swallowed it down. "She wasn't hurt," she said proudly. "Not a scratch."

"Then you could be looking at Mother of the Year here," he said, unable to help himself.

"What do you know, what I go through? Look at you." She broke the knot of her arms. "People make mistakes sometimes—and who are you, Mr. Tsk-Tsk college boy? The mistake catcher? A fucking hall monitor with a badge, what do you know about someone like me? I am a *real* person. I am a *single mother*."

"Your daughter is in the backseat of a state van, being driven by a stranger to the Department of Social Services. How long do you want to talk here?"

Krista stared, eyes dampening. Frawley was being hard, but it was working.

"What were you coming to see me about? You needed a babysitter? I tried to call you twice, you hung up both times."

She glowered at the waxy curtain, keeping her dusted emotions in check. "DSS only holds her for a while. There's an evaluation. Nothing happens until the evaluation."

"So maybe you want a lawyer here, then. Not the FBI."

She looked at him again, nearly amazed. "Why is it I'm always the one who gets used? Every man I know."

"Who's using you here? Who called who? Who's asking for help—me? I'm pretty sure I'm here because you want your daughter back. Because you can use me to get her."

"Real people make *real* mistakes—"

He talked over her. "This is not about you anymore, this is about your daughter. *Look* at this empty car seat."

She did, her eyes blinking wet.

Frawley went on, "You're going to need some sort of plea agreement on these charges now, in order to retain custody."

She looked up fast. "And my house. I want your guarantee."

"Whoa, hold up. I never said I could guarantee. I said I could *try*."

"You said—"

"I said I could *try*. And that is what I will do, Krista, that is my promise, provided you're straight with me here. And if that isn't good enough, maybe you want to wait for a better offer. How many more Get Out of Jail Free cards you got on you? Could your brother get you out of this jam? MacRay? Who? Fergie?"

Her eyes sparked to that.

"What, Fergie's your benefactor, is he? Why should a degenerate dust dealer help you out with your daughter?"

Nothing in her low-eyed look was telling—except the duration.

Frawley's stomach curdled. "Oh, Jesus."

She kept looking at him: defiantly, then starting to fall apart.

"You and the Florist . . ." Frawley had to stop himself from saying more. He was picturing the gangster's mashed face in a spasm of feral ecstasy, looming over her.

Krista's chin trembled. A hard woman crumbling was an awful thing to see. "Why you have to lean on me so hard? Why make me *beg* for everything I get? Treating me like I'm nothing, I don't matter. All you men."

Frawley summoned the memory of MacRay coming after him in the parking garage in order to sustain his anger, counterbalancing his sympathy for Coughlin's sister here. "You called me. That means you have something to trade."

She looked down, taking deep, shuddering breaths. "Duggy's going away with her after."

"Her?" Frawley stepped up. "What do you mean, with *her*?"

Krista looked up. She read the desire in his eyes, the anger, and said, "You too?"

He lost it. "What do you mean, *with her*?"

Krista was aghast. "What is she anyway? What does she have—Jesus Christ—to make all of you so fucking crazy over her?"

Frawley remembered himself, stepped back. "You said *after*. Going away with her *after*. *After* what?"

Krista turned to look at the clock—and Frawley's blood came crashing.

"Today?" he said, pouncing on her look. "Not Tuesday—today? Where? When?"

Her jaw quivered like mortar cracking off a facade. "My daughter. . . ."

"You need to be smart now, Krista. A life full of bad decisions, this is the one that could do you good, help turn things around. But their clock is your clock too."

"My daughter," Krista said, finally breaking. "She's retarded."

Frawley's breath was gone. He stood very still.

Krista spilled tears, her face collapsing in despair and defeat. "She's going to need things . . . special things . . . special schools . . ."

"Right," he gasped out. "Uh-huh."

She looked up, her face tired and tear-streaked. "For her I'm doing this. Not me."

"No," said Frawley, stealing another glance at the clock. 8:25. "Of course not."

"It's not for me . . . not for me . . ."

51
THE MOURNING OF

THE FOUR OF THEM standing around the hotel room, all in cop uniforms, guns and folded black duffel bags on the bed.

Rain fell hard outside the shaded window. A punishing rain was almost as good for a job as snow. It darkened the day, obscured loud noises, kept bystanders off the streets, and gummed up the city in general. Gloansy had picked up four bright safety-orange raincoats at the army/navy store the day before. The coats covered up the armored vests that bulked out their cop uniforms.

"Rain's good," Jem was muttering, walking back and forth from the drawn window curtains. "Rain's good. Rain's good. Rain's good."

Doug looked at the phone. He was barely there, the crashing of the rain outside like the shit coming down all around his head. He answered when spoken to and moved when it was required of him, but everything felt distant and rehearsed, occurring outside himself while he watched. The four of them going through their pregame rituals. He was having trouble placing himself in time, figuring out what led to what and how he had arrived at this hotel room at the end of the world, dressed like a Boston cop.

Dez cursed the bathroom mirror, having trouble with the hard contact lenses he wore on jobs. His face looked undressed without glasses, his nearsighted eyes small and lost in his face. *What's up?* Dez had said at the door, the last to arrive. *Nothing,* said Doug, until then hoping that Dez might stay away.

Gloansy gobbled down two pancaked slices of cold Domino's, while Jem's pacing and muttering and knuckle-cracking bordered on the lunatic. Where was the prejob ragging and the goofing that used to drive Doug nuts? Gone was all that crazy joy.

Would the G even let them leave the hotel? Or wait until they were going into the ballpark and nail them there, all packed up and loaded, a headline bust? Or would agents be waiting inside, wearing can guards' uniforms—a reverse Morning Glory?

Worse than the doomed feeling of the trap was knowing that he was the

only one aware of it. Asshole that he was. Falling for this creature of his imagi-
nation, this all-forgiving, all-healing girl—this magic, winning ticket. Trusting
her. Needing her. What was it about him that wanted a wounded girl to vanish
into? If the phone rang now, it would only be the G calling from the lobby,
telling them the place was surrounded and ordering them out, hands behind
their heads, one at a time.

It was not too late. He could tell the others what he'd done. They could all
change back into street clothes and ditch the uniforms and guns and walk away
clean—three of them heading back into Town, and Doug in a different direction. He had some money, he'd be all right. For a while.

But part of him still held out hope. Arguing that if there was going to be a
takedown, it would have happened already, there at the hotel. The G didn't
want them out on the streets, armed and unpredictable. Maybe Claire hadn't
told them anything. Every second that ticked toward Go time, Doug's hope
grew.

He went around wiping down the dresser and table with rubbing alcohol,
removing his prints from the room. Krazy Glue on his hands, krazy thoughts in
his mind. Glugging bleach in the bathroom sink and shower, blitzing the
drains, obliterating his DNA. Erasing every trace of his existence. The bundle
of cash he had buried shallow in the garden of a girl who hated him, and the
clothes piled up in Mac's old army bag by the door: they were all he had in the
world now. And these three guys.

Gloansy and Dez went around rapping fists, pulling on orange coats and
slipping out one at a time, down the hallway stairs to the rear door. Doug
watched from the window, the slapping rain providing decent cover for two
bright orange cops ducking out of a hotel and into a stolen car. They were leaving early to snarl the morning city commute before returning to the ballpark.
Doug watched them roll around the corner out of sight and envisioned them
being pulled over just outside the parking lot, boxed in at gunpoint by a road-
block shutting down Boylston Street. He closed the curtains as though tear-gas
canisters were about to come crashing through the window, smoke filling the
room.

Jem stood there with his 9mm drawn on Doug. Doug froze, losing it a
moment in Jem's sight, Jem holding the pose, grinning—then returning the
gun to his holster and snapping the leather catch. "You want the Tec-9?"

"Don't care," Doug said, dizzy. "Just put a gun in my hand."

Jem tossed him a loaded Beretta, Doug basket-catching it. Jem admired the
Tec in his hand, an oversized pistol with a clip feed in front of the trigger.
"Yeah," he said, then put it down on the bed and fit his thumbs into the front of
his gun belt, strutting around the room. "All those years watching *Cops* finally

paying off." He smiled, enjoying himself, grinding his jaw the way dust makes you do. "I'd've made a good cop. A *rich* cop." He stopped and tried his delivery—"License and registration, ma'am"—impressing himself, continuing his cop strut around the room. "Fucking ticket to *ride,* man. How you ever gonna walk away from this?"

Doug couldn't see any way to go forward or backward. To walk or to stay. He looked at the gun in his hand. *I'm not that guy anymore.* But here he was.

"By the way," said Jem. "I put you in after all."

Doug shook his head. "Put me in what?"

"The third floor. Shyne's dollhouse. I took the chance. Maybe you'll change your mind. You walked away once before and found your way back again."

FRAWLEY WAS STALLED IN traffic downtown, grappling with his car phone, wipers slashing rain. He couldn't get any numbers for Fenway Park from information. Nobody from the Task Force was in the Lakeville office yet, so the field office was calling New York for Provident Armored's headquarters number. He did manage to catch Dino at home and stop him from heading out to Lakeville. Now Dino was calling him back.

"My captain took it straight to the commissioner. You're *sure* now."

Frawley leaned on his horn. "I got it from the sister."

"Coughlin's sister?"

"They're going in strong. Some bullshit about a 'last job,' MacRay leaving after. That's all I know."

"Any clue how security works at Fenway?"

"None, but Dean—you gotta keep patrol cops away."

"There'll be nothing on the radio."

"And no helicopters to scare them off."

"Easy now, Frawl. We got Entry and Apprehension Team suiting up as we speak. That's our SWAT. They're on a scrambled freq. Do we know where these tea-pissers are jumping from?"

"We know nothing but the time." Frawley looked at his radio clock. "And it's fucking eight forty-five now! What's with this traffic?"

"That's another thing. It's the rain, but also my cap says they got two separate major jams, one westbound on Storrow, one in Kenmore Square."

"Kenmore Square?" said Frawley, punching the thin ceiling of the Tempo. "That's our guys!"

"A semi stalled across the intersection. The one on Storrow is an oversized rental van jammed under one of those height-restricted bridges. Both vehicles were abandoned, left locked up and running."

"Fucking—it's them, Dean!"

Frawley hung up and threw his phone, unable to bear the thought of missing these guys. Of not being there to hook up MacRay.

Screw the field office. Frawley bumped over a curb, gouging the Tempo's undercarriage on the street corner, swinging up one of the side streets climbing Beacon Hill, heading directly to Fenway.

DOUG SAT NEXT TO Jem in the backseat of the big Thunderbird, parked at the corner of Yawkey and Van Ness. Gloansy sat behind the popped ignition in front, Dez next to him. The windows were all cracked open in the drumming rain to keep their view from fogging. Doug saw the G everywhere, on the spilling rooftops, in surrounding windows, in every car that passed.

The can was three minutes overdue; the news radio station was in hysterics over the traffic tie-ups. Jem thumped his black shoes into the floor, marching in place as he sat, the sound like a pounding heart.

"I don't know," said Doug, going secretly crazy. "I don't know about this."

"Can's stuck in traffic with the rest of them," said Gloansy.

"I don't know."

Dez turned his head. "What do you mean?"

Doug was trying to give them at least a chance. "Doesn't feel right."

Jem said, "Everything's cool. We're gonna do this."

"I think something's up."

"Check this out." Jem unbuckled the clips on the front of his raincoat. In addition to the Glock in his holster and the semiauto Tec-9 strapped off his shoulder, he wore four fat pinecone grenades, World War style, affixed to his cop belt with black electrical tape. "From my gramps," Jem said. "Guy was a fuckin' war hero." He flicked at the little metal pins, still in place.

Dez said, "Those live?"

Gloansy said, "For Christ. You're gonna blow us up in here."

"Insurance, ant-dicks. You think they'd let anything happen to historic Fenway? These are our tickets out. One for each."

Dez glanced over the seatback at Doug, Doug fed up with his altar-boy disapproval.

Jem clipped up his coat again, white-blue eyes brimming with dusted confidence. "We're gonna do this. We're gonna do this."

Lightning brightened the street, Doug thinking it was a flash-bang charge, the G swooping down on them. He waited for thunder. There was none.

He couldn't sit still another moment. He opened his door and stood out of the T-bird, shutting the door before any of them could say anything, starting away through the rain.

He turned onto Boylston, the chime ringing as he pushed inside the package store. Bewildering, the lights, the colorful promotions—it had been a long time. He cut down a long aisle of wines to the back cooler. Two sixes of High Life longnecks waited for him on the rack. He grabbed both and brought them to the counter.

There was a cop waiting there: Dez, dripping on the floor. "What are you doing?"

Doug had no money in his uniform pockets. "Give me some money."

Dez said, "Put it down. Come on. Let's go—"

"Shut the fuck up." Doug turned to the cashier. "Put these on the police account." Without waiting for an acknowledgment, he walked out past Dez.

Dez caught up with him on the rainy sidewalk. "Duggy! What's happening to you? You don't need this—"

Doug shoved Dez back with an elbow. "I fucking told you not to come."

Doug returned to the car first, his wet coat crinkling as he sat. "The fuck was that?" said Jem, before seeing the twin caddies of tall boys.

Doug said, "Thought you wanted to be there for my first one back."

Jem's smile grew wide and fierce, all-encompassing. "Duggy Mac is *back*."

Doug passed one of the sixes over the seat to Gloansy as Dez returned, settling in, not removing his orange hood. Doug reached for his Leatherman, finding it missing. A twinge of panic as he pictured it sitting forgotten on his bureau—a tool he had carried with him on every job.

No matter. The trick, when you don't have an opener, is to use one beer for leverage, inverting it and hooking the cap of the beer to be popped, then twisting and pulling back the top one like snapping a stick in two. Doug cracked one for Jem and one for himself.

Genie mist escaped out of its small mouth. Doug's chest was pounding.

Jem waited for Gloansy to crack two, then said reverently, "To the Town."

Jem rapped fists with Doug, neither one spilling a drop. Doug said, "Here's how."

He brought the bottle to his lips, the beer splashing hard to the back of his throat, tasteless at first, swallowed like seawater. Then came the tang, the bite. His throat worked the brew along until the bottle was empty and weightless, the taste settling into his tongue like surf foam sinking into sand.

The first belch was an echo from a dark abyss. He popped open another and caught sight of Dez, slow to drink his first, disappointment and disapproval evident in the sag of his shoulders. Doug drank harder.

The other part of Doug was coming out now. The old Doug MacRay, the one resigned to his fate. The Jem in him who was damned and knew it. *Never prison again.* His only goal now.

No tomorrow: that was what Billy T. had been all about. No consequences, nobody to disappoint, not Dez, not Frank G., not even Doug himself. Nothing could touch him now.

Jem cracked open his third, ahead of Doug, meaning Doug was without another bottle to open his. He was working on the cap with his Krazy Glue fingers when Jem let out a war whoop.

The red light was on over the ambulance door on Van Ness.

The silver Provident truck turned off Ipswich, starting down the road, slowing at the rising door. It swung around, stopped, and began to back inside.

The black Suburban pulled up at the curb outside Fenway as the bay door closed.

Jem dropped his empty on the floor, kicking open his door to the street and the rain.

Doug stood out on the sidewalk, the downpour cracking loud against his hood. Dez got out in front of Doug, standing there, not looking at him, waiting for Gloansy. Those two started up Van Ness toward the Suburban as Doug crossed the street through blowing wet sheets, side by side with Jem, walking toward the Gate D entrance and looking for the G in every raindrop, thinking, *ambush, ambush, ambush*.

52
THE LAST JOB

JEM PULLED HARD A few times on the chained gate.

The red shirt sitting dry and comfortable on the folding chair inside looked up from his newspaper, then dropped it at the sight of the cops, hustling to the entrance.

Jem said, "Was it you who called?"

He was a young guy, cinnamon-skinned, puffy, maybe Samoan but not huge. "Huh?"

"Nine one one call, we got. Open up."

"I didn't . . . it wasn't . . ."

"Robbery call. Who else is here?"

"Robbery?" He looked around, panicked.

"There's no one else here?"

"Sure there is, but—"

"Call says you're being held up. Right now."

"Then I need to phone security."

"Phone whoever you want, but we gotta get in there first, do our jobs. Then make your call."

He nodded and unlocked the chain, admitting Doug and Jem.

Doug stiffened up to hide his jumpiness. "Go ahead, lock it back up if you have to."

As the red shirt did, Doug and Jem both unclasped the bottoms of their coats, baring their holsters. With the rain and the lack of lights, it was darker than a night game in there.

"Where's everyone else?" said Jem, starting down the ramp.

"Some around the corner there. Let me—"

"And what is your name, sir?"

"My name's Eric."

"Eric, point me in the right direction here. Let's make sure everyone's safe, then we can all sit down and make our phone calls."

Eric nodded obediently and showed them the way, moving down the slope toward the corner. Doug glimpsed the open Employees Only door, and then, wider, the tunnel.

The motorized flatbed pushcart was on its way toward the first aid station at the tunnel's end, loaded with thick bundles of plastic-wrapped cash. One gray-and-black Provident guard operated the cart's handle controls, the other backing him up with one hand on his holster. Doug double-checked their ears, seeing no wires.

Jem started after them, his voice booming inside the tunnel. "Who called 911?"

The guards stopped, turning fast, spooked.

"Who called it?" said Jem, hand at his waist, coattails flapping. Doug pushed Eric down to the floor, telling him to stay still, lie flat.

The guards looked at each other, hands on their holsters.

The anxiety in Doug's voice worked as he said, following Jem, "We got a distress call. Who made the call?"

The guards stayed between Jem and Doug and the money cart. "No call from us."

"Who called it?" said Jem, pressing closer.

"Hold on," said one guard, raising his off-hand.

"ID!" said Jem, not stopping. "Let's see some ID! Both of you!"

"Hold on, hold it, now," said the guard, half into a protective crouch.

"Whoa, *whoa!*" said Jem.

"Don't do that!" shouted Doug.

"We didn't hit it!" said one guard.

"We're on the job here!" said the other.

Two Fenway Park security blue shirts appeared at the mouth of the tunnel behind them. "What the . . . ?"

"Get down back there!" commanded Doug.

They put their arms out like this was all a big misunderstanding. "It's okay!" they yelled. "They're okay!"

Doug drew his Beretta, keeping it low at his hip, muzzle down. "Everybody on the ground, now!"

"For our safety!" said Jem, also drawing. "I want IDs from everybody!"

Twenty yards away, Doug just kept asserting himself. "Get down!"

"Wait, hey!" said the guards.

"On the floor!" yelled Jem.

The blue shirts lay facedown.

The panicky guard pulled his sidearm clear of his holster. Doug swung up his Beretta, aiming, bracing it on his opposite forearm. *"Gun!"* he yelled. *"Gun!"*

"Drop your weapon!" bellowed Jem, aiming his Glock. "Put it down *now!*"

"No, no!" said the other guard, covering his head, backing away.

Jem and Doug came at them gun-first, with legit tension: "Drop your weapon! We got a call! Put it down!"

Guard yelling, *"We did not call!"*

Doug stopped ten yards away. The four of them barking back and forth over drawn guns until the retreating guard dropped to his knee, took his hand off his holster, and laid on his belly, arms out.

"Stop resisting!" they yelled at the other one. *"Get down! Get down!"*

Cursing, the panicky second guard yielded, lying down arms-out, still holding on to his gun.

Doug and Jem came up fast, Jem stepping on the armed guard's wrist, covering both guards, Doug going to the blue shirts beyond the cash cart, gathering hands and binding them with plastic ties. The can idled just around the corner from the mouth of the tunnel, backed in—the driver unable to see or hear anything.

Doug ripped off the blue shirts' security radios and tossed them away. "Lie still," he told them, rejoining Jem, pocketing the other guard's gun and yanking his stiff hands behind his back. "Jesus *Christ*," spat Doug's guard, red-faced, gruff. "The fuck're you two doing? We're on the goddamn job here!"

"We got a call," said Doug, binding the guard's wrists. Doug then pulled up the black bandanna knotted around his neck, covering his mouth and nose and leaving only his eyes visible. Jem did the same as Doug turned and started back for Eric.

The puffy guy was already sitting up. Incomprehension, at first—masked cop with gun raised, coming at him—then Eric got to his feet and, with one hand on the tunnel wall, began to run for his life.

Doug yelled at him to stop as the round whizzed past. The crack of the gunshot echoed in the tunnel, and Eric turned, still galloping, his cinnamon hands reaching for the hip of his jeans as though trying to catch the bullet that had just entered his side. He ran like that a few more feet before collapsing—the shock of having been shot bringing him down, not the round itself.

Doug turned, seeing Jem with his 9mm still aimed, his knee and his opposite hand on the backs of the two squirming guards.

Doug rushed to Eric, who was gripping his wide hip in horror. But all four limbs were moving, and he had plenty of padding to absorb the round. Doug hoped the rain would do the same to the gunshot report.

He wrestled one of Eric's wrists away from the tiny wound, then the other, binding them behind his back. "There'll be help here soon," said Doug, leaning on his shoulder for emphasis. "Stay down and shut up."

He ran back to where Jem was, wasting a glare at him, then yanking his guard to his feet. The guard twisted and fought, Doug finally bouncing the guy off the wall, stunning him before muscling him around the corner.

Doug got the full view of the silver can there, the Provident medallion bold beneath the rear windows. He dumped the guard down against the brick wall and walked up to the passenger side of the cab to get the driver's attention.

He hadn't expected a woman. She was frizzy-haired and long-faced, throwing Doug off his game for a second.

She went white, jerking back and fumbling with the keys in the ignition, starting up the truck, diesel smoke coughing into the cave. Doug heard the locks automatically reset and watched the yellow rooftop beacon start spinning, the can going into lockdown. With the bay door closed in front of it and the iron girders behind it, there was nowhere for the truck to go.

Jem dragged the blue shirts over to the dazed guards, dumping them along the side wall. The driver peeked out the passenger window, now talking fast into the handset of a ceiling-mounted radio. "Assholes fucked up," snarled one guard. "Sandy's locked in there. She's calling the law."

Doug moved to the switch controlling the lamp outside, turning it off. He checked Jem standing over the four captives, bandanna puffing with breath, then started back past the trapped armored truck to the next bay door, pressing the call button on the cop-style two-way Motorola clipped to his shoulder. "Ready?"

"Ready," came back Dez's voice, breathless. "All clear out here."

Doug hit the switch and the second door crawled up the wall to the ceiling, rising on the crashing rain and Dez in his orange cop coat and black bandanna, holding his Beretta on the driver of the tail car: a swarthy bodybuilder type in a collared shirt and jeans, hands bound behind him, pissed off. Dez walked him inside, and then the big black Suburban followed them into the bay, backing in trunk end first. The wet tires slid to a stop on the downward incline, Gloansy jumping out wearing his bandanna, and Doug hit the switch that closed the bay door.

Gloansy took control of the tail-car driver, walking him back to the others at the Provident truck as Dez touched the radio wire looped over his ear. He blinked and squinted as he monitored all police channels plus the security net inside the park itself, muttering something about his contact lenses. "There it is," he said. "Call just went out from dispatch."

The driver had done her job, calling in a Mayday.

They jogged back to the idling can at the first aid station, where the mouthy guard was still going at it: "I put in twenty-two years as a guard at Walpole, I have friends that'll see to it you all live out the rest of your lives in rip-ass hell."

Jem pointed his gun at him and the guy shut up.

Gloansy and Dez stayed on the five hostages—the two uniformed can guards, the two Fenway security blue shirts, and the Suburban driver—while Jem and Doug worked the pushcart, Doug thumbing buttons on the electric handle to roll it past the back of the can and down to the open rear door of the Suburban. The cash was sealed in clear, tight, shrink-wrapped bundles, roughly the size of four loaves of bread packaged side by side. Jem scattered the paperwork off the top and dumped off two heavy racks of coins, the rolls bursting nickels and dimes on the floor. They pulled folded hockey duffel bags from their coat pockets, Doug spreading them open in the back of the Suburban.

Jem played baggage handler, tossing the parcels of currency at Doug as fast as Doug could pack them, six bundles to a bag. He was five or six bags in when Dez called back, "How much longer?"

Jem kept throwing. "What's up?"

"Scrambled traffic on one of the special cop freqs."

Jem stopped. Doug turned, seeing Dez in the flashing yellow light of the can beacon, his hand at his ear.

"Too soon off the initial call," Dez said. "Can't be because of us. Maybe something else going down somewhere."

Doug's heart was in his throat. He said, "I'll check it out."

"No," said Jem, already starting away. Doug watched him break open his coat on the Tec-9, stepping inside the tunnel.

Doug returned to the loaves of money, packing up the last bag, loading it as fast as he could.

FRAWLEY PULLED UP OUTSIDE the "1912 Fenway Park" facade at the original entrance to the park, Gate A, at the other end of Yawkey Way. All he had for rain gear was the blue Nautica jacket he had grabbed rushing out to the hospital that morning. He opened his trunk and threw his nylon FBI vest over his shoulders, good for identification only—bank agents don't carry body armor— and found an old orange Syracuse ballcap for his head. He grabbed what he had in there, sliding two extra 9mm mags for his shoulder-holstered SIG-Sauer into his pants pockets, emptying a box of shotgun cartridges into his zippered coat pockets, and pulling his Remington 870 twelve-gauge from its padded sleeve.

Dino's Taurus pulled up fast on the opposite sidewalk, Dino unfolding himself out of it, buttoning his trench coat to the downpour. "I looped the block," he said, concerned. "Nothing hinky. Looks tight. No vans around, nothing parked with handicapped tags."

Frawley gripped the brim of his cap, curling it one-handedly, cursing. A bad call here would ruin him, plain and simple. Good-bye, Los Angeles. Hello, Glasgow, Montana. "Maybe we're too early, maybe too late."

They turned to the blue Boston Police Department camper that had just arrived, the Entry and Apprehension Team mobile-command center parked outside a closed souvenir shop. Two pairs of black commando-types in balaclavas, Fritz helmets, and trunk armor, with the initials EAT on their backs, walked along Yawkey Way as though it were Sniper Alley in downtown Sarajevo, one team headed toward the nearby ticket office, the other away toward Gate D.

A silver Accord came by, slowing, a blond mom watching the show, her little boy in back waving. Dino said, "We gotta close off these streets."

Frawley was soaked with rain and doubt when he saw the EAT pair start sprinting from the ticket office down Yawkey toward Van Ness. Dino leaned into the open camper. "What?"

Two tactical cops were coordinating. "Voice inside, male. Says he's been shot."

Frawley saw the tac cops going in through the far gate and started running, thinking maybe he wasn't too late after all.

DOUG LEFT THE SUBURBAN'S rear door open with the cash-stuffed duffel bags, moving past the others toward the tunnel. Jem was more than halfway through it, walking slow. Doug could see Eric lying at the end, his thick legs kicking, groaning over and over again, "I'm shot, I'm shot." Doug was about to call Jem back when Jem dropped into a half-crouch.

Doug saw it too—a glint of light beyond squirming Eric. It was a small mirror on a long pole, extending across the mouth of the tunnel.

Jem opened up on it, cracking the mirror, the pole clattering to the stone floor. The echo of his fire was tremendous inside the tunnel, Doug going half-deaf, wincing, backing off and drawing his Beretta. Jem sprayed another volley at the mouth, then turned, firing mad bursts behind him as he ran back toward Doug.

The tunnel filled with fireballs. Fiercely bright but nonlethal Starflash rounds ricocheted off the walls, a disorienting salvo. Jem outran these sparkling bees toward Doug as Doug opened up, blasting cover fire at nothing but flashlight beams. He choked the trigger too tight, the Beretta coughing and jumping in his hand, the sound like firecrackers in a drum. Then Jem ducked past him and together they folded around the corner.

Jem broke off his empty magazine and reloaded, howling curses.

"What the fuck!" said Gloansy, panicked, edging away from the guards.

"We got dimed!" said Jem, leaning out, spraying the tunnel with fire, then leaning back again, the Tec smoking. "Fucking *dimed*! "Mother*fucks*!"

Three gunshots cracked from a different direction, Gloansy shrieking and twisting, hit, falling forward to the stone floor.

Doug ducked, looking around wildly, then grabbed Gloansy's ankle and dragged him to the side of the can by the rear right tire. All five hostages were squirming and yelling and covering their heads. It hadn't come from them. Gloansy had been hit from behind, and Doug peered out behind the can, back toward the Suburban. No one he could see.

Gloansy sat up swearing, reaching for his lower back. His vest had saved him, but it still hurt like hell.

Then more cracks over their heads. Jem opened up against the hull of the can, wasting rounds, the ricochets pelting the floor near Doug. Doug howled at Jem, but at least now he knew where the shots were coming from.

The can driver. From the safety of the armored interior, she was potting them through the gun ports. Doug and Gloansy were safe where they were— crouched against its hull—yet pinned down.

Doug looked under the can and saw Dez's legs on the other side. Doug yelled but couldn't get his attention, so he ripped off his radio and threw it beneath the truck, hitting Dez's shoe.

"The door!" Doug yelled to him. "Open the door!"

Dez crawled to the front of the can and jumped up to punch the red plunger button, the bay door starting to rise.

"What the fuck!" yelled Jem from where he was trapped at the near mouth of the tunnel.

But Doug was right: the driver was panicking, and as soon as she saw the door go up, she jumped into the front seat and powered forward, scraping the side of the can against the brick doorframe, lurching over the curb and out onto Van Ness.

Doug stood in the now empty bay and hit the button, shutting the door. He pulled the guard's gun from his pocket and went next to Jem, sticking his arm around the corner of the tunnel and firing, the .32 going crack-crack-crack.

"We bail!" Doug yelled over the reports. "Now!"

"No fucking way!" said Jem. "The ride is loaded and ready to go!"

"Leave it!" Doug said, over the racket of return fire. "Bail out!"

Gloansy was on his feet again, hunched over but moving. He drew on the tunnel and fired into it blindly, then tugged down his bandanna, exposing his face. "I'm driving!"

"No!" said Doug.

But Gloansy was already hobbling to the Suburban, his tunnel fire keeping Doug from giving chase. Gloansy was hurt, he was flipping out, he wanted the presumed safety of a mobile cage of glass and metal. "Meet you at the switch!" he yelled.

Dez was closer to the Suburban, wavering, torn between staying behind or taking off with Gloansy. *"Fuck!"* he said, watching Gloansy slam the trunk door shut. Then Dez hustled back to Doug.

With a rebel yell, Jem curled out into the mouth of the tunnel and filled the passageway with fire and noise.

CLOSER, OVER THE RAIN and the sound of his own slapping footsteps, Frawley heard gunfire. He saw flashes inside Gate D and heard echoed yelling.

Then someone out on the street near him cried, "Here they come!"

He ran with Dino and the others to the corner of Van Ness. A silver armored truck came scraping out of the block-long brick wall, yellow beacon twirling, surging down the street toward them through the rain. Two sergeants who should have known better rushed to the sidewalk and wasted bullets against the can's grille and windshield.

Frawley worried about the gun ports. He tried to make out the driver but the wipers weren't going, and all he could see through the rain was a blur of frizzy hair—maybe a bad disguise. Whoever it was, the driver was running scared.

Dino yelled at the rest of them to get away as the truck wheeled past doing thirty. It turned hard right and went into a heavy skid on the wet road, the driver righting the wheels and briefly regaining control, then overcorrecting, the truck veering toward the sidewalk across from the ballpark, ramming the parked police camper head-on.

The blow was tremendous, the loudest, ugliest thing Frawley had ever heard, the camper buckling and grinding on its rims, all four tires exploding, tearing up the asphalt and taking out a hydrant before stopping some forty feet away. Cops tumbled out of the open end of the wrecked camper, falling hurt to the wet pavement and trying to crawl away from the fountain the hydrant made in the rain.

Dino and the rest of the lawmen ran to the truck, the crash bringing two tac cops charging back out of Gate D to investigate. The silver truck was unhurt, the driver grinding gears, still trying to flee. Dino warned the men back from the gun ports.

Approaching sirens drew Frawley the other way, back out onto Van Ness—just as a second vehicle, a big black Suburban, jumped from the park.

It started away in the opposite direction, but the screaming patrol cars forced it to reconsider, cutting its wheels into a controlled skid that ended with the truck facing Frawley's end of the street, then starting toward him.

Frawley couldn't see the driver at that distance. All he knew was that he had someone fleeing a shooting. He stepped left onto the curb, working the pump action and aiming low for the tires—*Blam!*—missing the first shot, kicking sparks off the asphalt, pumping again and leading the truck this time—*Blam!*—striking the right front tire, pumping again—*Blam!*—bursting the rear. The tires shredded and peeled back off the rims, and there was a spray of wet sparks in the road as the driver fought the steering wheel, losing control on the turn going the other way, jumping the curb and plowing into a Thunderbird parked at the corner.

Frawley ran wide around the rear of the Suburban, assuming all four of them were inside the tinted windows. A two-man tac team advanced with MP5 submachine guns off their shoulders, and Frawley backed away, letting them do their work.

THEY HEARD THE CRUISERS wheel past after Gloansy in the Suburban. Shotgun blasts in the rain. The sickening glass punch of the crash.

"They got him," said Dez, hands on top of his head. "Oh, fucking shit, they got Gloansy."

Jem wheeled and screamed, sending more angry spray down the tunnel. *"Who the fuck dimed us?"* he bellowed. *"I'll fucking kill them!"*

Doug swallowed hard, going after the two uniformed guards and pulling them to their feet, powering them back near the tunnel.

Jem was reloading again, gripping his weapon in anguish. "Gloansy, you fucking shithead . . ."

Dez's bandanna eyes showed dull shock, his gun hanging in his hand. Doug woke him up by thrusting the guards at him and making him hold them at gunpoint.

Doug ran down the length of the cave, hitting plungers and opening the other four doors, then running back.

One empty duffel bag remained on the floor by the pushcart, and Jem was kneeling over it, stuffing it with cash, the Tec dangling from his shoulder rig.

"What are you doing?" said Doug. Jem kept on loading. "The fuck are you doing? Leave it! Come on!"

When Doug went to grab him, Jem raised up the Tec.

It was the guilty way in which Doug backed off. Jem sensed it, standing, tasting it the way a shark tastes blood, realizing, bright-eyed.

"This is you," he said. "You fucking did this. Did you fucking do this?"

Dez shouted from behind, "Fucking *come on, assholes!*"

Jem stared in white-eyed astonishment. He kept the gun on Doug as he knelt and zipped the bag shut, then pulled the bandanna down off his bewildered face. "Why, kid?"

Dez didn't know where to point his gun, at the guards or at Jem. "Tell him you didn't, Duggy!"

More sirens now, Jem's face going grim. He hefted the bag at his side, eyes and gun never leaving Doug as he backed up the incline to the open bay door, pausing there before the rain.

Doug awaited Jem's bullet.

The Tec came down and Jem tucked it into his raincoat, dead-faced, then ducked his head and started out with his black bag into the rain.

THE DRIVER OF THE Suburban, whoever he was, was at the very least unconscious. The spotter could see his shoulders rising and falling through the windshield, but his head remained down on the bloodied steering wheel. It was a potential medical emergency, but the spotter could not get a clear view of the backseat or of the cargo trunk. The status of the other three—their very presence—remained unknown.

A cordon of cops surrounded the crash site—the smaller of the two wrecks on Yawkey—one of them with a bullhorn, trying to coax out the occupants.

Frawley was down on his haunches behind a patrol car angled across the intersection, holding his shotgun across his knees. The boots next to him belonged to an ear-wired tac cop standing with his submachine gun braced atop the rain-popping roof of the car, trained on the Suburban. Frawley was coasting on adrenaline, not even feeling the rain. Fucking Special Agent Steve McQueen. *I just shot out a car's tires in the street.* He looked around for Dino. He had to tell this to someone.

More sirens coming, flashing blues arriving from everywhere. Frawley liked the cavalry's sound. But then he remembered the two cruisers that had scared off the Suburban. Those early patrol cars—who had called them?

There'll be nothing on the radio, Dino had said. *They're on a scrambled freq.*

Frawley got up and started looking for Dino for real, finding him under a borrowed umbrella at the corner fence, talking to a police captain. Frawley stepped in between them, interrupting, jacked up on hormones though barely aware of it. "Where'd the patrol cars come from?"

The captain looked at the letters *FBI* on Frawley's chest. "Well," he said under the umbrella patter, "when a daddy patrol car and a mommy patrol car love each other very, very much . . ."

Dino rested a stop hand against the captain's chest. "This is my guy, Cap. Frawley, bank squad. Good cop."

The captain looked back at Frawley, nodding a grudging apology. "We got a 911. Radio distress call from inside the armored."

Frawley turned and looked at the silver Provident truck near the camper wreck, now empty—a distress call going out inside his mind.

"Dean," he said, and Dino registered it, completed the thought.

This crew never left things like that to chance. They went *around* alarms.

"Trip it on purpose?" reasoned Dino. "But why?"

Frawley stepped back to take in the car wrecks on Yawkey, the multitude of cops in orange coats attending. He turned and looked up Van Ness, seeing more orange coats. "They wanted police here."

He noticed one cop crossing the street carrying a loose black bag—walking away from the ballpark, moving too calmly.

DOUG STOOD WATCHING JEM go. Another arriving cruiser squealed past, and then Dez was yelling at him. Doug turned to find Dez still holding his gun on the guards. Flashlights and footsteps in the tunnel.

Doug pulled his Beretta and extracted the magazine. Only two rounds left. He pocketed that clip and pulled a full mag from his belt, reseating it, chambering a round. He took a guard from Dez and hustled them all down to the last door, the one farthest away from the tunnel, at the end of Van Ness.

Doug put his guard facedown onto the floor there, then holstered his gun and untied his bandanna from around his face. The guard was begging for his life, certain he was about to be executed, until Doug's bandanna across his mouth gagged his pleas.

Dez did the same, then stood, still wiping at his eyes, trying to blink his contacts right. "Can we do this?" he said.

Doug looked out the door at the rain. *"Fuck,"* he hissed, considering their chances, then turned to Dez. "It's life for me—I got no choice. For you it's just a couple of years. Cut a plea, give them everything you can. If I make it out, I'm gone from here anyway."

Dez stared, uncertain.

"Gloansy's already hurt," said Doug. "Give yourself up. It's what I would do."

Dez blinked, sore-eyed. "No, it's not."

Doug leaned out of the bay and saw cops coming up from both sides, almost upon them. He stepped right out into the rain and quickly waved over the nearest pair.

In orange coats they came running up the sidewalk, guns at their sides. Doug made sure they saw his empty hands, then pointed them around the corner to where Dez was standing over the bound and gagged guards.

The cops got busy immediately, one officer dropping his knee down hard on a guard's back, the other calling in their position. "Nice catch," said the kneeling cop.

The guards started to wriggle, grunting in protest, trying to talk with their eyes.

"Transport these two," said Doug. "We're going after the third."

Doug and Dez started across the street, briskly but not running. Doug glanced down the length of Yawkey to where the Suburban was bunched up at the corner, having smacked into their stolen T-bird, cops in orange all over it. A paramedic was at the driver's-side door, working on Gloansy, and a chill rippled through Doug.

To their left lay Landsdowne Street, beyond a pair of empty cruisers. Ahead was Ipswich Street, full of orange cops, the direction in which Jem had gone.

"Come on," hissed Dez, starting left, looking to slip the police perimeter.

Gunshots sounded on Ipswich up ahead. Doug felt the reports in his chest, the way you feel thunder or a woman's scream.

"Holy fucking hell," said Dez.

"Take off," Doug told him, then started alone after Jem.

THE COP HAD REACHED the end of Ipswich where it met Boylston, walking in the street along the left-hand row of parked cars. "Excuse me!" said Frawley, coming up behind him. "Officer! Hold up a minute there, please."

The cop stopped, the bag hanging heavy and low in his hand. A gas station was to his left, another one across Boylston, a Staples office supply store to his right. Traffic continued on four-lane Boylston as usual.

The cop did not turn at first, his slick orange back wrinkling as his free hand went into it. When he did turn, it was with a sweeping arm motion such that the rounds rattling out of his gun would have zippered Frawley up from feet through groin to head, dropping him dead in the street. But Frawley had spun away behind a small gold Civic hatchback, which the cop now fired into.

Two other cops nearby came under fire, dropping the blue Boston Police sawhorses they were carrying, and Frawley hazarded a look through the cracked auto glass at his assailant.

Frawley only caught a distorted flash, the wild face with its white-out eyes and upper lip ridge looking profane in cop blues, like a cannibal wearing a chef's apron. James Coughlin. He was backing away behind cover fire with the engaged smile of a teenager seeing his violent daydreams come true.

Frawley tried to get his shotgun over the roof of the car, but pedestrians scattered behind Coughlin, cars waiting for a green light. Then Coughlin swung back, turning with the shoulder-harnessed semiauto—an illegal Intratec-9— popping window glass out of the car.

It sunk in then that Frawley was actually being shot at, and he went into a tight fetal crouch, putting his shoulder into the hindquarters of the car. Many of the rounds went through-and-through, puncturing the roof and thumping into the wooden fence behind him.

Then the firing stopped. Frawley gripped his shotgun wildly, expecting an ambush.

What he got instead was a sound like a stone skittering across the road. The thing rapped against the curb and Frawley peered down under the car, watching it spin and settle.

It looked like an old hand grenade. Frawley couldn't believe it. And then of course, he did believe it—and jumped up, racing away, yelling to the responding cops to get back—

The grenade blew, and the Civic's gas tank blew, and Frawley and his shotgun went sprawling. He turned from the wet asphalt and saw the little import on its side, undercarriage aflame. The windows of the storefront Staples were blown in, and everywhere on Boylston Street people were leaping out of their cars and running. Coughlin was gone.

Frawley got to his feet, pissed. That mangy fucker had tried to kill him. And a guy who'd open up on a federal agent would open up on anybody.

Frawley regripped his Remington and took off after him.

DOUG CAME UP ON the burning car, its stinking black smoke rising into the rain.

The grenades. Doug couldn't believe it.

"Fucking crazy," said a voice behind him.

Doug turned, found Dez still there. "Get out of here—"

"You two!" barked a voice from the side.

Two other cops ran past them. The one yelling to them had rank.

"Pick up that left flank! We're gonna sweep up Boylston and shut this end down!"

Doug nodded and did as he was told—pulling his Beretta and moving past the abandoned cars to the far sidewalk, past panicked citizens crawling away in the rain.

"What are you doing?" said Dez, coming up at his side. "What do you think you can do for him?"

"Desmond," said Doug, furious. "Get out. Leave me."

Then Doug saw Jem break from the Howard Johnson's parking lot half a block up, orange coat flapping, the bag in one hand, the Tec out in the other. Four, maybe five car lengths behind him, a plainclothes guy with a shotgun cut across after him, wearing a nylon vest reading *FBI*.

COUGHLIN WANTED THE McDONALD'S, running toward it, probably for hostages.

Frawley could not allow that to happen. He ranged left, and as Coughlin reached the curb up the street, Frawley pulled the shotgun to his shoulder and fired wide, between Coughlin and the restaurant—*Blam!*—shredding a Free Apartment Guide stand on the sidewalk. He pumped, fired again—*Blam!*—this time killing a *Boston Herald* machine.

Coughlin jerked back from the exploding stands. He spun and fired into the street, finding Frawley, but not quickly enough. Frawley dived between parked cars, scraping up the skin on his elbows and his knees, hearing rounds pick through the side of the truck, *rap-rap-rap*, thinking, *I'm in a fucking gunfight.* He got up off the road, worried about ricochets, sitting on the front bumper of the truck with his feet on the tail of the next car. He went into his jacket pockets and reloaded the shotgun, spilling some shells.

Smatterings of small-arms fire behind him, a burst here, a burst there. Then only the rain. Frawley leaned out one way, looking up the sidewalk toward McDonald's, people streaming out of the back entrance with kids in their arms. The front of the restaurant was glass, and he could see in between the painted Mayor McCheese and the Hamburglar, Coughlin was not inside.

Frawley leaned out the other way, looking up the rain-swept street cluttered with abandoned cars, their wipers still going. Not there either.

Frawley pulled back patiently, thinking Coughlin was waiting to pick him off if he moved. Somebody was going to get hurt in the cross fire. Coming up toward him were two cops on his side of the street, still half a block away. They were orange just like Coughlin, and he checked them for a split second, remembering that MacRay was likely still at large.

Shots again, *rap-rap-rap* off the side of his truck, and Frawley ducked out the other way, charging up the sidewalk, determined to keep Coughlin in the middle of Boylston and moving west.

DOUG MADE THE FBI shotgun as Frawley—the sleuth propped up on the front bumper of a UPS van, stopping to reload.

Dez was rubbing his eyes, trying to see clear. "You gonna shoot at cops?"

"Fuck away from me, Dez."

"How you gonna save him? How?"

Doug could take out Frawley. If he wanted Frawley to be dead, he could do it right now.

"You don't owe him anything, Doug. You can't do anything for him except die with him."

Then rounds cracked and pinged off the parked car next to them, popping glass, kicking rain off the street.

Jem was spraying rounds at them—at cops—from half a block away. Dez stooped low, swearing. "Duggy. We'll be pinned down here. We gotta bail *now*."

Doug watched Frawley curl out from behind the truck. Sometimes just knowing you can pull off a thing is enough. He let Dez tug on him, and together they started back down Boylston toward the black smoke of the bombed-out car.

WHETHER OUT OF PANIC or confusion or just softheadedness, Coughlin started across the intersection where Boylston met the end of Yawkey. Cops lay in wait there, the rounds pecking at Coughlin's vest, dancing him, picking at his leg and his shooting arm. Still he turned and spit rounds back, silencing the service pieces but not the submachine gunfire. Controlled double-taps staggered Coughlin, who held the money bag in front of him now as a shield, retreating back to the corner in front of Osco Drug.

Bloodied and sniggering, he hobbled up the wheelchair ramp to the drug-store, where someone inside had had the foresight to lock the doors. A wasted stutter of gunfire broke some of the glass until his Intratec clicked dry. Frawley heard it clatter to the pavement from his position in the drugstore parking lot, flat against the wall, listening to Coughlin's half-laughed cursing and the drag of his wounded foot.

Coughlin rounded the corner and Frawley was there with the Remington. Coughlin grinned like he knew him, or maybe thought the letters across Frawley's chest were funny. Frawley was yelling at Coughlin. He didn't know what he was saying, and it was just as likely Coughlin never heard it anyway.

Coughlin laughed, the pistol in his bloodied hand starting to rise, and Frawley squeezed one blast low—*Blam!*—then pumped and—*Blam!*—squeezed one blast high.

Coughlin flew back, puppet strings of insanity keeping him on his feet, backpedaling until he fell off the wet curb and spilled hard into the road.

Frawley did not move, frozen in the shooter's pose, still feeling the jerk of recoil. A bloody pistol lay on the sidewalk where Coughlin had once stood.

Coughlin rolled over in the street and started crawling. He was dragging himself, the black bag still in his grip, reaching for the double yellow lines like they were the top ledge of a high building.

Frawley finally moved, keeping his distance behind Coughlin, knowing that he had killed him and it was just a matter of time. Tac cops came charging up alongside Frawley, guns trained on the bright wet orange target, everyone waiting.

Coughlin stopped, laughing blood, then rolled over and looked up at the sky spilling down on him, his chest bucking, his mouth smiling even as his throat groaned for air.

DOUG WATCHED JEM'S ORANGE form crawl into the middle of the wide road, stop, and roll over.

Cops were coming up near them now. "Doug," hissed Dez.

Doug backed away, turning, striding fast alongside Dez. He and Dez would go on the run together now. The switch car with their change of clothes was lost, but the Fenway Gardens were right around the corner. They'd dig up Doug's stash, hit the nearest clothing store they could find, then hop a taxi to the long-term parking lot at Logan, boost an older model car, head out of state. Then figure out what shape the rest of their lives would take.

All these things raced through Doug's mind until he realized he was alone. He turned and saw Dez wandering back into the middle of the street, looking down the length of the double yellow line at Jem. Dez was trying to see through the rain, rubbing at his contacts like a man disbelieving his eyes.

Vested Frawley and some commando cops were coming up slow on Jem. Doug didn't understand Dez's concern—until, at once, he did.

The grenades on Jem's belt.

"Hey!" Dez started to yell.

The commando cops would never hear him through the rain. "Dez!" said Doug, calling him back. Regular cops coming from the burning car.

Dez ran a few steps forward, waving an arm. His stand here had to do at least as much with getting some final triumph over Jem—thwarting his grand battlefield exit, Jem's plan to take a few of his enemies with him—as it did saving the cops' lives.

Dez drew his gun and fired it for the first time that morning, straight up into the rain, then a few times low at the road around Jem. It worked, the only way to back the cops away from that distance.

The blast was like a road mine exploding, Jem erupting into lumpy pieces. The bag coughed money into the air, cash fluttering like confetti shot out of cannon, drifting back down to the wet road.

The cops near the smoking Civic were drawing on Dez now, yelling. All confusion in the slapping rain, Dez trying to see, his eyes bothering him, arms rising to his face.

The first shot spun Dez around. The second jerked him the other way, his vest vulnerable at close range, Dez dropping to the asphalt with a splash.

Doug drew and started after him. But already half a dozen orange raincoats were advancing on Dez where he lay.

You gonna shoot at cops?

Doug watched Dez squirming on the ground until the encircling cops blocked his view. Dez was down. Gloansy was caught. Jem was dead.

Something washed over Doug then, with the rain. He holstered his gun and turned and walked away.

* * *

THE RINGING IN FRAWLEY'S ears was his mind screaming as he picked himself up off the wet road and stumbled back toward the pieces of Coughlin. It was snowing money now, and he moved gun-first through the flurry of cash to the double yellow line.

Coughlin's armored vest was cracked open like a bloody husk. The fucker had blown himself up and tried to take Frawley and everyone else with him.

Frawley looked down the road to where the shots had come from, his thoughts too shrill to even speculate about what had happened. Someone was in custody down there. Frawley only hoped it was MacRay.

DOUG SAT ON HER stone bench. The willow was weeping rain into her garden, and he was trying to understand what it was he was feeling, until finally he realized—he felt nothing.

He got down on his knees in the muck. Rain battered the purple impatiens as he thrust his hands wrist-deep into the soil, as though he could reach all the way down to his money, take it, and leave. As though he had anything to run to now. As though he had anything to run for.

Nothing left in him but vengeance. Sirens wailed out on Boylston as he stood and shed his orange coat, starting back toward the Town.

53
HOME

DOUG WALKED OFF THE T at the Community College stop and crossed over Rutherford Avenue on the elevated walkway, seeing the soaked Town before him, the shoulders of its twin hills shrugged against the rain.

He walked along Austin Street between the rink and the Foodmaster plaza toward Main Street, umbrella people nodding at this drenched beat cop passing them on the sidewalk, kids in slickers and rubber boots staring up at the man in blue. Doug didn't see any of it. The only thing he noticed other than the bricks at his feet was the State Police helicopter cutting through the rain over the city across the river, looking for him.

The bell over the front door giggled as he entered the flower shop. He heard harp and fiddle music, "A Little Bit of Heaven" serenading the thirsty plants and squatting stone gargoyles. Doug stood alone among the pale blooms for a few airless moments, until Rusty, the Florist's guy, pushed through the black curtain hanging over the door behind the back counter.

He wore a green tracksuit and was eating a lettuce sandwich out of tinfoil. He looked at the sodden blue cop in the store as just another customer, until he recognized the face.

For a moment it seemed that Doug wouldn't have to shoot the ex-IRA man. Rusty had nothing but a cold sandwich to defend himself with, and Doug thought the guy might just bend to the will of force and time and step aside.

But a glance at Doug's empty hands showed him that Rusty had too much pride. The Florist's guy dropped his sandwich and lunged for something under the counter.

Doug cleared his holster and fired twice, the white-haired Irishman falling back against the wall to the floor. Doug passed the counter on the way to the back, Rusty facedown and gasping for air.

Doug pushed through the black curtain gun-first. The Irish music was louder there, warbling out of an old turntable. The glass-doored walk-in cooler was empty, Fergie's workbench standing across the room.

Doug heard a toilet flush. He turned toward the latch door as it opened.

Fergie wandered out carrying a newspaper, wearing his tight, hooded sweat-shirt, long work pants, and maroon suede slippers. He saw the cop there with the gun in his hand and at first just looked annoyed. Then he pulled off his read-ing glasses for a clear look at the cop's face. The half-glasses fell against his chest.

He said Doug's name and Doug filled the air between them with smoke. Doug did not stop firing until Fergus Coln lay beneath the workbench, bare-foot among the stem clippings, condolence ribbons unspooling over him.

It was a while before the Irish music returned to Doug's ears. He never heard the bell over the front door.

Two gunshots punched him high in the back of his vest. Another round bit into his left rear thigh, a fourth skipping off his shoulder to slice into his neck.

Doug twisted and dropped to the floor, firing from there, aiming back through the curtain into the store. He heard something fall, then the giggle of the doorbell.

He pushed himself to his feet. The lead in his leg burned and blood was spilling down the front of his shirt over his fake silver-and-blue badge. He felt a warm, pulsing hole in his neck and closed it with his palm, pressing hard and hobbling to the doorway, tearing down the black curtain.

Rusty hadn't moved, dead where he had fallen. Among the floor pots in front lay a body on its side, a young guy quaking, his black boots thumping the tile. A tear in the back of his T-shirt was blooming red, just over the belt of his fatigues. Doug limped over, his left hand holding the blood into his neck, his right hand holding his gun.

One of Jem's camo kids. The giggling bell had been the other one getting away.

Doug stood over him, waiting, but the kid refused to look up, lying there shaking in the scummy pot water he had overturned.

Doug holstered his gun and started away, leaving the kid twitching on the floor.

FRAWLEY SAT INSIDE THE McDonald's, still trying to count all the shots he'd fired. There was going to be an FBI investigation as well as civil liability hear-ings, and he would be held accountable for each and every round. He had already surrendered his Remington for ballistics.

"I'm going to be fired," he said.

Dino was drinking a strawberry shake next to him. "Easy, now."

"Look out there." The street was filled with umbrella-toting city, state, and federal lawmen, Suffolk County coroners, city hall lawyers, and news crews pressing against BPD sawhorses. "Shots fired in Fenway Park. A goddamn grenade blowing up a car." Frawley sat up. "I killed a man in the street."

"You shot him pretty good, but technically I think it was that crazy mofo's hand grenades that cashed out his tab."

Frawley's wrinkled FBI vest lay before him. "They can't clip me right away. Wouldn't look good. Got to wait for the inquest to run its course. Transfer me somewhere cold in the meantime."

"You at all curious about that other one down the street?"

Frawley grimaced. "Okay."

"It was Elden. The one in the Suburban, that was Magloan—with what looks like the entire take in the trunk, minus whatever got blown up out there with Coughlin."

Frawley waited. "And MacRay?"

"We'll find him. Bringing in the Canine Unit to search the ballpark."

Frawley looked at the half-eaten breakfasts left on the tables by the windows, empty high chairs, open newspapers.

"Dean," he said, unable to look the older man in the eye. "I did some stupid things with this. I did some things I probably should have run by you first."

Dino looked at him, quiet, maybe counting slowly to ten.

"Nothing illegal," Frawley stressed. "But I pushed it. I put myself inside this. I got involved."

Dino took a long draw on his shake, then set the cup aside. He stood. "You're in shock, Frawl. Couple of hours, we'll talk. Rather—you'll talk."

Dino walked away, leaving Frawley staring out the window, thinking about cold weather. He still had his law degree. Maybe this McDonald's was hiring.

Outside, he watched two detectives jump into an unmarked Grand Marquis, driving fast out of the parking lot.

Frawley read excitement on the faces of the remaining patrolmen. He pulled himself together and went outside. He asked the youngest-looking uniform what was going on.

"The Florist's shop in Charlestown," said the cop. "A bloodbath, gangland style. Looks like somebody got Fergie."

Frawley's mind seized up like a fist. All that time he'd been sitting there on his ass in a McDonald's, feeling sorry for himself—

Claire Keesey.

He took off running across the street, back up Yawkey toward his car.

DOUG PRESSED THE BELL again and hung his head low so that the badge on his hat was in the spyglass.

Claire opened the door to the cop. She saw Doug's face and his bloody hand at his neck and her hand went to her mouth, eyes widening.

Doug's first step over her threshold was okay. He faltered on the second step and went down hard on the third.

Claire screamed.

He could not move his hand from his neck. Pressure was the only thing keeping him alive. This slow throb against his palm was his clock running down.

He got himself into a sitting position and used his free hand and the heels of his shoes to push back from the open door. Making it to her place was all he'd thought about in the rain. Now he just wanted to push in deeper. He got to the small table outside her kitchen and slumped back against the legs of a chair.

He went away for a little while. Then he came back.

"Made it," he said. He needed a yawn in the worst way, but couldn't get one.

Claire came toward him. Impossibly tall, her hands covering her mouth, eyes screaming tears.

Doug fought down a swallow. "Why?"

She started to kneel, hesitated, remained standing.

"In your garden." He spoke in hoarse bursts. "That last time. I wanted you . . . to tell me not to do it. I wanted you . . . to stop me."

She shook her head in horror.

"I wanted you . . . to give me a reason . . ."

"But nothing *I* could have said . . ."

She still didn't get him. "I would have done . . . anything for you. Even save myself."

She slipped to her knees, sitting on her heels at his outstretched feet, mystified. "Why? Why leave that to *me*?"

And there, in her bewilderment, he recognized his grave mistake. He had surrendered himself to Claire, just as Krista had to him. When you give someone the power to save you, you give them the power to destroy you as well. That was what Frank G. had been all about—not relinquishing that grip on yourself.

A man coming at him down the front hall, gun out. The sleuth, Frawley. Doug tightened his grip on the side of his neck.

FRAWLEY WENT IN THE open door, seeing the trail of blood and rain, his SIG-Sauer out of his armpit. MacRay was in a cop uniform, slumped against a chair on the floor, Claire kneeling before him.

MacRay's gun was in his holster. One hand was wet red and clamped over a neck wound, blood dripping from his bent elbow to the lemon yellow carpet.

No grenades on his belt.

MacRay, dying, frowned at Frawley's gun, then at Frawley himself.

Frawley came up behind his SIG to MacRay's side, smelling blood, reaching across and tugging the Beretta from MacRay's cop holster while MacRay sat there and watched him take it. Frawley backed away past Claire, easing up on his aim, putting the Beretta in his back pocket. He saw a telephone on the table and circled to it, picked it up.

"Don't."

MacRay's voice was as bloodless as his face. Frawley put down the phone, moving back into MacRay's line of sight.

Claire turned her head to look up at Frawley through tears. "Did you do this?"

Her words cut him. She was asking, *Did you do this because of me?*

MacRay worked hard to breathe, harder still to speak. "She dimed me?"

He seemed to know the truth already. Frawley said, "That's right."

MacRay swallowed with difficulty. He looked at Claire until his eyes fell, then blinked back to Frawley. "Why let it go so far? Why not take us . . . at the hotel?"

"What hotel?" said Frawley. "I didn't find out anything until an hour before-hand."

MacRay looked hard at Claire again. Something was going on there.

Frawley said, "We're talking about Coughlin's sister, right?"

MacRay's eyes came back to Frawley, so still and staring that Frawley thought MacRay was gone. Then MacRay nodded. He seemed to relax.

Frawley's heart was pumping hard enough for both of them. "You got the Florist."

MacRay blinked. "Tell Dez I did it for him. For the Town."

Frawley wanted to feel nothing for the crook, but to be in a room with a dying man is to die a little yourself. "You'll have to tell him."

The only reaction was a flicker in MacRay's eyes.

"The money." said Frawley. "Where's the rest of your stash?"

MacRay was falling into himself.

"Where's the money?" pressed Frawley.

Claire said, "Leave him alone."

MacRay was going. Frawley backed away, heavy-legged. He picked up the phone and dialed 911.

SHE CAME FORWARD AND took his empty hand, holding it tenderly in her own, as though the hand itself was the thing that was dying.

Doug said, "You were never going away. With me. Were you."

She held his gaze. Her wet-eyed expression said no.

He felt love streaming out of his hand into hers like electricity.

She would find it in the spring. The money he had buried like doomed hope in her garden. Like a note he'd left for her. Maybe she could use it to fund her work at the Boys and Girls Club. Maybe in time she'd think of him differently.

His left hand fell away from his neck as he focused on her face. He wanted her to be the last earthly thing he would see.

Even if a thing is doomed—there is that moment of absurd hope that is worth the fall, that is worth everything.

CLAIRE FELT THE SHOCK of lifelessness in his limp hand. She dropped it out of fright and would only later wilt at the shame of letting him go. Right now a dead man was lying on her floor and her mind was choking on this.

Why had he come to her to die? Dragging himself into her kitchen, just as he had dragged himself into her life. She despised him for the mess he had made, the blood on her floor like the stain on her soul. And yet. And yet as she looked at him now, she could not help but feel for the motherless boy inside. For Adam Frawley too, the vengeful one whispering into the telephone—these two lovesick sons she had gotten caught between. But for the men they had become, she had only scorn.

She recalled a news story about a woman who was accidentally knocked overboard a moored cruise ship. She came up to the surface unhurt, treading water, but trapped by the tide pushing the massive ship back against the dock. She would have been crushed to death if she hadn't wriggled out of her evening dress and kicked off her heels, swimming straight down into the blackness, feeling her way blindly along the hull to the deep bottom keel, then pulling herself past it and kicking free, lungs bursting as she surfaced on the other side, naked and alive.

Had Claire made it to the other side? Was she coming up for air now?

The police were already in her foyer, and she reached for Doug's hand one last time before they were separated forever. His body had settled against the chair, his hand impossibly heavy now and wanting to fall. She noticed dirt under his fingernails and darkening his cuticles, and thought immediately of her garden. She couldn't imagine any reason why he would have gone there—nor why she felt so certain that he had.

Walk to the water until you can feel it on your toes. Then take off the blindfold.

She felt the same sensation of passing as she had watching her young brother die: of something coming to nothing, yes, but at the same time, a conferring of responsibility, a covenant passed from the dead to the living.

Claire was taking off the blindfold now. She looked deep into Doug's dimming eyes, reminded of hearth fires and how, even after the flames died, the glowing cinders were slow to cool. She wondered what it was that Doug MacRay saw as the glow of his life faded. She wondered what died last in the heart of a thief.

54
END BEGINNING

"CAN'T DO IT," SAID Jem. "I can't fucking do it. He's turning my fucking stomach with this. We ordered these sandwiches what, twelve hours ago? You couldn't get cold cuts like the rest of us, Magloan? Sitting here with your soggy-ass steak sub, these fucking limp peppers."

Dez said, "Never mind that he's been eating the thing for like, three hours."

"This isn't eating anymore," said Jem, "this is lovemaking. He's getting it on with a steak sub. Somebody cover my young, impressionable eyes."

Dez said, "Joanie does usually go around with a smile on her face."

"Oh—no question Gloansy gives primo head," Jem said. "I can vouch for that."

Doug shushed their groaning laughter, not very concerned about the audio sensors inside the vault's antitamper package, but careful just the same. The four of them sitting on the floor behind the teller counter in dusty blue jumpsuits, the bank brightening with morning light, trucks and cars rumbling outside through Kenmore Square.

"Know what we need?" said Gloansy, still munching. "Those headsets with ear wires, like in the movies. So we can talk while we're in different rooms."

"Headsets are gay," said Jem. "You'd look like a girl folding pants at the Gap. Walkie-talkies—that's a man's radio."

"I'm talking hands-free," said Gloansy. "Gun in one hand, bag of cash in the other, capeesh?"

"Do not say *capeesh*. You sound like a douche." Jem got to his feet, stretched. "See, this is too fucking relaxed here. This isn't robbing. This, we could do back at my place. Why going in on the prowl sucks. All night, cutting a hole in the fucking ceiling. Like *working* for a living."

"Prowl is smart," said Doug.

"Prowl is pussy," said Jem.

Doug checked the wall clock. "You want strong, kid, we go strong in about ten minutes. Let's pack this shit up."

Gloansy said, "But I haven't finished my snack."

Jem snatched it out of his hands and mashed it, threw it into their trash bag. "You finished now? 'Cause I got a fucking bank to rob."

Doug checked his Colt's load and dropped it back into his pocket, knowing he was much more likely to hit someone over the head with the thing than he ever was to fire it. As obsessive as Doug was about the jobs they pulled, Jem's weapons source was the one detail he preferred to know nothing about. If indeed it was the Florist or one of the dust-brained kids in the Florist's employ, that would only piss Doug off.

Gloansy got to his feet without his Mountain Dew. Doug told him, "You gonna leave your tonic there, you might as well write your name and Social Security number on the wall in blood."

"I got it, I got it," said the freckled wonder, stowing it in the open work duffel near the bleach jugs.

They went on with their bickering for a few more precious preheist minutes, and Doug took a step back and realized that this was the part of the job he liked best. The intervals of downtime when they were all just kids again, four messed-up boys from the Town, so good at being so bad. He realized he never felt more secure, more at peace, more protected, than he did then, cooping inside a bank they were about to rob. Nobody could touch them there. Nobody could hurt them except each other.

Jem said, "Bad news, Monsignor. *Rolling Stone* said U2's next album is disco."

Dez rubbed at his eyes, prodding his contact lenses. "Not true."

"It happens, kid. These things can't last forever. Got to end sometime."

"We'll see," said Dez, wiring his police radio into his ear. "We shall see."

Jem pulled a paper Foodmaster bag out of the work duffel. "Game faces," he said, handing out black ski masks.

"This is it?" said Gloansy, pulling on the knit mask. "This what you been so top-secret about?"

Jem grinned his grin and went back into the bag. "Feast your eyes, ladies."

Doug received his goalie mask and looked it over—the oval eyes, the jagged, black, hand-drawn stitches.

"Gerry Cheevers," said Gloansy, awestruck, pulling it on over his ski mask.

Jem pulled a gun into his blue-gloved hand and said, "Let's make some motherfucking *bank*."

The other masks nodded, smacked fists all around, Doug looking at the stitched-up faces of his friends. Dez went to take his position inside the shaded front windows, Gloansy remaining behind the counter.

Doug turned past the vault, following Jem down the short hallway to the back door where they faced each other in the shadows, standing silent and still on either side. Doug had no dark premonitions about the job as he pulled the black .38 into his hand. The only thing bothering him now was that the fun part was already over.

A car pulled up outside, doors opening, shutting. "Fucking clockwork," hissed Jem's empty-eyed mask.

Claire Keesey. That was the branch manager's name. She drove a plum Saturn coupe with a useless rear spoiler and a bumper sticker that said Breathe! She was single, as far as Doug could tell, and he wondered why. Surprising, the things you could learn about a person from a distance, the impressions that you formed. Tailing her for so long, watching her from afar, had raised more questions than answers. He was curious about her now. He wondered, with the idle affection of a guy thinking about a girl, what she was going to look like up close.

ACKNOWLEDGMENTS

Debts owed to: Charlotte, for unwavering support; my father, source of strength and inspiration; my Melanie and my Declan; the uncanny NewGents; Richard Abate, Prince of Agents; Colin Harrison, who enriched this book in record time; Kevin Smith at Pocket; Sarah Knight and everybody at Scribner; and Nan Graham and Susan Moldow.

ABOUT THE AUTHOR

Chuck Hogan abandoned his career as a video store clerk when his first novel, *The Standoff*, was published to critical acclaim and translated into fourteen international editions. He lives in Massachusetts with his wife and family.